THE PRESERVATION OF SPECIES

PART I

RULE OF EXTINCTION

PART II

STRUGGLE FOR EXISTENCE

PART III

BEASTS OF PREY

THE PRESERVATION OF SPECIES

PART I

RULE OF EXTINCTION

GEOFF JONES

For Erin

RULE OF EXTINCTION

Extinction is the rule. Survival is the exception.

– Carl Sagan

ASCENT

Chapter One

Two Days Before Impact

David Williams grimaced at the ugly yellow ball glowing on the horizon. Astronomers predicted the comet would appear larger than the sun tomorrow, before it struck the Pacific Ocean sometime late the following day.

The sight of the Ender filled him with despair. His family would die, along with everyone else on Earth, and there wasn't a goddamn thing he could do about it.

He took another sip of Irish coffee from his travel mug, then started moving again. He and his children walked the dog around their Minneapolis neighborhood each morning after Lindsey left. The ritual had grown increasingly difficult as the end drew near.

They rounded the last corner and started up the block toward their house. "Come on, kids, let's get home."

His six-year-old son Barry took off up the sidewalk. "When will Mommy be back?"

David sighed. "Not till tonight, Bud. She's with your grandmother." Bitterness crept into his tone. Barry and Kim needed their mom. He needed his wife.

Kim, who was twelve, lagged behind, her mood somber. She tugged Kona's leash while the golden retriever sniffed weeds growing wild in the yard of a neighbor who'd vanished weeks ago.

A high-pitched whistle pierced the air, faint at first, but growing steadily louder.

Barry stopped in front of the house next to theirs. "What's that noise?"

David craned his neck, wincing at the glare of the bright sky, made worse by the triple shot of whiskey. He felt like an ass for needing a drink to walk around the block with his kids, but it helped him put on a less mournful face and maintain a small semblance of normalcy.

Barry walked back, tilting his head. "Is that the comet, Daddy?"

The boy never stopped asking questions, even after the Ender showed up and the answers became impossible.

"I don't think so." The comet wouldn't make any noise until it entered the atmosphere. At that point, it would all be over. He took another swig, feeling helpless.

Kim pointed straight up. "There, look."

David stepped into the street, checking both ways, even though there wasn't much traffic anymore. Their western Minneapolis neighborhood was still safe, thank God. Other parts of the country hadn't fared so well. Other parts of the world no longer existed.

A tiny object twinkled against the blue sky directly above, whistling like artillery in an old war film. Needles of dread pricked David's spine. Was it a missile strike? Had someone decided to end it all early?

Kona whined, her tail drooping between her legs.

Across the street, Mitchell Vaughn leaned against the porch railing of his white colonial. He looked up from an oversized smartphone. "Hey Doc, something's going on."

After eight years as an anesthesiologist, David had grown to hate the nickname. It usually came with a *you-think-you're-better-than-me* tone, especially from people like Mitchell.

"What's happening?" Barry asked, pulling David's arm. "Is it bad?"

He stroked the boy's sandy crew cut and tried to keep the fear from his voice. "I don't know. We'll find out, won't we?" The response had become a familiar litany.

Is it really going to hit Earth?

Are we all going to die?

What happens when you die?

David would hug his children, tell them he loved them, and give them the only answer he could. *I don't know. We'll find out, won't we?*

Kim rolled her eyes. She looked more and more like her mom, despite her recently-cropped hair and baggy cargo shorts.

"It's crazy," Mitchell said. "Everyone's going nuts." He tapped the phone's screen, his gut draping over the porch rail like a water balloon. "It's all over the news."

"We aren't allowed to go online anymore, Mr. Vaughn." Kim's tone dripped with pre-teen attitude. She glared at the comet on the northern horizon. "We're not even supposed to think about it. As if we can't just walk outside and see it."

"Hold on," David said. "What's happening?"

He hadn't seen anything on the news that morning. He checked every day, hoping to learn something that might save his family.

"There's these pods everywhere."

Barry tugged his arm again. "What's he talking about, Daddy?"

"What do you mean?" David asked. "What pods?"

"It's a chance to survive, Doc." Mitchell hefted himself down the porch stairs. He'd put on forty pounds in the three months since the Ender's discovery. Gluttony was a common reaction to the apocalypse. As the whistling sound increased in pitch, he stopped and looked up. "Holy fuck, is that one of 'em?"

David winced at the profanity, more out of habit than actual concern. His kids had been exposed to far worse as society fell apart in real time on television and social media.

The bright shape in the sky grew larger. It was coming straight toward them.

Kona pulled free and ran home to their yard, where she turned and looked back, barking.

The noise shifted to a pulsing hum, creating the impression of deceleration.

David grabbed both kids and pulled them toward the house, his heart racing. If this was the end, he wasn't ready. He didn't know what to do. He thought he had two more days. He still needed to make things right with Lindsey.

A round white object as big as a minivan slammed into the ground across the street with an Earth-shaking boom.

David and his children staggered back.

Barry whimpered.

Kona growled.

"What the hell?" David whispered.

Mitchell held his arms wide, as if trying to keep his balance. "Holy fuck, would you look at that."

A capsule sat in a crater of blackened grass in the yard next to Mitchell's. It looked like a sphere that had been stretched at the ends. Wisps of smoke rolled up its smooth white sides.

David held both kids against his body, trying to make sense of what he saw. He wished he hadn't been drinking. Everything felt fuzzy. He wished Lindsey was here instead of caring for her senile mother at a nursing home on the other side of the goddamn city.

"Mrs. Turner won't like that," Barry said. The house next to Mitchell had belonged to June Turner, an elderly woman who gave the kids root beer when they brought her mail up from the street.

"Mrs. Turner is dead, dumbass," Kim said.

"Stop it, Kim." David shook her arm gently.

She jerked away. "Why? We'll all be dead in two days. Barry knows that."

"Kim, enough. You guys stay here." David followed Mitchell over to the strange object, which was maybe twenty feet wide by eight feet high. It was difficult to gauge because the whole thing was so smoothly curved.

"Liar," Barry whined. "Mommy says the Ender might not hit."

David didn't respond. He'd given up arguing with Lindsey about the situation. It didn't matter what anyone believed. The Ender was going to hit. If Barry and his mother wanted to pretend otherwise, what was the harm? Hell, he even felt a little jealous.

"Do you smell that?" Mitchell asked. "Smells like rain."

David sniffed. "Ozone?" He circled the capsule, which was shaped like a giant egg that narrowed slightly on both ends instead of just one. He couldn't find any handles or openings. The curved white surface was entirely unmarked. He crouched. A ring of blackened grass extended a foot wider than the capsule, but he saw no exhaust openings or nozzles or anything that could have burned the ground. Or made the damn thing fly, for that matter.

Kona crept over, dragging her leash. She sniffed the object.

Mitchell waved his phone. "I'm trying to tell you. These things are falling all over the U.S."

Barry and Kim stayed back. They disliked Mitchell as much as they'd liked Mrs. Turner.

"What are they?" David asked. "Where're they from?"

Instead of answering, Mitchell reached for the shiny white surface.

"W-wait, don't touch it," David sputtered.

"Why not?" Mitchell glanced at the comet in the sky. "What've I got to lose?"

There were a million reasons why not. Something extraordinary was happening. It could be dangerous. They needed to analyze the situation, so they could make informed decisions, and those decisions should probably come from the guy with the medical degree, not the one who inherited an oil-change franchise and ran it into the fucking ground.

"I need time to figure this out." David didn't add the word "dumbass," but it was there in his tone.

Mitchell's jowly face tightened into a sneer. "I got here first, Doc." He extended a finger and poked the surface.

A black line appeared around the capsule's equator. David stepped back, stopping beside Barry and Kim, who'd crept close. Kona's hackles rose.

The top half of the capsule separated from the bottom and floated upward. The inside appeared black and empty.

"Mitchell, what are they saying online?" The son of a bitch had to be holding out on him. David forced himself to keep a calm tone. "Where did this come from? What is it?"

A bitter smile spread across Mitchell's face. "It's a lifeboat, neighbor." The top half of the capsule kept rising.

Barry tugged David's shirt. "How does it do that?"

"I have no idea." He found a stout branch under one of Mrs. Turner's trees and carried it to the capsule, bending over to peer through the gap. Nothing connected the top to the bottom. He stuck the branch in the empty space between them, to test for an air flow, or something. Anything. He felt nothing.

"Magnets?" Mitchell asked. The top half hung motionless in the air, three or four feet above the bottom.

David placed the end of the stick against the top surface and pushed. It didn't budge.

"Dad, do you think this was sent to save us?" Kim asked.

"Who would have sent it? The government? The Air Force?"

She glared at him like he was an idiot, a look she'd picked up from her mother, and pointed skyward. "Aliens, duh."

Mitchell moved in front of David, forcing him back. He stank of old sweat.

"It don't matter who sent it, Doc." He lifted a heavy butt cheek onto the rim. The inside was dark and concave. Mitchell ducked his head under the floating top half and pulled himself in. The surface gave slightly under his weight and the top half of the capsule began to lower.

"Hold on, how do you know it's safe?"

Mitchell pointed at the Ender and cackled. "Sure as hell isn't safe here." He scooted backwards to the center and patted the surface next to him. "Get in if you want."

The bottom half looked like an oversized papasan chair. At least five or six adults could fit. The top half continued to descend.

Kim moved forward but David pulled her away. "Wait. Your mom isn't here. We can't just leave her." He leaned over so he could see inside. He needed time to think this through, to come up with a plan. "Mitchell, what's going on?"

Everything was happening too fast and nothing made sense.

Mitchell cackled again, then the top half of the capsule connected with the bottom, silencing him.

David pounded on the surface. "Mitchell!"

There was no response.

The black seam between the two halves vanished with a pop and an oily shimmer rippled across the smooth white surface. A weighty hum came from the pod, so low David felt it more than heard it.

Kona tucked tail and ran.

"Get back, guys." David grabbed his kids and pulled them away.

The capsule rose from the ground and accelerated straight up without any obvious source of propulsion. Ninety seconds later, it was out of sight.

Chapter Two

David dialed his wife's number and turned on the kitchen television. The Minneapolis stations had shut down weeks ago, but two national networks still operated. Onscreen, a capsule just like the one that had slammed into Mrs. Turner's front yard sat on a city street. A young couple climbed inside and beckoned several other people to join them before the top half closed back down. When the black equator faded, the capsule lifted away. A reporter described everything as it happened, but clearly had no real information about what was going on.

It didn't matter. David felt something he hadn't felt in three months. Hope.

The call went through and started ringing, thank God. "Come on, Lindsey, answer."

Barry stared at the television. "What are we going to do?"

"We're going to try to escape," David said. "We need to get your mom home and we need to find another one." He should have stopped Mitchell from taking the one across the street, but everything had happened too fast. David was much better at planning than making snap decisions.

"Escape to where?" Kim asked. "Where do they go?"

The phone kept ringing, but Lindsey didn't answer.

"It doesn't matter. They go somewhere else." Mitchell had been right about that. He'd climbed in without a moment's thought, with just the clothes on his back. David's mind raced. They could do better. They could collect supplies, things that might be useful wherever the capsules took them.

The phone went to voicemail. He hung up.

Kim gestured at the television. "Oh my God, look."

A label at the bottom of the screen indicated footage from Omaha, Nebraska. Two men fought over another shiny white capsule. One knocked the other off his feet and climbed inside. When the top half closed, the guy on the ground scrambled forward and jumped on top. He rode the capsule thirty feet in the air before sliding off. The microphone on the camera picked up the sound of breaking bones when he hit the ground. Someone in the crowd screamed.

David muted the TV. "Kids, go get our camping stuff together." It wasn't exactly survival gear, but it was close enough.

On the screen, a car crashed into a crowd surrounding another capsule. David slid in front of the television, blocking the view.

Kim didn't move. "What's the point? They're all getting taken. We missed our chance."

He turned to his daughter. "You're right, they're getting snatched up." He raised one eyebrow, a trick Lindsey used to love. "But we can look for one in the middle of nowhere, one that no one else can find."

Barry scrunched his nose. "How?"

A broad smile transformed Kim's face from sullen and serious to excited and hopeful. "From the air."

David's heart ached. He'd missed his daughter's smile.

He and three other doctors owned a small Cessna that was hangared at an airfield less than an hour from the house. Kim had learned to operate the plane's radios over summer break, picking up the controls easily.

"That's right," David said. "We'll take the plane and look for a capsule nobody's found yet. We can cover a lot of territory."

Kim nodded and gave her father a hug. He buried his face in her short brown curls. Hugs were even harder to come by than smiles.

"Now go pack some stuff." He forced himself to release her. "Both of you."

"Like what?" Barry asked.

"Water bottles, sleeping bags, good shoes, snacks." David dialed his wife again. He waved the kids away. "Go." They disappeared down the basement stairs.

This time Lindsey answered, curt and cold. "Hello, David."

He shoved aside the friction of the past few weeks. "Listen, something's happening."

"I know. I'm watching the news."

"We had one land right across the street. Mitchell got in it."

The television now showed a capsule on a bright green golf course somewhere in Colorado Springs, according to the chyron. A guy in a black t-shirt drew a pistol and shot an elderly man standing between him and the round object. Bodies lay scattered on the fairway. David tensed at the thought of taking his kids near that kind of carnage.

"Linds, you have to meet us at the airpark. We'll find a capsule out in the country." If they stayed away from developed areas, maybe they could avoid any violence.

"Are you crazy? We're not getting in one of those things. Where do they go? Who sent them?"

David took a deep breath and spoke slowly. "Lindsey, we know what will happen if we stay here."

"We don't know for sure. No one does."

"Dammit, please. For our kids."

Astronomers had calculated the likelihood of the Ender hitting Earth at ninety-nine point nine-seven percent. David and Lindsey had debated ad nauseam over the remaining three hundredths of a percent.

The phone went silent for a moment. "Mom can't even get out of bed now. She's all alone."

"Lindsey, she's eighty-four and she doesn't know what's happening. It's a blessing."

"David—"

"Get in the car and meet us at the airpark. Your kids need you more than she does." He wanted to add, *I need you too*, but his pride kept him from saying it.

Barry tugged his arm. "Is that Mommy?" The boy hugged a sleeping bag against his chest. "When will she be home?"

David held the phone to Barry's ear. "Tell her to come right now or you'll never see her again."

Barry's voice cracked. "Mommy, I want you." Tears swam in his eyes. "I love you too." David pulled the phone away.

"Lindsey—"

"You're an asshole, David. I can't believe you would—"

"Lindsey, go get in the car." His skin grew hot. "This is our only chance. We have to try. The airpark. I'm leaving now. I'll prep the plane and wait for you. Hurry." He hung up. The nursing home was on the other side of the river and they were wasting time.

Ten minutes later, he backed their small SUV down the driveway. Kona sat in the cargo area next to a pile of camping supplies. David took one last look at the blackened crater in Mrs. Turner's front yard and pressed the gas pedal to the floor. He didn't bother to close the garage.

"Did you reserve the plane?" Kim asked, ever the rule follower.

He shook his head. The four men who shared the Cessna 172 booked flight time with an online reservation system. One of the other pilots had killed himself the same week as Mrs. Turner, but he'd used a revolver instead of Ativan. David hadn't shared this news with his family.

"What if one of the other guys has it?"

"I don't know," he said, annoyed he hadn't considered the possibility. "We'll find another plane."

"What do you mean? Steal one? We can't steal one."

David drew in a deep breath, trying to keep his temper. "You know what's going to happen the day after tomorrow, right?"

Kim didn't respond.

"Mommy says no one knows for sure," Barry said.

"Your mom is wrong. There's a reason they call it the Ender." The light ahead turned red. David scanned for traffic on both sides, then sped through. "Are your seatbelts on?"

Two clicks came from the back seat.

The drive to Lakeshore Airpark in the suburbs west of Minneapolis normally took just under an hour. They raced down a six-lane thoroughfare with shopping centers on both sides. All the stores had been looted and the strip-mall on the right was a blackened husk.

"Can I sit up front?" Barry asked. "I wanna be co-pilot."

"I need Kim's help with the radios."

"I can help. You never let me help."

Barry's whining made David's skin crawl. He glared in the rearview mirror and told himself not to yell. The boy was only six.

Kim pointed forward. "Dad, look out."

Two men in purple Vikings jerseys shambled across the road. David swerved around them. One lobbed a tequila bottle at the car. It shattered on the back window. Kona yipped.

"Barry, I need you to be quiet."

"Yeah, dumbass, you almost got us killed."

"Kim." David squeezed the steering wheel. "Both of you. Be quiet and don't give me any bullshit right now."

His profanity silenced them.

Traffic picked up as they moved from the suburbs into the industrial parks, but most of the cars were going in the opposite direction, back toward Minneapolis. Did the other drivers know something he didn't? Maybe the capsules only landed in urban areas. David clenched his jaw and pressed on. He had to stick to the plan.

When the airport was a few minutes away, he called Lindsey again. She answered on the first ring. "I'm in the car. I just left."

Thank God, he thought. "I'm almost to the airport. How far are you?"

"Ninety minutes. Maybe more. Traffic is bad." She sounded close to tears. "Everyone's looking for those pods."

He gritted his teeth. "We'll get the plane ready and wait for you." He swerved away from a gray minivan careening down the center of the road.

"David, don't leave without me."

"If you'd left when I told you to, you'd be right behind us." He regretted the words immediately, but he couldn't help himself. He never could keep his mouth shut when people ignored him, especially when they found themselves in trouble as a result.

"I had to say goodbye." Her voice cracked.

David's throat tightened. He wanted to take back everything he'd said, both today, and over the past few weeks. He hated hearing his wife in pain.

"Can I talk to Mommy?" Barry asked.

He passed the phone to the back, glad to be interrupted for once.

"Daddy says the Ender is really going to hit. No, Mommy, I believe him. I love you too." He handed the phone to his sister.

"Please hurry, Mom. Mr. Vaughn got in one. It looked fine. All four of us will fit. Five, even. We've got Kona in the back, and our camping stuff. Yes. I love you too."

David took the phone. "Please hurry."

"I've got to go." She sounded distracted. "Traffic's a mess."

"Okay. Call when you can." He bit down on his pride and added, "I love you, Lindsey."

The line went dead. He wasn't sure she'd heard his final words.

He turned into Lakeshore Airpark, home to two hundred private planes, and raced down a frontage road. Barry counted off the rows of hangars.

David drove onto the taxiway and parked beside his hangar door. "Please be here." He stuck his key into the hangar lock, clicked open the shackle, and pulled one of the heavy sliding doors. Kim and Barry pulled the other door in the opposite direction.

Light filled the hangar, revealing the four-seat Cessna Skyhawk. The tangy sweet smell of aviation gas filled David's nostrils.

Barry hopped in place. "Yay!"

"Help me get the stuff in the back, guys." He let Kona down to run around on the deserted taxiway, grabbed an armload of camping gear, and walked to the plane.

They stuffed their sleeping bags, flashlights, and a fishing kit through the small hatch on the side of the fuselage into the space behind the back seat. Kim handed him a cook stove.

"Do we have any propane?" he asked.

She shook her head. He tossed the stove to the back of the hangar where it landed with an angry bang.

Barry opened the door on the right side and climbed to the front seat, using the step on the wing strut.

"Barry, get in back," Kim said.

David slammed the baggage compartment and secured the latch. "Move it, Buddy. We don't have time for this."

"I always sit in back," he whined as he climbed over the seat.

David grabbed a stepladder from the side of the hangar and placed it under the wing so he could inspect the fuel tanks. He stopped halfway up when his phone buzzed in his pocket.

Lindsey sounded frantic. "David, you've got to go."

"What? Why?"

"The pods are getting snatched up. It's crazy. Everyone's fighting for them."

"We can wait a little longer."

"No. Go find one, then call me. Traffic's crawling."

"Linds—"

"If you don't find one now, they'll all be taken. I'm miles away."

A chill swelled in David's core. "I can't leave you," he whispered.

"I'll go west on highway two-twelve. Fly in that direction. Call me when you find one. You have to. For the kids. I love you too, David. Now go." The call ended.

His heart raced. He climbed down from the stepladder and kicked it out of the way. *Fuck.* Bitter uncertainty flooded his mind. Should he wait? Should he call her back? No. He should do what she'd told him to do. It was a smart plan, even if he hated it.

"Kona, come," he growled, folding the pilot's seat forward. He lifted her into the back next to Barry, then climbed into the front.

"Dad, what about the pre-flight?" Kim asked. "You always say the pre-flight's the most important thing."

"When's Mommy going to get here?" Barry asked.

"She's going to come meet us," David said. He put on his headset, which provided blessed silence. "Just be quiet and get buckled." His mouth felt dry.

Kim tapped his arm.

He slid one cup from his ear. "What?"

"You didn't even pull it out of the hangar yet."

"Dammit, Kim, be quiet. This is our last chance."

Kim clamped her mouth shut. David pulled his headset back into place.

"Okay," he muttered, trying to focus. "Keys, mixture, throttle." He stomped on the brake pedals and cranked the ignition. The propeller roared. Papers from the little desk in the back of the hangar billowed out around them. He nudged the throttle and the Cessna rolled onto the taxiway. Squeezing the radio button on the yoke, he announced his intentions on the airport's frequency. "Skyhawk six-papa-zulu taxiing, runway two-eight." He steered with his feet, turning the nose wheel with the rudder pedals.

No one responded to his radio call.

As they cleared the hangars, the ugly glow of the Ender came into view. He nudged the throttle and steered the plane to the end of the runway.

Nothing else moved at the small airport. Even the windsock hung still. David had never felt so alone. He crossed the hold-position markings without stopping. "Skyhawk six-papa-zulu taking off, runway two-eight, westbound."

No one replied. He shoved the throttle to the firewall and the plane accelerated down the long strip of concrete.

As they lifted from the ground, David wondered if he would ever see his wife again.

Chapter Three

Ten Days Before Impact

David pounded the front door. "Mrs. Turner?" Still no answer. He pulled the key from his pocket and stuck it in the lock. He liked living on a street where the neighbors gave each other keys. Everyone except Mitchell Vaughn, anyway.

A wave of rot and death assaulted him when he opened the door. He recognized it immediately and closed his eyes. At the hospital, antiseptic pine usually masked this particular smell.

June Turner lay on her kitchen floor in a puddle of rust-colored purge fluid, her fingers intertwined on her distended belly like a woman deep in thought. Flies crawled on her face, laying their eggs in the soft edges of her eyelids. An empty bottle of Ativan stood on the kitchen table, next to a half-empty bottle of root beer.

David's stomach clenched tight at the sight of her, threatening to blow for the first time since med school. He returned to the front door and didn't breathe until he'd locked it behind him. As he marched back across the street, he made up his mind. They had to get away. His kids could have walked in on her putrefying corpse, for Christ's sake.

When Lindsey returned home three hours later, the ambulance still hadn't come. David glanced across the street as he helped his wife unload the car. The ambulance would never come. June Turner would rot for the next ten days and the flies that hatched from her eyes would buzz around the neighborhood. Maybe right into his own house.

"Mrs. Turner killed herself," he said as he hauled the last pair of bags into the kitchen.

"Jesus." Lindsey stood at the counter, her shoulders slumped.

David placed his bags next to the others. "We have to get out of here, away from all this. Let's go north."

She began to unpack the first bag. "You want us to leave our home?"

He picked up a box of rice cereal with a smiling baby on the front. "Where did you get this?"

"Crestline Child Care." She held up a carton of vanilla wafers. "Nobody thought to plunder the day care centers." She placed it next to tiny jars of pureed fruits and vegetables.

David took her hand, stopping her. "Think about it, Linds. We can get back to basics. If this is all the time we have left, let's make the most of it. Let's *live* these last few days."

Her eyelids narrowed. Those hazel eyes usually made his knees weak, but right now, they felt like daggers.

He pressed on. "Remember summers during med school?" They had camped in the backcountry across the Canadian border. They would canoe north for two days until they found a remote campsite where they would spend a week fishing, napping, hiking, and reading. Decompressing.

David massaged the base of her thumb. "We can sneak out of the tent while the kids are asleep and watch the northern lights."

Her glare softened. On their first camping trip, David had kissed her awake at three in the morning, led her down to the canoe, and taken her out to the middle of the lake. Curtains of color rained across the sky. They made love out on the water, under a sea of shimmering green. They'd told close friends that Kim had been conceived under that glowing aurora, but in truth, they'd screwed like rabbits the entire trip. They made love in the tent, in the hammock, swimming in the water. The canoe trips had been all they could afford in those early days, when student loans seemed insurmountable.

"Then what?" she asked. "We just wait it out in the woods? We won't have any way to know what's happening."

"That's the point. I'm sick of knowing what's happening. It isn't good for us. I'm sick of our kids hearing all the crap on the news."

Barry had watched a story about a man who tied one end of a rope around his neck and the other around a telephone pole before speeding away in his convertible. The man's head popped off like a champagne cork. Barry had slept in their bed for days after that.

Lindsey pulled her hand away. "We can't be out of touch. What if the staff at the nursing home bails? We'd never know. Mom could be lying there without any food or water, in her own filth."

"I'll get a satellite phone. We can fly up to Ely. The plane will be right there if we need to come back. We don't even have to go deep in the backcountry."

Her eyes shifted from side to side. David held his breath, hoping.

"What are we supposed to do if the Ender hits, David? We'll be in a tent."

He opened and closed his mouth, grasping for a response. How could she ignore the facts? "What do you think we're going to do *here* when it hits?"

"The basement. One of the shelters downtown. Who knows? We might still get in at Gateway." She'd entered their names into a lottery, hoping to win one of five hundred spots in a converted limestone mine in Pennsylvania.

"Lindsey, that thing is going to hit in ten days and it won't matter where we are." The words came hot and angry. "The basement won't save us. If the people in that mine survive somehow, they're going to be eating each other once the food runs out. They won't ever come above ground again. It's going to be a wasteland for a half century. This isn't a goddamn tornado warning."

She turned away. Lindsey's father had sworn like a sailor before he died. Cursing pissed her off. "Nobody knows for sure what will happen," she said. "I'm not willing to give up. We can't just run away."

"What's the fucking point? Our lives are miserable. We watch the world fall apart on the news. We check online to see which of our friends have slit their wrists. We line up for rations downtown once a week." He grabbed a jar of pureed carrots and slammed it on the table. "You're plundering day-care centers, for Christ's sake. We're just waiting to die."

She crossed her arms. "What about the rocket missions?"

Four spacecraft had recently launched from Florida and New Mexico. There hadn't been any official explanation, but rumors had sprouted. Astronauts were going to stop the Ender. They'd blow it up or blow it off course, just like in the movies.

David had read enough reports to know that nothing would work. The Ender contained too much mass and its collision course was too direct. He clasped his fingers together and forced himself to keep a slow, even tone. "If those rocket launches somehow manage to save us, we can come back home and pick up our lives again. Maybe by then someone will have removed Mrs. Turner's rotting corpse from across the street."

She nodded slowly. "Maybe someone will have removed Mom's corpse by then, too."

"Open your eyes," David growled. "She's a vegetable. She might as well be dead already." The words hung in the air like a noxious cloud. *Fuck.* Why couldn't he just keep his mouth shut?

Lindsey's voice was ice. "You go off to the woods if you want, but if you do, you're going alone." She stood and stormed from the house, slamming the door behind her.

Chapter Four

"Shit," David muttered. The needles on the fuel gauges wavered below the one-quarter mark. The tanks had only been half full when they took off, almost three hours ago.

They'd watched at least a dozen capsules lift off in the distance, all rocketing straight up.

They hadn't seen a single capsule on the ground.

"Try your mom again."

Kim punched the redial button on David's phone, which was attached to his headset by an adapter. Regulations only allowed the use of the device while taxiing, but David wasn't exactly worried about getting a fine.

The call went straight to Lindsey's voicemail.

"Shit."

"Do you think she's okay?" Kim asked, her eyebrows arching toward each other.

"I'm sure she's fine," David said. What else could he say?

He turned the plane ninety degrees and crossed another empty field, scanning the ground. They would need to land soon. They could wait for Lindsey, but how could she find them if she never answered her damn phone? He prayed she was okay. Things weren't as dire in Minnesota as they were in places like Oklahoma, but even here, there'd been stories of murder and abduction.

He pulled back the throttle to slow the plane and buy a few extra minutes aloft. He reached for the GPS to search for the nearest airport, then stopped himself.

Maybe I should climb until the air gets so thin we pass out. Just get it over with.

The plane would eventually run out of fuel and plummet to the ground. In less than two days, a roiling firestorm would cover the planet, regardless of what Lindsey and the skeptics of the world believed. Maybe it would be better to end it all now.

"Wait, Daddy, go back," Barry called out.

The boy had sounded five false alarms so far. David circled and scanned the ground without any real hope.

A white capsule shone brilliantly from the center of an empty brown field, miles from the nearest road. It was all theirs.

"That's it. You did it, Barry."

Kim smiled, her second that day. "What do we do now?"

He weighed his options. They could land at the nearest small airport, which might have a loaner car in the parking lot if they were lucky. Failing that, they'd have to wait for Lindsey to arrive and pick them up, assuming she ever answered her phone. In either case, they'd be miles from this capsule. Anyone could come along in the meantime and take it.

"Kim, get my checklist. Find the section for Soft Field Landing."

She shuffled the laminated pages. "We're not going to an airport?"

From the back, Barry said, "Let me see the checklist."

"Not now, Barry. Kim, you got it?" David's heart thumped in his chest. He'd never landed on anything but concrete.

"Yeah, but why aren't we going to an airport?"

He looked out the window as he circled the capsule. "Someone else will get here first. There's no time."

"Maybe that guy wants it," Barry said.

At the far edge of the field, a gray pickup bounced across the ruts.

Desperate rage surged in David's throat. "We got here first. It's ours. Kim, read me that checklist."

"Uh, one, normal approach configuration."

David nodded and glanced at his daughter. "Climb in the back next to Barry." She'd be safer back there if the landing was rough.

"What about Kona?"

"Get back there. Keep her between you." He clenched the yoke as Kim climbed over the seat. "Buckle up, both of you, tight as you can."

He wiped sweat from his eyes and maneuvered the plane away from the capsule.

Lindsey, where are you?

David reached for the flap lever and pulled it all the way up. With his left hand, he pushed the yoke forward to keep the nose down. "Are you buckled?"

"Daddy, is this safe?" Barry sounded scared.

"I need you to hold Kona for me, Bud. Help her be brave." He turned the plane ninety degrees to the left.

A long plume of dust rose behind the pickup truck.

"Keep reading, Kim. What's next?" David turned another ninety degrees. They were now pointing straight back at the capsule. Lines of plowed soil ran below them like corduroy.

"Two, during flare, maintain nose-high altitude."

"Attitude," he corrected. "Got it. What's next?"

"Add power during flare before touchdown to keep elevator effective and hold weight off nose wheel."

David pulled back the throttle to let the plane descend. He glanced at the airspeed indicator, then pitched forward more to keep his speed above forty knots. "Don't stall, don't stall," he muttered. His arm trembled on the yoke and sweat rolled down his sides.

"Four. During rollout, set power to idle and increase back elevator to keep weight off nose wheel. Five, no braking during roll-out." She paused. "Why can't you use the brakes?"

"It brings the nose wheel down too hard. It might get caught in the dirt and flip us."

"Daddy, the truck's getting closer."

"We found it first," David said through gritted teeth. He pushed the nose lower and checked the airspeed indicator again. The plane was a thousand feet from the capsule and two hundred feet above the dirt. He stole a glance out the side window. A man stood in the bed of the pickup, holding on to the roll bar.

"Dad, have you done this before?" Kim asked.

"I've practiced this kind of landing many times." He didn't mention that he only practiced it on paved runways with a certified instructor next to him. "Are your seatbelts tight?" He reached down and cinched his own.

The plane dropped lower and David nudged the throttle to keep the wheels above the ground. The capsule was six hundred feet ahead.

He held the yoke back. The stall horn shrieked, making him flinch. Dirt raced by twenty feet below. He nudged the power and held the yoke steady, allowing the plane to descend.

When the rear wheels touched, he pulled back on the throttle and the yoke at the same time.

A jolt shuddered them as the plane's tail struck dirt. Kona growled.

David held the yoke against his chest with both hands, clenching his teeth. He flexed his feet to keep them away from the brake pedals. The plane bounced and rolled, straight down the ruts.

He smiled. He'd pulled it off. He had actually—

The right wheel caught on something and the plane veered sideways, bouncing hard across rows of dirt. Instinctively, David stomped the left brake to compensate. The nose dropped. His heart hitched when he realized what he'd done.

The nose wheel of the two-thousand-pound airplane plowed into soft soil. The propeller struck the ground and a horrible clanking filled the cabin as the engine tore itself apart. The front of the plane lurched downward.

David's chest pressed against his shoulder belt as the tail lifted into the air. He grabbed the dashboard to brace himself. *"No, no, no!"* The back of the plane continued to rise. They were flipping over.

Kim and Barry screamed. Kona howled.

The seatbelt dug into David's torso, holding him against his seat. Dust and debris fell from the floor. He closed his eyes and crossed his forearms in front of his face. The world turned upside down.

"Daddy!"

The Cessna 172 slammed on its roof and came to a stop, the engine silent. Avgas fumes choked the air. Kona lay on the roof below him, whimpering.

"Barry, Kim, are you okay?"

The pickup growled in the distance, growing closer.

"I think so," Kim said.

David unfastened his seatbelt and fell onto the roof. Kona licked his face. "Hey, girl." He crawled into the back and reached up for Barry's seatbelt. A shallow scratch ran down the side of the boy's face.

Kim unbuckled herself and fell next to him, trembling. "Dad?" She was terrified, but she didn't seem hurt.

"Get the door open." He unfastened Barry. "You okay, Buddy?"

Barry dropped to his hands and knees and vomited.

Kim shoved the front seat forward and pushed on the door handle. "It won't move."

"Get out of the way." He leaned back on his elbows and kicked. The door swung open two feet, then stuck firm in the dirt. "Can you fit through?"

Kim crawled out.

David shoved Barry through the half-open door behind his sister.

Several loud bangs echoed through the plane as he squeezed out behind his son. What the hell was making that noise? He stood and looked at the approaching truck. The man riding in the back held an oversized rifle. He tried to raise it, but stopped to grab the roll bar as the truck bounded over tilled soil.

"Goddammit, there's kids here!"

The white capsule sat twenty feet away. The pickup was less than a quarter mile back and coming fast. It accelerated.

David pushed his children toward the capsule. "Kona, come on."

"What about our stuff?" Kim asked.

"What about Mommy?"

David couldn't answer. Another series of shots rang out. Dirt danced around them. David turned back and shouted, *"There's kids—"* The front of his right thigh burst open.

"Aaaaahhhh!"

His leg buckled under him and he fell on his face, getting a mouthful of dirt. His thigh burned as if white-hot metal pressed into it. He reached down, finding thick blood.

"Dad!" Kim shouted.

He tried to stand but his right leg wouldn't hold his weight. He dropped to his left knee and spat soil. The capsule wasn't even open yet.

"Go touch it, Barry. Hurry!"

Kim grabbed his armpit and he limped to his feet. She was a slight girl, barely eighty pounds, but she pulled like a weightlifter. David grimaced and staggered forward. Blood pulsed from his leg with every heartbeat.

Barry ran the last few steps, wailing. He placed his hand on the smooth white surface. A horizontal seam appeared and the top half floated upward.

The truck's horn blared and a new volley of shots rang out. Geysers of dirt exploded around them. Kim helped David stumble to the side of the capsule. Putting all his weight on his good leg, he lifted Barry into the open gap. Tears ran down the boy's face. His screams became gasps.

The top of the capsule switched direction and began floating back down.

Kim stood next to him with Kona's leash in one hand. Somehow, she'd managed to get hold of the dog. Barking madly, Kona pulled toward the truck.

David patted the inside of the capsule. "Up, girl."

Kona jumped in next to Barry.

"Get in, Kim, go." The truck's horn blared non-stop. Kim had one leg up over the edge, then the other. She was inside.

The top half of the capsule was less than two feet from the bottom now.

"Dad!"

David looked back. "We could have shared it, assholes," he muttered.

The truck lurched to a stop. Up in the bed, a large man in a denim vest fumbled with his gun. He tossed a magazine off into the dirt and slapped at his pockets. "Get away from there!"

David's children grabbed his arms and tugged. He lifted himself onto the edge and pulled his bloody leg inside just before the top half of the capsule connected with the bottom, sealing them in complete darkness.

Chapter Five

David lay between his kids, pressing his hands against the wet wound on his thigh. He slowed his breathing, fighting dizziness and disorientation. He was on his back, but he could barely tell which way was up. He needed to figure out what was happening. Had they lifted off yet? The pain searing his leg made it impossible to focus.

Light appeared from Kim's mobile phone as she zigzagged it around. Everything was black. David reached for the ceiling, making contact somewhere above his face. The soft surface yielded slightly when he pushed, like the foam of Lindsey's yoga mat.

"Do you have a signal?" Maybe it wasn't too late to try calling her again.

"No. Nothing."

"Daddy, I'm scared," Barry said. "Where's Mommy? Why did we leave without Mommy?"

"We had to," David growled. "They were shooting at us. They fucking shot me."

Barry choked on a quiet sob.

Tears welled in David's eyes. "I'm sorry, Bud." He felt horrible for leaving without Lindsey, but he hadn't had any choice.

Blood dripped down the sides of his leg, pooling against the back of his thigh.

"Kim, are you wearing a belt?" he asked.

"Yeah."

"I need it."

She arched her back next to him and pulled her belt through the loops in her shorts. Her elbow socked his cheek and he grunted, stars dotting his vision.

"Sorry, Dad."

"It's okay. Help me put it around my leg." He lifted his thigh with both hands. Throbbing pain warned him not to raise it by flexing.

She poked her belt under his leg and reached around to grab it.

Kona panted in the dark somewhere near David's feet. How much oxygen did the capsule hold? How long before the dog huffed it all away?

David took the ends of the belt and held them together near the top of his thigh with one hand while he used the other to fumble with the buttons on his shirt.

"What are you doing?" Barry asked, his voice trembling.

"I'm trying to fix my leg, Buddy. Can you help me take off my shirt? I want to use it as a compress." He wore a fitted blue button-down shirt with a t-shirt underneath. The effort to wriggled out of it seemed like more than he could manage.

Barry moved around next to him, then handed him something. "Use my shirt."

David's chest swelled at his son's gesture. He wanted to wrap his arms around both kids.

They helped him fold Barry's shirt against the wound. He sucked air between his teeth and knotted the belt tight to hold it in place.

"I want Mommy," Barry said.

David reached over and cupped his face in the dark. "Listen. Your Mom found her own pod. That's what I'm hoping. We'll see her just as soon as ..."

"When?" Kim asked. "You have no idea where this thing is going, if it's really going anywhere. It doesn't even feel like we've moved."

There had been no sense of motion. The capsule hadn't made any sound either. Were they still sitting in the field? They'd be trapped until the Ender struck. They'd be broiled inside the capsule. *Jesus.*

"What if it never opens?" Kim asked.

How the hell was he supposed to answer that one? If they ran out of air, they'd die miserably, panicking as their lungs burned. "Just try to stay calm. Let's conserve our oxygen."

Kona panted away at his feet.

"What if it opens somewhere bad?" Barry asked.

"This thing showed up right before the Ender was going to hit," David said. "I think it was made for us. Made to save us."

"If it was made for us, why doesn't it have any lights?" Kim asked. "Or a window, or a screen, or something?"

More questions he couldn't answer. "I don't know. We'll find out, won't—"

"Dad."

David let out a long breath. "I'm sorry, Kim."

Kona whined.

"It's okay, girl. It's okay." The dog lowered her head, a comforting weight on David's feet. He tried to slow his breathing. A drumbeat of pain throbbed against his thigh.

David fished his own phone from the pocket of his chinos. It was also out of service. He used the light to look at Barry, who had his thumb in his mouth. The blood from David's hand marked his cheek like war paint.

He turned away, his eyes wet. He had to be brave for his kids. When he was twelve, David's family had taken a road trip to southern California. They stopped at Carlsbad Caverns along the way, but David's father froze at the mouth of the cave, refusing to go in, even though the tickets were non-refundable. It was the moment he realized his father wasn't all-powerful, afraid of nothing. He was just an ordinary man.

Barry and Kim had to believe he could protect them, no matter what happened. He needed them to believe it so that he could too.

He shined his light upward and pushed at the ceiling again. Unlike his father, he suffered from a fear of heights, not tight spaces, but this goddamn pod might change that. He flailed and reached, trying to find anything other than that smooth, soft surface.

Kim hugged his arm.

He turned to her, light-headed. How much blood had he lost? What if he died and the kids were stuck in here with his corpse?

Both phones flickered off. The air seemed heavy. David's ears felt stuffed with cotton.

Several minutes passed. Maybe hours. He couldn't tell. He closed his eyes and might have dozed off.

Barry broke the silence. "What's happening?"

A line of bright light pierced the darkness, circling them. It widened as the top half of the capsule floated upward.

Chapter Six

Kona wagged her tail as light spilled into the capsule. When the opening grew large enough, she jumped out, landing with a splash.

David sat up, hunching over until the top half finished rising. Barry wrapped his arms around him, clinging tightly.

The golden retriever bounded along a white sand beach, her leash flopping behind her. A wall of palm trees stood fifty feet away. Beyond that, a barren mountain rose into a cloudless sky. The air smelled fresh and clean.

Kim crawled to the edge and peered out. "Are we in Cancún?" Their last family vacation had been a trip to the Caribbean.

David's chest felt hollow. If the capsule had simply taken them to a beach somewhere, it was all for nothing. No place on Earth was safe from the Ender. "Kim, climb out and have a look around."

She scooted across the capsule, its top half floating magically above her head.

"No, no, no, wait," he said.

She looked back, silhouetted against the outside light. "It's okay, Dad. It looks safe."

"We have to get out together, in case this thing flies off again." He imagined the capsule closing on him after his children got out, carrying him away somewhere, separating them forever.

Her mouth formed a small circle and she nodded.

David's muscles moved with the numb stiffness of a rough night's sleep. Sharp pain shot through his leg when he attempted to raise it. The back of his neck ached. He lifted his thigh with his hands and inched forward, Barry's shirt still strapped against the wound. Moving slowly, he slid his good leg over the edge.

The capsule sat in a foot of water just offshore from a tropical jungle. Tiny ripples sloshed against the beach. The empty sky was the pastel blue of early twilight. A blurry smudge rose over the trees, like heat above a fire.

To the left, a rocky, double-peaked mountain thrust up from the jungle. David put it close to a thousand feet, the height he normally flew when approaching an airport. Below the peaks, a round green hill poked through the jungle canopy.

To the right, the island stretched for miles, a picture-perfect travel brochure.

"Kim, help me keep my balance. Barry, give us a count."

Barry bobbed his head and said, "One, two, three."

David gritted his teeth and dropped into ankle-deep water. He landed on his good leg and leaned against his daughter. Success. The water around his feet grew pink as blood dripped from his chinos. Holding Kim for support, he hopped four steps to the beach. Tiny stars danced in his vision.

Barry looked up at him. "Where are we, Daddy?"

David took a deep breath. He saw no sign of the Ender, which suggested the southern hemisphere, maybe the South Pacific. It looked like paradise. The sand was pristine, clear of debris or flotsam. There wasn't any real surf to speak of.

He forced a fake smile and raised one eyebrow. "I don't know. We'll find out, won't we?"

Kim narrowed her eyes but didn't complain. "What about the other pods?"

The beach lay empty in both directions, though they couldn't see very far to the left, where it curved behind the base of the mountain. If the other capsules were here, they weren't in sight. David fished his mobile phone from his pants. It was dead, though it should have still been half-charged.

"Look. More islands." Kim pointed offshore, where four green shapes sat on the horizon.

"Are the rest of the pods on the other islands?" Barry asked.

"Maybe," David said. The odds that Lindsey had found one seemed too much to hope for. "Let's get over to the trees. I need to sit down." Growing dizziness accompanied his pain.

They marched across the sand. The ground seemed to rise up around David. As an anesthesiologist, he'd sat with his patients while they drifted away before surgery. They often claimed they were falling, despite being completely motionless. *Shit. I'm going under.* He stopped walking and fought to stay conscious. If he passed out, his kids would be alone.

Kim stood next to him, eyes wide. "Dad? Are you okay?"

Barry squeezed his hand. He looked younger than six with his shirt off. "When's Mommy going to get here?"

"She isn't coming," Kim said.

Barry's face grew tight with anger. "Don't say that."

David ignored them both and concentrated on his breathing. The air temperature felt like the low seventies, but his undershirt was wet with sweat and he was parched. A fallen palm trunk lay ten yards ahead, tucked back in a little alcove at the edge of the jungle. He put one foot in front of the other. If he could crash-land his Cessna in a field, he could walk to that log without passing out.

He trudged forward, one step at a time, until finally collapsing against the log.

Nausea threatened his stomach, but he fought it off. He'd lost a lot of blood and didn't want to lose his breakfast too. Stale crackers and Irish coffee. He held perfectly still, willing his body to relax.

"What is this place, Dad?" Kim's voice wavered. She knelt next to him, her lower lip trembling and her eyebrows creeping toward each other.

"We're safe, Kim. For now, that's all that matters."

She nodded and bit down on her lip, clearly doubting him.

"How do you know?" Barry asked.

David gave him the best answer he could. "The Ender isn't in the sky." He looked at the capsule sitting at the water's edge, its top half still floating in the air. "Whoever sent those things must have been trying to help us. Why would they send us somewhere that isn't safe?"

"Do you think we're on another planet?" Barry sounded hopeful.

"I don't know," David said. He didn't know what to believe. They hadn't been in the capsule long enough to fly to another world.

"What do we do?" Barry asked.

It was a hell of a question. Until now, his only concern had been surviving the Ender. He tried to focus. "We should gather supplies. We should search for the other pods. We need water."

Most of all though, he needed to tend to his leg. He dreaded looking at it and he didn't want the kids to see it until he knew how bad it was.

Kim was fighting back tears. The sight broke his heart.

"What is it, Sweetie?"

"Nothing," she said, tugging a curl of hair behind her ear, the way she always did when she was lying. Her eyes darted in Barry's direction, then back to him. The tears broke loose and rolled down her cheeks.

Whatever it was, she wouldn't talk about it in front of her brother. David twisted around to look behind him. The underbrush was thin, allowing him to see a dozen yards or more. It looked safe enough.

"Barry, can you do a special job for me? I need you to find a walking stick. Nice and thick. Can you do that?"

Barry grinned. Collecting sticks was one of his specialties.

"Stay right back there." David pointed over his shoulder. "Do not go out of sight." He looked around. "Where's Kona?" He gave a feeble whistle, his mouth sticky and dry.

Kim yelled, "Kona!"

The golden retriever ran into their little alcove from somewhere out on the beach. She panted and wagged her tail.

"Keep her with you."

Barry took Kona's leash and walked around the log.

David turned to Kim, speaking quietly so her brother couldn't hear. "Sweetie, what's the matter?"

Her lower lip trembled. "Dad, are we dead?"

He let his shoulders drop, feeling a wave of relief. Finally, a question he could answer. He took her hand. "No, Kim. We are certainly not dead."

She pulled away. "How do you know? This could be heaven, couldn't it?"

"I don't think people ride to heaven in shiny white capsules." He smiled. "But the real reason I know we're not dead is that my leg really, really hurts."

Her eyebrows pulled apart a little. That was good.

"I need to look at it, but I need you guys to give me some space while I do."

"Alright." She wiped her cheeks. Her eyebrows returned to their normal positions, little brown arcs over her hazel eyes. The fear had subsided, at least for now.

"Water is our first priority. I want you and Barry to look for seashells or maybe some broad leaves we can use to collect rainfall." It was the only thing he could think of. Thirst, a symptom of blood loss, was hitting him hard.

Barry dragged three sticks over. "Are these good?" Kona stood next to him, her tail still wagging.

David chose one long enough to serve as a walking stick and stout enough to act as a club. "Perfect, Buddy."

"I found this too." Barry handed him something that looked like a coconut shell.

David studied the bowl-shaped object. It looked *exactly* like a coconut shell. Maybe they really were still on Earth. If so, what would hit them first, the wall of fire or the tsunami?

He sighed, handed back the shell, and gestured toward the sea. "Would you fill this with water for me? I can use saltwater to rinse off my leg." It wouldn't be sterile, but he didn't have any other options.

Barry and Kona crossed the beach to the shoreline. The top half of the capsule had lowered back down. What the hell did that mean? If they touched it, would it open again?

"Don't touch the pod," he called out. He didn't know what it might do.

"How bad is it?" Kim asked, nodding at his leg.

"I don't know. I need to look at it." It felt like his quadriceps had been shredded.

Out at the shore, Kona bent, lapping water.

"Shit. Kona, *no!*"

Barry looked up, but the dog continued to drink, her tail flapping back and forth.

David cupped his hands and shouted, "Barry, bring her back."

The boy returned with the coconut shell full of water. Kona trotted alongside him.

David scratched the dog's neck. "You can't drink saltwater, girl. It'll make you sick."

Barry handed him the shell. "How do you know it's saltwater?"

The question was simple, but it felt like a slap in the face. How did he know anything? David stuck his finger into the water and touched it to his tongue.

There wasn't the slightest hint of salt.

"Where the hell are we?" he whispered.

He needed water. He didn't know if it was safe to drink, but it had been good enough for Kona, and again, he had no alternatives. He raised the shell to his lips and took a sip. It tasted pure. He sucked down the rest, cooling the inside of his sticky mouth.

"Get me more water, please." It would help him recover from the blood loss. He just had to pray it didn't turn out to be toxic or filled with parasites.

Barry made five trips before David decided he'd drunk enough. He saved the last shell-full to rinse his wound.

"Listen guys, I need you to give me a few minutes alone so I can look at my leg. Go out on the beach." He pointed beyond the little recessed area where he was sitting. Even if they walked left or right, he would still be able to watch them through the palm trees. "Go see what you can find. More coconuts would be great, especially some that are solid. We'll need rocks to crack them open." A supply of rocks might come in handy if they had to scare off a wild animal, but David kept this thought to himself. What kind of animals lived here? It sure as hell wasn't the Caribbean or South Pacific. Not if the ocean was fresh water. He shoved aside his rising panic. Maybe it wasn't an ocean. Maybe it was just a giant lake in the middle of Africa or something.

"You got it, Dad." Kim rose to her feet.

David waved Barry closer. "Listen, Buddy, you stay right by your sister, okay? It's dangerous if you don't."

Barry took Kim's hand and they walked around the trees to the left. Kona followed them.

A heavy weight pulled on the bottom of David's stomach, the same feeling he got from heights. He wanted to go with them, to keep them safe. Instead, he forced himself to shift his focus to his leg. He had to take care of himself first.

The kids were only thirty feet away. They'd be fine for a few minutes. They had to be.

He used his elbows to climb onto the log. Once on top, he teetered backwards and reflexively shot out his legs as a counterweight. Daggers of pain jabbed his thigh. *"Shit."*

He sat still for a moment, both hands on the log, sweating. The peaty smell of rotting vegetation filled the air. Out in front of him, palm trees crowded in from both sides, framing his view of the white capsule at the shoreline, with cloudless blue sky behind it. Every few seconds, he caught sight of Barry and Kim through the trees on the left. Other than the kids chattering, he heard nothing. The trees were still. No birds or bugs chirped in the jungle.

"Maybe we are in heaven," he said. If only Lindsey was here.

He untied the belt around his leg and pulled away Barry's t-shirt, now sopping wet. Thankfully, it had been red to begin with. Rocking from one butt cheek to the other, he inched his chinos down until the wound was exposed.

Based on the pain, David thought his thigh had been destroyed. Two years ago, when a windstorm knocked down trees all over town, the hospital had been hit with four chainsaw accidents. The worst had been a man who ripped a gash all the way into his femur.

David imagined that his thigh must look about the same. What he actually saw left him feeling wimpy, embarrassed, and relieved.

The bullet had torn across the front of the rectus femoris muscle, leaving a gully barely big enough to hold a pencil. Crusted brown blood filled the gash. David rinsed the wound with water from the coconut shell and picked away bits of dirt. He focused on the injury from a medical perspective, trying to keep the pain at a distance. The flesh lining the edge of the laceration was gnarled and white. Serous fluid seeped from muscle fibers. As long as the fluid remained clear, he was free from infection.

The wound wasn't debilitating, but it still hurt like hell. David longed for the first aid kit from the plane.

And the camping gear.

And his wife.

He shrugged out of his button-down, leaving the black t-shirt underneath, which was more than enough to be comfortable. The air was neither hot nor cold. He folded the shirt into a new compress and pulled his chinos up over it to hold it in place. He would rinse the blood from Barry's shirt and give it back to him. David felt better after looking at the wound. The water he'd drunk also helped. He didn't feel quite so weak. Hopefully, it wouldn't make him sick.

He listened for animal calls in the jungle. Still nothing. The dribbling waves were inaudible from this distance. The silence felt unearthly.

He'd done it. He'd saved his kids from the Ender. Now what? He still had to make sure they were safe. What did that even mean? He needed to figure out where they were. They needed food, shelter, protection from the elements and whatever else was out there. He needed to find other people who could help them survive.

A cold chill settled over him. He would be doing it all without Lindsey. Unless she'd somehow found a pod on her own. Was that too much to hope for?

David sat, his heart aching every bit as much as his leg.

Somewhere out on the beach, Kim screamed.

A moment later, Barry squealed.

"What?" David called out. "W-what is it?"

Both kids took off running, their shapes flickering beyond the trees. Kona barked nonstop, the way she did when someone rang the doorbell.

David scrambled to his feet, ignoring the pain in his thigh.

Something ran past on the beach. His throat grew tight. He only caught a glimpse from the corner of his eye, but it was bigger than a person, and definitely not human.

"Kim! Barry!"

The creature raced after his kids.

Heavy terror sunk in his guts. David snatched the stick and started forward, leaning on it like a crutch. He staggered out from the alcove, heart pounding, sweat dripping down his back.

Somewhere in the distance, his children screamed.

Chapter Seven

David broke into a run. His leg collapsed under him. *"Fuck!"* He jerked his good knee forward and somehow managed to land on it instead of his face.

A wave of panic swept over him. He couldn't save his kids if he couldn't even reach them.

He pulled himself up with the walking stick and trudged down the beach, hissing between his teeth. Every time he tried to speed up, his leg buckled.

"Barry! Kim!" Tears stung his eyes. *Please be okay.* He couldn't see them or the creature that had followed them.

More screams came from the jungle, somewhere ahead and to the left. He pushed himself, managing a slow jog.

Shivers ran through his body and he huffed from exertion. *Don't hyperventilate. Don't pass out.*

Kona barked, then Kim screamed again, closer now. Screaming meant it wasn't too late. Not yet.

Something moved near a large tree at the edge of the jungle.

An eight-foot-tall creature strutted back and forth on two long, scaly legs, with an oversized vulture beak big enough to snap a sapling. Stunted wings hung from its shaggy body. It looked like a giant cassowary, but the proportions were all wrong, like something from a kids' book where you flipped parts of the page to mix various heads, bodies, and feet.

Kona feinted around the giant bird, barking. She darted close until it turned on her, then dashed away, tail tucked and hackles up.

"Barry! Kim! Where are you?"

"Daaaddyyy!"

The fear in Barry's voice ripped David's heart. Both children clung to branches just above the bird's reach. Sprawling limbs jutted in every direction, like on an old oak. Kim hung with one arm and one leg looped over a branch, watching the giant bird strut around below. Three or four other limbs forked above her. She could climb higher if she tried, but Barry had reached a dead end. His branch angled upward just beyond his grip. He hung with both arms and legs wrapped tightly around the limb. Blood smeared the side of his face.

The creature abandoned Kona and ran under the boy, tilting its massive head toward him. Its beak opened and closed with an audible scrape, like the sound of the arm blade on a schoolroom paper cutter.

"No," Kim shouted. She dropped her legs from her own branch and bicycled them in the air. "Hey! Hey you!"

The creature left Barry and moved back to Kim. It shook its scraggly wings, crouched, and leaped straight up.

Kim lifted her legs as the huge beak snapped shut right where her feet had been.

She'd just saved her brother's life. Barry was lower. If the bird jumped at him, it would slice him in half.

David sucked in a lungful of air and let out a primal roar.

The creature swung in his direction, cocking its head sideways on its thick neck.

He stood alone on the beach, exposed. Easy prey. The creature took a few slow steps, then hissed and charged.

Kona barked from the woods, but the bird ignored her, racing forward on black talons that belonged on a dragon.

David's heart rattled like a snare drum. The jungle was only fifteen feet away, but he could never make it to cover. He was too slow. He lifted his walking stick and held it like a club. He planted his feet wide, digging them in the sand, ignoring the tearing sensation in his thigh.

The giant bird closed on him and leapt, cocking its claws forward. David drew the stick back over his shoulder like Kirby Puckett with the bases loaded.

As the monster descended, he swung, letting himself fall sideways, out of its trajectory. Claws sliced air next to his head. The stick made contact on the side of its body and the swinging motion propelled David further out of the way. He landed on his back, sand running into his t-shirt. Blackness crept in from the edges of his vision. *No.* If he passed out, that thing would eviscerate him.

The creature fell in a flopping heap, head and legs jerking in the sand as it tried to right itself.

David lurched to his feet, bringing new slices of pain to his thigh, and staggered to the thrashing animal. He raised the stick overhead and slammed it down, breaking the creature's scraggly wing with a wet crack. He felt bones snap through the stick.

The bird screeched, pulled its legs under itself, and rose in one swift movement. Its huge beak towered over him.

Kona moved close, barking nonstop.

David pressed the end of the stick against the creature's chest and shoved, driving it backwards. His thigh howled in protest. The monster backpedaled and almost went down again. He pushed forward.

Kona snapped at the creature's feet.

The bird shrieked, revealing serrated edges on its beak, like teeth on a coping saw. *What the hell is this thing?* He swung again with his club, hitting the wattled pink skin on the side of its head.

The creature stepped back, turned, and fled, its injured wing flopping at its side. It raced along the edge of the jungle, then jolted into the forest and disappeared.

David swiveled toward the tree, off balance and utterly exhausted.

"Barry? Kim?" His throat burned, raw and dry. His vision darkened. He dropped to his good knee.

If the kids responded, he couldn't hear it over his heartbeat pounding in his ears. He shuddered from the adrenaline coursing through him. *Can't pass out.*

Kim helped Barry climb down. They ran to him and wrapped their arms around him. The top of Barry's scalp was sliced so deep David thought he saw bone.

"It's okay, it's okay," he gasped, holding them as tightly as he could, still on one knee.

Barry pressed his bloody face against his neck, wailing.

"We need more sticks," David muttered. "One for each of you."

If the bird came back, he didn't have the strength to fight it off again. A black shroud crept in from the sides of his vision. He fought to stay conscious.

Barry kept crying. David looked at the injury on his son's head, struggling to focus. Maybe it wasn't bone. Maybe it was just sliced skin. He forced himself to breathe deeply. He needed to stay awake. "We have to find someplace safe."

"I want Mooommy!"

"I know." He squeezed Barry and looked at his daughter. "Let's get back to the pod. Maybe we can open it and hide inside."

Kim looked past him at something, her eyebrows pulling together.

David tried to rise, but he collapsed forward, taking Barry with him.

"Dad," Kim said. "Someone's coming." She sounded far away, at the end of a long tunnel.

He wanted to ask who or what, but his mouth wouldn't work. Cotton filled his head, the falling sensation returned, and everything went black.

Chapter Eight

One Day Before Impact

When the end of the world began, Sierra Preston accepted that there wasn't anything she could do. She tried to appreciate the fact that she'd had a good twenty-three year run and was privileged to live out her final days in relative luxury and safety. She simply continued her routine as best as possible. A fifteen-mile-wide rock was going to strike Earth. Nothing could be done.

Yesterday, everything changed.

The country had gone insane over the pods. No one knew where they came from and no one knew where they went, but it didn't matter. They took you away.

Sierra had been glued to the news, which showed the best of humanity, along with the worst, and plenty of gray areas in between. She saw people work together to pack the pods full. She watched a man in Colorado shoot someone and march through a pile of bodies to claim a pod by himself. In Minnesota, a tearful family recounted the story of a pilot who crashed in their field and took their pod before they could get to it.

When it became clear that the pods were concentrated in a swath from the Great Lakes to the Great Basin, millions raced west from the Atlantic seaboard, despite the fact that all the known pods had already been taken.

Sierra didn't have any hope of finding a pod on her own. She knew only one person capable of pulling off the impossible. Unfortunately, she hadn't seen him for days.

She walked down the aisle of a cinema in Westwood, California, while Luke, Han, and Chewbacca walked through the throne room on the eighty-foot-wide screen above. Moving row-by-row, she scanned each face in the audience, searching for her father. If a pod remained anywhere, he could secure it. Her father made things happen. He brokered multi-million-dollar Hollywood deals. Nothing was impossible for Rick Preston.

The three heroes on the screen passed dozens of rebel pilots. *All those pilots*, Sierra thought, *and they gave one of their few spaceships to a kid they'd just met.*

Sierra's father hated when she pointed out plot holes. "Why can't you just enjoy it?" he would plead. Her father loved *Star Wars*. It was the reason he became a studio executive. When she learned someone had dug up a print of the classic film, she'd been sure she would find him here.

Rick Preston disappeared a week ago, right after the Ender became visible in the daytime. "Just a quick stop at the office, Kiddo." He never came back. She'd gone to the studio looking for him, but the lot was deserted. She called everyone she could think of. No one had heard from him.

After that, Sierra stopped searching. She had everything she needed in their Pacific Palisades mansion, including the Valium that helped her sleep. There was nothing to do but wait for the end.

Until the pods appeared.

Sierra squinted in the darkness. The crowd on the screen showed a bit more dignity than the audience in the auditorium, many of whom were drunk or high. Pungent smoke turned the light from the projector into a spectral beam. Almost everyone here was middle-aged and white, like her father, which meant she had to study each face carefully.

She passed a man grasping the waist of a woman bouncing up and down on his lap. His pants were around his ankles, but the woman's skirt kept them mostly covered as she rode him. The man leaned around her, watching the enormous screen with an equally enormous grin. Thankfully, he wasn't her dad.

Chewbacca roared and both crowds burst into applause.

As the credits rolled, Sierra crossed the bottom of the auditorium and started up the other side.

A shirtless man with puffy eyes offered her a bottle of vodka. Grey Goose, perfect for the end of the world. She wiped the mouth, drank a swig, and thanked him. He smiled. Tears moistened the bags under his eyes.

She moved on, checking the last few faces before walking out. In the lobby, she took a tube of lipstick from her pocket and wrote on a mirrored wall, "Rick Preston, please come home, Sierra."

She tried to keep her hopes tempered. She had a lot to be thankful for. Everything had been handed to her, and she hadn't let it ruin her. She hadn't ended up in rehab, like several of her friends. She'd graduated from college with a business degree. It had been a good run.

Her motorcycle sat on the sidewalk where she'd left it. She climbed on, cranked the engine, and drove west, not wanting to return home yet, but not sure where else to go. She threaded the bike between abandoned cars littering the road and even found a few stretches where she got up to thirty miles an hour, enjoying the breeze pulling her hair back. She didn't bother with a helmet, but she'd put on her favorite riding leathers, a two-tone white and teal jacket with a camisole underneath, and padded white pants.

She told herself her father couldn't have procured a pod anyway. Even Rick Preston had his limits. She'd given up her initial search for him days earlier, and now she had to give up again, which triggered a fresh wave of grief.

After passing under the interstate, she turned toward Sunset Boulevard, stopping when she spotted a crowd in the intersection ahead. The mob seemed focused on a convenience store. Someone must have discovered an unlooted storage room.

She decided to circle around to the south, down near the ocean. She would get to see the beach one last time. Sierra revved the throttle and planted her boot to pivot the bike.

"Wait, help!"

A white kid ran toward her from the crowd. His gangly arms and legs suggested that puberty had only just begun its work on him, putting him at fifteen, tops. He wore a gray hoodie with a sporting goods logo printed on the chest and one knobby knee poked through a hole in his jeans.

"You gotta get me out of here. Please."

Sierra looked past him. The mob had separated into two factions. A gunshot popped in the distance. The kid squealed and brought his arms up around his head.

She considered riding off. The kid would be fine. No one was looking this way. But he didn't know that. He was terrified. Round eyeglasses magnified wide brown eyes.

"Alright. Hop on." She gestured over her shoulder with her chin.

He climbed onto the bike and wrapped his arms around her. More shots popped behind them as she accelerated away. The boy's arms tightened around her waist.

"See those handles below your seat?" she called over her shoulder. "You hold on to those."

He did as instructed, removing his hands from her midsection. Sierra wove around abandoned cars, passed the golf course, and turned up the hill, unsure what to do with her new passenger. She stopped in front of a Montessori school, letting the engine idle, and turned to look at him.

He had a thin neck, lips so full they looked feminine, and wire-framed glasses that had gone out of style a decade ago. He looked like the kind of kid who got bullied.

"Where're your parents, kid?"

"Josh. My name is Josh. My parents are in Bakersfield."

"What're you doing here?"

"I was down here because my parents spend all day praying. I wanted to have some fun before I died."

She snorted. "You came to L.A. to get laid."

He flushed, his face splotchy and red. "No, I didn't."

"Fair enough," she said. He was lying, but she didn't need to embarrass him any further.

He locked eyes with her. "Yesterday a man threatened to rape me near Hollywood Boulevard." He trembled. "That's the closest I've been to getting laid."

"I'm sorry." The poor kid was too young to go through this alone. There were parts of L.A. that would beat him half to death and then eat him alive. Literally. There were still good people out there, too, but not on the streets. "Why don't I take you back to your parents? They'll be glad to see you."

Riding up to Bakersfield would beat sitting in her father's empty mansion waiting for the Ender to hit and feeling shitty about the fact that he'd disappeared right when she needed him most. She and Josh would cut through the mountains to the east, since Interstate 5 had been bombed. The sun and breeze would feel good, and so would doing something charitable right before the end.

Josh shrugged. "Sure, whatever."

"Perfect. We'll stop off at my house and get a few things first." She would grab some water bottles, snacks, and maybe the picture of her family from back before Mom moved out.

She gunned the throttle and continued up the hill. Her detour around the mob had taken her farther north than normal, putting her on roads she hadn't used in weeks.

She had to slow down as she approached the estate of retired quarterback Gil Alexander. Dozens of cars lined the street, some of them double-parked. Number eight appeared to be having an end-of-the-world party.

An ember of hope flared in Sierra's mind. Her father sometimes hung out with Gil. They'd attended football games in his stadium box. Even if Dad wasn't here, Gil might know something.

The gate was open and the line of parked cars continued down the driveway to the house, like traffic on the freeway. Sierra turned in, riding along the grass right up to the front door. No one met them. Another dozen cars were parked in Gil's courtyard, including a familiar red coupe. Hope swelled in Sierra's chest as she lowered the kickstand.

"Holy shit, is this your place?"

"No. It belongs to a friend. Listen Josh, I need you to wait here for a minute while I get my dad."

"He's here?"

"I think so," she said, pointing at the red convertible. "That's his car."

Chapter Nine

David felt a cool wet cloth on his forehead. *Lindsey*. She always held a washcloth on his face when he was sick.

"Good morning." The voice sounded like it came from an old chain-smoking cowboy. "Or good afternoon, I should say." Definitely not his wife.

David opened his eyes, squinting against the pale blue sky. "My kids?"

"They're okay. They're not far."

A weight lifted from David's chest. "The bird creature?"

"We haven't seen it. But everyone's keeping together. They're safe."

David felt groggy and disoriented. He wanted to sit up but wasn't sure he was ready.

"I'm Waldmire." The man even looked like an old chain-smoking cowboy. Scraggly white hair hung over pinpoint green eyes and a narrow face of folded wrinkles. "I helped haul you up here." He wore a heavy brown Henley shirt with all three buttons fastened to the neck.

Heat from a small campfire warmed the side of David's face. "Where are we?"

"We're on a hill in the center of the island. We can see in all directions." He gestured off to the side. "We spotted your pod down on the beach from up here."

David touched his leg near the wound. It still hurt, but the pain felt dull now. "How many are with you?" Without waiting for an answer, he added, "My wife?"

Waldmire shook his head. "I'm sorry. It's just me, a young lady named Sierra, and a boy named Josh."

"What is this place? Do you know where we are?" Moving slowly, David sat up and looked around.

The jungle extended for miles in front of the hill. Beaches ran along both sides, meeting at a thin point in the distance.

Waldmire scratched his white goatee. "I was hoping you could tell me. I can't figure it."

"Do you think it's an alien planet?" Saying the words out loud felt weird, especially to a stranger.

"It doesn't seem like Earth," Waldmire conceded. "But there's palm trees and figs. How do you explain that?"

Hunger twirled David's stomach. "Figs?"

Waldmire pointed. "There's a whole mess of fig trees on the other side. Sierra, Josh, and I passed them on our way up here."

"Is your capsule down there?"

"No." Waldmire pointed at the vast slope behind the hilltop. "Our pod landed on a thin beach on the backside of that mountain. We had to hike around."

David nodded and looked out to sea. A large island loomed offshore on the left, fifteen or twenty miles away, with a broad plateau rising up in the middle.

"Could be another planet," Waldmire said. "Could be another dimension."

David turned back and raised one eyebrow. "Why would you think that?"

A smile lifted the corners of Waldmire's mouth. David's eyebrow trick often had that effect.

"We weren't in the pods long enough to travel through space," Waldmire said.

"What if time is different in the capsules?"

Waldmire rubbed the back of his neck. "Hadn't thought of that."

"Where're you from?"

"California. The hills above Santa Monica. I was Sierra's neighbor." Waldmire paused. "A family friend."

The word "family" brought David's focus back to Kim and Barry. "Thank you for taking care of me and my kids."

"My pleasure," Waldmire said.

He seemed like a genuinely decent man.

"Where are they?" David asked. "Can I see them?"

"Of course. Let me call them." Waldmire walked toward the front of the hill and produced a piercing whistle.

The campfire sat on the center of a grassy hill rising above the canopy. Directly ahead, the jungle narrowed to a point at the end of the island, some ten miles out. David twisted around. Behind him, a barren slope rose up at least five hundred feet, ending in two rocky crags with a low spot between them.

Small nests of clothes surrounded the campfire, spaced out like numbers on a clock face. The grass around the area had been stomped flat. A stack of firewood sat off to one side. Next to the wood, several plastic water bottles stood in a line, along with a row of coconut shells, a toothbrush, a short stack of clothes, and a first aid kit.

"First aid?"

Waldmire nodded. "Just the basics, but it's something. We put antibiotic ointment on your leg and fed you some crushed-up aspirin. You were feverish for a while."

David didn't remember any of this. He felt confused and lost.

Waldmire walked back and offered him a water bottle. "Your kids'll be thrilled to see you awake. They've been by your side day and night."

He took a sip before it hit him. "Night? Wait, how long have I been out?"

"A day and a half."

His heartbeat quickened. "That means Earth is gone."

Waldmire held his gaze. "Probably so."

"Have my kids said anything about that?"

"Barry believes his mom got into a pod."

"Maybe," David whispered. Aching sadness rose up inside him. *Lindsey.*

Waldmire squinted, the wrinkles around his face tightening into a spider web. He handed David a walking stick. "Barry wanted you to have this when you woke."

He smiled, tears heavy in his eyes. His children had taken care of him. He stood slowly and tested his leg. Waldmire held his arm in a strong grip and helped him hobble across the top of the hill.

"Daddy!"

Kim and Barry ran up the slope. Waldmire stepped out of the way as they crashed into him.

"I thought you died," Barry said, wrapping his arms around his waist. Kim joined the hug and he pulled them both tight.

"It's okay. I just needed some rest." He squeezed them, blinking tears from his eyes. A rust-colored scab ran across Barry's scalp. David pushed both kids out to arm's length and studied their faces. "Are you guys okay?"

Barry nodded. He wore an oversized yellow shirt with "Hollister" on the front.

A young Black woman in a white jacket with teal shoulders crested the hilltop, followed by a gangly white teenage boy. Both carried cloth bags and heavy sticks. Kona ran alongside them, wagging her tail. The woman gave David a small wave with two fingers.

"That's Sierra," Kim said. "And his name is Josh."

The boy, who wore glasses and a gray hoodie, dropped his bags near the firewood. Strange fruit rolled out, red and green, like Christmas ornaments. Barry sat down and began to sort them by color, counting as he went.

"You hungry?" Sierra asked. Her wavy black hair was pulled tight in a ponytail. "We have plenty of fruit."

Barry ran over with an emerald object the size of a tennis ball. "I got most of it. I'm the best climber. You should'a seen me."

The fruit was smooth, like a mango. David dug in with his fingernail and peeled back the skin, revealing firm white flesh underneath. His mouth moistened at whiffs of cherry and vanilla. "How do you know it's safe?"

"Waldmire says most fruit wants to be eaten," Barry said, his eyes twinkling as if he was about to burst. "Do you wanna know why?"

"Tell me."

"So you spread around the seeds with your poop." Barry snorted. Kim rolled her eyes.

David broke off a small chunk and placed it in his mouth, tasting a hint of vanilla, but also a starchy blandness, like a potato that hadn't cooked long enough. He swallowed, immediately craving more.

"I named them konapples because Kona found them," Barry said. The smile on his son's face made David feel even better than the food.

"Hey, doggo." Kim tossed one to Kona, who caught it, dropped it between her paws, and tore into it with her front teeth.

"Sierra says I'm a monkey," Barry said. "There were real monkeys up in the trees, little blue ones. What kind of monkeys are blue monkeys?"

Sad monkeys, David thought, but Barry wouldn't get the joke. He felt overwhelmed by all the new information.

"Kim was too heavy to get the best fruit," Barry said. "She broke a branch."

"Shut up, Barry," Kim said. "Don't be rude."

Sierra called to Josh. "Hey, can you build up the fire? It'll be dark soon, and I want to try roasting those root things." She looked at Waldmire and David. "We dug up some purple tubers in a little clearing."

"I wanna help," Barry said, following Josh to the firewood.

David turned to Sierra. "Thank you for taking care of them. And me."

She shrugged. "Of course." She glanced at Waldmire, then back at David. "I don't suppose you have any answers. What is this place? Who brought us here?"

"We've been chatting," Waldmire said. "Nothing concrete. Just more speculation."

"Well, now that you're awake, we can start looking for answers," Sierra said.

"What do you have in mind?" David asked. He hadn't had a chance to think beyond hugging his kids again and getting more to eat.

"For starters, we need to find the rest of the people who got in those pods."

Her smooth, wrinkle-free skin put her in her early twenties, but she carried herself with the confidence of someone twice her age.

"We'll need all kinds of people to survive here," Waldmire said. "People who can hunt, people who know how to make tools."

David worked through the idea. "That makes sense. And there's safety in numbers."

Sierra nodded. "Yeah, and we need to figure out where we are. Who brought us here? Why? What do they want?"

David ignored these questions for the moment. They felt too big to get his head around. "How do we find the rest of the people?" he asked.

"We start with this island." She pointed to the right. "You arrived on that side." She hitched her thumb toward the slope behind them. "We landed back there, and then circled up on the left." In front of them, trees extended for miles. "We need to search the jungle. After that, we need to try the other islands."

"Yeah," Kim said, her eyes wide.

David frowned. He wanted to look for other people too, but he didn't like the thought of his kids wandering off into the jungle. Hearing that they'd been climbing around in the treetops while he was unconscious made him uncomfortable.

"We should start first thing tomorrow," Sierra said.

She was moving too fast. He took a breath and asked. "Have you seen any more birds like the one that tried to kill me?"

She shook her head. "We haven't seen anything but the little monkeys, and they jump away before you get close, which is a shame." She lowered her voice. "Otherwise, we'd be roasting one."

Kim winced.

"If there was one bird, there have to be more," David said. "And I need more time to recuperate before I'm ready for a jungle trek."

"Take whatever time you need," Sierra said. "I'm not going to sit around and wait."

"I'm not suggesting that," David said. "I just think we need to be careful. You can't expect to defend yourself with nothing but sticks."

"You defended yourself with a stick just fine, and you were barely conscious, from what I heard."

Waldmire held up his hands. "I think we're all on the same page here. We don't have to make any decisions right this second."

David clenched his jaw. Sierra was not one to back down. He needed to keep his mouth under control. These were good people. They'd taken care of him and his kids. And Sierra was talking about all the right things. "I'm sorry. I'm just trying to get caught up." He shifted back to her second point. "How can we find out who brought us here?"

She seemed to think about it for a minute. "Right now, the pods are our only clue. We should find a way to open them back up."

"Have you tried touching them again?" David asked.

"Josh tried with your pod," Sierra said. "It didn't do anything."

"If we get back in them, where do you think they'll take us?" Waldmire asked. "Earth, or somewhere else?"

"Good question," David said. He had to keep his kids away from them, especially Barry.

"How do we get them open?" Kim asked.

Sierra shrugged. "We'll make tools. A hammer or an ax. I don't know." She pointed at the slope rising behind them. "If we have to, we'll roll one up the mountain and drop it over the back. The cliff goes straight down."

David tensed, even though she was clearly joking. As a rule, he avoided high places. Just being near the edge of the hilltop made him uncomfortable, and it wasn't very steep.

"We'll figure it out," she finished. "We'll find a way."

This young woman clearly never gave up. Kim seemed impressed with her as well, judging from the gleam in her eyes.

"Hey, hey, hey." Sierra shoved past him. "What are you doing?"

Barry stood with a load of branches in his arms and a proud look on his face. "You said to build up the fire." The campfire flames roared six feet high.

Josh sat nearby, playing with a large knife, ignoring him.

"I didn't tell you to burn up half our firewood. You're going to have to help us collect more."

"You can't tell me what to do," Barry snapped. "When my mom comes, she's going to yell at you."

Waldmire fished out several branches and rolled them in the dirt to snuff the flames.

Sierra rolled her eyes. "Yeah, whatever."

"Take it easy," David said. "Barry, come here."

Barry ignored him and ran off. For a moment, it looked like he was going to run all the way back to the beach, but he stopped at the far edge of the hill.

"It'll be dark soon," Waldmire warned. "Pitch black."

The sky was the same soft blue of early dusk, without a single cloud anywhere. Clouds weren't the only thing missing. David froze. "Where's the sun?"

From up on the hilltop, they ought to be able to see it, unless it was blocked by the big slope behind them. But even that didn't seem right. The light was flat and even.

"No sun," Sierra said, "At least not that we've seen. No stars. No weather."

He craned his neck skyward, searching the heavens. "How is that possible?"

"Our best theory is that the stratosphere is high and thick," Waldmire said. "It diffuses the light from whatever star is close by." He shrugged. "It also explains why night gets so dark."

"It's like a cave," Sierra said. "Without the campfire, you can't see a single thing."

He shivered. This really was an alien planet.

"Bring your boy back over here," Waldmire said. "Night comes mighty fast."

David limped to the edge of the hilltop with Kona bounding alongside. His leg hurt, but he found he could put a little weight on it.

Barry stood with his lower lip stuck out and his hands squeezed into fists. "I want Mommy."

"Me too, Bud." David hugged him. "Tell me about the blue monkeys."

Barry looked up, his eyes wet. "They go across the tops of the trees. I wanna name them sky monkeys."

"I like it."

A throaty growl came from somewhere in the jungle.

Barry clung to him. "What was that?"

"Best come back to the fire," Waldmire said. "We heard a couple of those last night."

The growl had come from far away, but it sounded larger than a giant bird.

David took Barry's hand. "Come on, Bud, let's get back. We have to stick together, okay?"

"I wanna go home."

"Maybe the capsules can help us go home," David said, though he didn't believe it. Earth wouldn't be habitable for decades. But Sierra was onto something. The capsules were their only clue about who or what had brought them here. Studying them was a good idea.

He looked down at the beach, roughly a mile away. It ran to the left all the way out to the point, which David thought of as the front of the island, and disappeared to the right, where it curved back around the mountain behind them.

David froze. "Where's our pod? Waldmire said you could see it from up here."

The sky turned gray, darkening quickly.

"You could," Barry said. He pointed. "It was right there. It's gone now."

The light continued to dim. In less than a minute, complete darkness shrouded the jungle, the water, and everything in sight except for the campfire on the center of the hilltop.

Chapter Ten

One Day Before Impact

Sierra walked through the open front entrance of Gil Alexander's mansion. "Hello?"

Except for the echo of her boots on the marble floor, the house was silent. She walked to the back. Gil's twenty-foot-long dining room table was covered by an absurd green tablecloth with the markings of a football field. Liquor bottles, pill containers, bongs, and syringes filled the end zone. A mound of cocaine sat on the sideline next to several five-hundred-dollar bills rolled into straws. Sierra looked out the glass wall at Gil's expansive backyard.

Her breath stopped.

Dozens of bodies lay scattered around the swimming pool below.

She had attended a binge party shortly after the comet first appeared. Three people had died from overdoses and one from autoerotic asphyxiation. Those might have been accidents. The bodies in Gil Alexander's backyard all lay beside red plastic cups, each of which held the remnants of a bright blue liquid. These were suicides. Sierra shook her head. Why would anyone cut short what little time was left?

She scanned each face, telling herself to just turn around and leave, but she couldn't stop looking. It felt like a dream, where she was unable to control her body and could only watch.

Her father lay on the grass, arms and legs intertwined with two women she didn't recognize, staring lifelessly up at the sky.

Sierra's breathing came fast. She'd accepted the possibility she might never find him, but she never imagined finding him dead. She felt dizzy. Cotton filled her head, her ears, her lungs.

"Fuck."

She swallowed and took a deep breath. It would have been better not to know.

The Ender would strike in twelve hours and she would face it alone. She considered trying to do something with her father's body, but then became convinced that if she went into the backyard, she wouldn't be able to stop herself from kicking him. She also guessed she wouldn't last long due to the smell. Most of the bodies looked swollen. They'd died days ago.

A tear rolled down one cheek. She wiped it away and turned back to the dining room table, wondering if she should help herself to a snort of cocaine. No. She'd tried coke at a party once and spent the night shitting herself. She would take Josh to Bakersfield. At least he would get to see his parents one last time before the end.

A clear pitcher containing a few inches of blue liquid sat in the middle of the table. Several amber bottles stood next to the pitcher. Sierra picked up one that was still full and sniffed. It smelled like vinegar. The word "Pentobarbital" was typed on the label. She stuffed it in her pocket, just to keep her options open, and walked out.

Josh sat on the edge of a koi pond in the front courtyard, playing with a huge knife. "You find your dad?"

"No," she answered, not wanting to explain, and definitely not wanting to break down crying in front of this kid. She gestured at the blade. "Where'd you get that?"

"My dad gave it to me. It's from his favorite movie, *Rocky*."

Two thoughts popped into Sierra's head. The first was that Josh could have pulled that knife on her while they'd been riding, but he hadn't. The second thought was that there weren't any knives in *Rocky*. He must have meant *Rambo*.

"My father isn't here." She walked over to the motorcycle. "One more stop and then we'll go to Bakersfield."

"How did you know?" Josh asked.

"Know what?"

"That I came to L.A. hoping to get laid?"

She smirked. "You're a fifteen-year-old boy. It isn't hard to guess."

"Sixteen. I just turned sixteen." Josh slid the knife into a sheath on the back of his belt and joined her on the motorcycle.

They rode the winding street to Sierra's house. The Ender glowed in the northern sky, larger than the sun now, though not as bright. Pulling into her driveway, Sierra waved at her neighbor, Waldmire Bock, who sat in his gazebo with a book in one hand and a joint in the other. Waldmire waved back. He'd spent a lot of time in that gazebo over the last few weeks, almost like he'd been keeping an eye on her. With anyone else, it might have been creepy, but with Waldmire, it felt comforting.

Inside the house, she thought about calling her mother, but decided against it. Their conversations always made her feel worse.

At least Dad was with someone when he died, Sierra thought. She was alone. Josh didn't count. He was just a kid.

"Your place is badass," Josh said.

He walked through the living room and opened the curtains. Sierra had closed them ten days earlier after growing sick of the Ender's pissy glow.

Josh put both hands on the glass and stared. "S-Sierra." His voice hitched. "C-come here."

She walked over and looked out, barely recognizing her own backyard. The gardeners had quit weeks ago. Vines and branches overran everything. The privacy wall on the right buckled under a purple explosion of bougainvillea.

At the bottom of the property, a round white shape sat next to a row of stubby palm trees.

Sierra couldn't believe it. "Is that what I think it is?"

Josh sounded like he might be hyperventilating. "W-we can escape."

The damn thing was right in her own backyard, and if she hadn't brought Josh here, she might never have seen it.

Tears welled in her eyes. Her father had killed himself for nothing. She should be escaping with him, not this stupid kid. She clenched her throat to keep from sobbing.

"That might be the last pod in the whole world," Josh said. "What're we waiting for?"

"What about your parents? Don't you want to call them? They might be able to get here in time if they leave now."

"My parents ... they aren't ... good." He trembled as he said it, but he didn't turn away. "They got worse when the Ender showed up."

"What does that mean?"

"I don't want to talk about it. I'm not calling them."

"So you were going to let me take you to Bakersfield for nothing?"

"I didn't want you to leave me by myself. I didn't want to be all alone when ..."

She nodded. "When the Ender hit."

"You aren't mad?"

"Will you be honest with me from here on out?" she asked.

"Probably."

"Good enough." She reached for the door, still unable to believe it was right there in her own backyard. "Come on, let's go."

Josh held up a hand. "Wait. Let's grab some stuff. You know, supplies we might need."

"Like what? We don't even know where that thing goes."

He shrugged. "Food and water. Spare clothes. I dunno."

She nodded. "Okay, but let's hurry before someone else finds it." The foliage concealed it somewhat, but she didn't want to take any chances.

Josh inhaled. "Yeah, like that geezer across the street."

A smile grew on Sierra's face. She wouldn't be quite so alone. "That geezer is a friend," she said. "He's going with us."

Chapter Eleven

Sierra trudged up the mountain with Josh, Barry, and Kim. Her legs were sore, Barry was driving her nuts, and worst of all, she felt duped. David had manipulated everyone into doing things his way.

After learning that David's pod vanished last night, Sierra had decided to hike to the beach behind the mountain to see if her pod was still there. If it was, she wanted to secure it somehow. That pod was their only clue about whoever had brought them here.

Kona ran past her, sniffing rocks and chasing little black rodents that scurried under cover whenever she got close.

Sierra had been ready to set off this morning, eager for a break from Barry. She'd planned to take Josh, confident the two of them could scare away any giant birds they encountered.

She knew Kim and Barry would beg to go along, and of course they had. But she also knew David wouldn't let them out of his sight now that he was awake. She hadn't expected the resistance she got from Josh, who whined about how long it would take, or Waldmire, who thought their pod was probably already gone.

That's when David suggested they hike up the mountain to look for the pod from above. It was a shorter trip and since David could see the whole slope from the hilltop, he was willing to let his kids go, as long as they promised to keep away from the drop-off in the back.

Sierra sighed. David had found a way to keep everyone close by and Sierra was stuck babysitting again. His manipulation would have made her father proud.

"Carry me," Barry said. He stopped walking and stood pouting.

David had assigned everyone a job. Barry was supposed to come up with names for any plants or animals they found. Kim was tasked with surveying the jungle below for signs of habitation or anything out of the ordinary. David asked Josh to count the nearby islands and figure out which ones were closest. And Sierra was in charge. It was her job to keep everyone safe. As if anything could actually go wrong on this empty, never-ending slope.

Her legs ached and a blister burned on her heel. "I'm not carrying you, Barry. Wait here if you want. We'll meet you on the way back down."

David had swooped in and taken control of the situation by making them all feel important with their little jobs, just like her father would have. David even looked a little like Rick Preston, another self-assured middle-aged white guy. An aching mixture of admiration and sadness washed over her. Unlike her father, David hadn't given up.

The slope went on and on. Pale green shrubs with tiny spade-shaped leaves grew among the rocks.

Up ahead, Kona hopped into the air with her back arched. Her paws and mouth all came down at the same time and a tiny squeak punctuated her landing.

"What was that?" Kim asked.

"One of those mice zigged when it should have zagged," Josh said.

Kona padded over with a bloody muzzle. She sat down and chomped the critter apart between her paws.

Kim grimaced. "Poor mouse."

"It's a hill mouse," Barry said. "I named them hill mice. I'm in charge of taxing."

"Taxonomy," Kim droned.

Sierra sympathized. She wanted to search for answers, not babysit. "Good job, Barry. Are you gonna stay here or come with us? We're halfway."

Barry extended his hand, which was sweaty and gross. Sierra forced herself to take it. He started moving again, though it felt like dragging an anchor.

Behind them, Kim fired a barrage of questions at Josh. "Did you like living in California?"

"I guess."

"What did you do for fun? Did you surf?"

"Shooting."

"Do you miss your parents?"

"Sorta."

"I miss my mom. She and Dad weren't getting along so great lately."

"Oh."

"Do you miss your friends?"

"Duh."

The conversation was one-sided, but Kim kept it going with admirable tenacity.

Above, two barren peaks loomed, with a saddle drooping between them. The rocky point on the left jutted up higher, while the one on the right was short and stubby. A lone boulder sat in front of the shorter peak. The whole thing looked phony, like a set from a bad science fiction movie.

"Almost there," Sierra said each time Barry slowed down.

Kona reached the top ahead of everyone else. She stopped at the saddle between the two peaks, tail wagging and tongue lolling.

Sierra's heart stuttered when she caught up to the dog. The back side dropped hundreds of feet straight down. She squeezed Barry's hand as he leaned forward to look.

Far below, a thin beach bordered the base of the mountain. A thin empty beach. "Our pod is gone, too," Sierra said.

Kim peered over the edge of the cliff. "Dad would not like this. He's scared of heights."

"I thought he was a pilot," Josh said.

Kim shrugged. "He says that's different."

"Well, I'm glad we didn't spend all day hiking around back there for nothing," Josh said. "Your dad's pretty smart."

Sierra hated feeling played, but she had to admit Josh was right.

Learn from it, Kiddo, came her father's voice. He always said that when she was upset about something. Sierra looked back down the slope they'd just climbed. David and Waldmire were small dots by the hilltop campfire. They'd promised to crack open coconuts for lunch when everyone returned. At least she had something to look forward to. Coconut flesh melted in her mouth, sweet and soft, with the texture of sushi-grade tuna. At the same time, it didn't make a damn bit of sense. Why were coconuts growing here?

Beyond the hilltop, the island's long sides met at a point, with miles of jungle in between. She leaned over to Kim. "Spot anything artificial?"

"This whole place looks artificial. It's a perfect triangle." The girl sighed. "But I don't see any signs of civilization."

Barry tugged Sierra's hand. "Can you let go?"

"Only if you promise to keep away from the cliff."

"Fine." Barry pulled free and walked around to the front of the larger peak.

"Stay where I can see you," Sierra called.

"Shhh," Josh said. "I'm counting the islands." He walked in the other direction, around the front of the smaller peak.

Sierra sat down in the middle of the saddle, careful to keep her distance from the drop-off behind her. It felt good to rest her legs and the view of the island was spectacular. She glanced at Barry, who busied himself throwing small rocks. Kim sat down beside her.

"It doesn't make any sense," Sierra said. "Why are they hiding from us?"

"The aliens?" Kim asked.

"Yeah, I guess. Whoever sent the pods." They had to be alien. There was no other explanation.

"Why are you so determined to meet them?" Kim asked.

The answer seemed obvious. "Whoever saved us is incredibly advanced. We can learn from them. And who knows, maybe we can teach them something in return." She shrugged. "We're all that's left of humanity. If we don't represent our species, no one will."

"What if they aren't friendly?"

"Why would they go to the trouble of saving us if they aren't friendly?"

"Maybe they want something from us."

"Then why don't they come out and ask?"

Kim didn't answer.

"Josh is right. Your dad is smart," Sierra admitted. Saying it out loud felt good. David was an ally, not a competitor, and she needed to be wise enough to recognize the difference.

"Thanks," Kim said. "What was your dad like?"

The question hit her like a brick wall. Sierra swallowed. "Tenacious. Always knew how to get what he wanted. I miss him."

"Maybe he found a pod."

Sierra looked at the horizon, trying to forget the sight of Rick Preston's bloated corpse lying beside the pool. "No. He died a few days back."

"I'm sorry." Kim hung her head. "What about your mom?"

"She wasn't part of my life. She bailed when I was nine." Sierra started to ask about Kim's mom but stopped herself. The subject felt too raw.

They sat quietly. Sierra wondered if she should tell David about the pentobarbital. Maybe he knew some use for it. She'd hidden the bottle under a rock on the side of the hill. The last thing she needed was for Barry to find it and take a sip.

Never show all your cards, Rick Preston had taught her. *Always keep something in your back pocket.* Even if she trusted David, there was no need to tell him about the poison. He might make her pour it out, just to get rid of it.

"How long have you known Josh?" Kim asked.

"A couple of days."

"He's a perv. He stared at your butt the whole way up here. I was trying to distract him."

Sierra chuckled and held up a fist for Kim to bump. It was nice to have someone looking out for her, even if she didn't need it. "You should have told me. I would have made him stop."

Kim went pale. "Please don't say anything."

"I won't. But if he ever crosses the line, I'll feed him his balls." She turned toward the smaller peak, where Josh had disappeared. "Where is the little dweeb?"

"Oh my God, look." Kim pointed at the other peak. Barry had climbed twenty feet up and stood spread-eagle on a tiny ledge.

"Barry, get down from there," Sierra yelled. She never should have brought him along.

"I almost hit it," he said from his perch on the rocky outcropping.

"Hit what? What are you talking about?"

Barry took careful aim and hurled a small stone out into empty air. It arced across the pale blue sky and plummeted to the slope below him, where it bounced for hundreds of feet before coming to a stop.

He teetered, spinning his arms. If he fell, he would land on the same slope and roll all the way down to the campsite, probably breaking every bone in his body.

Kim squeezed Sierra's arm. "Do something."

Barry caught the edge of the rock wall and clung to it. "I'm stuck," he shouted.

"You got up there. Climb back down." David would kill her if he got hurt.

"Go get Daddy."

"Your father can't come up here." Sierra crossed the saddle, keeping clear of the drop-off on her right, then circled out onto the slope until she was below him.

"Hold on tight," Kim shouted. "Don't fall."

"I'll get him," Josh said.

Sierra spun on him. "Where the hell have you been?"

"Counting islands, like I was supposed to." He polished his glasses on the hem of his hoodie and pushed past her.

Josh climbed up until he reached Barry's feet, then tapped the boy's shoe and showed him where to step. Together, they worked their way down.

Sierra reached for Barry's wrist, but he stuck his hands behind his back and scowled.

Kim stomped over. "What were you doing up there, dumbass?"

"I was trying to hit the cloud," Barry said. "I'm going to tell Dad you cussed."

"What cloud?" Sierra scanned the sky. "There aren't any clouds here."

Kim shook her head. "Mom and Dad told you not to lie."

"I'm not lying. There was a cloud." Barry started down the hill. Kona ran ahead of him.

"You only think you saw something," Kim said.

"Shut up," he shouted without looking back. "I saw it."

Kim's lips grew small and she glared at Sierra. "You were supposed to keep him out of trouble." She followed her brother. Josh took off after both of them.

Sierra stood at the top of the mountain, alone and deflated. She looked around for any signs of a cloud, but saw nothing. If Barry really had seen something, it was gone now. She sighed and started down the slope.

They descended in silence. Hiking downhill hurt the parts of Sierra's legs that weren't sore from hiking up, especially her knees.

"There are sixty-three other islands," Josh said after a while. "Most are just dots on the horizon."

"Good job," Sierra said, trying to be positive. "Which one is the closest?"

He pointed forward and to the right of their island's narrow tip.

"That's where we should go first," Sierra said. "I bet there are pods scattered on each island."

"We have to find Mommy," Barry said.

"Mom didn't make it," Kim said. "You know that."

Sierra's heart clenched.

"Now you're the liar."

"Barry, you have to accept it." Kim's voice rose. "She's dead."

"No, she isn't. She found a pod."

"Your sister's probably right," Josh said. "There were only a few thousand pods. The chance your mom found one is pretty low. Unless she was in the upper Midwest. That's where most of them were concentrated."

Sierra winced. He actually thought he was helping.

"You stay out of it," Kim yelled.

"I hate you all." Barry cried, racing away.

"Barry, hold up," Sierra called out. "You're gonna break your neck."

He kept running, all the way down the slope, with Kona bounding along next to him. Tears welled in Kim's eyes and Josh looked sullen.

Sierra might have gotten everyone down the mountain safe and sound, but they were all miserable and she felt awful for Kim, who she was really starting to like.

At the camp, Waldmire offered her a shell full of fresh coconut.

Thank you," she said, though it didn't seem appetizing now.

"What did you see?" he asked.

"A whole lot of nothing. And our pod is gone, too."

"I saw a cloud," Barry said, red-faced and clinging to his father's side. "It followed me around."

Kim glared at him. "Yeah, and you almost got yourself killed."

"What happened up there?" David asked. Concern darkened his face.

"He's fine," Sierra said. "He just climbed on some rocks. The rest of us didn't see any clouds."

Barry's face scrunched into a knot of defiance.

"Did you see anything else?" Waldmire asked.

"No," Josh said. "Just a bunch of stupid mice."

Barry's face scrunched even more. "Hill mice."

Kim rolled her eyes. "You're such a baby."

"Shut up. I want Mommy."

"Mom didn't make it. Even Dad knows that. He just won't admit it."

David closed his eyes. "Kim that is not—"

"Don't say that," Barry shouted. "I hate you." He stomped across the hilltop.

Sierra considered going after him, but the boy would probably just run from her.

"Barry," David called.

Barry kept going.

"Kim, go get your brother."

"Why do I have to?"

"Kim, go get your brother," he repeated, using a tone that left no room for argument.

Barry disappeared down the side of the hill, heading toward the beach where his family's pod had been.

"I'll go with you," Josh said.

Kim gave him a side-eyed glare. "Fine. Come on."

David watched them walk off, then turned back to Sierra. "Do you think he really saw something?"

"I don't know," she said, wishing she'd taken him more seriously. "None of the rest of us saw it."

"I'll keep my eyes peeled," Waldmire said. "Just in case."

She nodded. "Well, we confirmed both our pods are gone. After lunch, I want to start searching the island for other people."

"Hold on," David said. "Give me another day for my leg to get better. I'm barely on my feet again. That will give us time to carve some sticks into spears in case we run into those giant birds or whatever is growling at night."

Sierra opened her mouth to protest, but Waldmire held up his hand.

He looked at David. "Miss Preston can be a bit impatient." He turned to face her. "Sometimes even impetuous."

She exhaled.

"We'll find the rest of the pods," David said. "I just need a little time."

He looked down, and suddenly Sierra understood. The odds that his wife had gotten into a pod were small, but until they found them all, he could hold onto hope that she'd made it. He needed that right now.

"I'm sorry," Sierra said. "I'll back off."

Kim shouted from the crest of the hill. "Dad!"

He turned. "What now?"

"Barry," she panted, hurrying to the fire. "He ran away."

"Jesus, Kim, he's only six. I told you to bring him back here."

Kim leaned over gasping, hands on her knees. "I tried. He said he wanted to find Mom's pod, and I told her she didn't get in a pod, and he got mad. He called me an asshole, Dad. He ran under some low branches and Josh wasn't any help and I tried to go after him, but I think I went the wrong way, because I couldn't find him."

"Let's go get him," Sierra said. "He can't be far."

"I'll stay here in case he makes his way back," Waldmire said.

David pointed at his daughter. "You stay here, too."

"I can help look."

"No," David snapped. "Stay here. Where's Josh?"

"He's walking to the beach, in case Barry finds his way there." Kim's eyes welled up. "I'm sorry, Dad."

David grabbed his walking stick and hobbled to the edge of the hilltop. The others followed. "Which way did Barry go?"

Kim pointed toward the middle of the island.

Waldmire placed two fingers in his mouth and whistled, holding a loud, high-pitched note for a full five seconds.

There was no response. Sierra wondered if Barry might actually be in danger. Whatever they'd heard roaring at night was out there somewhere.

David descended, taking tiny, pathetic steps. She ran down next to him. "Here, grab my arm." He clenched her bicep with his free hand.

"I'm sorry, Dad," Kim called from above.

"Just stay with Waldmire," he shouted. The fear in his voice sent a chill down Sierra's back.

"We'll find him," she said as they descended into the jungle. David's grip felt like it was cutting off circulation.

He gave her a hard, frightened stare. "We better."

Chapter Twelve

David's shoulders tightened as if squeezed by a giant invisible hand. He told himself everything would be okay. Years ago, he and Lindsey had lost Kim at a park on the edge of the Mississippi River in downtown Minneapolis. They'd crisscrossed the playground, the riverbank, the parking lot. The girl had simply vanished. They were convinced that Kim, four at the time, had either fallen in the river or been abducted.

Lindsey had called 911 and was stuttering through a physical description when David found the girl in a sandbox off to one side. They hadn't even bothered to check there. Kim hated sand. She hated getting it in her clothes and her shoes. She hated the way it stuck to her fingers.

Everything had turned out okay. *This will be just like that,* David told himself. Barry had probably found a new fruit or something.

When they'd reached the bottom of the slope, Sierra had broken off through the jungle, heading toward the beach. They were on an island. Every direction led to the beach. She would probably find him there, but David continued deeper inland, just in case.

He stopped. What if Barry ran into the creatures they heard roaring at night? He shouted his son's name, then stood listening. "Where did you go, Buddy?"

His heart jumped at movement nearby. A monkey the size of a housecat looked at him from a tree trunk.

"Go on, git," he shouted. The monkey bolted into the canopy. David plunged on through the jungle.

A few minutes later he stopped and called out again. "Barry!" He held his breath, listening. Nothing. He pushed on, his thigh throbbing.

Rustling came from behind. Hope flared. It might be Sierra or Josh, coming to tell him they'd found him.

Kona bounded through the foliage, her tail wagging.

"Hey girl, where's Barry?"

Kona stared.

"Go find him, girl."

The dog sat.

"Shit."

David started off again but stopped when a wall of thick vines prevented him from moving forward. Light suggested a clearing on the other side. A stream babbled nearby. There was no way Barry had come through this thicket. He ought to find the creek and follow it instead.

"Fuck it." He wanted to rip something apart. He shoved through. Vines tugged his arms. He tore back, pulling down a wall of vegetation.

The last tendril broke free and David tumbled onto an outcropping above a twenty-foot drop, with a small clearing below. He leaned back to keep from falling over the cliff. His bowels clenched and his heart thudded in his throat. He hated heights.

Kona gave a low growl.

"No shit, girl." David's legs felt wobbly.

He stood on a ledge with the jungle to his back. On the right, the stream bubbled out of the trees and over the cliff. What if Barry had come this way and fallen? Bracing himself on his good leg, David leaned out and looked down. The waterfall ended in a small pool, surrounded by moss. He saw no sign of his son, thank God, but felt plenty of vertigo.

He puckered his lips and blew in and out, calming his heart rate, then turned and splashed across the stream, following the cliff to the right, where it sloped downward. After fighting his way through more dense undergrowth, he circled back into the clearing.

He liked it much better down here. The mist from the waterfall felt refreshing. It seemed like the perfect place for a six-year-old to stop and play. He pictured Barry building a dam across the creek.

Kona growled again. David reached down to stroke her. Hackles stood on her back. Movement came from the brush ahead.

"Barry?" David said, suddenly chilled from the mist.

Kona stepped in front of him, her front legs digging into the ground.

Something moved in the jungle beyond the clearing. David bent, ignoring the pain in his thigh, and picked up a stone from the creek.

A tank of a man broke through the vegetation. He carried a giant slab of animal meat on his shoulder.

David tensed, squeezing the rock.

The man wore drab green work pants with a gun belt. A white t-shirt popped against his dark skin and the straps of a backpack curved over muscular shoulders. His bald head glistened with sweat.

"Daddy!" Barry ran out from behind the man and raced over.

Two other strangers emerged from the trees, a wiry man in a brown jacket and a woman with curly black hair. Both of them also carried bloody hunks of something.

David dropped the rock and hugged his son. "Oh my God, Barry, you scared me to death." He pushed the boy away, took hold of his shoulders, and shifted his tone, letting out some of his anger. "You cannot run away like that. Do you hear me?"

Barry nodded. He looked wiped out, exhausted.

The trio stepped forward.

David stood. "Nice to see some friendly faces," he said, hoping the comment would prove accurate.

The big guy extended his hand. "I'm Wayne." He shook with a crushing grip. "This is Randall and Juliana. We're pleased to meet you."

David gestured at the meat they carried. "What is that?" Each piece was a leg, he realized. They all ended in ugly black hooves.

Wayne's eyes flicked to the haunch on his shoulders. "This animal looked like a cross between a pig and a hyena, but as big as a horse." He nodded toward the woman. "Juliana thinks it's prehistoric."

She offered a small shrug, mostly with her face.

"That right there was a creature you do not want to run into," Randall said, speaking with a drawl. Puffy eyes poked from his gaunt skull. He appeared to be in his late thirties, but looked ten years older, the sort of man who didn't take care of himself.

"Wasn't nothing I couldn't handle," Wayne said. "Let's get this meat up to that hilltop of yours. We've got a lot of work to do before supper."

Chapter Thirteen

One Day Before Impact

Wayne Wilcox receded into the shadows of the parking garage as the hook-and-ladder from hell rumbled past on the deserted Oklahoma City street. Four corpses hung from the ladder out in front of the cab, like lures dangling from the head of a deep-sea anglerfish. A thunderous procession of motorcycles followed.

Wayne crouched beside his two companions. He turned and glared at Louis. "You said they were heading south, out of the city."

Last night, Wayne had asked Louis to monitor the caravan while he got a few hours of sleep. It pained him to depend on someone else for a mission critical job, but he couldn't do everything.

"They were," Louis said. "I swear it. They must've come back" His bald head, already scalded from the sun, flared even redder.

Before everything had gone to hell, Louis had been a plump department store manager. Now, baggy skin hung from his bones.

Wayne took a deep breath and glanced at the wagons loaded with food they'd pilfered from a deserted apartment complex. "We'll just have to give them time to clear out," he said, peeking over the concrete wall.

The last of the caravan passed the parking garage.

"Who are they?" asked Blondie, a tall knucklehead they'd met near the apartments. He looked pale, even for a white guy. Wayne still didn't know the man's real name.

"Ain't you heard of the Piper?" Louis asked.

Blondie shook his head. He stood over six and a half feet tall, had the shoulders and arms of a silverback, and was the biggest coward Wayne had ever met.

"Three weeks ago, this guy caught some punks beating up a family in a grocery store," Louis said. "He shot 'em, right then and there."

"So he's some kinda hero?" Blondie asked.

Louis rolled his eyes. "Hardly. He was looking for excuses to kill people. He pretended to be a vigilante at first, but that didn't last. Eventually, he and his gang started butchering anyone they could find."

"What about the cops?" Blondie asked.

"Where have you been?" Wayne hissed. The last of the engine rumbles faded in the distance. He checked his watch and decided to wait five more minutes.

"On the road," Blondie said. "I got to Oklahoma City two days ago."

"The mayor and the governor evacuated the city after the prison break," Louis said.

"Breaks," Wayne corrected. There had been several.

"Yeah, yeah," Louis said. "Anyway, the cops already had their hands full, what with the Ender and all. There wasn't nothin' they could do. They blew outta town just like everyone else."

Blondie's mouth hung open. "What about you guys?"

Wayne wiped sweat from his brow. "Some people weren't in any shape to evacuate. Louis and I and a few others stayed behind to help."

"The old folks you told me about," Blondie said.

"That's right," Wayne said. A few people from Wayne's church had moved the residents of four nursing homes into a high-rise luxury building on the west side of town. Wayne knew of a dozen other similar situations across the city and suspected there were more.

Blondie's mouth turned downward. "When I agreed to help, ya'll didn't say nothing about a street gang."

"That's because Louis here told me they'd gone ten miles south," Wayne said, his words clipped with anger.

Louis scowled.

"I'm staying here," Blondie said. "It ain't safe. I'm not even armed. How am I supposed to defend myself if they come back?"

"We need your help," Wayne said.

He and Louis could probably manage all three wagons on their own, but Wayne wanted to get Blondie to the tower. Even though he was a coward, the man seemed like a decent human being. It wasn't safe to leave him here.

Blondie stared, a proverbial deer in headlights.

"Tell you what," Wayne said. "You can borrow a gun, just till we reach the tower." He pulled his backup firearm from his shoulder holster and gave it to him.

Blondie stared at the gun in his hand like it might bite.

Wayne patted his arm. "I got your back. We'll leave one at a time and spread out. That way, if anyone runs into trouble, the others can cover him. It's only a few blocks. We got this." He stood and grabbed the handle of one of the wagons. "Come on. Let's get to the tower."

Somehow, between the gun and the pep talk, Blondie mustered the courage to start moving.

At the parking garage exit, Wayne checked the street, then motioned for Blondie to take the lead before he could chicken out. The tall man moved quietly, just like Wayne had taught him. They'd poured vegetable oil on the wagons' axles to silence any squeaks.

Once Blondie was halfway up the block, Wayne motioned for Louis to follow. Two minutes later, he took the rear.

In his right hand, he held his .45 caliber M1911. He wore his army boots and carried his rucksack, but other than that, he was dressed as a civilian, in drab green work pants and a white t-shirt.

Trash littered the streets and sidewalks. Overhead, a layer of stratus clouds hid the Ender from view.

Blondie was already halfway past the next block. Louis stopped and mopped his forehead with a handkerchief, glancing back.

Wayne nodded. Louis and Blondie were good people doing good work. Hard work, with no promise of reward. He would make sure they got to sleep in penthouse apartments tonight.

Louis stuffed his handkerchief back in his pocket and turned to start walking again.

A man wearing bike leathers appeared around the corner, four yards in front of him, holding a shotgun. "Looky here," he said, his voice high-pitched.

Wayne tensed, scanning the area. Red brick buildings stood on both sides of the street. Withered shrubs lined the storefronts, dead and desiccated. There wasn't any cover nearby.

On the next block, Blondie abandoned his wagon and stumbled into the street, gaping back at them.

Two other men came around the corner, both holding firearms. Orange prison jumpsuits peeked from their cuffs and collars. They were both white, like the first man, and they were facing Louis and Wayne. They hadn't spotted Blondie.

"What's in the wagons?" asked one of the men. Prison tattoos covered his face.

Wayne dropped the handle of his wagon. He kept his handgun pointed at the ground. "It's food for starving people."

Out in the street, Blondie had a clean line of fire. Thank God Wayne had given him the pistol. All he had to do was take a shot. He didn't even have to hit anyone. He just had to distract these assholes long enough for Wayne to raise his gun.

"We've got more than we need," Wayne said. "And Louis here is gettin' tired. Why don't you take his wagon?" He drew in a deep breath, bringing everything into focus.

The man with the tattoos sauntered closer. "We'll take both wagons and you fuckers are gonna pay the Piper."

Out in the street, Blondie raised his gun and fired five times.

The first four shots went wild. Glass broke on a second-story window. The fifth shot hit Louis. Red bloomed on the back of his shirt, right below his neck. He tumbled into a row of brown hedges.

Wayne sucked air. He wanted to scream. He never should have trusted Blondie with a gun.

The man with the shotgun aimed for his chest.

Wayne ran sideways into the street. He felt wind from the shotgun blast along his arm.

He raised the M1911 and fired three times, nailing the man with the shotgun once in the chest. Blood sprayed the two men behind him.

The street exploded with gunfire.

Wayne kept running sideways, giving them a moving target, but also making it difficult to return fire.

He aimed at the man with the tattoos and hit him center mass with his third shot, then fired at the last man, who wore a black leather vest and was spraying bullets everywhere with a MAC-10.

The shot grazed the man's arm. He screamed, clutching the wound. The submachine gun clattered to the asphalt.

Wayne kept firing until the hammer clicked on an empty chamber, but he was off balance and each shot missed. He reached instinctively for his backup piece in his shoulder holster, but that was the gun he'd given to Blondie.

The third man took off around the corner, still holding his arm.

Wayne ran to Louis, who lay on his back, eyes open and lifeless. He tugged the Desert Eagle from his waistband. The metal gunsight at the end of the barrel caught on Louis' belt. Wayne jerked it free, checked the magazine, then scanned the street from a crouch.

Nothing moved. The first two attackers lay dead in the street and Blondie had disappeared.

Wayne darted to the corner. The man he'd shot in the arm was a block away and still running. On the back of his leather vest, a skeletal hand extended its bony middle finger.

Wayne raised the Desert Eagle, lining up the gun sight, then stopped himself. He couldn't shoot a man in the back.

He returned to Louis, said a prayer, and closed the poor bastard's eyes with the heel of his hand.

"Hey Blondie," he called out, as loudly as he dared.

Blondie didn't answer. He was probably five blocks away by now.

Wayne piled as much food as he could onto two of the wagons and started off, flexing his arms wide to keep them from banging together. He saw no sign of Blondie or any more of the Piper's men.

Twenty minutes later, Pastor Edwin met him in the lobby of Barton Tower. "Bless you, Wayne," he said.

A woman in her thirties named Juliana helped haul the food up the stairs. The elevators had died when the power went out.

"Louis is dead," Wayne said as they climbed. "We met a fella out there who helped us, but he took off when we ran into trouble."

"I'll say a prayer for them both," Pastor Edwin said.

They carried the food up twenty flights of stairs. Juliana insisted on doing her part, even though she barely weighed more than the boxes in her arms. She wore old jeans and a faded purple sweatshirt, kept her hair tied in a brown knot, and hadn't said more than twenty words. Quiet women made Wayne uncomfortable. He never knew what they were thinking.

Pastor Edwin surveyed the food as they stacked the boxes in a kitchen. "This should last us to the end," he said. He took off his thick glasses and massaged the bridge of his nose. "Most of the people here only eat one or two meals a day."

They walked through the suite onto a balcony. The breeze cooled Wayne's skin. Twenty floors up, they could see downtown to the east and Will Rogers Airport to the south. No lights were visible anywhere. Pastor Edwin only allowed lanterns in the inner hallways, where they couldn't be seen from below.

"What now?" Wayne asked, feeling fatigued as the adrenaline drained from his system.

Juliana touched Pastor Edwin's arm. The expression on her face meant something, but Wayne had no idea what.

"We need to blockade the stairwells," Pastor Edwin said. "Juliana found a little Bobcat tractor a quarter mile away. She parked it by the back plaza. We need to fill the stairwells with rubble, so no one can get in."

Wayne tilted his head at Juliana, impressed. "You drove a Bobcat?"

"I managed." She looked out over the railing, her thoughts a confounding mystery.

"The guy in the Bobcat won't be able to get back inside once he's done," Wayne said.

Pastor Edwin clasped his hands together. "No, he won't."

"I'll do it."

"We're blessed to have your help," Pastor Edwin said. "I thank God every day for putting you in our service."

Wayne waved the comment away, humbled and embarrassed.

Pastor Edwin left to check on someone calling from the next apartment. A low chorus of snores filled the tower.

Juliana pulled Wayne aside in the hall, where candlelight danced on the walls. "Can I talk to you for a minute?" Old mascara shadowed weary brown eyes.

"We heard something on the radio," she began. "There are these pods. They're carrying people away, like, they're here to save us."

Wayne squinted. He'd heard a lot of nonsense in the past few weeks, and a lot of wishful thinking. "Where're they from?"

"No one knows."

"Have you seen them?"

She shook her head. "They're mostly north of here. Radio says there were some in Kansas, and one near the panhandle."

She must have seen the dismissal on his face because she reached out and touched his arm. "It's something to try for. You should head north."

He shrugged. "I got nowhere else to go."

Wayne descended to the ground floor and found the small tractor behind the building. For two hours of cold catharsis, he tore apart the fountain, concrete planters, benches, and most of the mailroom, bulldozing all the debris into the stairwells.

When he finished, he drove the Bobcat up onto the rubble in the last stairwell, opened the engine, and tore out every wire, cable, and tube he could find. No one would ever get in the building. If nothing else, the people here could live out their final hours in peace.

He didn't know what to make of Juliana's talk about pods, but he set off north. Like he'd told her, he had nowhere else to go.

Wayne walked for thirty minutes before he heard the distant pops and ticks of gunfire behind him.

He looked back, unconcerned. Pastor Edwin and his flock were secure. All of the tower entrances were blocked off. The Piper couldn't touch them. Hell, he'd need a fifty-foot ladder just to reach the first balcony.

Wayne's stomach dropped and his skin prickled. "Oh, Dear Jesus, how could I be so stupid?"

The Piper was driving around in a hook and ladder truck.

Chapter Fourteen

The sweet, smoky aroma of fat dripping onto hot coals intoxicated Wayne. He hadn't eaten anything but fruit and vegetables for three days. He wanted to tear into a slice of the meat, raw and bloody. He couldn't, though, not until the creature's haunch had cooked all the way through. Even if it came out leather-tough, they had to do everything they could to ensure it wouldn't make them sick.

Wayne adjusted the last haunch on the wooden drying rack they'd constructed off to the side of the hilltop. Most of the blood had drained from the meat, which would help prevent spoiling until they cooked it. Later, they'd need to scrape the muddy dirt onto hot coals so the smell of all that blood wouldn't attract predators.

Josh, a white kid stuck in the unforgiving grasp of adolescence, gaped at the forty-pound hunk of meat. "How'd you kill it?"

"I spotted it a mile up the beach when it came down to the shoreline for a drink. I tracked it with the binocs until I found it sleeping in the jungle. I crept up slowly. Took me thirty minutes to cover a hundred feet. When I got close, I put two shots into it before it ran off."

Josh's eyes looked huge behind his wire-rimmed glasses. Wayne felt like beaming with pride, but he held his expression solemn, keeping the boy entranced. "After that, I followed the blood trail till I got close enough to put it down."

Sierra and Randall walked up the hill, each carrying one last armload of wood. Randall licked his lips as he checked her out. Wayne watched him closely. He'd brought Randall into this group, and if that low-life beanpole tried anything ungentlemanly, Wayne would knock him flat.

"Do you think that creature was some kind of alien?" Sierra asked. The young woman had dark skin, almond eyes, and long wavy hair. When Wayne first met David and his little boy, he'd wondered if he was going to spend the rest of his life on an island full of white folks.

"It looked like an Entelodont," Juliana said.

Sierra tossed her firewood onto the pile. "What the hell is an Entelodont?" The best thing about Sierra was her spunk. They'd need all the spunk they could get if they were going to survive here.

Juliana repeated the story she'd shared when she first saw the carcass. "Several months back, before the Ender, I chaperoned a field trip to the museum. They had a creature like that on display. The fur was different, but the face was the same. Some kids were teasing a boy named Eric who had bad teeth. They kept calling him Eric the Entelodont. That's how I remembered the name."

Randall dropped his own firewood onto the pile. "Bullshit. There ain't no animals like that."

"I told you, it was in the prehistoric section," Juliana said. "With the mammoths and stuff." She'd let her hair down, a messy scraggle that hung to her shoulders and made her face look pale.

"Wait a minute," Sierra said. "Does that mean we've gone back in time?"

"What about the giant birds?" David asked. "Do you think those were prehistoric, too?"

Juliana shrugged. "We haven't seen them."

"You're lucky," Kim said. "One of them chased me and Barry up a tree." She was not quite a teenager yet and had a rugged sort of look to her. Short brown hair and a perpetually serious expression.

"They're mean," Barry said, cuddling in his father's lap beside the fire.

The idea that they'd gone back in time made Wayne uneasy. "Were the oceans ever fresh water?" he asked. "Was the atmosphere ever so thick you couldn't see the sun?"

David looked up. "I have no idea about the sky, but I would think the oceans must have been salty for hundreds of millions of years."

He had an honest face. Twinkling blue eyes with little crow's feet.

The answer was good enough for Wayne. "That settles it then. We did not go back in time."

This group seemed like good people. He had put them to work collecting wood and they'd all hiked up and down the hill without complaining. He'd told them to keep near the edge of the jungle, stay close together, and make lots of noise, and they'd done just as he instructed.

He walked over to the firewood, selected nine thin branches, then sat down by the fire. The others joined him. Fat bubbled on the creature's leg and a bacon-y aroma wafted across the hilltop. Wayne's stomach rolled in sync with the spit. He wasn't sure how long he could wait.

David looked up at Juliana. "Are you positive it's the same creature you saw in the museum?" He turned the haunch on the spit, cooking it evenly. Barry's little round face glowed in the firelight.

"No. How can I be positive of anything?" Juliana lowered her eyes. "But I think it was the same."

Sierra exhaled as if annoyed. "Can't you remember anything else about it?"

"I …" Juliana shuddered and wrapped her arms around her chest. When she spoke again, her voice was cold and controlled. "I have been working very hard to remember as little as possible."

"I'm sorry," Sierra said. "I'm just looking for answers."

Waldmire, the wrinkly old guy, placed his hand on Sierra's shoulder, as if he was telling Sierra to back off, but also letting her know he understood how she felt.

Wayne approved. The group was lucky to have someone like Waldmire.

They were also damn lucky to have Juliana. She'd cared for the seniors at Barton Tower and she would take care of the kids here, too. It was her nature to be nurturing.

Wayne rummaged in his bag and pulled out his knife. He frowned at the puny two-inch blade and turned to Josh. "May I borrow that fine Bowie knife on the back of your belt? I'll sharpen it for you when I'm done."

Josh nearly fell over himself as he pulled out the knife and handed it over. Wayne began to whittle the first stick, scraping bark from one end.

"Where's the rest of the creature?" Sierra asked. "Maybe we can study it. David could perform an autopsy or something."

Randall pointed out over the jungle. "Good luck with that. It's miles away."

"If there are others, and I'm sure there are, they're probably feeding on the remains," Wayne said. "Best to keep away."

"Are they mean?" Barry asked.

"Very," Wayne said. He ruffled the kid's sandy crew cut. "You best not run off like that again, son."

Barry shook his head, staring at the shiny black hoof on the end of the rotating leg.

Wayne turned to the boy's father. "Were you a doctor?"

"Anesthesiologist."

Wayne nodded. An anesthesiologist wasn't as good as a surgeon or a general practitioner, but it was better than nothing. He checked his stick for loose splinters. Satisfied, he picked up a second branch.

The sky darkened, turning quickly from daytime into night, with that empty blackness overhead that felt close enough to reach up and touch.

Sierra looked around the group, her face orange in the firelight. "So, if the time travel idea doesn't work, what's the next best guess? Do you guys think this is an alien planet?"

"What difference does it make?" Randall asked.

"Figuring out where we are might help us figure out how to survive," Sierra said. Her tone carried a hint of condescension, as if it should be obvious.

"If it's another planet, why are there coconuts?" Juliana asked. "And fresh water and breathable air?"

Sierra shrugged. "I don't know, but who else could have sent those pods beside aliens?" She perked up. "Hey, is your pod still there?"

Juliana shook her head. "It flew away yesterday."

Barry drew in a long breath. "Where did it go?"

"It lifted off the beach and floated out over the water," Juliana said. "We ran after it, but it was out of reach before we could get close."

"It got back to wherever it came from," Wayne added, now whittling his third stick. "All that matters is that we're here. And we should thank the good Lord that those pods came when they did."

Sierra made a derisive sound, half-chuckle, half-snort.

Wayne stopped whittling, annoyed. "Why you got to be like that?"

Josh nodded. "Yeah."

"I'm sorry," Sierra said. "The idea that God allowed a comet to destroy Earth but then dropped a few thousand escape pods on just one continent is kinda ludicrous."

"I never said God sent the pods. I just said we should be thankful." He jerked the knife in angry strokes. "You California folks always get sarcastic about God."

Josh nodded again, though he was also one of the California folks.

"Where do you think we are, Wayne?" Sierra asked.

He kept whittling. "This is whatever's next, simple as that."

"Do you think God sent the pods to save us?" she asked.

Wayne looked across the fire with a glare that usually made people turn around and walk the other way.

Sierra held up a hand. "I'm not trying to be snarky. I'm asking seriously." She looked around the campfire. "We have no idea. No clues. No evidence." She spread her arms. "Except, here we are."

"Barry thought he saw a cloud on that mountain behind us," David said.

"I did," the boy insisted. "It was blurry."

"Ain't no clouds here," Randall said.

Barry scowled at him.

Wayne didn't know what the boy had seen, but he was growing increasingly confident that everything was going to work out. The hilltop felt much more secure than the long sandy point at the tip of the island where he'd camped with Randall and Juliana.

Spotting the bonfire up here last night had been a stroke of luck. It was a good base of operations and a good group of people, with a doctor, to boot. He started working on another stick. "What else did you see from that mountaintop?"

"Sixty-three islands," Josh said. "The one in front is closest."

Wayne nodded. That island had looked tantalizingly near from out on the point. They had nine people now. He and Randall and Juliana had walked all the way across this island. It didn't seem likely that anyone else was here. It was time to look elsewhere.

When he finished the ninth stick, he stood and used the Bowie knife to carve slices from the haunch. He folded each piece of meat onto a stick and handed out the skewers one by one, starting with the ladies.

Once everyone had a kabob, Wayne took one for himself and ripped off a bite with his teeth. It tasted like gamey pork and reminded him of the way rich earth smelled. He loved it.

Feeding the group would show them he could be trusted, that he would take care of them and keep them safe.

Wayne sliced off another hunk and tossed it onto the grass in front of the golden retriever. She made happy snorting sounds as she tore into it.

They devoured the meat and Wayne sliced off seconds and even thirds for most of them. "The important thing isn't where we are," he said. "We're here. Nothing we can do about that. The important thing is finding the rest of the pods."

The little boy whispered, "Mommy."

"We reached the same conclusion," David said. "We just need to be cautious. Not everyone who got in those pods was good-natured. We saw that on the news."

Wayne wasn't sure what they'd seen on the news, but he doubted it could compare to what had gone down in Oklahoma City. He glanced over at Randall. Hell, not everyone in this little group was good-natured.

"We'll be okay," Randall said, squinting until his eyes nearly disappeared between those puffy eyelids. "Ain't nobody gonna fuck with Wayne."

David looked unconvinced, and maybe a little wary.

"You and Wayne seem pretty tight," Sierra said. "How long have you known each other?"

Wayne tilted his head, curious to hear how Randall might answer this one.

"We just met," Randall said. "Right at the end."

"What happened?"

"Things in Oklahoma were pretty ugly," Randall said. "I was in the wrong place at the wrong time, and then I was in the right place at the right time. That's all."

Wayne leaned back, willing to let Randall put his past behind him. He deserved a second chance. They all did.

Chapter Fifteen

One Day Before Impact

The Piper's fire truck sat at the base of Barton Tower, parked in the landscaped courtyard. Its ladder extended to the fifth floor, where the bodies strung from the end hung against the side of the building like a cluster of fish on a stringer line. A fifth body had been added.

Blondie.

"How could I be so stupid?" Wayne whispered, hiding in the trees at the edge of the property. He told himself it was a mistake anyone could have made. The Piper used the ladder to display his kills, not put out fires. It didn't make him feel any better.

The Piper would butcher the old folks in their beds. He killed for the sake of killing. Wayne had to act.

Starbursts flashed on balconies halfway up the tower. Gunfire. A spark of hope gave Wayne strength. Pastor Edwin was armed. Maybe it wasn't too late.

Two men stood atop the fire truck, aiming roof-mounted water cannons at the balconies, which would prevent anyone up there from getting a clear shot. Three other men climbed the ladder, dragging a hose with them. Wayne saw no one else.

He crossed the courtyard, trying to figure out how to get up onto the truck. As he rounded the front corner of the vehicle, he came face to face with a man in a black leather vest. Wayne raised his pistol, keeping command of the situation. The man's eyes went wide and his hands shot in the air.

The roar of water blasting from the truck continued, along with cackles from the men operating the cannons. Those bastards were enjoying themselves too much to notice what was going on below.

The asshole in the vest looked familiar. Wayne twirled his free hand. "Turn around." The man rotated. A patch on the back of his jacket showed a skeletal hand holding up its middle finger. "You followed me here," Wayne spat.

The man spoke over his shoulder. "Couldn't let you have all the fun."

Wayne glanced up at the fire truck. The two men on top continued spraying the building, but the ladder was now empty. Everyone else had climbed inside.

The thought of shooting an unarmed man in the back made Wayne feel hollow. The thought of the Piper killing all those seniors was worse. He pulled the trigger, blasting a hole in the embroidered skeletal hand. One of the men on the truck looked down at the sound. Wayne raised his gun, took aim, and fired. The man's head burst, turning the stream of water bright pink. The second man reached for his gun. Wayne shot him in the neck. He fell backwards and disappeared.

Wayne reloaded and climbed up the side of the fire engine.

The body of the first man slumped over the pump panel. Wayne shoved him off onto the grass below. Blood covered the metal levers used to activate the pumps. Wayne shut them off and the hose running up the ladder went flaccid.

The hiss of rushing water was replaced by popping gunfire inside the tower. He holstered his pistol and climbed onto the ladder. Halfway up, it swayed from side to side. Outrigger feet were supposed to brace the truck, but these assholes hadn't bothered to set them up. He climbed as fast as he dared.

The ladder took him to a fifth-floor balcony. Wayne drew his gun and entered a suite through a bedroom. He didn't find anyone until he reached the apartment's front door, where a guard stood facing out into the hall. There was no time to subdue him. Wayne leveled his gun at the back of the man's head and pulled the trigger. Brains splattered the opposite wall.

He followed the deflated fire hose into a stairwell, fighting the urge to vomit. He'd shot two men in the back now.

Gunshots popped somewhere above him. Contrition would have to come later. The seniors were on the highest floors, where the suites were more spacious. Wayne followed the fire hose up the stairwell to the seventh floor and peered into the hallway.

Four of the Piper's men huddled against a pair of apartment doors, facing off against someone up ahead. Three other men lay dead beside the end of the hose. Drywall dripped in tatters where they'd used the high-pressure spray to tear the walls apart. If their intention had been to open lines of fire and flush out their targets, the tactic was solid, but Wayne thought they were probably just trying to be destructive.

He stepped into the hallway and shot all four men in the back, bringing his total to six. He clipped the last one in the shoulder as he spun around. Wayne fired twice more to put him down.

"It's Wayne," he called out while reloading. "Hold your fire."

A hand waved from a doorway up ahead. Wayne approached, gun out. He found Pastor Edwin sitting against the door, his legs splayed out in front of him.

"I'm out of ammo," Pastor Edwin whispered. Blood draped the side of his face. His jaw had turned so pale it looked blue. "Thank God you came back. You saved me."

Dark stains covered his clothes and he sat in a growing puddle of blood. Wayne hadn't saved him. Nothing would save him. Hopefully, shock was numbing his pain.

"Where's the rest of 'em?" Wayne asked. "Where's the Piper?"

"I killed three on the balcony. God forgive me."

"Where's the Piper?" Wayne repeated.

Pastor Edwin shook his head with a blank stare. A tear rolled down his pale blue cheek.

Wayne started to rise. Pastor Edwin grabbed his arm.

"Wait," he said, his voice a whisper. He closed his eyes but kept talking. Each word came slowly. "People need you. Your strength." He took a breath. "Don't give up. Keep people safe." Tears ran from both eyes, still closed.

One final breath rattled from Pastor Edwin's mouth. Wayne cupped the man's shoulders and lowered him flat on his back.

He returned to the stairwell and continued to ascend, exiting on each floor to run the hallway loop. Most of the apartment doors were locked, and the few that weren't stood empty. On the tenth floor, the sound of a struggle carried to the stairwell.

Wayne crept into the hallway.

Halfway down the hall, a man in a heavy fireman's coat wrestled with Juliana. He had his hands clasped tight around her, pinning her arms, but he didn't exactly have her under control.

The man wore a black military helmet with goggles on top.

The Piper.

"Hold still, bitch!" His voice was shrill and mechanical, like the recording in a fun house.

A gun lay on the floor several feet away.

Wayne inched forward. He couldn't take the shot without the risk of hitting Juliana.

She put both legs up on the wall and shoved the Piper backwards, into the opposite side of the hallway. He still had his arms around her, restraining her, but now he was facing in the other direction, away from Wayne.

Wayne holstered his gun and started forward. He had this. All he had to do was close the gap. He would free Juliana and then beat the living shit out of the Piper.

The hard steel of a muzzle pressed into the back of Wayne's head. Someone had snuck up on him.

A voice came from behind. "Don't you move."

Juliana whimpered.

"Well done, Randall," the Piper said. "Well done."

Chapter Sixteen

David untangled himself from Barry, who was still asleep, and got to his feet, his muscles aching from a night on hard dirt. The flat blue sky overhead gave no indication of the hour, only that it was daytime.

Wayne sat off to the side of the hilltop, away from the campfire, with an arsenal displayed around him in various states of disassembly. Barrels, grips, and parts David couldn't recognize lay on pieces of cloth and flat rocks.

"What the hell is this?" David asked as he shambled over, wincing at the stiffness in his injured leg.

"Cleaning my gear, Doc," Wayne said without looking up.

David felt small, even standing over him. Wayne's trapezius muscles strained at the neck of his t-shirt. Sandpaper stubble covered his lantern jaw.

Last night, David had been excited about the new people. Wayne could teach them survival skills, that much was obvious, and he hoped to learn more about Randall and Juliana, to see how they could contribute. He hadn't expected to wake up to a blatant show of force.

Wayne threaded a piece of cloth through a metal block with fingers as deft as any surgeon's. Kona sniffed the edge of the display, then wandered away to relieve herself.

Josh walked over, holding his glasses and rubbing sleep from his eyes. "Whoa. How many guns do you have?"

"Not nearly enough," Wayne answered. "As far as we know, these are the last remaining firearms in existence, to say nothing of ammunition." He wagged his finger at a line of small cardboard boxes sitting off to one side with pictures of bullets on them.

David tried counting the guns, which wasn't easy because they were all in pieces. As a teenager, he'd shot empty soda cans with a twenty-two, but he swore off firearms after watching a seven-year-old girl die in the emergency department. Her skull had been blown open by her little brother.

Wayne had five pistols, including one that looked like an old-fashioned revolver. Two other firearms looked like submachine guns, with scopes on top and curved magazines stacked next to them. The pieces in Wayne's lap looked like parts of a shotgun.

"Need any help?" Randall asked.

Wayne looked up. "Yeah, bring everyone over here." He lifted the metal block to his lips and blew on it.

"You got it, boss."

"Good morning, Wayne," Sierra said, walking over. "Are you running a flea market or just trying to compensate for something?"

David smirked.

Wayne popped the trigger assembly onto a metal cylinder, ignoring her comment.

"How much for the shiny black one?" She knelt and reached for one of the half-assembled pistols.

Wayne froze. "Do not touch that."

She jerked her arm back, then raised both hands by her shoulders.

Waldmire and Juliana joined the half-circle that had formed around the armory.

Wayne looked from face to face. "Have any of you completed firearms training in the past year?"

"I can shoot," Randall said.

"Training?" Wayne asked, his eyes narrow.

"Nuh-uh." Randall's shoulders dropped.

Josh raised his hand. "My dad took me to the range every couple of weeks. Does that count?"

"Was he a certified instructor? Or was he just showing you shit?"

Josh scowled and looked down.

"I worked with a trainer," Juliana said. "My last session was four months ago."

"Perfect." Wayne picked up a long barrel and fed a piece of string through it. "Listen, we need to set out an agenda. I'm going to continue Juliana's training, in case we run into anything else in the jungle. Meanwhile, we're going to start building a raft. If we work together, we should have it done in a week."

David crossed his arms. "Why do you want to build a raft?"

"'Cause those other islands are too far to swim to, Doc."

Josh snorted.

"Hey, I want to look for people, too," David said. He didn't mention Lindsey. He couldn't bear to raise his kids' hopes. "But can we discuss this first? We don't even know if it's safe to go out on the water." He looked at the others, hoping someone would back him up.

Wayne snapped a piece onto the shotgun. He had to know this display was intimidating. "Listen, I did not survive the end of the world to sit around a campfire and roast marshmallows while we debate everything."

"I want a marshmallow," Barry said.

David patted the boy's shoulder. "He's just talking, Buddy. We don't have any."

Wayne picked up two new pieces of metal. "We got nine folks. Not enough to rebuild civilization. Until I saw your bonfire up on this hill, I thought Juliana, Randall, and I might be the only people in this whole world. Now we know better. We need to find the other pods. If we can find more people and band together, humanity has a chance." He slapped the next part into place.

On the other side of the group, Sierra nodded.

It was exactly what David, Sierra, and Waldmire had discussed, but having it shoved down their throats with this display of force made David want to pull the brakes. "We've barely explored this island," he said. "What else lives here? How many of those Entelodonts are there? We need to come up with a long-term plan before we go sailing off."

"I'm talking about the future of the human race," Wayne said. "Is that long-term enough for you? Right now, we're all that's left. It may take years to find other people. We got to get started." Wayne attached the barrel of the shotgun.

David's arms tensed. "We don't know anything. We don't even know where we are. It's a little premature to talk about rebuilding society. And I don't remember anyone putting you in charge. Let's discuss this and take a vote."

Wayne pushed shells into the shotgun with his thumb, locking eyes with David. "This ain't student council and I'm not gonna pussy-foot around. I'm gonna build a raft, whether you choose to help or not."

"A vote is a good idea," Sierra said. "We're all in this together."

David exhaled, relaxing a little. He wasn't alone.

"Well, if we're voting, I'm with Wayne," Randall said. "You tell us what to do, we'll get it done."

"Me too," Josh said, nodding so hard he had to push his glasses back up his nose.

"He's brought us this far," Juliana said, looking around at everyone. "He's a good man."

"I'm in," Sierra said. "Going to the other islands makes sense."

"I'm sorry, David," Waldmire said. "But he makes a strong case."

David's mouth dropped. He hadn't meant to take a vote right then and there. He felt alone again. Kim squeezed his hand, which only helped a little.

"It's settled," Wayne said. "This hilltop will be our base of operations. We'll stockpile food and firewood here." He used the shotgun to point toward the beach where David's capsule had arrived. "That's the closest shoreline. We'll gather the biggest logs we can find and build the raft there. We'll need to collect vines and braid them into rope so we can lash it all together." He pumped the shotgun. "Let's get to work."

Chapter Seventeen

One Day Before Impact

The muzzle pressed hard against the back of Wayne's head. An itchy drop of sweat rolled down his face.

"On your knees," came the voice behind him. Wayne's gun was pulled from his holster. "Now, or I blow your brains out."

Wayne didn't have a choice. If he died, these two men would have their way with Juliana. He dropped to his knees.

Juliana stopped struggling.

The Piper walked her forward and stepped on the gun on the floor, presumably his own, pinning it beneath a heavy black boot. He looked down his long bulbous nose at Wayne. "Shoot him, Randall."

"I got a better idea," Randall said. "Let's throw him off the balcony."

The Piper went wild. "Yeessss! Holy shit, Randall. I love the way you think."

"We gotta tie 'em both up first," Randall said. "Put the woman on her knees."

The Piper shoved Juliana down in front of him, facing Wayne.

Tears ran from her eyes. She mouthed Pastor Edwin's name.

"Dead," Wayne said.

Pastor Edwin had told him not to give up. Wayne wanted to laugh. He and Juliana would be joining him soon. He couldn't see any way out of this.

The Piper looked at Randall, eyes wide. "You got the zip ties?"

"Yeah," Randall said. "I got 'em right here."

A shot exploded, filling the hallway, and the Piper flew backwards, most of his face missing.

Wayne slowly turned toward Randall. He looked wiry and mean, just like the rest of the Piper's men. Smoke wafted from his gun. His eyes bulged with an idiotic expression, as if he couldn't believe what he'd just done.

Randall bent and placed his pistol on the floor.

Wayne scrambled, grabbing the gun. He charged at Randall.

"Wait, no," Juliana cried.

He caught Randall's forearm and slammed him against the wall. He brought Randall's gun up and pressed the muzzle under his chin.

"Stop," Juliana pleaded.

Randall bobbled his head up and down. "Yes, stop." Thick brows like wooly caterpillars rose above his puffy eyes.

"He's one of them," Wayne said, stepping back.

Randall stank of leather and weeks of accumulated sweat. He wore heavy black boots, black jeans, and a brown canvas work coat. Expensive-looking binoculars hung from his neck.

"I was one of 'em," Randall said. "But now I'm not."

Wayne grimaced. The man had a weaselly face.

"He saved us," Juliana pleaded.

Wayne shook his head. It moved only a fraction of an inch, but it felt like the hallway rolled back and forth. "Why?"

Randall licked his lips. "I found a pod." He looked over at the crumpled body of the Piper. "I couldn't tell him." His eyes bulged and he stood tall. "That fucker was crazy."

"Why not just shoot us and take it for yourself?"

"I still gotta get out of the building," Randall said. "Past the Piper's men. Past your men."

Wayne snorted. "I don't have any men." He gestured toward the Piper with a tilt of his head. "He doesn't either. Not anymore."

Randall's eyes, which already looked like they were about to pop out of his skull, grew even bigger. "Damn."

"Where?" The single word from Juliana contained so much hope it broke Wayne's heart.

"I'll show you. All three of us can go."

"Wayne, we have to try," Juliana said.

He wanted to scream. Everything was coming to an end, and this little shit was dangling false hope in front of them.

He patted Randall down and retrieved his M1911 from the pocket of his coat. "Show us."

Randall licked his lips again. "Okay, but I gotta say something first. Yes, I was running with Yates."

"Who?" Juliana asked.

"The Piper. The Mad Fireman. 'Cept he wasn't a fireman." He gestured at the body heaped on the floor. "His name was Yates. I rode with him, but I only did it so I wouldn't hang from his ladder. He was a fucking lunatic. I ain't like him and I ain't gonna die just 'cause I was with him. You understand?"

Wayne took a deep breath. "Yeah, I understand. You'll do whatever it takes to stay alive. Including lying to us."

Randall's wide eyes somehow expanded. "Oh, but there really is a pod. I seen it. You swear to let me live and I'll show you. We can take it. All three of us."

"Show us," Juliana begged.

Randall lifted the binoculars over his head and handed them to Wayne. "You'll need these." He led them back to the stairwell. They climbed to the top floor and walked out onto an apartment balcony. "Come on now. Have a look. See for yourself."

Small waves of light snaked around the Ender, which glowed big and bright to the north, like a second sun.

Wayne passed the binoculars to Juliana so he could keep his gun trained on Randall.

"Follow Hampden Street to that shopping center, right there," Randall said, pointing.

While Juliana adjusted the knob on the top of the lenses, Wayne followed Randall's gesture. He spotted a Walmart, a liquor store, a burger joint, and a Carpet Town. Most of the glass storefronts were gone.

"Okay, got it," Juliana said. "What am I looking for?"

"Everything's been looted but that carpet place." Randall laughed. "Nobody wants to redo their fucking floors at the end of the world."

Even without the binoculars, Wayne saw a shimmer reflecting off the store's unbroken front windows.

"Look at the roof," Randall instructed.

A gaping hole dimpled the expansive roof of the Carpet Town, almost directly in the center.

"That could have been a traffic helicopter," Wayne said. He'd been right not to raise his hopes.

"There's something in there," Juliana said. "White. Round. It isn't a helicopter." She lowered the binoculars. "Wayne, if there's even a tiny chance …"

"I trusted you." Randall's caterpillar eyebrows wiggled. "I showed you. Let's go. Time is short."

Juliana gave a faint nod.

"What about everyone else?" Wayne asked. "The seniors. We gonna just leave them all behind?"

"We ain't got time," Randall said, pointing at the comet. "Just a few more hours."

"We made their last days peaceful," Juliana whispered. "We made them comfortable. *You* did that." She touched his arm. "I can make my rounds one last time to check on them."

Wayne worked his jaw. "Okay. We'll go as soon as you're done."

He escorted Randall downstairs, and to his credit, the little weasel behaved himself, standing against the wall while Wayne filled his rucksack with guns and ammunition from the bodies of the Piper's men.

"Yates was a goddamn psychopath," Randall said. "I only did what I did to stay alive. You have to know that."

"I don't even want to know what you did," Wayne said.

"Ain't you never done things you're not proud of?" Randall asked.

He didn't answer. The men he'd shot in the back lay scattered around them.

They returned to the fifth-floor balcony where the ladder met the building. "Cut those bodies down," Wayne ordered.

Randall looked like he wanted to protest, but he kept his mouth shut and did as he was told. Juliana joined them as he finished up.

"Did you tend to everyone?" Wayne asked.

She nodded. "They've all got food and water, right by their beds. Most are asleep."

"Let's go then." He glared at Randall. "All three of us."

They climbed down and after a few minutes of trial and error they figured out how to lower the ladder back into place. Wayne took the driver's seat.

They saw no one on the drive to Carpet Town. The city was dead.

Wayne bounced over medians and curbs as he turned into the shopping center. An old compact Chevy blocked their path. The fire truck swatted it aside like a cardboard box. Psychopath or not, the Piper had chosen a hell of a ride. Wayne kept his foot on the gas as he approached the building.

Across from him, Randall braced his arms on the console. "What're you doing?"

Wayne grinned. "We need to get inside, don't we?"

The twenty-five-ton fire truck plowed through the front wall of Carpet Town at fifteen miles an hour. Juliana yelped. Randall gave a tittering laugh as they ground to a stop.

They climbed out and walked down dark aisles toward a glow in the middle of the store. Rolls of carpet looked like stacks of lumber in the darkness.

A beam of light shone down on a white pod sitting in a nest of Pergo flooring samples.

Randall gave another tittering laugh. "It's a get-out-of-jail-free card." He ran forward and slapped the side. The top half floated upward.

Wayne studied the capsule. He didn't know where it would take him or what he would find when it opened, but he knew one thing. Pastor Edwin had told him to keep people safe and that was exactly what he intended to do.

Chapter Eighteen

Sierra and Juliana walked along the edge of the woods, each carrying a shoulder bag filled with coconuts. After three days, the Entelodont meat had finally run out and Wayne sent them to collect more food. Sierra had bit the insides of her cheeks to keep from lashing out at the idea of "women's work." She had to stay on Wayne's good side if she was ever going to earn his trust. She wanted him to give her one of the guns, and more importantly, she wanted him to value her ideas and suggestions. She wanted to help make decisions for the group.

Wayne had reviewed Juliana's firearms training and she now carried a small pistol in a makeshift holster on her hip. She was the only one he'd been willing to trust with a gun so far. Wayne even made her return it to him each night.

Sierra was growing increasingly frustrated with him. He'd decided that he was in charge, and he wasn't interested in hearing from anyone else.

She and Juliana wove through the trees as they walked, circling back to the beach whenever the vegetation grew too thick. Wayne had instructed them to stay right at the edge of the jungle even though no one had seen anything other than monkeys for days. Sierra was convinced there weren't any answers on this island. They'd seen no signs of other survivors and they hadn't learned anything about where they were.

A few yards ahead, Juliana stopped. "Jackpot." She stood over a fallen palm tree hidden in the underbrush. The men had been forced to go farther and farther down the beach to find usable trunks for the raft, but they'd missed this one. Juliana bent and pulled on one end, grunting. "It's too heavy. We'll need to send them back for it."

Sierra stomped to the other end and tried to lift the log, sick of all the sexist bullshit. She managed to raise it a foot or two, but then let go, defeated. Juliana was right.

To her credit, Juliana didn't rub her face in it. She began gathering sticks. "Let's mark the beach to show them where it is."

Sierra collected an armload and followed her out of the jungle.

The raft would be done in a few more days. Hopefully, that would enable them to find other survivors. Figuring out where they were felt like a tougher problem to solve. She hoped they would find clues on the other islands, but honestly wasn't sure what to look for.

"Who do you think brought us here?" she asked. Talking it through might spark some new ideas.

Juliana poked a stick in the sand and swiveled it around, driving it down. "I don't know. We may never know."

"How can you be okay with that?"

"Most of life's biggest questions never get answered. You know that. There's nothing we can do about it. All we can do is take care of each other. Those kids, especially."

Sierra walked a few paces and pressed another stick in the sand. Juliana's response, noble as it was, could never satisfy her. She needed more. She needed answers. Still, it was nice to get the woman talking. They'd hardly spoken.

"Did you have any kids?" Sierra asked.

Juliana looked away. "I don't want to talk about it."

Sierra clomped her mouth shut. Everyone here had been through hell. She'd buried the memory of her father's body as deeply as she could. This poor woman had apparently lost her children. She could barely imagine her grief.

They kept planting sticks until they reached the shore. The markers looked like an unfinished fence, starting at the water and pointing straight to the log. Anyone coming down the beach would be certain to spot them.

Sierra followed the sticks back to the jungle. "Let's go deeper in and see what we can find." She marched forward without waiting for a response. Wayne had told them to stay close to the beach, but he had also told them to stay together. Juliana would have to choose which rule to obey.

After hesitating for a moment, Juliana followed. The jungle grew darker as they moved inland. Monkeys chittered in the treetops.

Figuring out where they were was only one step. Sierra also wanted to know why they'd been saved. What value did human beings have, in the eyes of their rescuers? Understanding that might make it easier to interact with them once they finally met.

Juliana gripped her arm. "Look," she whispered.

Sierra froze and peered through the foliage. Forty feet ahead, an eight-foot-tall bird bent its neck over its body, preening its feathers with an oversized beak. It looked like an ostrich on steroids.

"Shoot it," she whispered.

Juliana drew her gun, but then held up her other hand and pointed. A second bird sat on the ground near the first. The sitting bird's head swiveled back and forth like a security camera.

"Shoot 'em both," Sierra whispered. They needed the protein.

Juliana shook her head. "Wayne said conserve ammo," she breathed. "Self-defense only."

Sierra considered snatching the pistol from her, but if she did that, Wayne would never give her a gun.

Juliana leaned close. "Let's get back."

Sierra pulled away from her, crawling forward to a clump of shrubs. The vegetation hid her from the birds. She wasn't about to abandon this opportunity.

The roosting bird sat on a raised pile of sticks. Juliana crept up next to her, clearly annoyed.

"It's a nest," Sierra mouthed.

"Come on." Juliana tilted her head. "They look dangerous."

Their massive beaks swished like gardening shears when they opened and closed.

"A nest means eggs," Sierra said.

"We can tell Wayne."

Sierra shook her head. The creatures looked dangerous, but they also looked skittish. She pulled a coconut from her shoulder bag and lobbed it over the clearing, where it landed with a thud.

The standing bird flapped its stubby gray wings. The one on the nest periscoped its head toward the coconut.

Sierra and Juliana ducked lower. "You're going to get us killed," Juliana hissed.

"Nope." If one of the birds charged, Juliana would be free to shoot it in self-defense. But Sierra didn't think it likely. She grabbed another coconut and raised her head enough to peer through clusters of green and yellow leaves. Both birds were still staring away from them, toward the coconut she'd thrown.

"*Wahk,*" called the nesting animal. "*Wahk. Waaaahk.*"

Sierra rose and launched another coconut. It crashed into a branch above the nest and fell to the ground. Juliana jerked her back down behind the bush.

The standing bird ran circles in the small clearing. The brooding animal scissored to its feet. "*Wwwaaaahk.*" Four yellow eggs as big as melons sat in the nest.

Jackpot.

After a moment, the circling bird stopped and pecked at the coconut, its scrubby wings extended on both sides. It lifted the foot-long husk in its bright red beak and sliced it in half with a loud snap.

Juliana gasped. Sierra ignored her and lobbed another coconut over the clearing. It thumped to the ground on the far side of the nest and rolled across leaf litter. Both creatures turned to face it.

"*Wahk,*" said the first bird, strutting over to the coconut.

"*Waaaaaahk,*" answered the second.

Sierra took out two more coconuts and handed one to Juliana. She made a throwing motion and smacked the coconut against her raised palm, which flopped backwards. They would each throw a coconut directly at one of the birds. Sierra locked eyes with her. *We can do this.*

Juliana stared for a long moment, then nodded.

The birds still faced away from them.

Sierra held three fingers, then two, then one. They stood and threw at the same time.

The coconuts hit both birds. The one by the nest bolted as if set on fire, disappearing in the brush. The other bird circled once, then followed its mate, crying, "*Waaahkk!*" as it ran.

Juliana bent to her knees in a wheezing laugh.

Sierra pulled her up. "Hurry."

They darted around the underbrush to the clearing. Sierra grabbed an egg, holding it gingerly at first, but it was heavier than it looked and the shell felt like solid rock. She scooped up a second one and Juliana grabbed the other two.

"Come on." They took off, running back toward the beach. Sierra looked over her shoulder, carrying the eggs under her arms like footballs, but the giant birds were nowhere to be seen.

When they reached the sand, Juliana stopped and bent over, breathing hard. "Those were in the museum, too," she said. "Skeletons. There were a bunch of different kinds."

"Where you saw the Entelodont?" This felt like another clue. "Were they also prehistoric?"

Juliana nodded. "I think so. They called them horror birds. I thought it was silly." She stopped herself. "No. That isn't right. Terror birds."

Sierra blew out a puff of air. "Those two weren't so terrifying."

"Are you kidding? You could have gotten us both killed."

"But I didn't," Sierra said. She nodded toward the giant eggs. "What's in your hands?"

She saw a tiny spark in Juliana's eyes.

They followed the line of sticks out to the shore, then turned right, toward Williams Beach, the name Barry had given the stretch where his family's pod had landed.

"If the terror birds were prehistoric too, that seems like more evidence we've gone back in time," Sierra said, trying to make sense of it. "This place really does feel like Earth."

Juliana looked unconvinced. "David said the oceans were always salty."

"Maybe he's wrong," Sierra said. "Or maybe the science was wrong."

"That doesn't give me much confidence in science."

Sierra groaned. "That's the whole point. When new information comes along, science adapts."

"Why would aliens send us back in time?" Juliana asked.

She chewed on this for a moment. "You know, we still don't have proof they were aliens."

"Who else could have sent the pods?"

A new idea occurred to Sierra, and it felt like a good fit. "If the pods are time machines, what if someone on Earth sent them from the future?"

Juliana looked lost. "Huh?"

"What if some small number of people survived the Ender, figured out time travel, and sent the pods back to rescue us?"

"Why would they send us even further back?"

"I don't know," Sierra said. "Maybe time travel only works backwards. Maybe Earth in the future isn't safe." She couldn't wait to get back and run the ideas past David. He shared her curiosity, and he'd finally forgiven her for siding with Wayne about the raft.

They drew close to the work site, where two large trunks lay in the sand about six feet apart, with thin branches crossing them in an X shape. A dozen other logs lay stacked nearby. Sierra assumed they would go across the top to form a deck.

"Well, once the raft is finished, we can stop speculating about everything and go search for answers."

"I wouldn't be so sure," Juliana said. "We may find more people, but that's probably it."

"What makes you think that?" Sierra asked.

"It's obvious. Whoever brought us here doesn't want to meet us, or they would have shown themselves by now." Juliana sounded fine with the thought, which was annoying.

Worse though, was the fact that when Sierra stopped to think about it, Juliana's theory made sense.

Chapter Nineteen

David walked down the beach with Josh and Randall to retrieve the fallen palm tree that Sierra and Juliana had found. The hike got his injured leg singing again. He hid the pain, not wanting to show weakness in front of Randall and Josh, who both seemed to value strength over everything else.

"How long until the raft is done?" Josh asked.

"Just a couple more logs," Randall said.

David had come to terms with the plan. They needed to find more people in order to build a stable community where his kids could grow up.

He was still trying to come to terms with Wayne.

To his credit, Wayne kept everyone working and it felt good to be productive. It provided a nice distraction from everything that had happened. It also gave David time to think things through.

"How many people do you think we'll find on the next island?" Josh asked.

"There was nine here," Randall said. "Maybe each one is about the same."

"I sure hope there's more," David said. If a handful of pods had landed on each island, it would take forever to find everyone. His heart ached. Every day it became harder to hold onto hope that Lindsey was out there somewhere. At the same time, he couldn't mourn for her until they found all the pods. It felt like he was in limbo.

"Why's that?" Josh asked.

"I would really love to find my wife," David said simply. It was easier than trying to explain the emotions he was juggling.

"I don't blame ya," Randall said. "I'd like to meet some new people, too. A man has needs, don't he?"

Josh snickered.

"Seriously?" David blurted.

He'd heard far worse from surgeons changing in the locker room, but the comment rankled him, especially considering the maddening mix of hope and grief he'd been feeling.

Randall either didn't notice David's reaction or didn't care. "Hell, yeah. We're starting a whole new civilization here. We can rule this place. We'll be kings."

"Hell, yeah," Josh echoed.

David stopped and stood there, trying to figure out how to tell Randall he sounded like an ass without starting a fight.

Randall's bushy eyebrows lowered. His wiry body looked hard and mean. "What's the problem, Dave?"

He took a deep breath. He always had trouble keeping his mouth shut when people were being stupid. It had caused issues with family, friends, and sometimes even the hospital director. He formulated a calm response. "I think you need to be careful about how you approach any people you find. If you march in like conquerors, it might backfire."

"Is that right?" Randall asked.

Josh watched them both, eyes wide behind his little round glasses. David was glad he'd come along. It was good for the teenager to see some examples of thoughtful reasoning after all of the brute-force intimidation displayed by Wayne and Randall.

They started walking again.

David had come up with a three-step plan. Maybe if he laid everything out, Randall would see that it made sense. "First of all, if you do find someone, you should observe them from a distance before you approach them. See how they treat each other. Try to understand their social hierarchy. Make sure they're not a threat."

"A threat?" Josh asked.

"Some of the people we find may not be friendly," David said.

Randall snorted. "Wayne and I can handle 'em."

David ignored the comment and moved on to step two. "Next, you'll need to determine who has the better situation. Our island has giant birds and those Entelodont things, which are dangerous, but also sources of food. You'll need to figure out what sorts of assets and liabilities are present on their island to determine which one is best."

"Huh," Randall said. "I figured we'd just bring everyone back here."

That's because you haven't thought it through. David managed to keep the response in his head. "The third thing is to win them over, to convince them that it's advantageous to combine our groups."

"You really think they'd need convincing?" Josh asked.

David shrugged. "There's any number of reasons they might not be onboard with joining us."

Randall laughed. "They're gonna have to get onboard if they want to sail back over here. Get it? Onboard."

Josh chortled.

The joke felt like something Barry might have said. It almost seemed as if Randall exaggerated his little dumb hick routine to make people underestimate him.

"How do we convince them to join us?" Josh asked.

"You can make the case that there's safety in numbers," David said. "Also, everyone in both groups will have different ways to contribute. A large group will be more efficient and more effective."

They arrived at the row of sticks in the sand, fence posts without the fence, just as Sierra had described. Several yards into the jungle, they found the fallen log.

Randall walked over to the narrow end and bent to grab it. "Come on now, let's get back before something else comes out of them woods."

David tensed, looking around. They hadn't seen any more creatures like the one Wayne shot, but they heard distant growls after dark on most nights.

He and Randall hoisted the log onto their shoulders. Josh walked in the middle, holding the trunk from below.

As they trudged back out to the beach, the pain in David's thigh grew sharper. It subsided slightly when they reached the shoreline, where the packed wet sand made walking easier.

"What if the next island ain't got people on it?" Randall asked.

"Wayne intends to keep looking, doesn't he?" David answered, talking to the back of Randall's head.

"Naw, I mean what if the next island is full of aliens? The ones that sent the pods."

David had given this some consideration, too. Meeting whoever had brought them here could open doors to all sorts of scientific advances. "We have to find a way to communicate and then convince them we have something of value in exchange for their technology."

"What the hell do we have to offer?"

"We can tell them about Earth," David said. "That has to be worth something. It's probably part of the reason they saved us."

"What do you mean?" Josh asked.

"Our history, our culture. There's so much for them to learn."

"I don't remember all that much from my history class, Dave," Randall said, twisting his head back.

Josh chuckled. "Me neither."

This was one case where education didn't matter. "Things that seem mundane to us might be fascinating to them. You could tell them about the cities you lived in, the shows you watched." David almost mentioned books, but was quick enough to stop himself. Josh and Randall didn't strike him as voracious readers.

"I could tell them about my favorite music," Josh said.

"Exactly," David said. "Randall, I bet your job would fascinate them. What did you do for a living in Oklahoma?"

Randall had been evasive about his past. He was silent for so long David wondered if he'd heard him. Finally, he answered. "I managed a restaurant called 'Grandpaw's Chicken.' Finest barbeque you ever had."

"God, I miss barbeque," Josh said.

Randall hardly seemed like the sort of guy who could manage a business, but David didn't mention it. He was proud of how he was handling the conversation. "Perfect. You can teach them everything about inventory management, hiring and firing, marketing. They might even be interested in recipes and cooking practices. All of those things would be unique to Earth."

Randall didn't respond, and since David couldn't see his face, he had no idea what he was thinking.

He spotted the raft, a tiny dot ahead on the beach. He hoped his kids were staying together and keeping Kona close. He didn't like being this far from them.

"What if the aliens ain't friendly?" Randall asked.

"Why wouldn't they be friendly? They saved us from the Ender."

"Maybe we're supposed to be slaves for them. Or food."

"That's a lot of effort to raise food," David said. "Why go to the trouble?"

"Maybe we're a delicacy. Maybe this island is a big-ass stockyard where they fatten us up."

"I don't think any species advanced enough to send those pods would need to raise humans for food."

"How do you know they even think like us?" Randall asked. "Not everybody thinks the way you do, Dave."

The comment hit him surprisingly hard. Lindsey had often chided David for struggling to understand other points of view. When one choice was so obviously correct, how could anyone choose differently? He winced. If other human beings made inexplicable choices for unexplainable reasons, what sorts of decisions might an alien make?

They finally reached the raft, where Wayne's legs stuck out from beneath the main deck, like a mechanic working on a car. He pulled a vine rope down between two logs and cinched it tight.

"Looking good, Wayne," Randall said.

The raft had come together enough for David to picture the end result. A row of logs ran across two larger trunks to form a platform slightly bigger than a king-size bed.

Wayne certainly got things done, and he had put in as much effort as anyone. He'd helped haul most of the timbers himself, some of them single-handedly.

He crawled out from beneath the raft and examined the log on their shoulders. "Nice work, gentlemen. Drop this one here in the middle."

They maneuvered the trunk out over the raft and lowered it into place.

Wayne pulled a rope vine around the new log. "Just a few more days and we can set out."

Randall sat on a corner of the raft and flapped his shirt from his chest. "Dave here is worried you and I won't make a good impression on them other islands."

Wayne looked back as he knotted the vine, eyebrows raised.

David's neck grew hot. He hadn't expected Randall to report their conversation. "I've been thinking about strategies to make sure everything goes well over there," he said. "That's all."

"Sometimes I wonder if you think you know better than the rest of us," Wayne said.

"Of course not," David said, trying to sound convincing.

"He sure does," Randall said.

Josh stood watching a few feet away.

Wayne walked over. His shoulders and forearms bulged from his t-shirt, now brown with dirt and sweat. "What are you so worried about?"

David squared his shoulders, unable to back down. "I'm worried you'll scare off anyone you meet, since intimidation seems to be your only way of interacting with people."

Wayne crossed his arms. "A little intimidation can be useful. Like you said, some of those people may not be friendly."

"Yeah, Dave," Randall huffed. "You have to show people they better not fuck with you."

"It isn't that simple," David hissed. "You're going to need a nuanced approach." He should have stopped there, but he didn't. "Something you don't seem capable of."

Wayne's eyes narrowed and for a moment, David thought he would get punched.

"One thing's for sure," Wayne said. "I doubt we'll find anyone out there as arrogant as you."

David opened his mouth, but Wayne held up a hand, stopping him. "Go look after your kids, Doc."

David stepped away. "Come on, Josh. Let's get back."

"No," Josh said. "I'm gonna stay here and help."

A smug smile spread across Wayne's heavy jaw.

David walked off, heart pounding and sweat dripping down his temples. He was disgusted with Randall, disappointed in Josh, and angry at Wayne. Most of all, though, he was furious with himself for making things worse.

Chapter Twenty

Wayne sat by the hilltop campfire with an egg propped on his thighs, Josh's Bowie knife in one hand, and a rock in the other. He placed the point on the shell and tapped the handle with the rock. David sat across the fire from him, silently stewing. Wayne felt bad about their confrontation, but after giving it some thought, he'd found a solution that should patch everything up.

"I hope there isn't a fertilized chick inside," Juliana said.

Darkness had fallen. Without any stars above, it felt like the world simply ceased to exist eight feet beyond the campfire.

Everyone sat watching Wayne. He enjoyed being the center of attention. People needed his strength and it was his duty to serve. He would keep them safe.

Sierra chuckled. "Super-sized balut."

"What the fuck are you talking about?" Randall asked.

"Hard-boiled duck embryo. It's a delicacy in the Philippines."

Wayne looked up from the egg. "That sounds nasty." He went back to tapping the knife with the rock, finally producing a crack, which enabled him to pry off a piece of shell. He held the egg low so the flames could illuminate the inside. "You're out of luck, Hollywood. Orange yolk and a whole lotta egg white."

Everything was working according to plan. The raft was almost complete, the group had food to eat, and soon they would find more people to build their community.

Wayne opened the other three eggs, careful to crack them on the ends, so the shells could be used later as containers. He picked up a short stick that Josh had whittled for him and used it to scramble the yolks. Next, he poured the mixtures into nine coconut shells that had been soaked in water. He set the shells on hot coals and stirred the scrambles every so often while they cooked.

"That smells so good," Sierra said. "Reminds me of my mother's cooking."

Josh looked up. "I thought you lived with your dad?"

Josh might be an awkward little white boy, but he was paying attention to Sierra, remembering details about her.

"Mom moved out when I was nine," she said. "Before that, she cooked breakfast every morning. Biscuits and gravy. Grits. Soul food. She said it helped her connect with her roots."

"I take it your mother was Black and your father was white," Wayne noted.

Sierra opened her mouth with an expression of exaggerated awe. "You could be a detective."

He smiled. There was that spunk again.

"The great Rick Preston never made breakfast?" Waldmire asked.

Sierra shook her head. "He was always off to work before I got up. He would leave me a twenty on the counter so I could pick up something on the way to school."

Randall whistled and Wayne raised his eyebrows. Sierra didn't know how good she had it. Twenty bucks a day, just for breakfast. Her leather jacket and those fancy white motorcycle pants probably cost more than his whole wardrobe back home.

Once the eggs congealed, Wayne drew the coconut shells from the fire and passed them around. "Ladies first."

Juliana took a bite. "Oh my God, that's good."

Wayne agreed. The eggs were richer and creamier than chicken eggs, with a hint of sweetness from the coconut.

"Too bad we aren't eating drumsticks," Sierra said. She gave Juliana a wicked glare.

Juliana stood her ground, God bless her. "If I had shot one, the other one might have attacked us. We might both be dead now."

Sierra glanced over at Wayne's rucksack. "If I'd been armed, too, we could have shot them both. We might have a feast now."

After what had happened with Blondie, Wayne wasn't about to give anyone a gun until he was one hundred percent certain he could trust them.

"When's the last time you shot an animal, Hollywood?"

"I've never shot an animal, Wayne. I've also never stolen eggs from a terror bird, until today. And I bet David never landed an airplane in a field before last week." She looked proud of herself for coming up with this clever little retort.

"He trained for it, though," Wayne said, turning to David. "Didn't you? You had a checklist. You practiced."

David gave a reluctant nod, warming Wayne's heart. David was smart, and despite his arrogance, he would probably make a good ambassador. Wayne had decided to put David in charge of meeting new people, giving him exactly what he wanted.

Sierra's mouth puckered as if she was trying to find another argument. Wayne welcomed it. He could take whatever she threw his way.

Waldmire changed the subject. "It looks as if the raft is nearly done."

"Yes," Wayne said. "We should be able to finish it and get everything ready in two days. We'll set out at daybreak the following morning."

"And you're still aiming for that island to the right of the point?" Waldmire gestured off in the dark.

"That's correct."

"How long do you plan to be gone? Will you explore the whole island?"

Waldmire was asking smart questions. "We need to be thorough," Wayne said. "If anyone is there, we'll be sure to find them. We'll look for signs of habitation along the shore. People would likely come down to the beach for water. We'll circle the whole thing if we have to."

"If you don't find anyone, will you come back, or go on to the next island?" Waldmire asked.

The whole group had grown still. Every last person was focused on him. "We'll come back first, so we can help replenish the food stores. While we're gone, the people who stay here will need to restrict themselves to the hilltop, for their own protection."

"And if there are people over there, how are we going to approach them?" Sierra asked.

Wayne extended his hand toward David. "I understand Doc has given that some thought."

David nodded. "Yeah."

Wayne smiled. "I appreciate that. You'll be our emissary, our ambassador."

David looked puzzled, not pleased.

Kim whispered, "Dad?" Her eyebrows arched toward each other.

David gave Wayne a hard look. "I'm not leaving my children."

This was not the reaction Wayne had expected. "You're the one who said we need a nuanced approach. You'll keep us honest." He inhaled deeply through his nose, trying to keep his irritation at bay. "You'll be our moral compass."

Randall snorted. "Every ship needs a compass."

Wayne rolled his eyes.

"Who else are you taking?" Waldmire asked.

Wayne looked around the group. It should be obvious, but apparently he had to spell it out. "It's like David said. We don't know what kind of people we'll find. We need to make a strong showing." He massaged the back of his bald head. "We need all the men. Me, Randall, David, and Waldmire."

The campfire burst into argument.

"I'm not a kid," Josh whined. "I want to go."

Juliana said, "There isn't enough room. We can't all go."

Barry wrapped his arms around his father. "Daddy, you can't leave."

"Seriously," added Kim.

"What is this?" Sierra asked. "The nineteen-fifties?"

"We need upper body strength for rowing," Randall said. "You and Juliana couldn't carry that log, could you?"

Sierra looked like she might explode. "That's bullshit. The raft can hold six."

"And we need room to bring people back," Randall countered. "Wayne's in charge. Quit arguing with him."

"We ought to discuss this further," Waldmire said.

David stared across the flames, silent.

Wayne's blood rose as he listened to their chatter. They didn't understand. These people needed him. He was here to keep them safe. It was Pastor Edwin's dying command.

"Now listen," Wayne said.

The tiresome jabber continued. Sierra got to her feet.

"*Now listen,*" Wayne said again, almost roaring.

Silence.

He stood, grabbing the shotgun as he rose. Sometimes a little intimidation could be useful. "I was sent here to keep you safe, and by God, you will do what I say."

Faces danced in the firelight. They looked scared. Hopefully, he'd finally gotten through to them.

Chapter Twenty-One

Sierra shouldered her bag and started up the path from Williams Beach to the hilltop. Kim and Josh led the way, also carrying bags of fruit. They'd spent the morning collecting even more coconuts, spicy oranges, and the purple tubers that Barry named "barneys."

The hilltop camp already looked like the produce section in a supermarket, but Wayne insisted they keep gathering food.

Sierra had to find a way to make him listen to her and recognize her value without threatening his precious sense of authority. She needed to do it soon, too, because she was determined to join him on the expedition, no matter what he said.

"Wait up," Juliana called from the beach. Behind her, Barry played fetch with Kona while the men struggled to position a large log.

Sierra waited for Juliana to run over, uncomfortable about letting Kim and Josh get too far ahead. The path was well-traveled and they hadn't seen terror birds near here, but she didn't want to take any chances.

Once Juliana caught up, they set a quick pace, rejoining the kids around the first turn in the tunnel of foliage. The trees near the beach, which were mostly palms, grew apart from one another, but as the path approached the hill, dozens of other types of trees crowded in, along with a mix of broadleaf plants and dangling vines.

Josh and Kim chatted as they walked. Sierra and Juliana followed several paces behind, listening.

"Barry gets to name the plants and animals," Josh said. "We should think bigger than that. We should name this island, or maybe this whole planet."

"What would you call it?" Kim asked. "Josh-land?"

He chuckled. "At least you have a beach with your name on it, Miss Williams."

"That's just what Barry started calling it," Kim said. "I think it's silly."

"This place isn't like Earth," Josh said. "We can do whatever we want here. There aren't any rules. We could be kings."

"And queens," Kim added.

Sierra chuckled, glad to see Josh talking like a kid for once, instead of trying to be one of the grown-ups.

Juliana seemed amused as well. "What kind of rules would you make, your majesty?"

A rustle came from the underbrush ahead. Everyone stopped. "What was that?" Kim whispered.

Something moved beyond the wall of ferns on the right.

"Probably just one of Barry's stupid monkeys," Kim said.

Josh held out his hand toward Juliana, "Let me use your gun. I'll shoot it and we can have stew for dinner."

"Sorry," Juliana tisked. "Wayne made me promise." She drew the gun and crept past the kids, leaning her head from side to side to peer through the plants.

A blue monkey burst from the foliage, ran across the path, and bounced up a tree on the other side.

Kim squealed. Sierra's whole body clenched.

The monkey stopped halfway up the tree, where it hung by one arm and hissed at them.

Josh made a gun with his finger. "Ka-pow."

To her credit, Juliana kept her cool. Sierra probably would have pulled the trigger out of shock.

Juliana looked back at the others. "Come on, let's get to camp."

A creature bigger than a bull burst from the undergrowth, slamming Juliana across the path. She crumpled on the ground, wailing.

Kim screamed, the fingers of both hands splayed on either side of her face.

Sierra grabbed her and Josh, pulling them both backwards. Her heart lurched in her chest and she felt short of air.

The creature trotted to Juliana and stood over her, like a dog guarding its food. Raspy rumbles came from deep in its chest.

Sierra, Kim, and Josh froze. The monster stared at them.

Wayne had said the Entelodont looked like a mix between a hyena and a pig, but that only began to describe it. This beast towered seven feet tall. Bony cheeks protruded from its long hairless snout like on a warthog. Yellow teeth jutted from oversized jaws. Ragged black hair hung from its sides.

"What do we do?" Kim whispered, shaking.

"Back up slowly," Sierra said, keeping her eyes on the beast. The Entelodont stood in the center of the path, between them and the hill. The beach was more than a quarter mile behind them.

On the ground, Juliana moaned. "My arm, my arm."

Everything will be okay, Sierra told herself, trying to keep panic at bay. It was just a broken arm. David could set it, though Sierra couldn't quite imagine how. Juliana's arm twisted in three places.

She had to get the kids away from here, and she had to get the creature away from Juliana. She pushed Kim back down the path and sidestepped toward the trees on the left.

The Entelodont pawed at the ground. Its filthy black hoof caught Juliana in the gut. She shrieked. Thick saliva dripped from its mouth, pattering on the jungle floor like rain. Several globs landed on the woman. The creature stank of musk and rot.

Sierra held up her hands. "Over here." She stood at the edge of the path, by the wall of trees. If she lured the monster this way, she could climb a tree to escape. She could keep its attention while the kids ran to get Wayne. That son of a bitch should have given her a gun. She scanned the ground for Juliana's pistol but couldn't find it.

The Entelodont flicked its tail and glanced her way. Its eyes were big black globes.

"That's right," she called. "Over here."

Kim and Josh crept backwards, inch by inch.

The animal leaped over Juliana's body, bounding toward them.

Sierra's stomach lurched. "No! Wait!" She waved her arms.

The Entelodont stopped, but kept watching Kim and Josh, its head towering five feet off the ground. Kim whimpered. Josh turned pale. He pulled his knife from his belt and held it, shaking, in front of him. It might as well have been a toothpick against a creature so large.

Sierra slid her bag of fruit from her shoulder and flung it at the monster, striking its massive neck. The Entelodont snarled and turned to face her. Hairy cone-shaped ears rotated forward. Slime glistened on jagged teeth poking from its snout.

"That's right. Over here." She waved her arms again, trying to keep its attention on her.

On the path, Kim looked around, as if preparing to flee.

"Don't run," Sierra hissed. "You'll draw it after you."

Branches swayed in the canopy above and leaves floated down. It had to be that stupid monkey, scampering away, because there was no wind here. Sierra kept her eyes trained on the creature.

"Juliana, where's your gun?" she called. "Can you shoot it?"

Juliana moaned.

The Entelodont lolled its head back and forth between Sierra at the edge of the jungle and the two kids out in the middle of the path. It snorted, blasting dirt and leaves across the ground. Sierra trembled, then gritted her teeth to stop herself. She couldn't let it see her fear.

"Keep backing up slowly," she called. "Get Wayne." The monster turned her way again. "That's right, you ugly shit." She reached back, feeling for the closest tree. If it charged, she could slip behind the trunk, putting it between them. "Come on!"

The Entelodont's head seemed to split apart as it opened its jaws. A cold jolt ran up Sierra's spine. But the monster didn't charge. Instead, it turned around. Juliana tried to ward it off with her good arm. The creature closed its teeth on her shoulder and lifted her from the ground. She howled.

Sierra ran out onto the path, horrified and desperate. "No!"

The Entelodont's head lurched, engulfing Juliana's torso with its crooked teeth. Her legs hung from one side of its mouth and her arms dangled from the other.

Sierra froze, only four feet away.

The beast shook its head like a giant pit bull. Blood spattered Sierra's face and a gag rose in her throat. Juliana's foot swung into her chest, knocking her away.

Sierra pinwheeled her arms as she tumbled backwards. She landed on her butt near the trees.

Kona burst up the path, barking like a junkyard dog. Froth flew from her mouth and the hair on her back rose straight up. She slid to a stop in front of the Entelodont, paws stretched wide.

The creature dropped Juliana on the dirt and growled at the dog, who jumped left and right, a swarm of canine fury. The monster snapped at the golden retriever, but Kona dodged away.

David and Wayne ran up. David grabbed Kim and Josh, pulling them farther back. Kim held her hands over her face, shrieking.

Wayne raced forward and dropped to one knee beside Sierra. He fumbled with his rucksack.

Kona barked nonstop.

Wayne pulled a big gun from the bag, then froze, staring up toward the creature.

"Hurry," Sierra cried, still on the ground.

Kona ran a half-circle around the Entelodont. The monster turned, tracking her, then swung back to the people on the path.

"Shoot it," Sierra yelled.

Wayne raised the gun, but it was too late. The Entelodont leaped away, leaning like a motorcycle as it ran. Kona chased it a few yards, still barking, until it disappeared in the jungle. The thunder of its hooves faded in the distance.

Sierra crawled across the path, tears flowing. Juliana's wide eyes stared ahead, lifeless. Torn flesh showed part of her cheekbone.

"Somebody, do something," Kim wailed.

Sierra shook, sobbing uncontrollably. There wasn't anything anyone could do. They should have stayed on the beach. They should have waited until the whole group was ready to walk back together. She should have made Wayne give her a gun.

She cradled Juliana's head in her arms and cried.

Chapter Twenty-Two

David saw his first corpse in medical school, a heart attack victim who donated his body to science. Death had become a real thing then, no longer an abstract concept, and his sleep had been fitful that night.

Now Kim and Barry stared at Juliana's body, pale and stale, as the pre-meds liked to say, while the adults dug her grave. He didn't want them here. Dried black blood rimmed the wounds on Juliana's crushed torso. He didn't want his children to see this, but he had no choice. He had to keep them close.

They had decided to bury Juliana in the glade where David first met her, Wayne, and Randall, after Barry ran away. The endless babble of the waterfall droned in the air. Bright red flowers decorated the trees and thick moss covered the ground.

They used sticks and rocks to loosen the soil and coconut shells to scoop it out. Soon they were all filthy. Wayne insisted they go down as deep as they could. He didn't want an Entelodont to dig up Juliana and feed on her.

They lined the bottom of the grave with palm fronds, lowered Juliana in, and covered her with a layer of broad leaves.

Barry pointed in the hole. "If I die, are you going to do that to me?" Tears traced lines through dirt on his cheeks.

David's chest felt hollow, right beneath his sternum. "That isn't going to happen, Buddy."

He prayed it was true. He needed to tell Wayne he wouldn't go anywhere on his goddamn raft. He couldn't leave his kids. Wayne would have to shoot him first.

Wayne spoke about Juliana for a few minutes. She had buried three children in the months before the Ender, right after her husband disappeared. Despite all that, she'd spent her final days caring for several dozen seniors who didn't have anyone else. She'd never stopped trying to do the right thing.

Kim's mouth stretched into a grimace and the tears fell. David pulled her close. He didn't know what else to do. None of his parenting books had included anything about the trauma of a twelve-year-old who saw a woman get mauled to death.

Sierra reached over and rubbed Kim's back.

Wayne looked around to see if anyone else had anything to say, but was met with solemn faces. He shoved dirt into the hole. Everyone joined in to help.

When all of the soil had been moved on top of the grave, Wayne stabbed a crude wooden cross into the ground. He stepped back and looked at the others. "I saw her spirit."

"What?" David asked. "What do you mean?" It was the last thing he'd expected to hear.

Wayne's eyes looked heavy. "I saw a ghostly shape up in the trees when that creature killed her. It was Juliana, looking down on her body as she floated away."

Josh's mouth hung open. "Her soul."

David hadn't seen anything, though he'd been focused on Kim and the monster in front of her, not the damn treetops. He believed in an afterlife, but to him, the soul was something ethereal, a vague positive energy, not anything tangible. In the hospital, he'd witnessed numerous deaths and never once saw a departing spirit.

"How is that possible?" Sierra asked. Grime covered her face, leaving crinkles around her eyes where she squinted, making her look older than twenty-three.

"There's something about this place." Wayne's response was flat and matter-of-fact. "When you die here, your soul is visible."

Wayne had definitely seen something. David had come to realize that Wayne never lied. Still, he wanted to take an analytical approach. "Did you actually see it come out of her?"

"No." Wayne said. "She was dead when I got there."

"What did it look like?" Waldmire asked.

"A breath of mist," Wayne said. "A thin cloud, barely visible."

Barry squeezed David's hand. "That's what I saw on the mountain."

David looked back and forth between his son and Wayne. "Wait, do you think it was the same thing?"

"Did I see a soul?" Barry asked. "Was it Mommy?"

David's heart melted. He didn't think so, but Jesus, after all the crazy shit they'd been through, anything could be possible.

"It's the aliens," Sierra said. "It has to be."

Everyone looked up, but they saw only the trees surrounding the glade, with their little red flowers.

"It wasn't an alien, Hollywood," Wayne said. "It didn't even have a shape."

David latched on to Sierra's idea. It was the only thing that made sense. "Maybe they don't have a physical form, like we do. Maybe they're a swarm of microscopic beings or something."

Wayne scowled. "What are you even talking about?"

"I believe you, Wayne," Josh said. "It was Juliana. It was her soul."

Kim looked up, tears in her eyes, and maybe a hint of hope. "Dad, what if they're right?"

David didn't believe it, but he also didn't want to crush his daughter's spirits. "Look, if anyone sees something else floating overhead, point it out," he said. "We need evidence. We don't really know anything."

"I know one thing," Sierra said. "I need a gun." She locked eyes with Wayne. "If I'd had a gun, this wouldn't have happened."

"Juliana had a gun," Wayne said. "It didn't save her."

Sierra didn't back down. "Train me," she said. "Now." She stood motionless.

Finally, Wayne nodded. "We'll start with some drills. Trigger discipline, breakdown, cleaning, and assembly."

"Why does she get training?" Randall blurted.

"Yeah," Josh said. "I want a gun, too."

Wayne held up a hand. "Everybody will get a turn. For now, the whole group stays together at all times. Nobody goes off alone." He walked to his rucksack and picked up his shotgun. "Let's get back to camp."

Chapter Twenty-Three

Sierra sat next to Waldmire with her feet in the sea, braiding vines into rope. The tiny ripples lapping the shoreline belonged at a lake, not an ocean. She dipped her hand every few minutes to soak her fingertips, numb from hours of weaving the coarse fibers. Kona splashed nearby.

"I still can't believe it," she said, her heart heavy with grief. "I keep wanting to go back in time, to do something different, to stop it all from happening."

"I know," Waldmire said. "Juliana was a good person. At least she's in a better place now."

"How do you know that?" In Sierra's mind, Juliana was just gone.

"I don't know it," Waldmire said. "I believe it."

The sentiment made her uncomfortable. "What if you're wrong?"

Waldmire raised his eyebrows. The expression smoothed the creases around his eyes but somehow made him look older. "What if I'm wrong? What difference does it make? I believe because believing helps me."

"How does just believing in something help you?"

"It grounds me." Waldmire smiled. "It comforts me. Faith gives me strength when I need it most."

"I don't think I can believe in something just because I want to." The idea that Juliana had gone to a better place was appealing, not to mention the idea that her father had gone to a better place. But she didn't believe it. Sierra saw death as simply the end of existence. It was all the more reason to live a good life.

Rick Preston had raised her without religion. He didn't believe in anything he couldn't put his hands on or secure in a business deal and he always cautioned her to stay out of religious debates. *Never argue with faith, Kiddo. You can't win.*

"That's okay," Waldmire said. "I won't hold it against you." His response lifted her sadness a little. She wanted to lean into him. She needed a hug, but she wasn't sure how he'd react.

Kona ran over, dropped a stick, and shook, spraying them. Waldmire tossed the stick into the shallows. Nobody had seen anything in the water, not even a minnow.

He turned and looked at Sierra, his eyes sparkling. "You want to go on that expedition, don't you?" A hundred feet up the beach, the others were putting the finishing touches on the raft.

She looked sideways at him. "Oh, I'm going. I just haven't figured out how to make it happen."

He smiled warmly. "I believe you will. You've got Rick's tenacity."

Kona dropped the stick again. Sierra tossed it as far into the water as she could. "I wish he was here. He'd know what to do. He always knew what to do."

Waldmire laughed. "Trust me, Sierra. Rick Preston did not always know what to do."

He was right, of course. Whatever had happened between Rick Preston and her mother had not gone well, and neither of them ever talked about it. She considered asking Waldmire if he knew why they split up, but decided against it. She didn't want to know. Instead, she asked, "Do you really think Wayne saw her spirit?" She'd been watching the sky all day and hadn't seen a thing. Certainly not a ghost.

"He saw something. Wayne's no bullshitter." Waldmire held a piece of vine between clenched teeth and pulled two strands tight, then checked his work. The rope held. "Maybe it was her spirit. Maybe it was the ghost of someone who died when the Ender hit, here to show her the way. Maybe it was something else entirely. We don't know enough about this place to say for sure."

She tied off her own piece of rope and coiled it on the sand beside her. "Do you really think ghosts are real?"

"I told you, Sweetie. I don't think they're real. I believe it."

The answer only frustrated her.

Never argue with faith, Kiddo. You can't win.

She glanced over at the raft, where Wayne hefted a bag of fruit onto the deck. "He's so sexist. He thinks the only way to make a strong showing is with men."

Waldmire put a hand on her shoulder. "You'll never change someone like him. Don't even try."

Sierra dipped her sore fingers in the water. "Are you saying I should give up?"

He smiled broadly, which made him look almost noble. "Never. It isn't in your nature to give up. If Wayne is sexist, you've got to make a sexist argument. Turn his weakness against him."

The approach was simple, yet she'd been too angry to see it on her own. "You really think something like that could work?"

"You, my girl, are pretty convincing." He put one arm around her. It was half a hug, but it would do. She leaned into him and realized she trusted Waldmire without reservation. Maybe that was her kind of faith.

When the vine ropes were finished, Sierra carried them over to the raft. Blisters on her fingertips had burst from braiding them. They felt like a badge of honor.

The raft was complete. A row of palm trunks formed the deck, with thin branches bracing them above and below. Underneath, a pair of bigger trunks served as pontoons, raising the deck two feet off the beach.

Wayne stood, gazing out to sea.

She stopped in front of him. "Can I talk to you for a minute?"

Randall took the new vines and looped one of them around the logs. Josh sat on the deck, where he tied palm fronds onto a Y-shaped branch, making a paddle.

"I've been thinking about this expedition," Sierra said, looking up at the huge man.

Ridges lined Wayne's forehead like furrows in a field. She couldn't tell what he was thinking.

"If you take all the men, that leaves Josh, Kim, Barry, and me. That might not be a strong enough group. After what happened yesterday—"

"As long as you stay on that hilltop and keep the fire going, you'll be fine." Wayne spoke with confidence. "Nothing will bother you up there."

"It isn't just that," Sierra said. "I know you want to make a strong showing, but what if you find a camp that's mostly women? Or *all* women."

On the other side of the raft, Randall made a humming sound. Josh giggled.

Sierra ignored them. "If you find a group of women, you ought to have a woman along. Someone who can talk to them. If you show up with just men, they might hide from you."

Wayne narrowed his eyes.

"I only want the mission to be a success." The line felt hokey as she said it, but she managed a straight face.

"Ho-ho," Wayne said. "That's all you want?"

She smirked. "Okay, yes. I want to go." She held up her hands, showing off her blisters. "Haven't I earned it?"

A grin spread across Wayne's big square jaw.

David approached from further up the beach, where he and his kids had been cracking open coconuts. "We've got fresh coconut juice for everyone," he said, holding out shells. "Wayne, I need to talk to you." David's lips were drawn tight and white.

Wayne held up a finger. "You know, I've been thinking, Doc. You got to stay here and look out for your kids. Hollywood should go instead."

Josh looked up. "Why does she get to go?"

"In case we run into other women," Wayne said. "If we show up with just men, it could be intimidating." He gave Sierra a wink.

The tension drained from David's face and he nodded. "Okay."

Sierra smiled, happy her negotiations were benefiting them both. Even better, she felt like she and Wayne were finally beginning to understand each other, and maybe even respect each other.

"That's not fair," Josh whined.

Wayne looked over his shoulder. "You can go in her place if you wear a dress."

Randall snickered. Josh crossed his arms and scowled.

Wayne turned back to David. "You'll be in charge here, Doc. You got to set some ground rules. Everyone stays together the whole time we're gone. Every one of you, including the dog. There's enough food and water up on that hilltop for several days. You shouldn't need to come down from there."

Wayne was the one actually setting the ground rules, but David didn't seem to care. *Give someone what they want, and they'll agree to anything.* It was another one of Rick Preston's favorite sayings.

"We'll be fine," David said. "You just make sure you all come back safe."

"Not to worry," Wayne said. "I got this."

Chapter Twenty-Four

The raft scooted along at a satisfying pace. Wayne had once paddled a canoe five miles across Lake Thunderbird, just outside Oklahoma City, with a steady headwind that turned a two-hour excursion into an all-afternoon affair. Paddling here was a piece of cake. "There's no wind," he said aloud. "That should make for an easy trip."

Randall glanced back from the front of the raft. "Don't you go saying that. You'll jinx us." He looked angry, but then, with those bushy eyebrows, Randall always looked angry.

"There hasn't been any wind since we got here," Sierra said.

Randall wrinkled his nose. "You're right. Funny we didn't notice."

"It can be hard to notice the absence of things," Wayne said. He'd observed the lack of wind on the first day, but didn't mention it. No need to be arrogant.

"How can a place have no weather?" Randall asked, resting his paddle across his lap.

"Weather is caused by the uneven heating of the Earth's surface," Wayne said. Meteorology had always fascinated him. "On this world, the upper atmosphere keeps everything steady and constant. Everything 'cept your paddling."

Randall lowered his paddle back into the water. "Is that why we can't see the sun?"

"It must be," Wayne said. "The stratosphere is extra thick here." He chewed on the possibility for a moment. "You know, maybe we went forward in time. Maybe everything got messed up after that comet hit." He pointed up. "Maybe we're back on Earth and that's just what the sky looks like now."

"It's a plausible theory," Waldmire said. "Einstein predicted space travel would make time go by faster. And the Ender certainly would have sent lots of debris into the sky. Maybe the atmosphere has been fundamentally changed."

The old guy reminded Wayne of his first commanding officer. No matter what happened, he was always even-keeled.

Wayne was able to stomach the idea of going forward in time. Going back meant nothing mattered. Nothing he did here would make a difference if history had already been written.

"That makes more sense than an alien planet," Randall said, letting his paddle trail in the water. "'Cause there ain't no aliens here."

Sierra glared at him. She obviously didn't like Randall, which was smart on her part. Wayne wondered if he ought to tell her and the others about Randall's involvement with the Piper. Reborn, or not, a week had passed and the guy still seemed full of spite.

"How do you explain the lack of salinity?" Sierra asked.

Randall glared right back. "I don't know. I ain't no goddamn scientist."

That settled it. When they returned to the hilltop, Wayne would need to pull the others aside and give them a little background info on Randall.

"It's one more reason to find whoever brought us here," Sierra said. "Hopefully they can explain it." She dug in with her paddle as she spoke. The island in front of them loomed large, at least three times the size of the one they'd left. "If we ever get there, that is."

Wayne heard the message, loud and clear. "Randall, if you don't keep paddling, you're going to swim the rest of the way."

Randall dipped his paddle and finally put some effort into it.

Wayne doubted they would see any aliens. He expected to find people. Three pods had landed on their island. It stood to reason that the other pods had landed on the other islands. David was right, though, there was no telling what kind of reception they might get. The Doc's plan for how to approach people was solid. Wayne added his own bullet point. He intended to keep the size of his group secret, just in case.

He considered passing out firearms to the other three. Wayne followed Roosevelt's policy on the projection of power. *Speak softly and carry a big-ass stick.* If the whole group was armed, they'd make a strong first impression.

No. After watching Blondie blast a hole in Luis, he could never give a gun to anyone until he was one hundred percent sure he could trust them with it.

Except for the shotgun, which he kept close at hand, Wayne had wrapped his guns and ammo in plastic bags in his rucksack to keep them dry.

He scanned the beach in both directions with the binoculars. An inlet cut into the woods on the right. He looked for campfire smoke rising above the trees but saw only clear blue sky.

David had asked them to look for Lindsey. It was a long shot, but he loved the idea of bringing back the Doc's wife, not to mention the kids' mother. He longed to witness their reunion. They needed more miracles here, especially after what had happened to Juliana.

Wayne had been sent here to protect these people, but he hadn't been able to keep her safe. He paddled harder. He had to do better. He had to be strong. He paddled so hard that the raft started to turn. Instead of backing off, he added a J-curve to the end of his stroke to compensate.

The trip took most of the morning, or at least what passed for morning here, but eventually the raft struck the shore with a gentle lurch.

This beach seemed no different from the one they'd left a few hours earlier. Wayne hopped off and sloshed ashore. "Let's drag her up a little," he instructed. All four of them heaved the front of the raft onto the sand. "That's far enough. We don't have any waves to worry about."

"Or tides," Sierra said, her mouth hanging open. "That means this world must not have a moon."

Wayne hadn't considered this. He'd assumed the moon was up there, hidden from view like the sun and the stars. "Nice observation, Hollywood. I missed it." The idea that the moon was gone unsettled him, but he didn't let it show.

She patted his back. "It can be hard to notice the absence of things."

He grinned as he shouldered his rucksack. He'd spent an hour yesterday showing her trigger control, shooting stance, and sight alignment with his thirty-eight. She'd picked it up quickly, asking smart questions. He was glad he'd brought her instead of David. The Doc would be fretting about his kids the whole time.

Randall shoved past them. "It still doesn't make this an alien planet." He put his hands to his mouth and shouted. "Hello! Is anyone here?"

Silence.

Sierra pointed to the right. "Wayne, let's follow that river. If someone's here, maybe they set up along the bank. And it'll help us find our way back."

"Good call," Wayne said as he started across the beach. "Let's go find some people."

Chapter Twenty-Five

Sierra watched for fish as they followed the river inland. The water was clear and shallow, passing over a mossy bottom. It was also as lifeless as the sea. Dark woods crowded the banks on both sides. The trees here were taller and straighter than on their island, feeling more like a forest than a jungle, but along the bank, the vegetation was thick, and growing thicker.

"Where does the river come from, if there's no weather here?" Waldmire asked.

"It must spring up from the ground somewhere," she said. "We should look for the source." Maybe it would lead to a clue. She didn't really think so, but she was desperate for ideas. They'd walked for almost an hour and she was growing discouraged.

"To hell with that," Randall said. He kicked his way through a waist-high bramble with tiny oval leaves. "There ain't nothing here."

The thickening underbrush had been slowing their pace for the last twenty minutes or so. When they weren't weaving around clumpy plants that looked like miniature palm trees, they were wading through a sea of ferns.

"We ought to look for high ground," Waldmire said. "Maybe we could see more."

"Where?" Randall spat. "There ain't no high ground. We should head back."

Upstream, the brush grew even thicker, encroaching all the way to the river.

Sierra wasn't ready to give up. She peered through the trees, where the vegetation wasn't so dense. "What if we cut through the woods for a bit and then curve back to the river? If the going doesn't get any easier by then and we don't see anything new, we can turn around."

"It's just gonna be more of the same," Randall said. "This place is deserted."

"I like Sierra's idea," Wayne said. "It'll give us a change of scenery, if nothing else."

"Then what?" Waldmire asked.

"We'll row around the island and see what we can find that way," Wayne said.

Sierra led them into the woods, thrilled Wayne was running with her suggestion. If they were able to keep working together like this, they could handle the dynamics of just about any group they encountered.

"I'm gettin' hungry," Randall said.

They'd stockpiled plenty of food back at the hilltop, but they hadn't brought much for themselves. Wayne had been certain they'd find fruit along the way.

Most of the trees here looked like pines or spruces, and a bunch of them just looked like telephone poles with fern-like clumps growing from the top. None of them held any fruit.

At least the walking was easier in the woods. Sierra kept their path parallel to the river and they continued for another fifteen minutes or so. Her eyes slowly adjusted to the dim light, not that there was anything interesting to see.

She was just about to suggest they turn back when she noticed movement through the trees ahead. She froze, holding her breath, and raised her hand. Behind her, the others stopped. Her instincts told her to back away slowly. Her curiosity kept her going.

Wayne crept next to her and unslung his shotgun.

They inched forward together until they got a clear view.

Ten yards ahead, five creatures clustered together on the forest floor, each the size of a turkey. Red and blue feathers covered their bodies. They looked like birds, but they had short, stubby wings and long snouts instead of beaks.

She tapped the binoculars hanging from Wayne's neck. He handed them over and she brought them to her eyes.

"Are those the ones with the eggs?" he whispered.

She shook her head. These were nothing like the terror birds.

The animals dug at the ground with the ends of their wings.

"They have hands," Waldmire whispered. "What kind of birds have hands?" Curved black claws scratched the dirt.

"Aliens?" Sierra asked under her breath.

"No way," Randall said. "Those critters didn't build any pods."

Sierra leaned close to Wayne. "It's going to be a long day," she whispered. "Dinner would help."

He nodded and raised the shotgun.

"Hell, yeah," Randall said.

One of the animals froze at the sound. It turned to face them.

In a heartbeat, all five creatures bolted, zigzagging off through the trees.

"Dammit, Randall." Wayne glared at him.

"It ain't my fault."

"It certainly is," Waldmire said. "You scared them off."

"Why don't you say that again, old man."

Sierra shoved between them. "They went the same way we're headed. Let's keep going. Maybe we'll find them again."

"Randall, take the rear," Wayne said. "And keep quiet."

After another few minutes, low growls rumbled through the woods. The sounds seemed bigger than the noises small bird-creatures might make. The memory of the Entelodont took hold, raising the hair on Sierra's neck.

She slowed her pace as they approached a clearing. Something moved beyond the trees. Something big.

Taking small, quiet steps, they all crept closer. The forest gave way to a mudbank along the river, which curved in from the right.

Sierra stared in disbelief.

Giant beasts wandered the clearing. Some had four legs and horns. Taller ones stood on two legs with horse-like snouts. Long tails waved in the air behind both kinds. The little blue and red bird-creatures ran among them.

These were not the plastic, reptilian monsters from the movies. They were brightly colored, with tufty feathers, and they were caked with mud and scarred with old wounds. There were more than three dozen. Babies and juveniles wandered among the adults.

"This can't be," Waldmire muttered.

One of the tall ones emitted a goosey bark, scaring off one with horns when it got too close. The four-legged horned animal scrambled away, faster than a creature that size should move, shaking the ground.

"Dinosaurs," Randall whispered. "Mother-fucking dinosaurs."

Chapter Twenty-Six

Wayne shook his head, breathing hard. "It doesn't make sense. Where are the people? There were thousands of pods."

"We're in the goddamn Jurassic," Randall said.

Wayne glared at him. "No, we aren't."

Sierra held her finger to her lips.

"That time machine theory is sounding better and better," Waldmire said.

"No, it isn't," Wayne growled. He wished everything would just slow down. He couldn't get his head around what he was looking at.

The creatures with horns dominated the watering hole. They were as big as elephants, with spiky frills rising high above their necks. The biggest ones were rust-colored. Iridescent patches of gold shimmered on the haunches of the smaller ones.

Sierra still had his binoculars hanging from her neck. She raised them to her face.

"Maybe it's like *Journey to the Center of the Earth*," Waldmire said. "Maybe we're somehow inside the planet and that's why there's no sun."

"That doesn't make any sense," Wayne said. Nothing made any sense.

One of the horned dinosaurs approached the edge of the woods.

Wayne's heart pounded in his chest. A barricade of trees stood between them and the dinosaur, like bars on a jail cell, but he still felt defenseless. Four-foot-long horns protruded above the creature's eyes and a shorter horn sprouted over its beak. Two other horns stuck out sideways from its cheeks and a starburst of spikes ran along the top of its frill.

"It's coming for us," Randall said.

"We're okay," Sierra said. "It can't get through the trees."

The gaps between the trunks were too narrow for its massive head to fit, at least directly in front of them.

"Is that a Triceratops?" whispered Waldmire.

"Too many horns," Sierra said.

The creature stared into the woods at them, its breath whooshing in and out like a bellows.

"So you're a goddamn dinosaur expert?" Randall barked.

"Triceratops has three horns," Sierra said. "That's where the 'tri' comes from." She put her hand on Wayne's forearm. "There aren't any people here. We should go."

"Yes," Randall hissed. "Let's go."

The horned dinosaur lowered its head to the ground and snorted.

Wayne's feet wouldn't move.

Sierra pulled his arm. "Come on. It isn't safe here."

The dinosaur butted its head against two thick trunks. Splinters of wood exploded from the impact with the sound of thunder. Randall shrieked and took off. The trunks toppled forward until their upper branches caught against the next row of trees.

Wayne squeezed his shotgun, which was a twig compared to the beast, then finally got his feet to move. He backed away.

The animal's snout poked between the two leaning trees. It snorted and gave a deep guttural moan. The top of its frill brushed against the bottom of the canopy.

Wayne turned and picked up his pace, looking back over his shoulder every few seconds. Waldmire and Sierra ran side-by-side. Randall was a dozen yards ahead of them.

They raced through the woods, not stopping until they reached the riverbank.

Wayne gasped for air, twisting the shotgun in his hands. His face felt slimy with sweat. "This ain't right. I wasn't sent back in time." He didn't know what to think. He didn't know what to do. He shook his head and started downstream. The others followed.

"Maybe those weren't Earth dinosaurs," Randall said. "Maybe they're alien dinosaurs. They looked funny. They were all furry."

"Those were feathers," Waldmire said. "They've been finding fossils with feathers for years now."

Wayne sped up. He needed to get back to the first island. He couldn't keep people safe from dinosaurs.

He stopped to catch his breath when he spotted the raft on the beach.

Sierra drew close to him. "Hey. Are you okay?"

"No," he snapped.

She flinched.

Wayne felt awful. He didn't want her to be afraid of him. He needed her. He didn't know what he was supposed to do now.

He walked out to the middle of the beach, trying to clear his head.

The others continued toward the raft, giving him some space. The first island stood on the horizon. From here, the two prongs rising at the peak made it look like a volcano. Wayne tried to center himself. He needed to focus.

"We've had company," Randall said, pointing at the sand. A line of three-toed footprints ran back and forth from the woods to the raft. They looked like bird tracks, except bigger. Much bigger.

"The sooner we get out of here, the better," Waldmire said.

Something rustled in the woods behind Wayne. Something large. He spun around.

A twenty-foot-tall monster emerged from the trees. Its jaws stretched wide, filled with dagger-like teeth. Two muscular legs supported a heavy torso. Even Wayne knew this one. *Tyrannosaurus rex.* A pair of fingers twitched on each of its stubby arms. Scraggly brown feathers hung from its sides in brindle stripes. Deep black scales surrounded yellow eyes.

Wayne's heart stopped, then it sank.

He had enough firepower to take down this monster. Two shooters could spray its belly with semi-automatic bursts. They could triangulate their fire from the sides. Two others could aim for its eyes with high-caliber rounds. If they didn't blind it, they would drive it off.

Wayne couldn't breathe.

He had all the firepower he needed, and it was all packed up tight in his rucksack, because Wayne didn't trust his team.

The shotgun trembled in his hands. The monster stood between him and the woods. There wasn't anywhere to go.

"Get to the raft," Sierra shouted, somewhere behind him.

The Tyrannosaurus blinked. Its eyes darted from one person to the next. Wayne was closest. Sierra was several yards behind him. Randall and Waldmire were already at the raft.

"Sierra, hurry," Waldmire yelled.

The Tyrannosaurus took a step forward.

"Come on, Wayne," Sierra said.

He shook his head. He couldn't outrun the monster staring down at him. There was only one option.

He could buy time.

Chapter Twenty-Seven

Sierra's skin grew cold. The Tyrannosaurus took another step toward Wayne. Its tail undulated in the air behind it. Shaggy feathers hung from its sides in matted clumps.

Waldmire and Randall shoved the raft into the sea.

"Come on, Sierra," Waldmire hissed.

Wayne backed up slowly, still holding the shotgun in front of him.

"Get away from there," she whispered, willing him to flee.

Maybe it wasn't hungry. Humans weren't its normal prey. Maybe it was defending its territory, and it would ignore Wayne once he moved away. He just needed to turn and run.

"Sierra, now," Waldmire yelled.

The Tyrannosaurus raised its head toward her. It took a step in her direction, ignoring Wayne.

Fear sparked down Sierra's spine. She turned and fled. At the shoreline, she grabbed a paddle and splashed to the raft, already several feet out. She hoisted herself onboard and looked back.

Wayne raised the gun and fired. Distant screeches erupted from the trees.

The creature stopped. It looked curious, not hurt.

Wayne pumped the shotgun and fired again. He had to be hitting it. The monster stomped toward him, its mouth gaping wide. He stumbled backwards.

The Tyrannosaurus bounded forward, leaned down, and snatched Wayne between its jaws. Blood rained on the beach. Wayne's legs kicked in the air, then his body broke apart as teeth crunched shut around him. Pieces thumped onto the sand.

Waldmire clamped his hand over his mouth. Randall screamed.

Sierra paddled, pulling water as fast as she could. *No, no, no.* It hadn't happened. It couldn't have. She looked back. The Tyrannosaurus bent and fed, snapping Wayne up chunk by chunk, until nothing was left.

She leaned over the water and vomited, then quickly resumed paddling.

On the beach, the Tyrannosaurus looked up at the raft again, blood covering its chin. It lumbered forward and stepped into the sea.

"Faster," Sierra shouted. She pulled and pulled. The raft lurched with each stroke. Randall, who had barely done anything on the trip over, worked his arms in a frenzy.

The Tyrannosaurus stood knee-deep in the shallows, its tail high in the air behind it. Brown and yellow feathers shimmered on its neck and shoulders. Wayne's blood dripped from its teeth.

"It can't swim, can it?" Waldmire asked, breathing hard.

Randall chanted, "Go on back, go on back."

Sierra looked down, trying to gauge the depth below. Maybe the water was over its head here.

The Tyrannosaurus slumped onto its belly, creating a four-foot wave that rolled toward them.

"Oh shit," Randall shouted. "Shit, shit, shit."

The dinosaur's head remained at the surface, like a crocodile. Its arms and legs tucked against its body as its tail swished back and forth, propelling it toward them.

The wave hit the raft, boosting them away from the monster.

Sierra turned forward. Their home island didn't look any closer. It would take hours to paddle the distance.

"What do we do?" Randall shouted.

Sierra's gut clenched. "Keep paddling." She wanted to go back for Wayne, but *oh fuck,* he was gone. The clench in her stomach tightened. His guns. All the guns were gone. Wayne had been wearing the backpack when the dinosaur ate him.

"It's gonna catch us," Randall shouted from the back of the raft. The Tyrannosaurus was thirty feet behind and gaining.

"What if we all jump in and swim in different directions?" Waldmire asked.

Sierra's arms burned. She tried to imagine swimming beneath the monster, then resurfacing after it passed. It would never work. The dinosaur would reach down and snatch her like a bird spearing a tadpole. "Keep paddling," she shouted.

The creature grew closer, ten feet away now. Its nostrils opened and closed, spewing thin mist. Both eyes locked on the raft. Only its head and tail were visible above the water line.

"It's on us!" Randall pulled his paddle from the water and scooted away from the back.

As the Tyrannosaurus approached, its upper jaw rose above the surface. Water flowed past eight-inch teeth. It would tear the raft apart.

Someone had to do something.

Sierra clambered to the back. She swung her paddle down on the monster's nose, feeling stupid as she did it. Wayne's shotgun had done nothing. What would a stick do? The dinosaur didn't flinch.

The gap narrowed. The front of its face was a foot from the raft.

She pressed the end of her paddle against the dinosaur's snout and shoved, pushing away from the beast. The surge from the monster's movement washed them forward at the same time.

"Paddle," she barked.

Randall took Sierra's position across from Waldmire at the front.

The Tyrannosaurus moved closer again.

Sierra's breath came in choppy bursts. She stole a glance over her shoulder. Their island was impossibly far.

The monster swished its tail and surged closer. She pressed her paddle against its snout and held it there instead of pushing off. She dropped to one knee and braced herself as the dinosaur drove them forward.

"He's pushing us," Randall shouted.

Waldmire used his paddle like a rudder, fighting to keep them from spinning.

Sierra squeezed her own paddle under her arm, the other end braced against the dinosaur's nose. She jammed her back foot against a log.

Wayne's binoculars dangled from her neck just above the water, which poured through yellow teeth only inches away.

The creature's eyes fixed on her. Short black quills grew from its head. Its tail swung back and forth, but no matter how hard it swam, it couldn't get any closer.

Sierra gritted her teeth and squeezed the stick for dear life. Her arms trembled. Just when she thought she couldn't hold on any longer, the Tyrannosaurus stopped pushing and the raft drifted off. She teetered and backed up from the edge.

"We're fucked," Randall said.

She took a deep breath. "We're alive. We're still alive. Keep going." She kneeled and joined the others in paddling. "It stopped."

"Why?"

"How the hell should I know? It got tired."

"What do we do if it swims all the way over?"

Their island didn't seem any closer, but Randall had a point. If they tried to land the raft, the Tyrannosaurus could just walk out of the sea and kill them.

"We're so completely fucked right now." The tendons and muscles stood out on Randall's arms as he paddled.

A terrible thought occurred to Sierra. Randall sat on his knees at the side of the raft, leaning over as he stroked. A quick kick would send him in. If the Tyrannosaurus went after him, it might buy them time to escape.

"What're you looking at?" Randall asked. "Get paddling."

She thrust her paddle in the water and pulled. She told herself to keep thinking. She couldn't sacrifice someone to save herself, not even somebody as loathsome as Randall. There had to be another way.

"It's still back there," Waldmire said. "It isn't coming after us." The face of the dinosaur fell farther behind.

"Hot damn," Randall said, "It gave up."

"Why did it stop?" Waldmire asked.

"Maybe it's full." Sierra shuddered.

"Bullshit," Randall said. "Wayne was just a bite. Most predators will gorge themselves when there's easy food around."

Sierra squeezed her eyes shut as she paddled. Wayne had been chomped to pieces. Nausea threatened again, though nothing was left in her stomach.

She looked back, expecting the Tyrannosaurus to resume the chase, but it just floated like a log as they pulled away. The animal's legs hung below it in the clear water. Its tail floated motionless at the surface.

They steered the raft toward the side of their island, heading toward the mountain on the far end.

After a half hour, the dinosaur was a small brown hump in the distance.

The profile of their island stretched out as they moved alongside it. Sierra lost track of time. It felt like she'd been paddling for days. The green curve of the campsite hill eventually became visible above the trees. When the hill was finally straight in, they turned and paddled toward the shore.

Randall looked behind them. "It's out of sight now. Hot damn, we lost it."

Sierra checked with the binoculars. She couldn't see it.

"Hey, Ms. Preston," Waldmire called out. "Nice job back there."

Randall snorted. "No shit, girl. You saved us."

Sierra's arms felt like jelly, but their words gave her strength.

"We're going to stay on this island, now, right?" Randall said. "No more expeditions."

A thin wisp of smoke rose from the hilltop campfire.

"I don't know," Sierra said. "We— we can't give up. We have to figure out what to do next." She couldn't spend the rest of her life on that damn hilltop with just seven other people.

Six other people, she corrected herself.

They rowed the rest of the way in silence. Sierra checked the water behind them with the binoculars every few minutes but saw no sign of the dinosaur. Eventually, they reached the shore, not far from where the raft had been built. "Come on, pull it up on the beach." They heaved the front of the raft onto the sand and walked to the jungle.

Sierra held herself, gripping her arms, as they trudged along the path to their camp.

The image of yellow teeth ripping into Wayne kept playing in her mind. She longed for a drink to take the edge off, or better yet, a Valium. For all his faults, Wayne had pulled their group together, built the raft, and got them across the sea. A lead weight sunk through her chest. She didn't want to tell David and the others what had happened. She ground her teeth together and walked on.

A half mile in, they passed the spot where Juliana had been killed, marked by flowers Kim had laid on the trail. Ten minutes later, they came to the base of the hill.

Josh stood waiting at the crest above. "Where's Wayne?" he cried.

David appeared next to him and put a hand on his shoulder.

Sierra, Waldmire, and Randall climbed to the top and Kona bounded over to greet them. Kim and Barry crowded around.

"Wayne got eaten by a motherfucking *T. rex*," Randall said, breathing hard. "He's dead."

Josh's face contorted. He shook his head back and forth.

David leaned in, squinting. "I— I don't ..."

"What?" Kim winced. "How? Are you sure?"

"That island is full of dinosaurs," Sierra said, looking from face to face. "Maybe the pods really were a time machine. I don't know." She wanted to make sense of it, but right now she was jittery from exhaustion, amped from adrenaline, and heartbroken. She just wanted to lie down.

Tears filled Josh's eyes. "Where are the guns?"

"They're gone," Randall spat. "They were in Wayne's backpack. It ate 'em up."

Josh turned pale.

David held up his hands. "Okay, start from the beginning. This doesn't make any sense."

"It can't swim, can it?" Kim asked, looking back and forth between Sierra and her father.

"Yes, it can," Randall said. "It followed us halfway here, then it gave up."

Josh pointed off in the distance, past Sierra, his finger wiggling in the air. His chest heaved so much it looked like he was hyperventilating. "Are you sure?"

Sierra spun around. Below on the beach, less than two miles away, the Tyrannosaurus rose from the sea and stepped ashore.

Chapter Twenty-Eight

David shook his head, unable to process what he'd learned, unable to comprehend what he saw.

Down on the beach, the Tyrannosaurus leaned over and pawed the raft with one foot. Heavy logs rolled into the water as the vine ropes tore apart. A split-second later, the sound of clattering timber reached them.

"What the fuck?" Randall backed away from the group. "It swam all the way over."

Barry stood on a rock to get a better look. "What's it doing?"

The Tyrannosaurus walked away from them, heading toward the point at the far end of the island.

"Keep going," David whispered. From this distance, it looked small, just a shorebird on the beach.

Waldmire waved everyone back from the edge of the hill. "We need to find someplace else."

"Why?" Josh asked. "It's way down there. We're fine." He looked at each of the adults. "Aren't we?"

The Tyrannosaurus stopped and returned to the raft, its nose low to the ground. When it reached the jumble of wood, it turned and walked toward the trees below them, straight toward the path in the jungle.

Kim tugged David's arm. "What do we do?"

His heart pounded. He didn't answer. He didn't know what to say.

"It's following our scent," Sierra said.

Below, the Tyrannosaurus reached the edge of the jungle, where it disappeared from view.

Waldmire pulled Sierra toward the campsite. "Let's move."

David turned to him. "Where? Where can we go that it can't follow?"

"Up the mountain," Sierra said. "If we get high enough on the rocks, we'll be out of reach. Come on."

David looked at the barren incline rising above the hilltop. "Then what?" They needed a plan.

Sierra and Waldmire were already at the base of the slope. "Come on, everyone," Sierra called.

David and his kids followed. They passed the campsite. Coals and embers smoldered in the fire pit.

"Can we scare it off with fire?" He searched for a torch, but saw nothing substantial enough to grab.

On the slope, Randall took the lead, passing Waldmire and Sierra, with Josh close behind. Kona bounded up alongside them.

David gave up on the fire and left the campsite. The others were already ten yards ahead. There wasn't time. He had to get moving.

They climbed.

David's leg throbbed after the first hundred feet. He looked at the horn-shaped peaks above. *What are we supposed to do when we get up there, sit and wait?* If the Tyrannosaurus followed them, they'd be trapped. He wanted to ask about Wayne's guns again. Maybe he'd misunderstood something. They couldn't all be gone.

Josh, Sierra, and the others pulled away. "Come on, Dad," Kim pleaded.

David looked back. The treetops shook along the jungle path, indicating the dinosaur's progress from the beach to the hillside. He picked up Barry and carried him a few steps, but his injured leg screamed. Breathing hard, he put the boy down. "Kim, go on ahead."

"No. Here." She took his hand and they formed a train, with David pulling Barry in the back. They managed to speed up a little.

Above them, Randall had almost reached the saddle.

Josh turned and pointed down. "It's there." His voice came out an octave higher than normal.

The Tyrannosaurus climbed up the side of the hill. There was no cover between them and the dinosaur now, just the barren scrabble of the long mountain slope.

"Why is it coming after us?" Josh whined. "Why can't it leave us alone?"

"'Cause we're easy prey," Randall said. "We're soft. All the other dinosaurs had horns and shit to put up a fight."

The monster approached their campsite, its brown hide rippling. It lowered its head to the fire and sniffed, blasting sparks into the air with each breath.

We wandered around a lot down there, David thought. Maybe it would catch a scent and move away. Maybe it would go down the front of the hill, where all the men went to piss.

The Tyrannosaurus raised its head and looked up the mountain. It roared, a stuttering bellow like the blast from a train horn, then lumbered over to the slope.

Josh screamed. He raced ahead of the others, passing Randall. He arrived at the saddle between the two peaks and pinwheeled both arms, staggering back from the precipice.

David's heart pounded in his chest, even though he hadn't seen the drop-off yet. He picked up Barry again and sped up, despite his throbbing leg. The boy whimpered, his breath hot in David's ear.

"Where now?" Randall shouted. "It's coming." He stood with Josh at the top of the saddle, halfway between the pointed rocky peak on the left and the stubby one on the right.

Sierra caught up to them, with Waldmire close behind. "This way." She pointed left. "Climb up the front."

David and his children arrived at the low area between the two peaks. His legs went numb from the sight of the small beach hundreds of feet below. He looked back down the front of the mountain.

The Tyrannosaurus was halfway up the slope and still climbing. Kona barked.

Sierra led the others to the front of the taller peak, where the rock face was jagged and irregular. She guided Waldmire to the first handhold and he started up. As soon as he climbed high enough, Randall shoved forward and followed.

David's stomach churned at the thought of climbing that steep face, but it was the only place to go.

Sierra helped Josh onto the rocks next. The handholds were only wide enough for one person at a time. She looked over at David, shaking her head, then down at the Tyrannosaurus climbing the mountainside.

"What do we do, Dad?" Kim asked.

Kona kept barking.

Barry whimpered.

"Climb faster," David shouted. Randall and Josh inched higher. The Tyrannosaurus would arrive before they got far enough to make room for him and his kids.

Keeping away from the drop-off, he spun to look at the other peak, which was shorter and rounder. A lone boulder sat in front of it, barely big enough to hide one of them, much less all three. David's heart pounded.

The Tyrannosaurus roared again. From this angle, it was all face and jagged teeth, less than two minutes away. Its eyes tracked David. The realization that this monster was looking at him knocked his breath out, like a plunge into cold water.

Barry was crying now. Kim's eyebrows stretched toward each other. The fear on her face stabbed his gut. "*Daddy?*"

David leaned over the cliff. The drop was almost eight hundred feet. Just looking at it made him afraid to move.

"Fucking hurry," Sierra pleaded.

Josh was trying different handholds about ten feet up. He looked like a lizard holding onto a wall. Above him, Waldmire reached the top, where the peak flattened out again. Seeing him up there made David dizzy.

"Daddy?" Kim repeated.

David opened his mouth, but nothing came out. He had no plan.

The lower peak wouldn't put them much above the dinosaur's head. Hell, it wasn't steep enough to prevent the bastard from just walking up the side. David reeled.

He looked over the cliff again. Ledges and cracks crisscrossed the wall below. He pulled Barry up to the edge, horrified at the thought of what he was about to do.

He had no other choice.

David dropped to his knees, grabbed his son's hands, and lowered him over the cliff on the backside of the mountain. Every fiber of his being told him this was a terrible idea. The beach was eight hundred feet below. He squeezed his eyes shut for a second, fighting off vertigo.

The ground trembled as the dinosaur approached, sending grit over the edge into Barry's face.

David held the boy by his arms, suspended over open air. He stretched his legs out behind him, lying prone at the top of the cliff.

"Daaaaddyyyy!"

"Find a ledge for your feet." Tears clouded David's eyes. His hands grew slippery with sweat. He lowered Barry as far as he could. The edge of the cliff bit into his armpits.

Barry kicked at the wall. For a second, his hands slipped, then the boy's weight lessened. His toes had found a ledge.

"That's it. Now hold on." He placed one of the boy's tiny hands against a crack in the cliff wall and let go. "Hold tight, Barry. Oh my God, please hold tight."

"Dad," Kim cried from behind. "It's close."

Barry looked up. "I'm scared."

"Do not let go, no matter what." David forced himself to release his son's other hand. It was the most difficult thing he'd ever done.

He rolled sideways and waved Kim over. "Hurry."

Taking Kim's hands, he lowered her onto the cliff next to her brother. Forty pounds heavier, she pulled him forward an inch, then her feet found purchase. She let go of his hands one at a time, grabbing cracks in the rocks.

"Just stay there. Both of you." David pushed himself to his feet.

She looked up, crying. "What about you?"

Good question. The Tyrannosaurus was now a hundred feet away. It stank of musk and mold and wet decay. Filthy clumps of feathers hung from its sides.

On the front of the rocky peak, Josh had climbed a little higher, but still not enough. Sierra stood below him, jerking her head back and forth, looking for some other place to go.

David ran to the base of the shorter peak and ducked behind the lone boulder. His bad leg howled as he pulled it in tight. The rock would hide him from view as long as the dinosaur didn't bother to take two steps in this direction.

Kona followed and stood right next to him, still barking.

Terrific.

David tensed. When the Tyrannosaurus came his way, he could throw himself back down the slope. He could try to lure it after him. If he stayed on his ass, he might slide all the way to the campsite without killing himself. Then he could try to lose it in the jungle below.

Fat chance. He would shatter every bone in his body rolling down that slope.

Across the ridge, Sierra yelled, "Move it!" Josh had crept a few feet higher and Sierra finally started up. She made eye contact with David. She wasn't anywhere near high enough. The dinosaur would snatch her.

She must have reached the same conclusion because she climbed back down and circled around to the middle of the saddle.

The dinosaur's face crested the ridgeline. It turned its head toward Kona, barking near David's boulder, and then over to Sierra, some twenty feet away. It walked straight up to the low stretch between the two peaks and looked over the drop-off. Claws from one foot curled over the edge just above Barry and Kim.

Leaning out, the dinosaur sniffed the air.

Barry cried, "Daaddddy-y-y-y!"

"It can't get you, Bud!" David shouted, desperately hoping he had done the right thing. For all he knew, the Tyrannosaurus might be able to lean over and pluck his children right off the wall. He couldn't let that happen. David rose from behind the boulder, ready to scream if it lowered its head.

On the peak directly across from him, Sierra jumped and grabbed a thin edge two feet above her. She pulled herself up, the toes of her boots slipping against the flat surface. David tensed. She was still way too low. One foot got traction and she scrambled up until she was roughly the same height as the monster's mouth.

The Tyrannosaurus turned toward her, its tail now extending across to David, close enough to grab. The end drooped, heavy with ragged feathers. Its left leg, the lower one, slipped on the rocky scrabble at the front of the slope. It caught itself on the cliff edge with its uphill foot and started forward, no longer above the kids.

David allowed himself to breathe.

A small chunk of the cliff edge broke off under its right foot and fell straight down. The dinosaur stepped away, wobbling slightly.

"Slip, you fucker," David growled. If it slid down the slope, it would break its bones just as easily as he would.

The dinosaur regained its footing and lifted its head toward Sierra. Its tail dropped to the ground.

An insane thought came to David. He often moved his one-ton Cessna around in the hangar by pushing its tail, far from the center of gravity. If he could somehow nudge the dinosaur's tail, he might throw it off-balance enough to fall back down the slope.

A low rumble came from the creature's throat. It stretched, reaching for Sierra.

She kicked loose a rock the size of a cinder block. It bounced down and hit the monster's shin.

The Tyrannosaurus growled, shaking the mountain top. Josh and Randall screamed.

Panic struck David. He hadn't heard his children in more than a minute. They could have fallen.

Sierra climbed higher and pushed a much larger rock with both legs. The rock broke out from under her, but it bounced past the Tyrannosaurus, tumbling down the front of the mountain.

She lost her footing and slid down into the hole left by the boulder, well within the dinosaur's reach.

"Sierra!" Waldmire called out, too high above her to help.

She flapped her arms against the cliff, trying to find a handhold, but she only loosened more gravel underneath her.

The monster's massive head darted forward with a wet chomp. *Oh, Jesus, it got her.* David felt cold and hollow and helpless, but a second later, Sierra kicked off its nose and climbed back up, out of reach.

Holy shit. He squeezed his hands into fists, willing her to climb higher.

Kim cried out from the cliff. "Dad, I can't hold on."

The sound of her voice brought a tiny taste of relief. She was still alive. "You have to, Sweetie. Find a better grip."

The Tyrannosaurus turned around on the saddle. David ducked behind his boulder, heart thumping. Kona moved directly in front of him, quiet now, her teeth bared. He peered out past the dog.

The dinosaur crept closer, stumbling in the gravelly dirt between the two peaks. It stopped and looked at Kona. "Go on," David shouted. "Lead it away." He hated the thought, but he was willing to sacrifice his dog to save his kids.

Crying continued from the cliff. The sound tore at David's heart, but it meant they were hanging on.

The dinosaur shifted its weight and stretched its head over the void, sniffing. Its tail curved down on the slope behind it, keeping it balanced.

Yellow saliva dripped from its teeth. *It can reach them*, David thought. *They aren't low enough.* He stepped out from behind his rock.

The monster's head was already close to the ground as it balanced on the precipice. One foot grasped the cliff's edge and the other clawed at the slope, several yards back. It leaned over. It would lower its neck and pluck Kim and Barry off the wall.

"No!"

David sprinted toward the Tyrannosaurus, screaming. A low rumble came from deep in the creature's chest. It twitched in his direction. He turned and dashed alongside the dinosaur, gaining speed as he ran downhill. Six hundred feet of incline lay below him. If he kept going, there would be no stopping. He would bounce and break all the way down.

Instead, he reached out with both hands and grabbed the dinosaur's tail. Tufts of feathers ripped free. He was about to slip past. He lunged, wrapping both arms around the tail in a hug, squeezing and clenching. Pain seared his fingertips as two nails tore to the quick. His grip caught and momentum flung his legs out from under him.

Pebbles shifted under the dinosaur's downhill foot. The animal slipped backwards. David weighed two hundred pounds, a tiny fraction of the creature's weight, but he was all the way at the end of its tail, throwing off its balance.

The Tyrannosaurus shifted its mass toward the top of the cliff. David's stomach lurched as the tail lifted him twenty feet above the slope. He hung on, wrapping his legs around it like a body pillow. The feathers were coarse and rough, and stank of metal and chalk. The animal stepped forward, raising him even higher. It shifted its weight to the very top of the saddle.

The *CRACK* of breaking rock exploded between the peaks.

The edge of the cliff broke away, collapsing under the monster's weight.

The body of the dinosaur fell into the hollow where the top of the cliff had been. Its tail dropped to the ground, flapping. David sucked in feathers and dirt.

The creature tumbled forward over the precipice. Its tail slithered up the slope, pulling David along with it. Pain dug into his sides.

The Tyrannosaurus screamed, a horrible squeal like an animal caught in a trap.

David wrestled his arms free, letting go just as the tail disappeared over the edge.

The cliff wall that his children had been clinging to was gone, replaced by a jagged crater.

"No, no, no."

Bawling and bloodied, David crawled to the top. He peered over the drop-off where the rock had broken away under the dinosaur's weight. Dust billowed from the avalanche below.

The Tyrannosaurus crashed onto the beach. Blood and guts exploded outward, showering the sand.

A small whimper came from the side.

Kim and Barry stood together on a ledge to the right. They must have shimmied sideways before the cliff broke away. David's chest swelled. "Hang on, guys. Just hang on."

Half-laughing, half-sobbing, he scrambled across what was left of the ridge and lay flat on the ground, reaching to pull Barry up. Sierra appeared next to him and lifted Kim.

David wrapped his arms around his children and shook with relief.

Randall, Josh, and Waldmire joined them. "Holy shit," Randall said, looking over the cliff. "Holy fucking shit." He clapped David on the back.

They all collapsed on the ridgeline, exhausted. David sucked at the bloody, pink flesh where his fingernails had been. Pain stabbed his knees, his shins, and his elbows. He felt moisture under one arm that was probably blood. He reached for it and felt a sharp pain in his chest. He'd cracked a rib. Maybe more than one.

Josh dropped to his knees and vomited.

Waldmire put a hand on his shoulder. "It's okay, son."

David squeezed his children against his chest and held them there. Kona licked the side of his face.

Randall paced back and forth. "What the fuck do we do now?"

"We go back to camp," Sierra said. "David needs to be patched up."

He felt like he actually *had* tumbled down the hill. Every part of him was sore, burning with pain. But he didn't care. He kept hugging his children.

Below, a thin line of smoke rose from the remains of their fire on the hilltop. David looked to the right where the Tyrannosaurus had come ashore. The shattered raft was a tiny smudge from this distance. Beyond the beach, the island of the dinosaurs loomed on the horizon. They could never go back there.

He turned to the left, to the other side of their island.

A large shape moved through the water, just offshore. David blinked. Air drained from his lungs. "What now?" he whispered. It looked like another raft, but twice as large as the one Wayne had built. Something moved on its surface.

Three human figures jumped off, splashing in the shallows. They pulled their boat ashore.

DESCENT

Chapter Twenty-Nine

Five Days Before Impact

Alice Cameron flew down Mauna Kea in the cool dark of night on her carbon fiber road bike. The wind stroked her hair. There was no point in wearing a helmet. Not with the world ending in five days. Not when she was guilty of treason.

Self-defense, she rationalized.

She'd rationalized a number of questionable decisions over her twenty-nine years, but killing a commanding officer topped the list.

Cameron leaned into the turn, banking almost forty degrees. Her tiny LED headlight barely lit the road. No matter. It had been days since she'd seen anyone on this part of the island. The Pohakuloa Training Area where she was stationed had been abandoned and the observatory at the mountain's peak was deserted. Hawai'i had become a ghost island after it was reported the Ender would strike the Pacific. Commercial airlines discontinued flights from the mainland weeks ago.

Thousands of stars sparkled in the black sky overhead. The Ender was too far north to see. For now.

Cameron felt no qualms, no regret. *That cocksucker got what he deserved.* She let off the brakes, allowing the bike to pick up speed.

A swath of light moved across the horizon like a lighthouse beacon. As the beam swung closer, she recognized it as headlights coming her way.

"Get off my ass," she hissed, swerving to the shoulder. Maybe someone had found out about Lieutenant Collins.

Rubber squealed on asphalt as the car barreled down behind her.

She pedaled harder, on the inside of a long turn. The headlights chased her, but wouldn't reach her until the road straightened. If it wasn't someone tracking her down, just some idiot out for a drive, he wouldn't be watching for bicycles in the middle of the night. He might run her over before he even saw her. She had to get to the end of the turn before he caught up, so his headlights would finally illuminate her.

Cameron intended to bike to the top of Mauna Kea again in five days and watch as the Ender crossed the sky and struck the ocean to the southwest, a once-in-a-lifetime opportunity if there ever was one. The vapor cloud would billow into the atmosphere and the blast wave would follow soon after. She'd planned her final moments and she wasn't about to let this asshole run her down and take that away from her.

She squeezed the rear brake and feathered the brake on the front wheel as much as she dared, glancing back. The car was on top of her. She jerked right to get out of the way, releasing the brakes. Her front tire hit soft sand on the shoulder and pulled out from under her. She straightened the wheel to stay upright, which pulled her farther off the road. Her stomach dropped as a dirt berm launched her upwards.

Brakes screeched. Cameron tumbled through cool air. She tucked for landing and hit the ground rolling. Scrub branches snapped beneath her and a thousand jabs of pain needled her skin.

When she finally came to a stop, she lay still, hurting all over. The hair above her ear was wet and the side of her head burned so fiercely it felt like she'd been scalped.

Twin cones of light stabbed the dusty air overhead as the car stopped. The driver scrambled down the shoulder, puffing hard. Was he coming to finish her off?

Cameron lay still, an ambush predator flush with adrenaline.

When the driver knelt beside her, she struck, clenching her fingers around the asshole's neck. She'd killed one person today. What difference would a second make?

"Are you okay?" The words escaped just before her grip tightened. A feminine voice with an Indian accent.

Cameron's fingers trembled. She could crush this woman's windpipe in less than a second. Part of her wanted to. Instead, she released her grip.

"No, I'm not okay. You ran me off the road, bitch."

"I'm sorry," the woman gasped. "I didn't see you."

"No shit." Wet liquid pooled in Cameron's ear. The open wound on the side of her head throbbed. She needed to get pressure on it before she lost too much blood.

"Can you move?" The woman leaned over her. "I have to get to the mainland. There's something coming."

"No shit," Cameron said again. "We're getting incinerated in five days."

"No. I'm not talking about the Ender. There's something else."

Chapter Thirty

Torchlight danced at the edge of the hill. Kona growled. Sierra stroked her back. "It's okay girl."

The all-encompassing darkness had hit soon after they descended to the hilltop. Josh and Kim built up the fire to help the newcomers find them. Sierra hoped they were friendly. If not, she wasn't sure what she could do. She was exhausted, her group was unarmed, and David was beat half to hell.

The torch crested the hill, followed a moment later by three figures.

Sierra rose, holding Kona's leash, hoping to appear strong. Kona was a sweetheart, but the strangers didn't know that.

Two men and a woman stepped into the circle of light around the campfire. All three carried long spears. One of the men held the torch. All were white.

"Hello," Sierra said, trying to muster the confidence Wayne always exhibited. "We saw you down on the beach a few hours back. We would have come to greet you, but it's been a shitty day. I'm Sierra."

One if the men stepped forward. "I'm Charlie." He wore jeans and a plaid shirt buttoned tight over a round belly. Dirty blond hair hung from his brow and deep laugh lines bordered lips that looked sculptured. He'd been handsome once. Maybe even movie-star-handsome. "This is Cameron and Morrie," he added.

Morrie raised his torch in greeting. He had a young face and curly red hair.

"Glad to meet you." Sierra introduced her companions one by one.

Cameron raised her chin. She was tall and lean. A shiny scar ran through short blond hair above her ear. "Is it just the seven of you?" She seemed suspicious.

"There were two more," Sierra answered. "A woman named Juliana died two days ago. A man named Wayne was killed today. Like I said, things have been rough."

Cameron and Charlie looked at each other.

"What happened?" Charlie asked.

Josh answered. "Wayne got eaten by a *Tyrannosaurus rex*." The words came out sad and angry. "Juliana was killed by a giant wolf-pig."

Waldmire put his arm around the kid.

Cameron raised her spear and scanned the black night surrounding them. This woman appeared to be wound tight.

Sierra held up a hand. "It's okay. The wolf-pigs never come up here. We think they keep away from the fire."

"And the Tyrannosaurus?" Morrie asked.

"It's dead."

"Dad made it fall off a cliff," Kim said with pride in her voice.

Charlie turned toward David. "You killed a dinosaur?"

"Awesome," Morrie said.

Cameron tilted her head back, also clearly impressed.

"Gravity did most of the work," David said. He smiled at his daughter and patted Barry on the shoulder. "I always told you guys that heights are dangerous."

It looked like he was trying to hide how much pain he was in. Sierra had taped gauze over his missing fingernails and dabbed antibiotic ointment on his scraped side. He'd even agreed to take one of their few aspirin tablets, believing he'd fractured a couple of ribs.

"Are there more of them around?" Charlie asked.

Sierra shook her head. "It came from a different island. We went searching for other people. The Tyrannosaurus followed us back."

Barry looked up from his father's lap. "Will another one come?" The boy had not left his side since the mountaintop.

David rested his chin on his son's head. "No, Buddy. We're safe."

"How do you know?" Barry asked.

David looked around the fire as if hunting for an answer. "As long as we stay away from that island, there's no reason for another one to come over."

"Dinosaurs," Charlie said. "I wonder what that means."

Sierra leaned forward. "I've been wondering about that, too. Do you think the pods could have sent us back in time?"

Charlie shrugged. "That theory makes as much sense as any. You should talk to Priya."

Sierra started to ask who Priya was, but Cameron's hands cinched tight around her spear at the mention of her.

Morrie clicked his tongue. "Well, we've got a bunch of big-ass rhinos and some little squirrel things on our island, but no dinosaurs."

Charlie elbowed him. "What about Carol Mulligan? She's practically prehistoric." He leaned toward Josh. "She isn't dangerous, though. Not many teeth left."

Josh chuckled.

The laughter was nice to hear, even if it was slightly tasteless.

Charlie opened his hands. "We'd like you to join us. All we ask is that you help out as best as you can."

"How many people do you have?" David asked.

"Thirty-seven."

A hush fell over the group. Sierra had expected another ten or twelve at most.

Barry asked, "Is Mommy there?"

Kim rose up on her knees. "Is there a woman named Lindsey? From Minnesota?" The eagerness in her voice crushed Sierra.

Charlie's eyes turned soft. "No. I'm sorry." He sounded like he meant it.

A knot of tension loosened inside Sierra. These people were okay. Better than okay. They seemed genuinely nice.

Sierra squeezed Kim's shoulder. She grasped her hand and held it tight.

"That doesn't mean your mom isn't out there somewhere," Charlie said.

"That's right," Sierra said. "Three pods came to our island. You must have had what, a dozen? The rest have to be somewhere. With your raft, we can keep searching. Have you been to any other islands?"

"Charlie and I came here once," Cameron said. "We must have missed you."

Charlie nodded and pointed off into the darkness. "Two men also went to the big island out in front of yours. They never came back."

"That's the one with the dinosaurs," Josh said.

"Well, that explains it," Morrie said. "What a shitshow." He glanced at Kim and Barry, then added, "Sorry."

"It's okay," Kim said. "We've had our own shitshow here."

Sierra smiled. She loved that girl.

"Will you join us?" Charlie asked.

Sierra looked around the fire. "What do you guys think?"

Rick Preston had taught her to invite the opinions of others even when the answer was obvious. *Especially* when the answer was obvious. It was an easy way to make people feel important, and a great way to build camaraderie.

"I'm in." Randall nudged the fire with a stick. "No offense, but it'd be nice to see some new faces for a change."

"Me, too," Josh said.

"Tell us a little more about your group," David said.

Sierra smiled at the newcomers. "David likes to gather information before making decisions. He's what you might call a planner."

"Dad, we can't stay here," Kim said. "It's too dangerous."

"I know," he said. "I just want to make sure they don't have a bunch of crazies over there."

Charlie gave a small belly laugh. "We've definitely got crazies."

"That's putting it mildly," Cameron said.

Charlie smiled. "Not everyone gets along, that's for sure, same as on Earth, but nobody's killed anybody yet."

Sierra decided right then and there that she could trust him.

David must have reached a similar conclusion. "We'd love to join you," he said.

"Yay," Barry said.

Waldmire nodded.

"I think we're in agreement," Sierra said, happy about how the decision had played out. Everyone was onboard. They would meet more people and the new island sounded much safer.

"It's settled, then." Charlie said. "We'd like to collect some food before we head back."

Sierra gestured at the mound of dark shapes behind her. "We actually have a pretty good stockpile of produce here. We're happy to share it."

Cameron relaxed her grip on the spear. The scar along the side of her head flashed, shiny in the firelight.

"Make yourselves comfortable," Sierra said.

She unleashed Kona, who sniffed each of the newcomers. Charlie got her to shake hands, which affirmed Sierra's assessment. If Kona trusted him, she did too.

Morrie and Charlie sat in the spots that had belonged to Wayne and Juliana. Waldmire offered them tubers that had been roasted over the fire.

"No thanks." Charlie patted his big belly. "I ate too much fruit on the hike up here. I love those spicy oranges."

"Fireballs," Barry whispered.

Waldmire sat back, watching the newcomers. "What have you got to eat on your island?"

"We planted a garden," Morrie said. "We've got corn and these little squashes that look like green pumpkins. They're bland, but the seeds are good when you roast them."

"We're always on the lookout for more protein," Charlie said. "The squirrels are getting harder and harder to find."

"A while back, Charlie killed a giant rhino." Morrie looked over at him. "When are you going to do that again?"

Randall's tongue snaked across his lip. "What the hell does rhino taste like?"

"It's greasy, with a nutty aftertaste," Morrie said. He brought his fingers to his lips and parted them with a kiss.

Josh chuckled.

"Wait, what do you mean 'giant' rhinos?" Kim asked.

"Priya thinks they're prehistoric," Charlie said. "They're as big as elephants."

Sierra leaned forward. Priya really sounded like someone she wanted to meet. "If they're prehistoric, that brings us back to the time travel idea. Have you seen anything in the sky? Weird clouds floating around?”

Charlie shook his head. “No clouds at all, ever. What kind of clouds have you seen?”

“I saw a little fuzzy shape,” Barry said. “It was hard to see, but it was there, I promise.”

“Wayne saw it too,” Sierra said. “He said it looked like a breath of mist.”

“We haven’t seen anything like that,” Morrie said.

“We should watch for it though,” Charlie said.

“Yes,” Sierra said. “We should all be watching for it.” Charlie seemed just as interested in finding answers as she was. “What about your pods?” A glimmer of hope rose in her chest. “Are your pods still there?”

“No. They disappeared on the second day.”

“Same here,” Josh said.

“Where did you all come from?” Waldmire asked. “Before the Ender.”

“Cameron was from Hawaii,” Charlie said, gesturing her way. “We met up in California and found a pod in Nebraska.”

“I came from Colorado,” Morrie said.

Sierra and David outlined their stories.

When it was Randall’s turn, he said, “I was in Oklahoma. I found a pod with a tough sumbitch named Wayne. Juliana was with us, too.” He paused and looked around. “I’m the only one left from that pod now, ain’t I?”

The group grew silent.

“Why don’t we all get some rest?” Charlie said. “We’ve got a big day tomorrow.”

Barry yawned. David slid him off his lap and stretched out beside him.

“Are there any kids on your island?” Barry asked.

Charlie’s eyes twinkled. “There are four. How old are you?”

“Six and a half.”

“We have one who’s younger and three that are a little older. They’ll be excited to meet you.”

Barry’s face lit up.

Sierra smiled. They'd finally found more people. The rest had to be out there somewhere. She couldn't wait to compare notes with them. Her mind raced with questions.

Finally, things were starting to look up.

Chapter Thirty-One

Five Days Before Impact

Cameron took her third swig of rum and tried to parse the woman's story into the important pieces. "You haven't told anyone about this?" Every inch of her body hurt, most of all the flap of scalp now held against the side of her head by an Ace bandage.

The woman, an astronomer named Priya, shook her head. "There isn't anyone else at the observatory. Everyone left to be with their families."

"You're still here."

"My family is in Jaipur." Priya paced back and forth through her studio apartment. "That's in India."

"Yeah, I know." The rum hit Cameron harder than she expected, probably because she'd lost so much blood. She had drifted in and out of a hazy consciousness on the drive to Priya's apartment in Waimea. Her head was patched up now, as well as a nasty road rash on her hip. It was almost three in the morning. "You saw a swarm of objects heading toward Earth, just like the Ender?"

"Not just like the Ender. I told you. The objects are following a disparate trajectory and approaching at a faster velocity." She sounded frustrated, as if talking to a child.

"Don't take that tone with me, Priya. I lost a lot of blood when you ran me off the fucking road."

Priya didn't flinch. "I'd like to point out that I never actually hit you. You ran off the road all by yourself and I could have easily left you there. What kind of moron goes riding a bicycle in the middle of the night on Kea, anyway? And if you're having trouble understanding what I'm saying, then perhaps you should lay off my Koloa Rum."

Cameron grinned and took another swig, just to spite her.

Priya continued pacing.

"How many of these objects are there?" Cameron asked.

"It's impossible to tell. They are too far away and too small." Priya waved her fingers. "Hundreds. Maybe thousands."

"And you're sure they're going to strike the mainland?"

"Yes. I interfaced remotely with the McDonald Observatory in Texas to corroborate my observations on their equipment. The objects will strike the Midwest two days from now."

"Wait, do they know about these objects in Texas?"

Priya's eyes darted around. "No. I hacked into their system."

"Why? Why aren't you publicizing this?

"Have you seen the news lately? People are doing crazy things. If word of this got out, it could cause riots, more panic."

Cameron squinted. She thought Priya was telling the truth, but maybe not the whole truth. Maybe she wanted to keep this discovery all to herself. Or maybe she was afraid she might be wrong.

"If the objects turn out to be real, we can report them to the authorities," Priya said.

"Won't these things just create more impacts and cause more damage?"

Priya looked uncertain. "If they just crash into us, yes. But I don't believe they will. I believe they are from an extraterrestrial intelligence. I believe they are some sort of landing craft."

Cameron narrowed her eyes. "Bullshit."

"They are tiny objects grouped tightly together. Nothing moves through space like that."

"Okay, what if it's an invasion?"

"If it's an invasion, it's the most incompetent invasion ever." Priya spoke with mousey condescension. "They're coming to conquer a planet two days before it becomes uninhabitable."

"There's that tone again," Cameron said, though Priya did have a point. "So you think this is some kind of rescue mission?"

"Look, if I'm wrong and it's actually an attack, or just another planetary impact, then what have we lost? We die two days early."

Cameron plucked a cactus spine from her thigh. She would probably be picking spines from her skin until the Ender hit. "So what's your plan?"

Priya sat down across from her. "I want to go to the airport and try to find a flight to the mainland."

"You won't," Cameron said.

"How do you know?"

"I was stationed at the Pohakuloa Training Area on the western slope. I know things."

Priya stood up. "Wait? You're in the Army?"

Cameron gave a sloppy salute, careful not to touch her head wound. "Warrant Officer Alice Cameron."

"Can you contact your commanding officer and try to get us a flight?"

"My C.O. died yesterday in an accident." Cameron forced herself to keep a straight face. "It was very tragic."

Excitement brightened Priya's eyes. "Why are you even here? Why aren't you in the survival cave?"

Cameron smirked. The news had reported that military personnel on Hawai'i were moving into a dormant lava core on Moloka'i, with supplies stockpiled to keep them alive for a hundred years.

"There is no survival cave," she said. "It's bullshit."

Priya's face darkened.

"There were other plans, though," Cameron admitted. It was illegal to speak about them to a civilian, but after killing Lieutenant Collins, disclosure of classified information seemed a bit trivial. "There are a few dozen contingency projects. Bunkers. Remote stations. Most of them will fail. Probably all of them."

"Why aren't you at one of those?"

The question bit deep. Cameron wanted to smack the annoying little twat. That wasn't fair, though. Priya didn't know what had happened. How could she?

Cameron drew in a deep breath. "I was on the shortlist for a deepwater lab. My C.O. was ready to make it happen. All I had to do was agree to fuck him."

"And you wouldn't? Not even for a chance to survive?"

Cameron rolled her eyes. Lieutenant Collins was a repulsive slug who would have kept her under his thumb and under his sheets for the rest of her life. "That wouldn't be surviving."

Priya slumped. "I guess we're stuck here."

Cameron let her stew for a minute. She still had favors to call in. A flight to the mainland could be arranged if she pulled the right strings. But this woman had run her off the road and then had the gall to challenge her about damn near everything. She deserved a little friendly torture.

Priya took the bottle of rum, poured herself a shot, threw it back, and collapsed onto a wicker chair.

Cameron took another sip herself, savoring it. The buzz from the alcohol finally started to mask the throbbing on the side of her skull. "Hold on now," she said finally. "There might be something we can do."

Seven hours later, they hitched a ride on an Air Force KC-10 Extender flying to Northern California.

Chapter Thirty-Two

David held his breath while Cameron dabbed a fresh layer of antibiotic ointment on the scrapes along his ribcage. "Why didn't you want to hike up there with the others?" he asked.

"Somebody had to stay here and stand guard," she said. "You looked like you were going to sleep the day away."

He pulled his shirt back down. "Killing dinosaurs is hard work, you know."

She crossed her arms. "I still can't believe you actually took down a Tyrannosaurus."

Waldmire, Kim, Josh and Barry sat a few yards away, slicing fruit. Randall sat alone by the fire, poking at embers with a stick.

"He did," Kim said. "All by himself."

David smiled. "You could have gone up to see the body."

Sierra had taken Charlie and Morrie up the slope behind the campsite sometime before David woke. They were now heading back down and were finally close enough to look like people instead of ants.

"Nah, I believe you," Cameron said. "I gotta say, that's pretty badass."

The compliment was as much a salve as the ointment. David couldn't remember the last time anyone had called him "badass," especially not someone as self-assured as Cameron. She was lean and lithe, and he found her attractive, in spite of the fact that she looked tough enough to beat him up. Maybe partly because of it.

"You should have met Wayne," Josh said. "That guy was badass."

"You can say that again," Randall muttered.

"I wish I'd known him," Cameron said. "Hell, I wish we'd known you guys were over here all this time. It's weird we didn't run into you back when Charlie and I came over."

Waldmire stopped slicing fruit and turned toward her. "Wait. What do you mean?"

"Charlie and I came to this island once for food," she said.

"When?" Waldmire asked. "Our pods opened eleven days ago. How long have you been here?"

Cameron's eyes narrowed. "Two and a half months. Priya knows the exact count." She frowned. "You all got into pods on Earth, right? Just before the Ender hit?"

"That's right," David said. He felt a hollow tug on his guts, similar to the sensation he got from heights.

"So where have you been for the last two and a half months?" Cameron asked. She looked every bit as confused as he felt.

No one answered her.

Kim walked over. "We got in our pods. They were closed for a few minutes, then they opened. We've been here for eleven days."

"That doesn't make sense," Cameron said.

Sierra, Charlie, and Morrie reached the bottom of the slope and started across the hilltop toward them.

"Guess what," Sierra called out.

"These new people have been here longer than us," David said.

"Yes." She beamed. "Isn't that awesome?"

"How is it awesome?" David asked. It made him uneasy.

Sierra and the others walked over. "It's another clue. We just need to figure out what it means."

She was right. The news was unnerving, but it didn't change anything. It didn't hurt them in any way.

"It does bring us back to time travel," David said. "If we all got sent back in time somehow, maybe we got sent to slightly different days."

Kim, Barry and Josh passed out coconut shells. "Hilltop fruit salad," Kim said.

Randall pointed at the slope with his charred stick. "Y'all see anything new up there?"

"Nope," Sierra said. "No sign of the cloud. The Tyrannosaurus is still down there on the beach."

"It damn near exploded," Morrie said.

Charlie shook his head, grinning. "It's pretty amazing how you did that."

David had only been trying to protect his kids, but the accolades were nice to hear.

"You're gonna be a celebrity when we get back to the village," Morrie said.

David turned to him. "When you say, 'village,' what do you mean exactly?"

Charlie shrugged. "There's a perimeter wall and six buildings in the center. Four cabins and two storage sheds."

David nodded. "Well, I guess if you've been here for a couple of months, it makes sense that you've started building things."

Charlie looked sheepish. "Naw, naw. I should have explained that. The buildings were there when we arrived." He chuckled. "It's been so long, I guess we take 'em for granted."

"Who built them?" Sierra asked. "What are they made of?"

"They're artificial. Like cement, or fiberglass, or something ... except different. Priya thinks it might be some kind of 3D printing. There aren't any seams."

David looked over at Sierra. "More clues," he said. More clues had to mean they were getting closer to answers.

"Does your group have any other ideas about who brought us here, or why?" Sierra asked.

"The going theory has always been some sort of aliens," Cameron said.

"If aliens brought us here, why ain't they shown themselves?" Randall asked.

Charlie gave a shrug with his face. "Priya and I believe we're under quarantine."

David nodded. "Our needs are all met. We have food and water. A quarantine makes sense." It was nice to be brainstorming with more people. "How long until they determine that we're safe?"

"That's the question, isn't it?" Charlie said.

"What's life like on your island?" David asked. The news about the buildings made him realize he didn't really know what to expect.

"Everybody pretty much does their own thing," Charlie said. "There's lots of work to go around, but enough people pitch in."

"What kind of work?" Josh asked.

Morrie held up his hands, which were thick with calluses. "Preparing food, cleaning, cutting firewood, weaving. Most of it's mindless, but it can be fun figuring out how to make things."

"Like what?" Barry asked.

"We learned how to weave reeds into mats and blankets and things like that. There's a group experimenting with pottery. We've got a decent set of tools, like axes and hammers." He chuckled. "We even built some outhouses."

David exchanged another glance with Sierra. She looked hopeful. This was exactly what they'd been looking for. People coming together to build a community.

"What if you don't want to work?" Josh asked.

"Nobody's forced to do anything," Morrie said. "That's the problem."

Charlie offered a sheepish tilt of his head. "Everyone's been through a lot. We all lost people we loved. It doesn't seem right to make anyone work if they don't want to."

Morrie frowned. "Idle hands are the devil's playthings."

Charlie waved him off. "The village gets along fine. We don't need help from Thad's little group."

"Who is Thad?" David asked.

"He's a wacko back in the village. Older guy." Charlie took a long, slow breath. "Thad thinks we're in Purgatory. He's convinced a few other people. It's just an excuse for them to slack off while the rest of us do all the work."

"What's Purgatory?" Barry asked.

"Some people believe it's a place you go between Earth and Heaven," David said. "Your sins have to be forgiven there before you move on."

"Do we believe it?"

David shook his head. "No, Bud. Even if we did, that isn't where we are."

"How can you be sure?" Kim asked.

"Purgatory is somewhere you go after you die, if you believe that, anyway. We didn't die. We came here in shiny white pods. It's nonsense."

"Amen," Cameron said. "Thad won't bother you. He and his flock keep to themselves."

Morrie looked down, shaking his head.

"Sorry man." Charlie patted his back. He looked around at the group. "Morrie's brother is wrapped up in Thad's nonsense."

"And your sister," Morrie said.

Charlie looked down. "I saved her from the Ender. I only wish I knew how to save her from herself."

Chapter Thirty-Three

Three Days Before Impact

Cameron rode shotgun in Charlie Rourke's semi-truck cab while Priya lay in the back, where she'd been snoozing off and on since the Sierra Nevada Mountains. Cameron wasn't sure why she stopped to get Charlie, other than the fact that his house had been on the way. Maybe it was because he was good at handling things. If there really did turn out to be aliens at the end of this insane road trip, he should be the one to greet them. He'd know what to do. He always knew what to do. It was why she'd fallen for him all those years ago.

She'd needed only five minutes to convince Charlie to join them. His one condition had been that they take his semi instead of the wheezing rental car she'd lifted at Travis Air Force Base.

Cameron had expected to feel sparks. She hadn't seen Charlie in nearly a decade. He still had those ridiculous full lips, but he was no longer the lean machine of his twenties that he'd been back when Cameron had been finishing her teens. She didn't feel sparks, none of that primal yearning, but seeing him still felt good. Familiar.

Now she wondered if picking him up was a mistake.

"You're not going to talk me out of this, Cam," he said, his eyes on the road. They passed a sign promising Salt Lake City in three hundred and fifty miles.

"She's a nut job."

"She's my sister," Charlie countered. He spoke with calm, even tones, in that buttery voice that had charmed off Cameron's pants once upon a time. "She's had a hard life, Cam. You know that."

Priya leaned forward from the back of the cab. "When you say 'nut job,' what do you mean exactly?"

Charlie winced.

Cameron smiled. How long had she been listening?

"Lily never learned to think for herself," Charlie said. "Dad died when she was in junior high and Lil dropped out to take care of Mom."

"Your mom's even nuttier. I suppose you'll want to pick her up too?"

"Mom wasn't crazy." Charlie's tone grew dark. "Mom was cruel. She died last January."

Good riddance, Cameron thought.

"Lily's been doing better," Charlie went on. "She even dated a guy for a while."

"What about him?" Cameron mocked. "Why don't we pick him up too?"

Charlie was silent for a moment. "He bailed on her when the Ender showed up." His voice became hard. "Listen, Cam. You appear at my doorstep with a crazy-ass story about aliens landing on the Great Plains. I agree to take you there, in my truck, right where my sister lives. If there's any chance of saving her, I'm doing it. You'd understand that, if you ever loved anyone as much as yourself."

She sneered and stared out the window. He'd insisted on taking his truck so he could be in control. Charlie was always one step ahead. That's what she'd liked about him, even more than the charming voice and the pretty-boy lips.

"I say we pick her up," Priya said.

Cameron looked back. "You don't know this woman. She's *lōlō*."

"Oh come on, she can't be any crazier than you, Cameron."

Charlie laughed, a deep belly shake that had been sexy back when there was less belly. "I like how you think, Priya."

Cameron sat back in her seat, giving up. When Charlie made up his mind, there was no changing it.

The tan desolation of Utah drifted by as they continued east.

Fifteen hours later they rolled into Griffith, Nebraska, a town stuck in the middle of the twentieth century. Most of the buildings on Main Street looked like they'd been shuttered for a decade or more.

Charlie turned at the sole stoplight and parked two minutes later in front of a prefab home with cream siding. Out stepped a broadly-built woman with thin lips, a bang-cut that looked self-inflicted, and cheeks as round as grapefruit. A young boy hid between the folds of her dress.

"Is there something you forgot to tell me, Charlie?" Cameron asked. He hadn't mentioned anything about his unmarried fundamentalist sister having a child. *Hypocrite.*

Charlie ignored her and climbed down from the cab. Lily engulfed him with Paul Bunyan arms.

"You look good, Lil," Charlie said.

"I haven't been eating well. It's hard to get anything hearty these days. Just vegetables from the neighbors. I've lost weight."

Even so, she was still a bear of a woman.

Charlie stepped back. "You remember Alice Cameron, don't you?"

"I do." Lily kept her arms at her sides.

Cameron clasped her hands together in front of her chest and exclaimed with a drawl, "Oh, Lily, it's so good to see you."

"Knock it off, Cam," Charlie said.

Lily looked down her nose at Priya. "Who are you?"

Cameron could tell from her tone what she was thinking. Lily hadn't changed a bit. "She's a terrorist," Cameron said, her eyes wide. "You can tell by the brown skin."

"Oh, for fuck's sake," Charlie said. "Knock it off."

"I don't like that language in my house," Lily said, despite the fact that they were still in the front yard. She clamped her hands over the boy's ears.

"She's Indian," Charlie explained, as if it should even matter.

Lily squinted. "I'll have you know I have several Indian friends."

"Those are Lakota," Cameron said, doubting she understood the difference.

Priya stepped forward. To her credit, she didn't appear to let any of this get under her skin. "My name is Priya Rami. I'm an astronomer and I believe we are going to have visitors tomorrow. Someone is coming to help us."

Lily took the news as if she'd been expecting it. "I knew we would not be forsaken."

Priya looked down. "And who is this?" The boy retracted into the folds of his mother's dress like a hermit crab.

"This is Isaac. He's almost four." Isaac peeked out. "Say hello to your Uncle Charlie."

Isaac said nothing.

Lily waved her hand. "Oh, you must come in. All of you. Even you, Alice. How long have you been driving? I'll put some coffee on."

As they walked to the house, Cameron leaned over and warned Priya to avoid the coffee. "It'll give you the shits."

They sat at a sparkling Formica table with aluminum trim while Isaac stacked empty Tupperware containers on the floor. He built a tower, knocked it down, then built it up again.

"I've been praying for a miracle." Lily closed her eyes briefly, apparently firing off a quick follow-up. "Now Charlie, what is this all about?"

Charlie looked across the table at Priya. "Tell her what you saw."

The twinkle in his eyes made Cameron uncomfortable. Was he developing a spark for the little nerd girl?

Priya sat up straight. "I work at an observatory. Three days ago, I spotted something new coming towards Earth. Something other than the Ender. It's a swarm of several thousand small objects. I calculated their trajectory and I believe they will arrive in a band between the Great Lakes and the desert southwest.

Lily sipped her coffee, one pinky pointed in the air. "And what are these objects?"

"Don't know," Charlie said. "Priya thinks they're something new."

Priya nodded. "They have an unnaturally high albedo and they're following a parabolic trajectory which cannot be explained by gravity."

Lily looked annoyed. "Okay, but what are they?"

Charlie took a deep breath. "This is something mankind has never seen before."

"Bingo," Priya said. "They clearly have an extraterrestrial origin. That, coupled with the unnatural properties of the objects themselves and the timing of their arrival indicates an intelligent creator."

Lily nodded with a pious smile. She'd heard the magic words.

Cameron rolled her eyes.

Charlie took his sister's hand. "Whatever they are, we're going to look for them tomorrow morning. I want you to come with us."

"And Isaac?"

"Of course. We'll make a perfect greeting party. Man, woman, white, brown, young, and old."

Don't forget smart and stupid, Cameron thought.

Later that night, Lily showed Cameron and Priya to a pair of twin beds in the guest room. Charlie took the couch.

"How long did you and Charlie date?" Priya asked as she got into bed, trying way too hard to sound casual.

"A couple of years, off and on." Those had been good times, mostly.

The answer seemed to satisfy Priya. Cameron had long since gotten over Charlie, but she still didn't like Priya's interest. She added, "He was my first, you know." This wasn't strictly true, but Cameron didn't want to unwind that unpleasant coil.

The next morning, they ate a breakfast of undercooked oatmeal, then departed in Charlie's truck, leaving early to avoid any questions from the neighbors. Lily and Isaac sat in the back of the cab with Priya. Isaac opened and closed each storage compartment and switched all the lights on and off. Incessantly.

They drove north with no specific destination in mind.

After two hours, Charlie stopped on a bluff that was quite literally the middle of nowhere. Not a single car passed by. Everyone climbed down from the cab to stretch their legs. The Ender glared from the northern sky, bigger than ever.

"They should be here by now," Priya said, pacing. "Maybe the objects changed course since I last observed them. Maybe my calculations were incorrect."

Charlie put a hand on her shoulder. "You can't know what you can't know." Priya seemed to grow a foot from his touch.

Cameron sneered and walked off by herself, listening to the silence of the prairie. A whistling sound stopped her in her tracks.

"Do you hear that?" Charlie called out.

Cameron had already spotted the first object. Two others were visible from the bluff, small white dots against the blue Nebraska sky.

The closest one landed four miles up the road. They drove north and found it sitting in the grass a hundred feet from the blacktop.

Charlie stopped the rig and everyone climbed out. He beamed at Priya. "You were dead on the money."

"It looks like a giant white football," Lily said, pressing her hands together above her hefty breasts.

Priya walked around the object with a huge smile on her face, a kid at Christmas. "It's a triaxial ellipsoid."

"Dweeb," Cameron said.

"Is that a mathematical term?" Charlie asked. "It's good to be precise."

Cameron glared at him, annoyed by how quickly he'd jumped to her defense. Charlie held a small Ruger, maybe a P90, pointed up, his finger outside the trigger guard. She didn't know where he'd been keeping it, but she was glad to see it. She kept her own Beretta out of sight.

Lily walked down and stopped right in front of the object, where she lowered herself to her knees, hands together, praying. Isaac stood behind her with his pinky in his nose.

"What do we do?" Charlie asked. The object hadn't moved or shown any sign of life. The plains were silent.

Cameron strutted forward and knocked. "Hello, anyone home?"

"Cam, wait," Charlie said.

The object split apart. Cameron jumped back. Priya grabbed Charlie's free hand. They watched in silence as the top half rose three feet in the air.

"I don't see anyone," Isaac said, peeking out from behind his mother, who remained kneeling with her head bowed.

"How does it do that?" Priya asked.

Cameron leaned in and looked around. A plush black surface lined the interior. It was concave, a giant cushioned bowl.

Lily rose and stepped forward. "Second Kings, two eleven. Behold, there came a chariot of fire and carried Elijah up into heaven on a whirlwind."

"I don't see any fire," Isaac said.

"Let's all just calm down for a minute," Charlie said. For some damn reason, he was still holding Priya's hand.

Lily hoisted Isaac into the pod and climbed in after him.

"Hold up, Lily," Charlie called to his sister, finally releasing Priya's grip. "We don't know what this thing is."

"I know what it is, brother." A sanctimonious smile broke on Lily's face. "It's our salvation."

"Salvation?" Charlie looked from Priya to Cameron. "Are we supposed to get in?"

The top half of the pod lowered slowly.

"Oh shit." Charlie grabbed Priya again and pulled her forward. He helped her climb in, putting his hand right on her tight little Indian butt, and then pulled himself up after her. "Come on, Cam."

Cameron froze. The thought of being trapped inside that thing made her skin crawl. Especially with Lily.

Charlie beckoned. "Cameron, get the hell in here." The top half continued to lower, now two and a half feet from the bottom.

If she stayed, she could try to find another pod. But if she failed, her final hours would be spent in Bumfuck, Nebraska.

She dove through the opening. A moment later all five of them were sealed in total darkness.

Chapter Thirty-Four

While the others bagged up the food, Sierra traversed the side of the hill that had been designated as the women's bathroom. After making sure no one was watching, she moved three rocks from a small pile at the base of a shrub. Underneath sat the ugly amber bottle of pentobarbital that had killed her father. She didn't want to leave it behind. She might need it someday.

She slid the bottle into her jacket pocket and returned to the hilltop, where she helped load the remaining fruit into spare shirts with the sleeves tied off. The rest of their belongings had all been bagged up.

"This is a good haul," Charlie said, "But I really wish we had some protein."

"What about the Tyrannosaurus?" Morrie asked.

"We don't have tools to butcher a carcass that size," Charlie said.

"We could use this." Josh pulled out his knife, nearly slicing Randall.

"Hey, careful," Randall hissed.

Charlie reached for the knife. After a moment of hesitation, Josh handed it over.

"It's worth a try," Charlie said. "We could take a few chunks back with us. If it's decent eating, we could send a team over for the rest."

"How long is the hike behind the mountain?" Cameron asked.

"Another couple of hours, once we reach the beach," Sierra said.

"Let's just get to the raft first," Cameron said. "It's a long hike down, and we've still got a lot of rowing ahead of us." She started off without waiting for a response. Charlie shrugged and followed her.

Sierra took one last look at the campsite that had been her home for eleven days and headed after them, excited for a fresh start. She was eager to see what the village looked like and meet new people, especially Priya, who sounded every bit as curious as she was.

They descended the hill with Cameron and Charlie leading the way. The pink scar on the side of Cameron's head looked like something she could have grown her hair over, Sierra realized, but she kept it cropped short, which made the injury seem like a badge of honor.

As Cameron stepped over a fallen tree trunk, a flash of silver appeared beneath her shirt in the back. Sierra kept watching until her shirt rose up again, confirming her suspicion. Sure enough, a pistol grip stuck from her waistband.

"What made you come to our island yesterday?" Waldmire asked.

"Your big fire," Charlie said. "You had a blazing bonfire a few days back. One of our people spotted it from the beach."

"That was you, Barry." David said. "Remember when you put too much wood on the fire?"

Barry smiled.

"Does the village have any sort of leader?" Sierra asked. "Is anyone in charge over there?"

"Nah," Charlie said. "We talked about it, but decided it wasn't necessary. We discuss whatever needs to be done each day and then everybody chips in to make it happen."

"Not everybody," Morrie said. "Some people seem to think everything will just be provided."

"For a while, that was true," Charlie said. "There was plenty to eat, everywhere we looked."

"It's still true," Morrie said. "It's just that the rest of us are doing all the providing."

"Charlie is selling himself short," Cameron said. "He may not make all the decisions or tell everyone what to do, but he's definitely stopped some people from losing their shit."

Charlie chuckled. "I think that makes me more of a referee than a leader."

A low growl came from Kona. She froze and stared into the jungle.

"Easy, girl," David said. He wrapped the end of her leash around his fist.

Cameron looked back, concern on her face. "Do you think she smells something?"

"*Waahk!*" The sound came from ahead and to the right. Sierra craned her neck and spotted the red beak of a terror bird off between the trees. "*Wwwaaaahk!*"

David grabbed his children and whispered, "Keep close."

The bird blinked and rotated its head in short, jerky movements, then bolted away through the jungle.

Charlie looked at Cameron with a dazzling grin. "Fresh meat."

"We've got plenty of food," Cameron said. "And what about the dead dinosaur?"

"If David can take down a *T. rex*, I can handle that bird," Charlie said. "I'm going after it, with or without you."

Sierra felt a smile spread across her face. This guy grabbed on with both hands when opportunity came along.

Shaking her head, Cameron pulled the bags from her shoulder and handed them to Morrie. "Get everyone to the raft. We'll meet you there."

Charlie and Cameron took off after the bird, spears raised.

Sierra shoved her bundle of clothes at Waldmire. "I'm going with them." She ran into the jungle, ignoring his protests. She wanted to get a first-hand look at these two in action. If she was lucky, she might even be able to help. She could earn a place on the team.

Charlie and Cameron moved quickly but quietly. Sierra kept her distance, not wanting to screw up the hunt. She ducked through branches, slid down short slopes, and wove between tree trunks for several minutes, unsure if they still had the terror bird in sight or were just following its tracks.

The sound of breaking branches came from ahead, then a series of shouts.

Sierra caught up to Charlie and Cameron, who stood in a small clearing surrounded by thick foliage. She stayed back, hoping she wouldn't distract them.

The terror bird had climbed onto an old deadfall and gotten its feet stuck in the rotten branches.

"He's trapped," Charlie said.

The terror bird tried to lift a foot, but its talons were caught beneath the crisscrossing limbs. It squawked, flapping its scruffy brown wings. Feathers floated around the glade.

Charlie crept forward, holding his spear in front of him.

"Slow down," Cameron said, moving sideways to flank the animal. "Why don't we shoot it?"

"Save the ammo," Charlie said, stepping forward. "It's trapped."

The terror bird swung its oversized head back and forth.

"You aren't as young and quick as you think," Cameron said. She sounded frustrated.

"Sheesh, Cam. Give me some credit. I got this."

The terror bird stopped struggling. It stood motionless, knee-deep in the branches. It could have been a museum display, except for its eyes, which darted back and forth between Charlie and Cameron.

Charlie lunged, driving his spear forward. The tip struck the bird squarely in the chest and slid right off. He stumbled sideways and dropped to one knee. "Fuck."

"What happened?" Cameron yelled.

"Bounced off," Charlie grunted. "Breastbone." He used his spear to climb back to his feet.

The bird exploded from the deadfall. Chunks of wood flew everywhere. It flapped as it leaped, legs cycling in the air. When it landed, it charged at Charlie, knocking him on his back. It raked his torso with its talons.

Sierra sucked in her stomach. *"No."*

The bird leaned over Charlie's head, its giant beak stretching wide.

Cameron charged, screaming. She shoved her spear deep into the monster's thigh, forcing it away from Charlie.

The creature lurched, snapping its beak inches from her face.

Charlie groaned, clutching his gut. Sierra ran to him, but didn't know what to do. She was afraid to move him and wasn't sure she could anyway. He was more than twice her size.

"You're okay, dude," Cameron yelled, holding the bird at bay with her spear. "You're going to be okay."

Charlie didn't look okay. A dark, lumpy stain smeared his tattered shirt. Sierra felt helpless.

The terror bird swiped at Cameron with its free leg. She dodged sideways, shoving with the spear, still buried in the creature's thick thigh. Its claws missed her by inches. A cobra hiss spewed from its gullet.

"Mother fucker," Cameron hissed back, wrestling the spear, which flexed and wobbled as the bird tried to advance. The creature snapped again, stretching for her face.

Sierra had to do something. The gun. Cameron couldn't use her gun without taking one hand off the spear. She ran behind her and pulled the pistol from her waistband.

Cameron flinched but kept her focus on the bird. "Shoot it. Hurry."

The gun was heavy as a brick. Sierra almost dropped it. She aimed for the bird's head, but it moved around too much. She lowered the pistol to its body and pulled the trigger.

Nothing happened.

"Safety," Cameron shouted, sounding angry and annoyed.

Sierra looked for the switch, trying to remember everything Wayne had taught her. Where the hell was the safety on this one?

The animal dug into the ground with three-inch claws and stretched its neck towards Cameron. Blood glazed its leg below the spear. It drove the woman backwards until she slipped in the undergrowth and fell on her butt.

The terror bird pressed its attack, reaching with its huge beak, but still held at bay by the spear in its thigh. Cameron growled, her arms trembling as the creature's head closed on her.

Sierra found a switch and thumbed it off. The bird jerked around so much she didn't trust her aim, even at this short distance. The animal extended its neck, reaching for Cameron.

Sierra marched forward, raised her arm, and placed the barrel against the bird's head, right behind its eye. She pulled the trigger and the gun roared, flying up and back. A red mist exploded. Sierra's arm felt like it had been slammed in a door.

The terror bird dropped in a heap.

She whooped. She'd done it. Holy shit, she'd actually done it.

Cameron pulled the spear from beneath the animal, stepped on its beak with a heavy black boot, and shoved the point through the bullet hole in its head, pinning the corpse to the ground. Panting, she turned to Sierra. "Nice job."

She barely heard the words over the ringing in her ears.

Cameron snatched the gun and ran to Charlie, still flat on his back. His shoulders trembled and both hands covered his belly. "Come on, let's have a look," she said. "You're going to be okay."

Charlie shook his head. The color was gone from his face. Even his lips were pale.

"Don't be a pussy." Cameron moved his hands aside and pulled apart the shreds of his shirt. Three gouges split the skin. Beaded blood glistened in the slashes, dark against yellow layers of fat.

Sierra's stomach rose. She looked away.

"You're gonna be okay, Charlie," Cameron said again.

His eyes widened. "For real?"

She swallowed and nodded. Sierra thought it was a lie.

"God damn," Charlie said, sounding tired. "Don't leave me, Cam."

She shook her head. "I won't."

"David's a doctor," Sierra said. "He'll know what to do." That might also be a lie, but she didn't know what else to say. "I'll get him."

She took off in the direction she hoped led to the beach, despair darkening her thoughts. Everything had been going so well. She had to find David and get him back here before it was too late.

Chapter Thirty-Five

Three deep lacerations ran across Charlie's blood-smeared abdomen. Dirt contaminated the wounds. *This man needs a surgeon*, David thought. *Not an anesthesiologist.*

"Do something." The desperation in Cameron's voice broke his heart.

David nodded. He was the only one with a medical background and he would do everything he could. He studied the wound. Three inches of belly fat had protected Charlie's internal organs, which was something. He hadn't bled too much and he was unconscious, both also good. His breathing was shallow but steady. David checked his pulse. Strong. If the cuts hadn't penetrated his abdominal wall, he might survive.

The terror bird lay a few feet away with a spear sticking straight up from the side of its head. It looked bigger than the one that attacked his children when they first arrived. The sooner they got the hell off this island and joined the other group, the better.

"Clean and seal, clean and seal," he muttered, a mantra from his first year in medical school. He snatched a water bottle from Randall's hand. "I need more water. As much as possible. As clean as possible."

Randall shrugged. "The rest of our water bottles are all back at the beach." Sierra had found them at the newcomers' raft and brought everyone here to this tiny clearing. "It'll take half an hour to go get 'em."

"Then we better hurry," Cameron said. She pointed to Morrie, Josh, and Randall. "You three. We're running." She looked down at David. "Don't you let him die."

"I won't," he said, hoping he could make good on the promise.

They took off in the direction of the beach.

David splashed water across the wounds, washing away a layer of muddy blood. Sierra handed him a second bottle, which he used to clear stringy clots from inside the lacerations.

He dug into the first aid kit for the tube of Bacitracin, pulled out the gauze and surgical tape, then put them back. There wasn't enough to cover the slashes.

Waldmire grasped his shoulder. "How can we help?"

"After I clean the wound, I want to close everything up as tightly as possible. We'll need the cleanest shirt we have and some vines to tie it."

Waldmire nodded, then steered Barry and Kim away.

"Keep them close," David said without looking up. "Kona too."

Sierra knelt next to him and held out a brown bottle. "Can you use this?"

The label looked like it had been produced on an old typewriter. "Pentobarbital?" He'd used it as a preanesthetic to help patients relax before surgery. "There's enough here to kill an elephant. Where did you get this?"

"Long story."

"Do you have a syringe?"

She shook her head.

"I could use it to sedate him, but he's already out. Do you have anything else?"

She shook her head again.

He looked at his hands. Filthy gauze covered torn fingernails, which throbbed painfully. "Show me your fingers."

Sierra tucked the bottle back in her pocket and held out her hands. They weren't sterile, but they looked better than his. And more importantly, they were small.

"Okay, you're going to pluck out the larger bits of debris."

Her eyes widened.

"Your hands are cleaner and smaller. We need to clear the wound and we need to do it before he wakes up." He put his fingers on the skin around the shallowest laceration and pulled gently to widen it.

Sierra took a deep breath, then followed it with a retching cough. The biting stench of blood and sweat wafted up from Charlie's body.

"You can do it," David said.

She reached in and plucked out a pea-sized nugget of dirt. "That's it." David kept his voice calm and reassuring. She removed several more pieces, one at a time.

Blood oozed through layers of fat and pooled in the bottom of the wound. The last clump of dirt was too deep for Sierra to reach. She found a twig on the ground and extended it toward the slash.

"Wait." David snapped the twig in half, peeled off the bark, and handed it back. "It still isn't sterile, but it's better."

Sierra dipped one end of the twig in the blood to moisten it, then touched the dirt clump. It lifted right out.

"Just like Operation." Sweat beaded on her face. "The game."

"Yeah, I've played it." David held the second wound open. The bird's talon had sliced the peritoneum, but the damage appeared to end there. "Don't touch the intestine," he instructed. A hint of purple coil was visible deep in the wound. Sierra shuddered and plucked out dirt.

When they moved to the third gash, the deepest, David's heart sank. Thick brown chyme oozed through a tiny hole where the intestine had been perforated. It smelled like dog shit and ammonia. Sierra turned away, gagging.

"It's okay," he said. As an anesthesiologist, most of his time in the operating room was focused on measurements and monitoring devices. It had been a while since he'd been this close to the action. "You're doing great. Better than I could, even."

Waldmire and the kids returned with loops of vines as Sierra cleaned out the third gash.

Barry crept closer, peering over her shoulder.

"No, Buddy, you don't want to see this," David said.

Waldmire steered the boy over to his sister, where she was studying the terror bird.

When the last chunk of dirt was out, Sierra sat back, dripping with sweat.

"You did great," he told her. "Take a break. You earned it. Go help prep the vines."

She nodded and hurried away.

Charlie's forehead felt clammy and cold, a sign of shock, but his heartbeat felt regular, which suggested he wasn't getting worse. Hopefully a low-grade fever would come on soon, to kick his immune system into high gear and help fight infection.

David had to do something about the perforation on the small intestine, though. He found the gauze in the first aid kit, tore off a small rectangle, and smeared it with antibiotic gel. Bacitracin wasn't meant for internal use. It might harm his kidneys and it might kill off his gut bacteria, but David was short on options.

Cameron ran into the clearing, breathing hard. "How is he?" She dropped a canvas bag filled with water bottles next to Charlie.

David looked at her. "I'm doing everything I can, but you know this isn't good."

She handed him a bottle.

He motioned for her to sit across from him and instructed her to roll Charlie toward him while he irrigated the wounds, trying to clear out smaller contaminates. He used all of the water, praying it was clean enough.

"Now hold the big wound open for me."

When she did, Charlie made a rattling gasp. "Wake up, dude," Cameron whispered.

"No," David said quietly. "We want him to stay unconscious a little longer."

She nodded. She didn't look happy about it, but she seemed to trust him, which was all he could ask.

David lowered the rectangle of gauze into the largest wound and placed it over the gash in the intestine. He used Sierra's twig to press down on the sides so that it covered the perforation.

"Will that work?" Cameron asked.

"A suturing kit would be better, but I think this will help."

Together, they passed the vines under Charlie's body. Waldmire took off his Henley and folded it into a square. The old man's torso was pale and wrinkled.

"We want this to be tight," David said. He and Cameron pushed at Charlie's belly, closing the lacerations. Fresh blood oozed out, which would hopefully expel any remaining foreign matter.

Waldmire positioned his shirt over the wound while they tied it in place with vines. When David let go, Charlie's belly sagged. The wounds might have reopened under the shirt, but for now it was the best they could do.

Randall, Morrie, and Josh arrived, carrying coconut shells filled with water. David stood and took a drink, his mouth dry. He used what remained to rinse the blood from his hands.

Cameron got right up in David's face, so close he could smell her sweat. "Thank you." The pain on her face told him she knew. Charlie would probably die.

"I wish I could have done more." He felt like he'd let her down.

They spent the next half hour building a stretcher out of branches and vines. Charlie moaned a few times but remained unconscious. David checked his forehead periodically, and by the time they hefted him onto the stretcher, a febrile response had kicked in. If he got too hot, David would crush some aspirin and place it in his mouth, but for now, he would let Charlie's body fight off any pathogens that might be in the wounds. Aspirin would also help with the pain when Charlie woke up, but it would impede clotting, so he needed to keep the dosage low.

Waldmire and Randall tied the bird carcass to a stout pole and lifted it onto their shoulders. Cameron and Morrie carried Charlie's stretcher. They walked through the jungle to the beach and then turned left, toward the raft.

Barry ran up the shore with Kona, throwing a stick into the water for her to fetch. Kim chatted quietly with Josh. David couldn't make out what they were saying, but he heard her giggle once or twice. He took solace from the fact that his kids were making the best of a shitty situation.

Sierra dropped back to walk with him. "Do you think he'll live?" she whispered.

He looked at her without saying anything. It was answer enough.

"I really liked him," Sierra said.

"Me too." David had known Charlie for less than a day, but the man had a quiet confidence that put everyone at ease. "Where did you get that pentobarbital?" he asked. "That wasn't hospital stock."

"My father killed himself with it," she said, staring ahead, her face blank. "Him and a few dozen others. Suicide party."

"I'm sorry."

She touched his arm. "Let's keep that bottle a secret."

"What are you planning to do with it?"

"Don't worry, I'm not going to kill myself." She raised her hands, palms up. "It just feels like an ace up my sleeve, you know? *Our* sleeves."

It was nice to be part of a team, a secret conspiracy. It made David feel a little less alone. "Just make sure my kids don't find it. Too much is deadly." Sierra looked away, and David silently cursed his stupid mouth. "I'm sorry about your father."

She nodded but didn't say anything else.

When they arrived at the raft, Cameron ordered everyone to collect firewood. "It's too late to set out," she said. "We'll camp on the beach." She set a guard schedule. Each adult would take turns standing watch overnight.

The newcomers' raft had an outrigger hull on each side and a raised platform in the middle. It was twice as big as the one Wayne had built. Several reed baskets of fruit sat undisturbed on the deck, along with the supplies they'd brought down from the hilltop. Waldmire rummaged through his belongings and found another shirt.

Charlie's stretcher was positioned close to the fire and David made a pillow for him with a bag of clothes. He touched the man's forehead. The fever had lessened and David dared to hope he might live. He considered untying the bandage to see if he could close the lacerations more tightly, but opted instead to just let him rest.

David lay down close by and fell asleep almost instantly.

Sometime later, Sierra shook him awake. "Charlie's making noises," she said.

The others were all asleep, but the campfire was still blazing.

"Wake Cameron." David crawled over to Charlie, trying to clear the cobwebs from his mind.

A hissing sound came from between Charlie's teeth and he opened his eyes.

David felt a wave of relief, along with a hint of pride. He hoped Cameron was impressed. It was starting to look like he'd done it, like he'd saved this man. He placed his hand on Charlie's arm. "You had us worried, my friend."

Cameron moved close. "Hey dude, you feeling better?"

Charlie grimaced.

"David's got you all patched up," Sierra said. "You're going to get through this."

Charlie's eyes moved around as if searching for something. "I don't think so." He spoke slowly, taking a breath with each word. "You had my number, Cam. Not as young and quick as I thought. You always had my number." He clutched at her hand. "Watch Joe."

David and Sierra exchanged a glance.

"I can handle Joe," Cameron said.

Charlie frowned. "He's trouble. Watch him." He took a deep breath. "Tell Priya …"

"Fuck you," Cameron said, tears creeping into her voice. "You tell her yourself."

"Tell Priya I loved her." Charlie closed his eyes and his face relaxed.

"Charlie," Cameron said, shaking his shoulder. She looked at the others. "The asshole went to sleep again."

David touched Charlie's neck, searching for a pulse. He felt nothing. He'd done everything he could. Hell, he'd done a great job, considering the circumstances. He pressed harder, shifted his fingers, and held his breath.

Finally, he pulled his hand away and met Cameron's eyes. "I'm sorry. He's gone."

Cameron's face became a mask, cold and grim.

"Who's Joe?" David asked. He'd heard about Thad, but no one had mentioned anyone named Joe.

"Don't worry about it," Cameron said. "Go to sleep. I'll stand watch."

The look in her eyes told him not to argue.

Chapter Thirty-Six

They set out across the sea just after dawn. Cameron put her anger and grief into her paddling. The trip was a disaster. Her relationship with Charlie was ancient history, but losing him still crushed her. He was her only connection to what life was like before everything went to shit. Hell, he was her only real connection, period. Now she was completely alone.

More importantly, the village needed him. Charlie had kept things from teetering over the edge several times.

They'd loaded the raft in silence, Sierra working twice as hard as the rest, like she was trying to prove herself, like this was all some big adventure, a mystery to be solved, not a goddamn struggle for existence.

The three kids and the dog sat up on the deck with the baskets of fruit and vegetables, Charlie's body, and the bird carcass. All six adults sat on the pontoons, paddling. Except for Randall, who mostly just pretended.

"How many days did you say you've been here?" Sierra asked, breaking the silence once they were away from the shore.

"Seventy-something," Morrie said. "Priya keeps count. But the days aren't really days, I guess."

"Why aren't the days really days?" Barry asked. The boy had his father's dimples.

"The days are shorter here," Cameron said. "Twelve hours of light and ten hours of night." Priya had timed it with a mechanical watch. She had buckets of discipline. Maybe that explained why Charlie liked her so much. Discipline had never been Cameron's strong suit, even in the Army.

Sierra's eyes danced back and forth, like she was cataloging this new information. She looked perfect with her black hair pulled tight in a pony-tail and her caramel skin. After months without any direct sunlight, Cameron probably looked like a corpse.

"Can you tell us anything else about the giant rhinos?" Sierra asked after a while.

"They're enormous," Morrie said. "Their horns are five feet long. They look demonic."

"They're animals," Cameron said. "Nothing more."

"But they aren't a threat?" David asked.

She liked David. He'd done everything he could to save Charlie, and seemed genuinely sorry it hadn't been enough. There was also something vaguely cute about his chiseled face. Too bad he was such a mom.

"Nah. They're all up on the plateau." Morrie pointed at the wide shelf rising up from the middle of the island. "Our village is in the woods. They can't get down."

Cameron wasn't a hundred percent sure that was true. The island was maybe half the size of Moloka'i, and they'd only explored one side of it, along with a small chunk of the plateau.

"How confident are you that they're prehistoric?" Sierra asked.

"Talk to Priya," Cameron said. "She's the one with the theories."

"You may not want to hit her with twenty questions right away," Morrie said. "Charlie was her boyfriend."

Cameron ground her teeth.

Charlie's body lay on the front of the raft, covered with broad palm leaves. Cameron had insisted they take him home to bury him there. He would have wanted that.

The terror bird was in the back, its legs hanging over the edge and its claws dangling in the water. Christ, they needed the food, but not at this cost. They should have gone after the dinosaur carcass instead. At this point, though, everyone just wanted to get to the village.

Given the smells coming from the corpses, she wondered if something might catch their scent and follow them. Hopefully, the aroma wasn't strong enough to reach the island with the dinosaurs. At least there wasn't any wind to carry the stench.

"How do you get up to the plateau?" Waldmire asked.

Cameron liked the old guy. His raspy voice reminded her of a country singer.

"There's a way up at the end of the canyon," Morrie said. "It's where our pods opened."

"Your pods weren't on the beach?" Sierra looked over. "All of ours were on the beach."

"Ours landed in the canyon, packed in like an egg carton." Morrie's tone grew sad. "They opened up and there was Thad, first one out, welcoming everybody and going on about how we all needed to be cleansed before we could move on to heaven."

"Why did people believe him?" Kim asked.

Cameron looked over her shoulder, curious to hear Morrie's answer. His brother had been one of the first to jump on Thad's bandwagon.

"Thad always has an answer," Morrie said. "He told people to pray for food and then he led us straight to an apple tree, just like the Garden of Eden. We were euphoric. We'd survived the end of the world. Thad took it from there and ran with it." He looked down. "Religion has that effect on some people."

"That doesn't sound like religion," Waldmire said. "That sounds more like manipulation."

Cameron chortled in agreement. Waldmire was as wise as he looked. "Thad is an extremist," she said. "A fundamentalist."

She paddled harder, wanting the trip to be over. Of course, it would go faster if everyone pulled their weight.

"Hey Randall, should we ask one of the kids to take your place?" Cameron allowed anger into her voice, which somehow made the paddling slightly easier.

Randall's eyes narrowed between puffy eyelids, like he was thinking about it, then he dipped his paddle in the water and gave a decent pull. Even David, who'd been hurt, paddled harder than that lazy son of a bitch.

As they inched forward, stroke by stroke, she steered the raft toward the beach at the end of the forest path.

David pointed to three long shapes on the sand. "What are those?"

"Canoes," Morrie said. "Dugouts. We made those before we built this raft. We rowed all the way around the island. Didn't find a damn thing."

Cameron didn't care about the canoes. She was more concerned about how empty the beach looked. "We were gone for two days. Someone should be watching for us." She paddled harder as the boat closed the distance.

When they finally drew close enough, Kona hopped down, swam to shore, and squatted to pee.

Cameron jumped into the shallows and pulled them the last few feet. "Why isn't anyone here? I don't like this."

Everyone climbed off and they dragged the front of the raft onto the beach. David winced as he pushed. He was definitely hurting, but he wasn't letting it slow him down, which was admirable.

She adjusted the palm fronds covering Charlie. He felt cold. Touching him made her feel cold. "I don't want to show up carrying a corpse. We can send some people down for him later." She led them past the dugout canoes to the opening in the trees, setting a quick pace on the path, just shy of jogging.

"Each island is like a different environment," Sierra said as they walked through the woods. This one feels like Sequoia National Park."

Kona bounded alongside them, a blur of yellow weaving through green ferns. Every so often she stopped to sniff the pine needles and leave her mark.

After fifteen minutes, the beige perimeter wall came into sight. Beyond it, the huts and shacks stood clustered in the center of the village, just above the fields.

"That definitely doesn't look man-made," David said.

Cameron remembered feeling baffled the first time she saw the village as well. The wall ran in a perfect circle, with three openings. The one in front of them stood at the six-o'clock position, another one on the right sat at three, and a narrow one on the far side opened at twelve, where the little stream flowed in.

Sierra ran her hand over the rough surface. "It's like a weird mix of plastic and plaster."

"Nobody's doing the weeding," Morrie said.

The fields inside the eight-foot wall were empty, except for tiny green shoots poking from the soil. Charlie had tried to get everyone to plant crops a long time ago, but they weren't terribly motivated back when food was plentiful. Now it was nearly too late.

A row of work tables lined the far end of the fields, where people usually milled about, preparing meals. Today, nobody was there.

"Is it normally this quiet?" Sierra asked.

"No," Cameron said, more harshly than she intended. She felt stupid standing here in the entrance gawking, but she couldn't quite bring herself to move forward. She wasn't ready for more bad news.

"Maybe with Charlie gone, the whole place is slacking off," Morrie said. "They're all asleep in the cabins."

"Joe would never let that fly," Cameron said.

"Who's Joe?" Sierra asked.

"He's just a guy," Cameron said. The full explanation was a bit more complicated than she felt like getting into. Joe had been losing his temper more and more in the last several weeks, usually over something stupid, like a broken tool. Every time he went through one of his rants, it seemed like another screw wiggled loose.

"Are you sure everything's okay here?" David asked.

Cameron ground her molars. Nothing was okay. She and Charlie and Morrie never should have left. "Come on. Let's find them."

As she stomped into the village, Charlie's dying words echoed in her mind. *Watch Joe. He's trouble.*

Chapter Thirty-Seven

One Day Before Impact

Joe Walker stared at the floor of Yosemite Valley, two thousand feet down. Half Dome loomed across the gulf to his right and Yosemite Falls spilled down across the valley to his left. What a majestic place to die.

No, a majestic place to *fly*. All his life, Joe had dreamed of flying. His best childhood memories involved reading Superman comics to his drunk father.

"I can do it," he said aloud, though he was completely alone. Joe hadn't seen a soul on the six-hour climb to Glacier Point.

He extended his middle finger across the valley at the Ender, where it hung in the northern sky, larger than the sun now. Its dull yellow light gave everything a second shadow.

You're gonna splat like a mother fucker, Joe's daddy said, his raspy voice haunting him all the way from prison.

Joe tried to ignore him. If he was going to go through with this, he had to make himself believe.

He needed a running start. Joe pictured himself dipping down a little before rising up and soaring across to the far side of the valley. He walked away from the cliff's edge, kicking a few rocks aside so he wouldn't trip on take-off.

Thirty feet back, he stopped near a clump of stunted red pines, his heart pounding in his chest. A television report estimated that a hundred million people had committed suicide in the last several weeks. What was one more?

"Dammit, believe. Gotta believe."

Joe stretched one foot behind him and put his hand on his knee like a track and field sprinter.

"One."

"Two."

He stood up straight. What was he thinking? He had to find a spot to land. If there was even the tiniest chance he could fly, he needed a destination.

Joe returned to the lookout point and picked up the binoculars he'd stolen from the deserted gift shop. Half Dome was too high. He swung left. The opposite side of the valley was wooded and uneven. He kept turning until Yosemite Falls came into view. From here, the falls were silent, but he imagined how they must thunder up close. Above the falls and to the right, he saw a lookout point just like the one he was standing on. Perfect.

When he landed on the other side, he would walk into the mist to cool off. Maybe the thunder would drown out his daddy's voice.

As Joe lowered the binoculars, something white glinted in the trees. He'd already started to turn around when it registered that nothing up here glinted like that.

Over the past twenty hours, seventeen hundred pods had been discovered in a shotgun pattern from the Great Lakes to southern Nevada. Another thousand or so were believed to have gone unreported. Only a tiny handful had been found in California. People had climbed inside every single one and flown away.

On their final phone call, Joe's momma had told him the pods were sent to deliver the worthy up to Heaven. She had not been given one because she'd looked the other way while Joe's father beat him and his sister. Joe's sister lived in a home for disabled adults where she had almost learned how to bathe herself.

Shaking, he raised the binoculars. Two miles across the glacier-carved valley, an oblong white shape gleamed in the afternoon sun.

The pod lay at the bottom of the upper falls, where the terrain flattened slightly. Below that, the lower falls dropped straight down to the valley. Joe opened his mouth, breathing harder than he had on the hike up. He felt dizzy, unable to believe his luck. Joe Walker never got lucky.

According to the news, the Ender would send firestorms of vaporized air around the globe. The heat would extend seventy feet below the surface. Some of the atmosphere would burn away.

Joe threw the binoculars aside. "You really are going to fly, you lucky son of a bitch." For the past day, everyone had speculated about where the pods went. A man in Kansas had been on his phone, talking with a news station while he climbed in. The call ended the moment the pod closed.

They took you somewhere else. That was all that mattered.

Joe checked his watch. The Ender would strike the Pacific in eight hours. He pulled out his map and found a trail going up the opposite side of the valley. It went right past the shelf where the pod sat, then zigzagged up to the lookout.

He started down the path to the valley floor. The hike up had taken six hours. He thought he could make it down in less than four, but then he would have to climb the other side. He picked up his pace.

What if he ran into someone? What if they tried to take the pod? *You can't let that happen*, his daddy said.

Joe had left his Smith & Wesson 629 in his truck so he wouldn't be tempted to use it. He'd been determined to fly, or die trying, as the saying went. If someone else tried to take that pod, the revolver would come in handy. He'd only drawn it once, years back, when a pair of thugs attempted to rob him in Stockton. Just pointing it at them had done the trick, which was good, because Joe didn't think he could actually pull the trigger.

"Sometimes you have to do things you don't want to," his daddy liked to say after the third drink kicked in and he started growing mean. "People must be punished."

Joe pressed on. In twenty minutes, he arrived at the grueling switchbacks, which were a hell of a lot easier now than on the trip up. He was making good time.

He wondered if there were supplies at the campground he could use. He made a mental list of items to collect. Food and water. Spare clothes. Survival gear. He didn't know where the pod would take him, but it would pay to be prepared.

Blisters bit his heels after the first hour. He added a first aid kit to his list, along with a backpack to carry everything.

By the time he reached the parking lot, the sun had dropped behind El Capitan to the west. Fortunately, the bone-yellow glow of the Ender provided enough dusky light to see. It just didn't provide any warmth.

Joe's daddy let out a barking laugh. *That'll change in a few hours, won't it?* Joe glanced over his shoulder. That gruff voice sounded so real sometimes.

He unlocked his truck and retrieved the Smith & Wesson from under the seat, along with several boxes of forty-four magnum loads. He shoved the gun into the front of his pants. It made him feel safe. Other people couldn't be trusted. Joe's daddy had taught him that much, and everyone else had proven him right. They'd all looked the other way when Joe showed up with a black eye or a broken arm.

He grabbed his jacket and a spare water bottle from the back seat and put them in his backpack, which already held a khaki shirt and a box of peanut-butter crackers. It wasn't much. He closed the door and set out across the valley floor, hoping to find more food and maybe a first aid kit before starting up the other side.

The path led through a campground with a few tents under the trees and an old banged-up camper by a water spigot. The tents looked like they had been there for weeks.

Joe checked his watch. Just under five hours to impact. The hike to the pod would take at least four. His legs felt rubbery. He had to hurry.

The closest tent sagged on its poles and the zipper door hung open. Joe doubted there was anything inside, but he dropped to his knees and leaned in, just in case.

An old man lay on a sleeping bag, mumbling quiet whispers toward the tent's roof. Joe froze, every muscle tense, hoping he wouldn't be noticed. He backed out slowly through the mesh flap.

Don't you say nothing, Joseph Walker, came his daddy's voice. Something was wrong with the geezer in the tent. He should check the other tents and maybe the camper near the water spigot. The clock was ticking.

Joe took a few steps, then stopped. His father was a grade-A asshole. He didn't have to be like that. He could be the good guy, somebody who helped others instead of hurting them. Besides, he had the revolver to keep him safe. There was still time if he hurried.

Back in the tent, he shook the man's ankle. "Hey pops. Can you get up?"

The old man sprang forward and Joe scrambled backwards to get out of his way.

"What do you want?" the man asked. He unfolded himself as he climbed out of the tent. Joe stood six-four in his boots, yet this guy towered two inches over him. He wore an off-white sweater and brown corduroys, and stank of stale menthol.

"I'm trying to help you," Joe said, his hand hovering near the pistol. The old guy had moved fast.

The man's cobalt eyes wandered all over him, examining. He shook his head. "You can't help me. Judgment's upon us."

"Look, I don't have much time," Joe said, growing angry.

"Time's all we got left." The man's eyes flitted to the sky. The Ender was hidden behind the ridge to the north, but its pale glow filled the valley.

Sweat trickled down Joe's sides, ice water on his skin. "I found a pod," he blurted. "It's the last one."

You're asking for it, retard, Joe's daddy said. *That man ain't right. Leave him be.*

The man stared. Gray tufts of hair fluttered over his ears and his bald head glowed yellow in the dull light.

"I'm trying to save you," Joe said. "Don't you want to be saved?"

The man gave a desperate nod. "I do want to be saved."

Joe pointed toward Yosemite Falls. "You're gonna have to climb with me."

The nodding continued.

"I'm Joe. Joe Walker." He chuckled. "Like the whiskey. What's your name?"

The man didn't smile. "Thad Lipton. Like the tea."

Chapter Thirty-Eight

Sierra followed Cameron up the path between irregular rows of small green plants. The smell of freshly-turned soil hung in the air.

Even though she'd heard about the pre-built village, actually seeing it made her feel like she'd collected another puzzle piece. She still didn't know how they all fit together, but she thought she might finally have enough to complete the picture.

They stopped in the center of the village, at a row of crude wooden tables that had clearly been built by people. Tendrils of smoke rose from several small campfires, as well as a large fire pit on the right, which was surrounded by a wide stone hearth.

"Hello," Cameron called out, her hands around her mouth. "Where is everyone?"

Log benches fanned around the main fire pit on one side. Kona wove between them, sniffing every few feet.

Barry ran past the benches to a wooden structure that looked like a homemade swing set. A solid-looking horizontal beam was held ten feet off the ground by two sets of angled support posts. Vine ropes hung from the beam at regular intervals. Barry grabbed one and swung on it like Tarzan.

"Is that for drying meat?" Josh asked.

"Yeah, that's where we field dress the squirrels," Morrie explained. "The rhino, too."

"What does that mean?" Barry asked, still swinging.

"It means they hang dead animals from those ropes and cut them open," Kim said.

Barry let go and brushed flakes of dried blood from his hands. "Eww."

Kim snorted.

Sierra stopped by several crude wooden tables with instruments scattered across them. Handmade tools of wood, rock, and vine lay alongside utensils that had obviously been brought from Earth. She saw spoons, forks, and a few small knives, all of which had been worn down from use.

David picked up a folding multi-tool. It looked like something they could have used to pluck the dirt from Charlie's wounds.

Two off-white structures stood behind the tables. Each was a single uniform object, with curved corners and edges.

"Those are for storage," Morrie explained. "Food goes in one and supplies in the other."

Sierra touched the surface of the supply shed, which looked like Styrofoam, but felt firm and solid, just like the perimeter wall. Both sheds looked identical. "Who built this? How did they build it?" No one answered her.

She stepped inside and Waldmire leaned in behind her. The structure was only big enough to hold two or three people. A rudimentary wooden shelf leaned against the side wall, stacked with clothes, baskets, and more tools.

"Where the hell are they?" Cameron poked her head in the other shed. "Check the cabins."

Kim's eyebrows crept toward each other, the way they always did when she was scared. "Do you think some new creature showed up?"

"There isn't any sign of a fight," Sierra said. The village looked abandoned, not attacked.

"Maybe the aliens took them," Barry said.

Sierra glanced at the boy, then up at the sky. She saw only robin egg blue, surrounded by the forest on all sides.

Four larger structures dotted the slope beyond the sheds. They also looked injection-molded and all four of them looked exactly the same. Each had a door-sized opening in the front wall and small square windows about six feet up on the side walls. All of the corners were rounded and smooth.

Reed mats draped in front of the doors, with heavy rocks anchoring them on flat roofs. The makeshift curtains weren't part of the structure. They had to have been added by the people living here, undoubtedly to create a little privacy.

Morrie pointed at one of the cabins. "Half the women bunk in that one." He looked at Sierra and Kim. "They'll probably make room for you, if you want."

Kim turned to her father, eyes wide, shaking her head. Sierra couldn't blame her. Sleeping in a room full of strangers would have terrified her at twelve. Even at twenty-three, she didn't much care for the idea.

David pulled Kim against his side. "You don't have to."

"If she don't want to sleep there, I will," Randall said.

Josh giggled.

"Randall, shut up," Sierra said.

"Why don't you fuckin' make me?"

Waldmire stepped between them. "These structures are all human-sized. Could that mean that whoever brought us here has the same body shape as us?"

Randall scowled and backed away.

Sierra shrugged. "Either that, or they were built specifically for us." She pretended to ignore Randall, but watched him from the corners of her eyes.

A tired, creaky voice came from one of the cabins. "Who's there?" An old woman pushed aside the mat hanging over the doorway.

Cameron rushed to her, with the others close behind. "Where is everyone?" she demanded.

"That's Carol Mulligan," Morrie said. He held the back of his hand next to his mouth and added, "Kinda senile."

Carol looked distraught. "They've all gone up to the canyon."

"Why?" Cameron gave her shoulders a gentle shake.

The old woman's eyes moved from face to face, taking in the newcomers. "You found someone."

David waved. Sierra offered a smile.

Morrie snorted. "Nothing gets past her, does it?"

"Knock it off, Morrie," Cameron said, her jaw clenched. "What happened?"

"Thad held another baptism down at the beach this morning." Carol spat the words with distaste.

Morrie huffed. "Jesus. How many baptisms do they need?"

"They saw Matt and Grace ..." The old woman stopped herself and glanced at Kim and Barry. "Matt and Grace were having relations."

Randall chuckled.

Cameron glared at him, anger in her eyes. And maybe a little fear.

"So what?" Sierra asked.

"Thad said his people were being corrupted." Hope bloomed in Carol's eyes. "Maybe Charlie can calm him down."

Cameron stepped back. "Charlie is dead."

The old woman's face fell, making her look ancient. "Thad marched his people up to the canyon. Once Joe heard about it, he rounded up everyone else to go after them. It wasn't long ago." She wrung her hands. "He was angry."

"He's got every right to be angry," Morrie said. "Thad's group doesn't do anything to help out around here."

"Come on, let's go." Cameron led them behind the sheds and the big fire pit to another opening in the wall, about half as wide as the one they'd come through below the fields.

Carol remained behind.

Outside the wall, three thin structures stood in a row at the edge of the forest. Like the tables and benches, these had been cobbled together from rough-hewn wood. They looked nothing like the prefabricated buildings.

"Ew." Kim held her nose. The acrid stink of outhouses emanated from the structures.

Cameron turned left and ran alongside the wall, following a path up the gentle slope.

Sierra looked back into the village as she followed. The eight-foot wall surrounded an area roughly the size of the field at Dodger Stadium, which made it more than four hundred feet in diameter. Except for the openings, it was a perfect circle.

They followed the wall until they met a stream flowing into the village. The water entered through a gap that was barely wide enough for someone to squeeze through. Kona lapped noisily at the creek. Sierra hadn't seen the stream when they were inside.

"Where does that go?" she asked.

Cameron had already pushed on, turning right to follow the stream into the woods. Waldmire craned his head through the opening to look back inside. Randall cupped his hands for a drink just upstream from the dog.

"The creek? Oh, it runs down behind the huts," Morrie said. "It separates them from the camping area, then it sorta peters out and seeps under the wall."

"Camping area?" David asked.

Morrie flicked his hand toward the far side of the village, where a few dozen trees grew inside the perimeter. "Some people prefer to sleep under those trees there." He took off after Cameron.

Sierra hurried to keep up, following the stream through the pine-filled woods. David moved alongside her, with Kim and Barry close behind.

"Do you think this is a good idea?" he asked quietly. "Maybe we should wait in the village until whatever's happening blows over."

"If there's anything we can do to help, we have to try. It's probably just a couple of hotheads who lost their tempers."

David held her gaze for a moment. "I hope you're right."

They pressed forward.

The forest ended at a towering wall of gray rock split down the middle by a tall, narrow opening, almost like an alley between two skyscrapers. The creek streamed out through the flat bottom. Inside, the walls were almost perfectly vertical and they met the ground at right angles.

Randall stood with his hands on his hips. "What the hell is this?"

"Welcome to the plateau." Morrie said, looking up. "Now you see why the rhinos can't get down, huh?" The smooth stone rose at least five stories, maybe more.

"Come on," Cameron said. She followed the little stream into the opening.

The flat floor dipped slightly in the middle, keeping the stream in the center, like in the flood-control spillways that crisscrossed Los Angeles, except here, the walls towered straight up on both sides. The canyon zigged and zagged so they could never see more than a hundred yards ahead.

"This isn't natural," Sierra said. Above, she saw only uniform blue sky. If giant rhinos were up there, they weren't looking down. "How far does the canyon go?" she asked.

"It cuts most of the way through the plateau," Morrie said.

His reply didn't really answer her question, but she let it slide. She'd find out soon enough.

After another ten or fifteen minutes of walking, angry voices echoed from ahead. Cameron glanced back at the others, concern pinching her face.

They rounded a corner and came to a crowd gathered at the end of the canyon. A thin waterfall poured from an opening high on the back wall.

"What's going on?" Cameron called out.

The crowd turned and parted, moving to either side of the creek. Someone shouted, "New people!"

Sierra tried to take it all in. There were roughly two dozen people standing around. Beyond the crowd, several others lay along the edge of a small pool at the base of the waterfall.

"Joe, what's going on?" Cameron asked again.

A man holding a huge silver gun stepped forward. "That's what I'm trying to figure out."

A knot of fear clenched inside Sierra. The people lying along the edge of the pool weren't just lying there. They looked dead.

Chapter Thirty-Nine

Five Hours Before Impact

Joe didn't have time to pillage the other campsites or the beat-up camper by the water spigot. The old man would slow him down on the hike to the pod.

Joe's daddy barked a hoarse, sputum-filled laugh. *You're gonna die, you dumb fuck.*

"Shut up," Joe said.

Thad cocked his head, puzzled. "What?"

"Just come on." He started across the parking lot toward the trail.

A shrill voice called out. "Where you going in such a hurry?"

Two men stepped out from the camper. The lead man chewed on a toothpick. He had the jowly face of a bulldog. The other man held a hunting rifle. An ugly sunburn blistered his face.

Joe's daddy let out another lung-cancer laugh.

The men blocked the trailhead. The one holding the rifle aimed it at Joe's chest.

"I'm hiking up," Joe said, thinking fast. "I'm gonna watch the Ender from the top."

Thad stood next to him, silent.

The bulldog chewed his toothpick. "Looks to me like you and gramps are heading into the woods to get nasty." He looked at his companion. "Ain't that right, Pete?"

Pete laughed. Both men wore white dress shirts and dark slacks, as if they belonged in offices somewhere, not a national park.

Pete leaned in. "Grandpa, why you got to be so nasty?"

Thad was a statue.

The bulldog tongued his toothpick from one side of his mouth to the other. "Let's rumble." He brought up his fists, knuckles crusted with old blood.

Joe had to do something. He'd found a pod, for Christ's sake. His hand inched toward his pistol.

"Easy," Pete said, stroking the rifle's trigger.

"What do you want?" Joe asked.

The bulldog grinned. "We want to beat the living shit out of you, that's what."

Rage boiled inside Joe. These fuckheads wanted only to inflict pain, just like his daddy.

Pete gestured with the rifle. "Hand over your gun, nice and easy."

Thad stepped forward. He kept his arms straight down and bellowed at the men. "Cowards and murderers will be cast in a lake that burns with fire."

Joe stepped back in awe. Thad sounded like that old wizard from the movies, yelling at the big demon on the bridge.

The bulldog let out a tittering laugh and the toothpick fell from his lips.

Thad stepped closer. "Topheth has been prepared. A pyre and a torrent of brimstone awaits."

Joe didn't understand what the old coot was saying, but he saw the rifle track away from his chest and toward Thad. This was his chance.

You can't do it, though, can you? Joe's daddy whispered. *You ain't got the balls. Just tiny little peanuts.*

Yes, I can. Joe drew the revolver and pulled the trigger. A hole opened on Pete's chest and gore spewed to the ground behind him. Buzzing filled Joe's ears as the gunshot's echo ricocheted around Yosemite Valley.

Pete fell backwards like a cut tree.

Joe's throat drew in, so tight he couldn't get air. Jesus. He'd killed someone.

Thad didn't flinch. He took another step toward the bulldog. "Remember what you heard and repent. I will come, a thief in the dark. I will bring blackness to consume you."

With great effort, Joe shifted the revolver toward the bulldog. He didn't think he could pull the trigger again. His shoulders trembled. He couldn't believe what he'd done.

"Mother fuck," said the bulldog. He seemed more frightened of Thad than Joe, even though Joe was the one pointing the gun at him. He turned and ran.

On the ground, sticky air hissed from the tunnel in Pete's chest as his lungs emptied.

Joe's arm felt numb. He fumbled the revolver back into his pants. He almost threw it away. He still couldn't breathe.

"We have to leave now." Thad's voice was small and simple, nothing like the wizard roar from a moment ago. He didn't look at the body. He walked to the gate at the trailhead, corduroys buzzing.

The old coot was right. Time was running out.

A spark of happiness struck Joe. His daddy had been wrong. If Joe hadn't gotten Thad out of that tent, those two assholes would have beaten him to a pulp. Joe's throat finally opened and glorious air filled his lungs, along with the taste of gun smoke. He'd done the right thing. He'd saved Thad and Thad saved him.

Joe turned toward the trail, then stopped and went back for Pete's hunting rifle. Only for hunting, he told himself. Only for hunting.

Yeah, right, Joe's daddy said. *You got the taste now.*

Joe ignored him. He caught up to Thad at the bottom of the first stair climb. "Thank you. You saved me."

"The Lord above saves." Thad looked up.

"Okay," Joe said. His mother had been religious, but it hadn't kept her from getting beaten every week. Whatever. Joe could deal with a little religion. They climbed without talking. The mountainside was silent except for the distant gush of the falls and the buzz of Thad's corduroy pants.

The old fart didn't stop once. He was a hell of a lot tougher than he looked. Joe was beyond exhausted and his feet were raw with blisters.

After nearly three hours, the trail passed the lower falls. The cool mist felt good. Joe wished it would clean him off. He wanted to make sure he didn't have any of Pete's blood on him.

They kept going for another half mile, and then Joe called for Thad to stop. "We need to leave the trail and head that way." He pointed across the slope toward the base of the upper falls.

They hopped a little fence and Thad followed him through the woods without a word. Joe's heart pounded from a mix of exhaustion and fear. What if the pod was no longer there? What if they couldn't find it? He looked at his watch. They only had twenty minutes left.

The trees thinned out, giving way to a boulder field, steeper than Joe had expected. Out in the middle, the pod glowed yellow in the light of the Ender. "Yeah, baby," Joe said. His legs trembled and he'd be sore for days, but it didn't matter. They'd made it. Joe was going to fly.

Thad stared with a blank expression. "What is that thing?"

"How long have you been at the campground?" Joe asked.

Thad made his fingers dance, counting. "Weeks."

He hadn't seen the news. He didn't know about the pods.

Joe put his hand on Thad's shoulder. "You get in and it flies away."

"Where?"

"Nobody knows. Away from here."

They scrambled across the boulders.

Thad stopped a few yards from the pod and narrowed his eyes. "How do we get in?"

"It opens when you touch it," Joe said. It was one of the few things people knew about the pods. A black smear of bird shit ran down one smooth side. "Why did you come with me?"

"Propitiation."

Joe didn't know what that meant, but before he could ask, the light changed to the orange of sunset, all at once instead of gradually. Above, the Ender burned across the sky, splitting the heavens. A wide contrail broiled in its wake. It looked like the surface of the sun. The roar of a million jet engines followed a moment later.

Joe pulled Thad the last few feet and placed his hand on the pod. It felt cool and slick.

The top half lifted magically in the air.

An immense light flared from the west. The Ender had struck. The shockwave was on its way. Joe grabbed Thad's bald head and maneuvered him inside, like a cop shoving a crook into a patrol car.

As soon as they touched the black surface of the interior, the top began to lower.

Thousands of miles away, the world began to burn. Joe smiled. Somewhere out there, his daddy would burn, too.

Chapter Forty

Sierra's limbs felt numb, like dead weights. Ten bodies lay side-by-side at the edge of the shallow pool. Several looked small. *Children.*

David walked forward. Hope rose in Sierra's heart. Maybe it wasn't too late. Maybe he could do something. David stopped short and the hope drained away.

"Why?" she whispered. Her eyes crept to the smallest bodies. Their feet made little "v" shapes. She counted four. Four children and six adults.

Morrie ran to the line of bodies and dropped to his knees. He buried his face in the chest of a man. It had to be his brother.

"Where's Charlie?" Joe demanded. He stood alone on the far side of the crowd, holding a silver pistol with the barrel pointed down. Jet-black hair swept away from a hard, tight face. Khaki sleeves were rolled up past thick, hairy forearms.

Beyond Joe, an old man knelt off to the side of the pool, his fingers interlaced on his head, like a prisoner of war.

Several people sobbed in the crowd.

Sierra didn't know what to think. It looked as if Joe had killed the people lying in front of the pool and the old guy on his knees was next.

"Where's Charlie?" echoed a short young woman with an Indian accent. "Why isn't he with you?"

"Charlie's dead," Cameron said. "I'm sorry, Priya."

Priya looked from Cameron to Sierra to David, as if searching for some hint that Cameron was wrong, or that she'd misheard, or something.

Sierra swallowed, her face tight. She shook her head slowly.

Priya fell to her knees. "No, no, no, no, no." Several people crowded around, embracing her. A few others went to Morrie's side.

"This just keeps getting better," Joe hissed, his face dark with anger.

Everything was happening too fast. Sierra turned to look for David, hoping he could help her make sense of the situation.

David was working his way backwards, toward his kids and the dog, who lingered near the last bend in the canyon.

"Charlie has gone to his final reward," said the man kneeling by the pool. He was bald, with wisps of white hair above his ears. He smirked. "Or perhaps his punishment."

"Shut your goddamn mouth, Thad," Joe barked.

A burly man with long black hair shouted from the crowd, "Joe, you gotta do it. I'm telling you." His arms bulged from a sleeveless t-shirt with a picture of Abraham Lincoln on the front.

Joe's eyes danced around like tiny searchlights. He twitched and looked off to the side, as if someone else had spoken to him. Sierra followed his gaze, but there wasn't anyone there.

The heavy, paralyzed feeling in her arms and legs grew stronger. Something horrible had happened here and it was only going to get worse. She stepped forward, every muscle tense, her instincts screaming that she should turn and run, but she had to do something. "Are you Joe? My name's Sierra." If she got him talking, maybe he would calm down.

Joe gave her a grim, angry look.

"We found them on the other island," Cameron said. "Seven of 'em, plus the dog."

Joe swung his head around. "Tell me you also found some food."

"Yeah, we got a big-ass bird," Cameron said. "And lots of fruit, potatoes, stuff like that."

Murmurs came from the crowd. Sierra spotted three other Black people, but everyone else except Priya was white. There were at least two sets of couples and five women in their twenties who clustered together. They all looked haggard.

Except for Joe, no one appeared to be armed.

"They found dinosaurs, Joe," Cameron added. "On the big island to the left."

"Dinosaurs?" blurted a man wearing a navy blazer.

"Bullshit," said the guy in the Lincoln t-shirt.

Sierra hitched her thumb down the canyon. "Why don't we go back to the village? We'll tell you all about it." It would give them a chance to defuse the situation.

"No." Joe pointed his gun at the kneeling man. The barrel looked like a cannon. "We have to deal with this business. There have to be consequences."

"What happened here?" she asked, trying to keep him talking.

"That's what I want to know," Joe said, his voice rising again. "Because it sure looks like Thad killed his goddamn followers."

"I killed no one," Thad said, raising his chin. His eyes sparkled like sapphires.

"Liar." The brute in the sleeveless t-shirt jabbed his finger at Thad. "You went Jonestown on 'em."

He was the kind of guy Sierra crossed the street to avoid. His wide-set eyes and down-turned mouth gave him a mean face. On his shirt, President Lincoln also wore a sleeveless t-shirt, and a label below read, "Abolish Sleevery." The absurdity seemed appropriate. Everything had gone mad.

"We came up here and found Thad praying by the pool," said a large woman with skin as dark as Sierra's mother's. "His followers were all laid out there. He insists he didn't do it. He says they were already dead." She dabbed her eyes with the back of her hand.

Sierra pointed at the dead children. "Where are their parents?"

"The parents are lying next to them," Joe said. "Except for her." He used his gun to point at a broad-shouldered woman in a blue dress.

Cameron walked over to her. "Lily, what happened? Isaac?"

Lily's eyes flitted to the row of bodies. The lips of the children were blue, their skin colorless. One of them was this woman's son, Sierra realized. A chill ran through her.

"Lily was at the village the whole time," said the large woman. "Several of us saw her there. She kept trying to break away and come up here."

"The bitch was in on it, I'm telling you," spat the brute in the sleeveless shirt. "It's like you always say, Joe. People must be punished."

Thad spoke up. "The angel Gabriel came to us." His voice boomed in the box canyon.

"What?" Sierra asked. "What are you talking about?"

Thad looked at her, and there was no doubt in the old man's voice. "The angel floated overhead while we witnessed the fornication." His cobalt eyes lasered into the crowd, where a man and a woman stood together, arms around each other.

"We thought we were alone," shouted the man, pulling the woman close. "How were we supposed to know those freaks were watching?"

"I don't get it." Cameron turned to Thad. "You and your followers saw Matt and Grace banging on the beach. So, why did you kill your own people? Why didn't you kill Matt and Grace?"

"Hey," shouted Grace. She glared, eyes fierce.

"The sinners will pay soon enough," Thad said.

"You're insane," Matt shouted.

Something clicked into place and Sierra thought she understood. She looked at Thad with disgust. "You didn't kill your people, you saved them."

Still on his knees, Thad rose up, straightening his back.

Sierra nodded, her throat tight and dry. "You didn't want them to get corrupted by anything else."

"Their very souls were at risk," Thad said quietly.

Sierra turned to Joe. "He drowned them to save them. In his mind, everyone here is already dead." She tried to imagine how it went down. Did the parents stand by and watch? She felt like vomiting. They had to have waited further down the canyon until they were called up for their turn. Parents couldn't watch that, could they?

Thad grinned.

Joe pulled back the hammer on his revolver. The click echoed in the canyon. "You figured it out, Sunshine." He pointed the gun down at Thad's face.

Sierra held up her hands. "Wait, wait, wait. Joe, let's do this right." If he shot Thad, she really would puke. "We'll hold a trial."

"Yeah, a trial," someone shouted from the crowd.

Someone else yelled, "Shoot him."

"Sierra, Sweetie, back away," Waldmire called out.

She stood her ground. "People shouldn't watch this, Joe." She swung her arm toward Kim and Barry, standing further down the canyon with their father. "Those kids shouldn't see this. It's barbaric."

Joe looked off to the side, then back at Sierra. The silver gun trembled in his hand, still pointed at Thad.

He can't do it, she thought. There was hope.

Yellow teeth appeared inside Thad's crescent smile. He tilted his head, looking past Joe to Kim and Barry. "You found more children," he said. "Let me save them, too."

Joe pulled the trigger.

The sound boomed off the walls as the top of Thad's head exploded. His body slumped backwards. Dark chunks of gore splattered the ground. Several plunked into the pool.

Sierra looked away. She actually wanted to vomit now, but she couldn't. How had everything gone so horribly wrong?

For a long moment, no one said anything. The only sound came from the waterfall splashing into the shallow pond.

The brute in the ludicrous t-shirt broke the silence. "What about Lily? I'm telling you, Joe, she was in on it."

"He's probably right," Morrie said, still on the ground next to his brother's body.

"She was in the village," insisted the large woman. "We all saw her."

Joe swung the gun around, parting the crowd. Lily thrust out her broad shoulders. She looked at peace.

Sierra felt dizzy. Would this madness never end? She took a deep breath. "That's exactly what she wants. Thad couldn't kill himself because he thinks suicide is a sin. She wants you to do it for her. Don't give her what she wants, Joe."

Lily glared at her and Sierra knew she was right.

Joe gave Sierra the slightest nod and lowered his gun. He narrowed his eyes at Lily. "You can spend the rest of your days thinking about how your little boy drowned."

Chapter Forty-One

David pulled his children's faces against his chest. Dear Jesus, how much had they seen? They certainly knew what happened. There was no escaping the roar of the gunshot.

Kona pulled on her leash, whimpering.

He squeezed his eyes shut. These lunatics were killing each other. He'd wanted to find other people. He'd wanted to build a community where his kids could be safe. Instead, they'd come to a place where they killed children, and now a madman was carrying out public executions.

When David opened his eyes again, he saw something new.

A blurry cloud floated thirty feet above Joe's head, a smear in the air, drifting in front of the waterfall.

He squinted. The shape hovered directly above the crowd, where none of them could see it without looking straight up. But from back here, away from everyone else, it was in plain sight.

Thad claimed he saw an angel when he ran into that couple screwing on the beach. Wayne had seen something overhead when Juliana was killed. And Barry had seen it on the mountaintop.

David blew out a sarcastic huff. "There's your stupid angel." It wasn't any angel, of course. It had to be something alien, some weird part of this horrible screwed-up world.

Joe looked his way. "What?"

David pointed. "Just look."

Most of the crowd turned their heads toward the waterfall spilling out from the back wall.

The warble of air rose upward and passed out of the canyon, becoming virtually invisible against the blue sky.

"It's what Thad saw," David stammered. "It, it … it's gone."

"Come here," Joe said, waving him closer with his gun. "All you new people, gather around."

David didn't know what to do. He wanted to take his kids and run, but he wasn't sure what would happen if he tried. Would Joe shoot him, too? Plus, he couldn't just abandon Sierra, Josh, and Waldmire. He shuffled Barry and Kim behind him. "I don't want any trouble," he called out.

Joe's face softened. Somehow it made him even more frightening. "It's okay. We're all going to be okay. Come on over."

Josh, Waldmire, and Sierra crept toward Joe. Randall was already close to him.

"Dad?" Kim's eyebrows pulled together.

David glanced back at his kids. "You guys stay here," he said under his breath.

Barry was silent. David hoped the boy didn't understand what was going on. He resisted an insane laugh. *He* sure as hell didn't understand what was going on. He walked toward the others.

"Those your kids?" Joe asked.

David swallowed. "Yes. I don't want them to see the bodies. They've been through enough. My son's only six." He also didn't want them to see Thad's brain matter scattered across the ground.

"Fair enough." Joe held his arms wide and ushered everyone away from the pool, meeting David halfway. A few people still had their hands over their ears from the gunshot.

The crowd of two dozen villagers clumped together and moved to one side of the shallow stream, staring at the new people. David joined Sierra, Waldmire, Josh, and Randall on the opposite side. He looked up, hoping the cloud would reappear, but saw only pale blue sky.

Joe swiveled his head from the newcomers to the villagers. "Pay attention now. Things are gonna change around here. We're going to have some rules. Everyone needs to pull their own weight." He jabbed two fingers toward the ground. "I'm not going to bust my ass while half of you wander off to pray all day."

"The people who did that are dead now," said a middle-aged man wearing a blazer.

Joe shot daggers from his eyes. The man looked down and Joe continued. "I'm going to keep everyone safe. Including you new people."

Several heads nodded. Others scowled.

"What do we do about them?" asked one of the villagers, gesturing toward the bodies.

The crowd rustled, many of them sniffing back tears.

Joe swung his head around. "We've got a lot of burying to do. I want graves dug before dark."

Cameron stepped forward. "I need a group to come with me to the raft to get the food. The bird we killed has enough meat on it for everyone."

David took a deep breath and tried to formulate a plan. He and his kids would help unload the raft. Joe could have the goddamn food. Once everything was unloaded, they would row back to the first island.

And then what?

They couldn't survive there alone, not with Entelodonts and terror birds running around.

Joe's eyes narrowed. "How big is this bird?"

"It's like an ostrich." Cameron said. "We also brought some supplies. Clothes, binoculars, even a small first aid kit." She looked over at a short young Indian woman. "Charlie's body is on the raft, too."

The woman nodded softly. Her dark pupils were dilated with shock.

Joe turned to the long-haired thug in the Lincoln t-shirt. "Burt, take some men down to the raft and collect everything. Put it all away in the sheds."

Burt nodded. "You got it, boss."

Josh looked at David and Sierra. "I left my knife on the raft." He turned to Joe. "I'm keeping it." His lower lip trembled. "It was my dad's."

"I'm sorry, son," Joe said.

David couldn't believe his ears. "You can't just take our property." His wallet was in one of those bags, with his only photo of Lindsey.

Joe stared off to the side for a moment, as if someone was calling to him, then stepped closer to David. "I can't keep everyone safe, unless you all do what I say."

"Safe?" David spat. "Are you fucking insane? You just blew a hole in that man's face." He could almost see Lindsey shaking her head at him. Why couldn't he keep his mouth shut?

Joe put one hand on David's shoulder. He flinched. The gun was in the other hand, down by his side. "I did what had to be done." Up close, Joe's skin was clammy and his breath smelled like shit. "I'm responsible now. You got that?"

David pursed his lips. Sweat trickled down his back. "Sure."

Joe stepped away and swung his head around. "Everybody just needs to calm down." He pointed at the bodies. "We're going to establish some order around here, so we don't end up with any more of that."

Some of the people in the crowd nodded. Others looked away.

David kept his mouth closed.

"Come on," Joe said. "We've got work to do."

Chapter Forty-Two

Sierra dug in the soil with a flat stone, her hands raw and dirty. Thad's head exploded again in her mind, an after-image she couldn't shake.

The bodies of Thad's victims lay several yards away, against a backdrop of pine trees, waiting to be buried.

She crouched in a shallow grave next to Waldmire, scraping dirt loose with her rock while he scooped it into a reed basket.

"We have to get out of here," he whispered.

"Where? Back to the island where everything wants to eat us?"

"We can find a way to keep clear of them," he said.

"If you're wrong, we're dead," Sierra said. "Besides, that puts us back at square one, and it means abandoning everyone here."

"Everyone here is crazy," Waldmire hissed. He lifted his basket and dumped the dirt on a growing pile at the head of the grave.

"That isn't fair," Sierra said. She'd seen their faces in the canyon. Most of them had been terrified. She knifed her stone through the dirt, frustrated.

Waldmire hung his head. "I know. You're right."

They were in the woods beyond the side opening in the wall, just past the outhouses. Above, Joe paced between the graves and the bodies, one hand resting on the gun in his belt. Randall and David worked together a few graves over. Several of the villagers were digging the rest of the holes, while another group prepared the bodies, wrapping them in reeds and leaves.

Lily sat beside her son with her legs folded under her. She wiped his ash-colored face with the hem of her blue dress.

"Thad murdered children," Sierra whispered. "Maybe Joe didn't have a choice."

Waldmire's face fell. "There's always a choice."

Joe stopped above their hole. "What was that?"

She looked up but kept digging. "We're just sad about what happened," she said. "Thank you for letting us help with the graves. It's the least we could do."

Joe stared for a moment, then moved on.

"You don't execute people in public," Waldmire whispered. "Like you said, you hold a trial."

Cameron and Burt approached through the woods, carrying Charlie's body on the wooden stretcher. They placed him next to the others and Priya sat down beside him. She lifted a palm leaf from Charlie's face and cupped his cheek with her hand.

Lily rose and started toward her. Cameron moved to block her path.

"He was my brother," Lily said.

She was bigger than Cameron, with a neck like a telephone pole and the shoulders of a swimmer, but Cameron stood her ground, not saying a word. Lily grimaced and returned to sit by her son's corpse.

Burt walked over to Joe. "Everything's off the raft. We hung the bird on the butcher's rack. Crystal and a couple of the women are carving it up."

"Good," Joe said. "That'll tide us over a little longer."

"They brought some decent gear, too," Burt said. "Binoculars. Water bottles. No more guns, though."

Sierra touched her jacket pocket, feeling the bulge from the vial of pentobarbital, glad she'd kept it with her.

"The little punk tried to keep his knife," Burt said. "I told him he couldn't have it, but he wouldn't listen." He grinned like the Cheshire Cat. "I made him listen."

Anger rose in Sierra's throat. Josh was just a kid, with no one to look out for him. She stood and stepped out of the hole. "What did you do?"

"Sierra, stop," Waldmire hissed. He reached for her hand, but she shook him off.

Burt laughed, making Lincoln jiggle on his belly. "Don't worry, babe. He'll be okay."

"Answer the girl," Joe said. "What did you do?"

Burt's eyes glistened. "I gave him a shiner."

Joe leaned forward until he was right in his face. "You can't go hittin' kids."

"What the fuck, Joe?" Burt looked hurt. "You always say that people must be punished."

Joe jerked his head off to the side, as if listening to a distant voice. He swung back to Burt. "Did anyone see?"

"Naw. We were down at the beach, by the raft."

"Is Josh okay?" Sierra asked.

"I'm sure he'll be alright," Joe said. He smiled wide enough to show his molars. "Kids are like rubber. Trust me. They always bounce back." Black stubble covered his chin and he stank of musk and sweat.

Sierra breathed through her mouth. "You have to understand, I'm responsible for Josh. I saved him on Earth. He wouldn't be here if not for me. He's like a kid brother."

Joe put his hand on her shoulder. She took a deep breath to keep from flinching. "I saved Thad," he said. "I'm the one who brought that psychotic son of a bitch here." He glanced over at the bodies. "So, you have to understand, I'm responsible for everything now."

Nodding, she stepped into the grave, eager to get away from him.

She dug silently until Joe wandered out of earshot, then whispered, "Do you think Josh is okay?"

"I expect he's probably fine," Waldmire said. "But I'll check on him to make sure."

"Thank you," she said.

"What are you going to do?" he asked.

"I don't know." She felt wiped out, both physically and emotionally. *Power through, Kiddo*, Rick Preston liked to say. "Maybe the worst is behind us. Maybe once everyone has a chance to cool off, Joe will ratchet down a few notches."

"And if he doesn't?"

Sierra shrugged. "Let's talk to David and see if he has any ideas. If we get enough people together, we can stand up to Joe. Or set off for another island. I don't know."

"It's a good plan."

She chuffed. "It doesn't feel like any sort of plan at all."

"Maybe not," Waldmire said. "But you're focusing on the right things. Let's just keep a low profile in the meantime. We'll figure it out."

His words gave her the strength she needed. She tore into the dirt. She was numb and exhausted, but at least she wasn't alone.

Chapter Forty-Three

The smell of roasting bird made Randall Pond's stomach gurgle with anticipation. If only he had a beer to go with it. He wondered if anyone here knew how to make beer.

Burt stood in front of him in line, his back a brick wall. He was Joe's bouncer, his muscle. The lazy sumbitch had bossed people around all afternoon. Randall needed to figure out how to get that job. But right now, he just wanted to eat and lie down.

His shoulders ached, knots groaned in his back, and he was covered with dirt from digging graves all afternoon. It wasn't fair. Josh only had to haul stuff from the beach and Dave's kids hadn't been made to do a damn thing.

A sexy-thin woman placed a huge yellow potato on Burt's plate. The asshole stood watching until she added a second one. Randall's mouth watered. It was good to see so many women. He stepped sideways and held out his woven-reed plate. It looked like the sort of thing they used in piss-poor countries in Africa.

The woman placed a medium-sized potato on Randall's plate, between the slice of bird meat and the pile of mushy squash. She turned to the next person in line.

"'Scuse me, ma'am," Randall said. "Could I get another? I'm awfully hungry." He gave her his most charming smile. On the hilltop, Randall had been able to eat whatever he wanted.

"Sorry, hun. Rules are rules. You don't wanna get me in trouble, do you?" Three big diamonds were inked in a row on her bicep, the winning combination on a slot machine.

Randall kept his smile going. "Oh, I bet you know how to find trouble all by yourself, ma'am."

"I ain't old enough to be called 'ma'am.' Call me Crystal." She had to be in her thirties, maybe even late thirties, like him. She smiled wide, showing crooked teeth and equally crooked intentions. She did not hand over another potato, however.

Randall walked to the next table, but there wasn't any more food. Instead, a man wearing a suit coat used Josh's knife to scrape the skin and gristle from the severed head of the terror bird. Randall chuckled. Josh had whined all day about his damn knife, when he ought to be thankful they weren't making him do that nasty work. The man looked up with a curious expression. Randall moved on.

A reed basket filled with feathers sat on the next table, along with a pile of personal belongings from Randall's group. Water bottles, wallets, cell phones, and lots of clothing. The binoculars Randall had used in Oklahoma peeked out from beneath a pair of panties.

He wandered over to the main fire pit. Dave and his kids sat out in the middle of the benches, surrounded by villagers. Kona wandered through the crowd, sniffing crotches and begging for handouts.

Jasmine, the big Black woman, was talking to everyone about ice cream flavors. "French Vanilla, Mint Chocolate Chip, Rocky Road." She was obviously trying to take their minds off everything that had happened.

The crowd rewarded her with nods and mumbles as she named their favorites. It was all pointless. It reminded him of the shit people would talk about in lock-up. There hadn't been any ice cream at Cushing Prison and there sure as hell wouldn't be any here. Someone called out, "Monkey Madness," which had to be made up. Who the fuck would eat ice cream named Monkey Madness?

Randall didn't want any part of that nonsense. He chose a spot off by himself and sat down with his plate on his lap. He ate the little sliver of bird meat first. It was reddish orange and tough to chew, but it tasted okay, kinda like the dark meat on a turkey. He immediately wanted more. He picked up the potato and took a bite, skin and all. It tasted like dirt, but he needed all the calories he could get. Between the rowing and the digging, it had been a long fucking day.

He definitely had to get in tight with Joe. It might take time, but he could work his way up. He'd done it with the Piper, and before that, he'd done it with the most powerful gang at Cushing. It was just a matter of endearing himself to the right people.

Someone stepped over the bench and sat down next to him. Randall shifted to make room. He didn't like being crowded. It felt too much like prison. A weight dropped onto his plate. He looked down and saw a new potato, bright yellow and bigger than the first. He looked up and saw a row of diamonds. *Jackpot.*

"I saved you one," whispered Crystal.

"Thank you." Randall took a bite, tasting more dirt, but happy for the food. "Where you from, anyway?" Asking people about themselves was the easiest way to be endearing.

"Henderson, Nevada. It's basically a Vegas suburb. I went to school in Cedar City, but flunked out. Too many weekends in Vegas. So, I moved to Henderson. Once you live there, it's not so alluring."

Randall didn't care two shits about her life story, but he liked the way "alluring" rolled off her tongue. Crystal was pretty fucking alluring herself. Her lips were big berries and her hair was the color of brandy. He had to remember to tell her all that when the time was right.

"They got you staying outdoors?" she asked.

"Yeah," Randall said.

After they'd finished digging the graves, Cameron had taken him to an empty patch of dirt under the trees on the far side of the village. He liked it better than the cabins. The one he'd peeked in smelled like feet and the walls felt as close as a prison cell.

"Were you friends with any of them people that drowned?" Randall asked. It was good riddance as far as he was concerned. Fewer mouths to feed.

"Not really. They mostly kept to themselves." Crystal looked down. "I liked the kids, though. They didn't deserve that."

Randall made a sad face he hoped was sympathetic. "Did those people really believe this is some kind of afterlife?"

Crystal smiled, her teeth as crooked as a bucket of fish hooks. "I know, right?"

He smiled back, imagining her with her clothes off. "What do you believe?"

"I believe in luck."

"We both found pods," Randall said. "Hard to get luckier than that."

"Sometimes you have to make your own luck." Crystal's words came out smooth and sweet. "I'm pretty good at that."

Randall's prick stirred in his pants. "What do you mean?"

She looked at him sideways. "Well, I'm lucky Joe is in charge now because he likes me." She tapped the remains of the potato on Randall's plate. "I get extra privileges."

"How do you manage that?"

She gave him a sultry grin, which looked especially nice because she wasn't showing her teeth. "I give Joe extra privileges from time to time."

Clever girl. They both knew how to endear themselves.

"Do you have any ideas about how I might get on Joe's good side?" Randall made a sad face. "'Cause I'm not as charming and pretty as you are."

Crystal blushed. "What're you good at?"

"I'm good with guns. I did a lot of hunting and shooting." He didn't mention the fact that most of his targets in the last month had been of the two-legged variety.

"I'll put in a good word for you." She stood, placing her hand on his shoulder for a moment. "I have to go clean up dinner now."

"Thanks for the tater." He winked. "I owe you one." He watched her round ass bounce along as she left and thought about how he might like to repay her.

After finishing his supper, he headed to the camping area. The last thing he needed was to get roped into dish duty. He hopped over the little creek and wandered under the trees. Smoldering campfires dotted the ground, each one surrounded by little nests where people slept at night. Clothes hung from branches all over the place, like in a homeless camp.

Waldmire sat by a small fire near the perimeter wall. Josh lay a few feet away, between the roots of the closest tree. The wall curved off in the darkness in both directions, another goddamn reminder of prison. Randall had liked the open hilltop better. He sat down and warmed his hands.

"Have you learned anything new?" the old man asked.

"I learned that digging graves is a pain in the ass." He turned around and put his back to the fire, letting the heat soak his muscles. Josh left the tree and came to sit with them. The kid had a black eye.

"These people are assholes," Josh said. "We need to get our stuff back and leave." The bruise around his eye shone in the firelight.

"Why ain't you in one of them cabins?" Randall asked. "I'm sure Dave would let you bunk with him."

"Mr. Williams is a wuss," Josh said. "All he ever does is talk. I want to stay out here with you."

Randall couldn't remember ever having a kid look up to him. "Well, if you don't wanna be a wuss, you can't let people give you any shit," he said. "You have to show 'em you won't put up with it. Otherwise, once they start, they never stop." It was a lesson he'd learned the hard way.

Josh nodded slowly, his eyes wide behind those little round glasses. One of the lenses was cracked. The kid was actually listening to him.

Randall lay back next to the fire and laced his fingers under his head, proud of himself. He'd done his good deed for the day.

Chapter Forty-Four

David held Barry against his side while Jasmine pulled back the reed curtain to one of the cabins. She gestured for them to enter. "We want y'all to stay here, at least for a little while."

Jasmine had shown David and the kids around the village, offering tidbits of information about each person they met. Names, former occupations, and where they'd come from. There were twenty-five people here, and most wanted an introduction. David was so tired he didn't think he could remember any of them.

He followed Kim into the dark single-room structure. A worn blanket lay across a pile of dried grass in one corner, forming a makeshift bed. Two short stacks of clothes sat along the wall. Kona padded over and sniffed them.

"Do those belong to someone?" Kim asked.

Jasmine picked up the clothing. She was moderately overweight but moved with a comfortable grace. "Charlie and Priya stayed here. Priya is going to stay in the women's cabin for a while. We don't want her to be alone right now." Jasmine's voice rose and fell in a sing-songy rhythm.

The cabin felt safer than camping out under the trees. Here, they'd have walls around them and Kona would let them know if anyone came to the door.

"Thank you," he said. "Tell Priya we'll be happy to move out when she's ready."

"That's very kind of you." Jasmine shook her head, cradling Priya's belongings in her arms.

"How the hell did things go so horribly wrong here?"

"Dad." Kim squeezed his arm.

His heart lurched. It felt exactly like something Lindsey would have done.

"I'm sorry," he said. "Sometimes my mouth runs off on its own."

"It's okay," Jasmine said. "That's a fair question. Until today, everybody mostly just stayed out of each other's business." She stared off into space. "Maybe that was the problem. Maybe if more of us had taken time to connect, this wouldn't have happened."

David reached out and clasped her hand. "I'm so sorry. As bad as today was for us, it must be hell for you."

The muscles on Jasmine's face twitched. "Thank you. Hopefully, things will be better now."

He wanted to ask if she really believed that, but he was afraid to hear the answer. He didn't know what to think. "Thank you for the cabin, and for showing us around. You've been very gracious."

Jasmine gave a small nod and left.

David walked over to the back wall and slid to the floor. Distant firelight passed through high windows on the side walls, creating a soft glow on the ceiling that filled the room.

Barry pulled back the blanket and inspected the straw under the bed.

Kim ran her hand along the back wall. "Who do you think built this?"

"I don't know," he said, too tired to give it much thought. "The aliens who brought us here, I guess." He reached out to ruffle Barry's hair. "I saw your cloud, Buddy. It floated over us in the canyon."

Barry's face lit up, and the sight of it gave David strength. "I told you it was real," Barry said.

"That's what you were pointing at?" Kim said. "What was it? What was it doing?"

He shrugged. "I don't know. Floating. Watching."

"Did you tell Sierra?"

"I haven't had a chance. I've barely seen her."

"She's gone to bunk in the women's cabin," Kim said. "She thinks it will help her get to know everyone. She's smart. Mom would've liked her."

David blinked away tears. Kim was talking about Lindsey in the past tense. He crawled over to the crude bed and held his arms wide, inviting his children to join him.

Barry lay on his bicep. "I miss Mommy."

David pulled both kids close. Kona snuggled up next to them.

Everything hurt. His ribs, his leg, his torn fingernails, and his heart. He hoped he would feel better in the morning. He needed a clear head to come up with a plan.

Kim moved around, unsettled. David had no idea how to reassure her. The thought of staying here with Joe in charge frightened him, but so did the idea of taking his kids back to the first island.

He slowed his breathing and tried to relax his mind. He would go to Sierra in the morning. They could talk quietly with a few people, like Jasmine and maybe Cameron, and try to get a better sense of what was happening here. Once they had enough information, they could figure out what to do.

Chapter Forty-Five

Cameron waited for everyone to leave the center of the village. Most had wandered off to the cabins shortly after dinner, eager to put a shitty day behind them. Three women lingered near the clump of trees behind the butcher's rack, waiting for a turn in the outhouses just outside the wall.

When the area around the main fire pit was vacant, Cameron walked to the work tables. She had quietly confiscated Charlie's Ruger and wanted to give it a good cleaning. Cleaning a gun always made her feel better.

The work tables were lit by the cookfires and nearby torches, but she didn't want to risk anyone coming along and spotting the gun. She entered the supply shed and felt around for an empty shelf in the darkness. This was something she could do with her eyes closed.

Within minutes, the pistol was disassembled. She used an old shirt to wipe down each part, then began putting it back together. As each piece snapped into place, she felt a tiny sense of satisfaction.

"You were supposed to keep Charlie safe," Priya said, standing in the entrance to the shed.

Cameron took a deep breath, frustrated she'd allowed someone to sneak up on her. "It was his own fault," she said. "He got foolish in his old age." *Foolish for charging after a giant bird and foolish for chasing this little mouse*, she thought.

"He talked about you a lot," Priya said. "He never stopped caring for you."

Was this her way of salting the wound? "Charlie never gave a damn about me." Believing that made everything easier. Cameron went back to reassembling the Ruger.

Priya shrugged. "Whatever you say, Cameron." She shifted on her feet. "We need to talk about what we're going to do now that Charlie is gone."

"You mean who you're going to fuck next?"

Priya looked away. "Don't be an asshole, Cameron. You're better than that."

Cameron smiled. Priya never was one to back down. "We don't need to do anything. Thad took care of the crazies and Joe took care of Thad. Everything's fine now."

"Don't be naive, Cameron. You're better than that, too." She stepped into the shed and lowered her voice. "Joe is more dangerous than Thad. He's been unraveling ever since we got here."

Watch Joe. He's trouble.

Charlie had obviously discussed Joe with Priya. Cameron's heart felt like stone. She should have been the one Charlie was confiding in, not Priya.

"What do you expect me to do?" she asked as she clicked the Ruger's slide lock into place.

"Find out what he's planning," Priya said. "He's holding a meeting. He'd never let me sit in on it, but I bet he'd let you."

Cameron tucked the gun into her pants. She sighed. She wanted to lie down and sleep. "When and where is this meeting?"

"Behind his cabin," Priya said. "Right now." She turned and walked away.

Cameron waited a moment, then wandered through the village to Joe's cabin, which sat in the back, beyond all the rest. Firelight flashed behind the small building.

Morrie, Burt, and Harold sat beside a small campfire while Joe paced back and forth, occasionally stopping to glance down. She wasn't surprised to see Burt and Harold there. They were Joe's biggest bootlickers. But Morrie seemed out of place. He wasn't a tough guy like the others. He looked so young he probably still got carded when he ordered a beer. Then again, Joe had avenged Morrie's brother today. Maybe that explained why he was here.

Cameron walked toward them.

Joe stopped pacing when he noticed her. "We were just talking about you."

"Words every girl loves to hear," she said.

Joe stared, seemingly unable to understand her sarcasm.

"Where did Charlie kill that rhino calf?" Morrie asked. He used a stick to tap the ground beside the fire, where he'd sketched a map in the dirt. The plateau was shaped like a giant bow tie. A jagged line representing the canyon bisected the narrow section in the middle, where the knot would be, starting at the bottom and ending just before it reached the top.

Cameron used her boot to indicate a spot on the left side, a third of the way from the center. "Somewhere around here."

"Where is that?" Burt asked, squinting and shaking his head.

Burt really was as dumb as he looked.

Morrie traced the zigzagging line. "This is the canyon." When the stick came to the end, he tapped the ground. "The ladder is here, by the waterfall."

"Where Joe shot Thad," Burt said, suddenly catching on.

It had been the perfect coup. Joe had solved the village's biggest problem and established his authority in one single act. No one had challenged him.

"That's right," Morrie said. He waved the stick over the whole sketch. "Climb up the ladder, and all of this is the plateau. Got it?"

Burt grunted. Joe resumed his pacing.

"Are the rhinos on both sides?" Harold asked.

His ridiculous hair was hidden beneath a black knit cap, but the silly bee tattoo was visible on the side of his neck. Apparently, it was a football thing, as in soccer. Harold was from Britain, where they took that shit seriously. Lucky bastard had been in Vegas when the pods showed up.

Cameron took Morrie's stick and swiped it back and forth along the top of the bow-tie's knot, just beyond the end of the canyon. "Yes. The rhinos can cross from one side of the plateau to the other on this little strip of land."

"How much of the plateau did you explore?" Joe asked.

She tapped the left half of the bowtie. "Maybe a third of this side. We stopped at a watering hole out in the middle. We didn't want to get too close to any of the herds."

Joe gazed off into the night. "We need meat. We need to make another kill."

Cameron dug at the ground in front of her with the stick, roughly where the village would be if Morrie had included it in his map.

"I'm telling you, we should just shoot one," Burt said.

Joe glared at him. "Did you figure out how to make ammo and forget to tell the rest of us?"

Cameron chuckled, happy that Joe wanted to conserve the few rounds they had left and even happier to see Burt put in his place.

"We're good on food for a bit, aren't we?" Harold asked. "We just got that ginormous bird." Somehow, he managed to make a British accent sound whiny.

"There's barely anything left of the bird," Joe said. "We ate most of it tonight. And we'd have a hell of a lot more food if you'd planted the fields when Charlie asked you to, but you were too goddamn lazy."

Burt chortled, making Honest Abe wobble on his t-shirt.

Joe leaned over him. "What's so fucking funny? You didn't do any better."

Burt crossed his arms and looked away.

"Why don't we go back to that other island?" Cameron asked. "There's fruit over there, giant birds, and even those pig things." She wondered if they should move there. This island had been picked bare.

Harold shook his head. "No way. They said there's dinosaurs over there, didn't they?"

"The dinosaur wasn't from there," Morrie said. "But that island is definitely not as safe as ours. Charlie was killed by that bird."

"A fuckin' bird," Burt said, shaking his head. "Charlie was soft."

Cameron clenched the stick and moved it in a circle, widening the hole. She tried not to let her anger show.

Joe jabbed two fingers in Burt's direction. "That's right. He was too goddamn soft. Look where it got us."

Morrie lowered his eyes.

Joe put his hand on the pistol grip sticking out from the front of his pants. "We're down to thirty-two people, and that's counting the seven new ones. Charlie should have done something about Thad a long time ago."

Cameron drew in a deep breath through her nostrils. Conflicting emotions swirled in her chest. He was right about Thad, but it wasn't fair to blame Charlie.

"We're staying on this island," Joe continued. "We don't know what's out there, and I'm not gonna risk any more lives to find out." He looked at Harold. "It couldn't have been a dinosaur. They all died thousands of years ago. But whatever it was, we're not going to lure another one here. There's plenty of those rhinos. We just need to figure out how to get one of them off by itself."

"What about the dog?" Burt asked. "It's got some meat on it."

Joe's mouth dropped open. "Great idea. Brilliant. Maybe we should dig up the dead people and cook them too?"

Burt looked down.

"Charlie killed a rhino shortly after we got here." Joe said, tapping the map with the toe of his boot. "If he could do it, we can do it. We just need to figure out how."

"Charlie got lucky though, didn't he?" Harold said. "Those rhinos, they'll run you over."

Cameron rolled her eyes. Harold was such a pussy.

"Priya might have some ideas," Morrie said, looking around at the others. "She found the salt and showed us how to preserve meat with it."

Harold nodded. "Yeah, yeah, maybe some of Charlie's smarts rubbed off on her."

Burt laughed. "That's not all he rubbed off on her." He somehow looked angrier when he was laughing.

Harold giggled.

Cameron imagined thrusting her stick into Burt's eye, all the way to the back of the socket.

Joe stood still. "Priya's barely a hundred pounds soaking wet. What the hell is she going to know about hunting?"

"How is Priya doing?" Harold asked.

It took Cameron a moment to realize the question was directed at her. "She'll survive."

What else could she do? What else could any of them do? The dead were gone. She'd cared about Charlie, too, but nobody asked how she was doing.

"What about the new people?" Joe asked. "I hear the thin guy with the puffy eyes is a good hunter."

"Randall," Cameron said.

Joe nodded. "What about the others? Any skills we can use?"

"Yes," Morrie said. "David is a doctor."

Joe snorted. "When was the last time anyone got sick here?"

Morrie looked down. "Never."

"Exactly."

Cameron rolled her eyes. Joe was ignoring the fact that people could still get injured.

"What about the others?" Joe asked.

"Waldmire is a retired judge and Sierra just completed her MBA," Morrie said.

Joe swung his head sideways, staring off into space, as if listening to something. He nodded. "Yep. They're all just more mouths to feed. Which brings us back right where we started. We need meat."

"When's the last time anyone's even seen those rhinos?" Burt asked.

"Nobody's been up on the plateau for weeks." Joe said. "We need to scout it out. That'll give us some ideas. First thing tomorrow, Harold, you and I will go, and let's take Randall with us. That'll give us a chance to check him out, too."

Everyone got up to leave. Cameron watched Joe walk to his cabin.

Charlie had been right. Joe was definitely trouble. The guy seemed to be holding on by a thread. But she was glad to see him prioritizing food. If they were able to kill a rhino, the extra meat would help everyone feel better. Maybe they could put all this ugliness behind them.

The most important thing was to give Joe a chance to cool off. Once he saw that everyone could work together and get shit done, he would dial down the rhetoric.

Thankfully, the village was silent. Nobody was going to cause any problems tonight, not after ten deaths and an execution.

Chapter Forty-Six

"Dad." Kim's voice pulled David awake.

It took a moment to realize where he was. The cabin. The village.

"What's the matter, Sweetie?" he whispered, trying not to wake up Barry.

"I ... it's nothing." She tugged her hair.

David put his hand on her cheek.

"Is it Mom? I miss her too."

Kim let out a puff of air. "Mom, my friends, everything." Her voice hitched and she hugged him. "I miss her so much."

He pulled her tight, ignoring the pain in his ribs. "I know."

She tensed. There was something more.

"What's going on?" he asked.

"Josh wasn't at dinner. He didn't eat." Her voice trembled. "I took him some food after."

"I thought he annoyed you," David said.

"Of course he annoys me," Kim said. "But he's the only other kid left now besides me and Barry." Her voice went quiet. "He's all alone."

"He'll be okay, Sweetie," David said.

"He's going to get caught."

A worm of worry crawled up David's spine. "Caught doing what, Kim?"

She was silent for a long while before answering. "He's going to steal his knife back."

David exhaled. As his body deflated, he felt the hard ground beneath the thin layer of straw.

"Please talk to him," Kim begged. "He doesn't have any parents. He doesn't have anyone to help him. Even back home, I don't think his parents were very good. He needs someone like you."

Warmth filled David, and not just from his daughter's praise. Her empathy for Josh made him proud. "Okay. I'll say something to him. First thing."

"No, Dad, tonight."

He turned to face her. "What?"

"He's going to do it tonight."

David sat up, his ribs complaining against the motion. "He's camped out with Waldmire and Randall, right?"

"Yes."

"Okay. Stay here."

He rose. Kona tried to follow him to the door, but he told her to stay. He wanted her to keep watch on the kids.

As he left, Kim whispered, "I love you, Daddy."

He smiled. Her words made it worth the trouble.

The air temperature was the same at night as during the day, which still felt unnatural. A few small fires flickered around the village, giving him enough light to make his way toward the camping area. Everyone seemed to have gone to bed.

He was glad Kim had confided in him. And she was right. Josh didn't have anyone. The boy had looked up to Wayne, but now he was alone. He had to be terrified after seeing the execution, not to mention those dead children.

A small crash came from the center of the village. It sounded as if something wooden had fallen over. David detoured in the direction of the supply sheds. Short flames danced in the main fire pit. Three reed baskets sat just outside one of the sheds.

Inside, Josh mumbled to himself and dug through wooden shelves in the dark, knocking things over as he went.

"Josh," David whispered.

The teenager spun, his fists in front of him.

"Easy. It's David."

"What do you want?" Supplies littered the ground.

"I want to keep you out of trouble."

Josh huffed. "I'm already in trouble. This whole place is trouble. They're assholes."

David smiled. "Yes, some of them are."

Josh's face softened. A small hematoma darkened the skin under one eye. "The asshole with the long hair hit me." He sounded close to tears. "He's like three hundred pounds, and he hit me."

"Jesus. What happened?"

"I tried to stop him from taking my knife."

"And you think taking it now is a good idea? Josh, you're only going to make things worse."

Anger and defiance filled Josh's face.

"I'm sorry. Look, why don't you come bunk with me in the cabin." That way he could keep an eye on him. "Tomorrow, I'll talk to Joe about getting your knife back."

Josh said nothing.

David picked up a basket. "Come on. Let's put this stuff away before someone finds us here, okay? Where does this go?"

Josh yanked the basket from him. "I'll do it."

Thank God. He'd gotten through to him. David reached for another basket sitting outside the entrance.

Inside the shed, Josh said, "A-ha!" He spun around, holding the knife in front of his face. "Nobody will give me any shit now."

David sighed. "You know that isn't true." He extended his hand. "Come on. Please give it to me."

Josh pulled the knife away.

"We'll figure out how to get it back. I promise."

The boy stared at the blade. Finally, he handed it over.

David squeezed the grip. It fit his hand perfectly, and he had to admit, it made him feel powerful.

"What the fuck is going on?" Joe asked.

David swung around, holding the knife in front of him. Joe jumped back, as if dodging the blade, even though it missed him by a mile. Burt loomed behind him.

Heavy dread fell on David's chest.

"Stealing weapons," Burt said.

"It isn't stealing," Josh said. "It's mine."

David kept his voice slow and even. "I can explain." He lowered the knife.

"I don't want to hear it," Joe snarled.

Burt snatched the knife from David's hand, moving fast for someone his size. "This tough guy came at me today," Burt said, holding up the eight-inch blade. "I bet he was planning to come at me with this."

Joe glared at David. "You're attacking my people?"

David winced. Joe was confused. He hadn't attacked anyone. Burt was obviously referring to Josh.

"Just calm down. You don't understand." Condescension and frustration crept into his voice. "That is *not* what—"

"I understand plenty," Joe growled. He moved closer, getting right up in his face.

David's chest tightened. He brought up his hands to push Joe away. "Back off and let me explain."

Joe punched him in the gut.

David doubled over, sucking air.

Josh whimpered. Burt laughed.

Morrie ran up. "What's going on?"

David tried to focus, but tiny motes swam in his vision.

"One of our new people is a thief," Joe said. "I can't let this go. I just can't. You all saw what happens when there's no discipline."

"What're you going to do?" Morrie asked. The fear in his voice sent a cold shiver up David's spine.

"He needs to be incarcerated," Joe said.

Morrie nodded. "I'll put him in his cabin." He reached for David, but Joe shoved his arm down.

"No. I want everyone to see what happens when you break the rules." Joe turned and pointed at the wooden structure behind the main fire pit. "Tie him to the butcher's rack."

Burt snickered. "I love it."

"What about the boy?" Morrie asked.

David held up his hand. He concentrated and spoke slowly. "Josh didn't do anything. He was trying to stop me."

Joe looked down at the boy. "Is that right?"

Josh's lower lip trembled.

"Get out of here," Joe said. "I don't even want to see you. If you try anything, you're next."

Chapter Forty-Seven

Sierra couldn't believe her eyes. She'd gone looking for David as soon as she woke up, only to find him standing with his wrists over his head, tied to the wooden frame behind the main fire pit like someone about to be interrogated by Russian mobsters.

She shoved through the small group gathered nearby.

Burt rose from his seat on the edge of the fire pit. "Joe said no visitors." A big black gun hung from a strap around his neck.

"Untie him, now," Sierra said, continuing forward.

Burt put his hand on the gun and slid in front of her. "Joe was explicit. No one goes near him."

"Come on, Burt," said one of the villagers.

"It's okay," David muttered. "I'm fine."

Sierra made fists at her side and looked up at Burt. "Why are you doing this?"

"Mine is not to question why, mine is but to do or die."

He was as mindless as he was ugly.

She turned and looked at the villagers. A couple of them lowered their faces.

"It's okay," said a man wearing a blue baseball cap. "We won't let things get out of hand."

She chuffed and pointed at David "This is already well out of hand," she said. "What happened?"

"He tried to take something that wasn't his," said a young woman standing off to the side.

Sierra was sure there was more to the story, but it didn't matter. She'd never get anywhere arguing with Burt. She had to find Joe. She stomped away.

A large hand grabbed her arm as she passed behind one of the cabins.

"Now where are you going in such a huff?" Jasmine asked, her voice melodious. The big woman pulled her aside.

She hitched her thumb over her shoulder, back toward David. "I'm going to make Joe stop this bullshit."

Jasmine struggled with a load of wooden bowls in her other arm. One fell to the ground with a wet thunk. "Just calm down before you go making things worse." Her eyes darted back and forth.

"I can't leave him there."

"Oh, yes you can." Jasmine's eyes widened and the tower of bowls started to fall.

Sierra caught them, getting sticky gruel on her arms. "What're his kids going to think when they see him like that?"

"They're fine, Shug," Jasmine said. "Dee and Felicia are keeping them busy."

The word "shug" jolted her. Short for "sugar," it was something her mother had called her, back when Sierra was a little girl. Back before she'd left.

"Reggie's keeping an eye on David," Jasmine continued. "He's watching Burt, too."

"Which one is Reggie?" Sierra asked.

"Blue baseball cap." Jasmine ushered her away from the cabins and upstream along the creek. "Help me with these dishes and give yourself time to cool off." They stopped at the perimeter wall, right where the creek entered through the thin gap, and Jasmine got to work, humming as she scrubbed.

"Why isn't anyone doing anything?" Sierra asked. "Why are they letting this happen?"

Jasmine made a disapproving click with her tongue. "How old are you?"

"Twenty-three," Sierra said. "What difference does that make?" She snatched a wooden bowl caked with grain mush and dunked it in the water.

"I would think that after twenty-three years, this wouldn't be the first time you've seen people standing around doing nothing while somebody with power was causing trouble."

Sierra scowled. "Yeah, I've seen plenty of that. That doesn't mean I understand it."

"People are scared," Jasmine said. She pointed off in David's direction. "The whole point of that nonsense is to send a message. Go against Joe and you'll be punished. Besides, You know what just happened. People here are hurting, too. I lost a friend. Morrie lost his brother."

"I'm sorry," Sierra said. Everything Jasmine said made sense. She was a smart woman. Not just smart, astute.

"Thank you," Jasmine said.

"So what are we supposed to do?" Sierra asked. She scratched food off the bowl with her fingernails.

"Give it time. Let everyone cool off. Once things go back to normal, Joe will calm down and quit trying to boss everyone around."

Sierra stopped scrubbing and looked Jasmine in the eyes. "How old are you?"

"More than forty." Jasmine said, straightening up as if to own her age. "Why?"

"I would think that after forty years, you would have learned that once a guy like Joe gets hold of power, he doesn't let go."

Jasmine's shoulders fell. She knew Sierra was right. It was clear on her face.

The sound of people walking came from outside the wall. Sierra craned her head through the narrow opening. Joe passed by, with Randall close behind, and a third man she didn't know.

This was her chance. She would talk to Joe and find some way to make things right. She dropped her dish and stood.

"What're you doing, girl?" Jasmine asked.

She answered with a Rick Preston classic. "Powering through." She squeezed through the gap in the wall.

"Be careful," Jasmine called out.

"I will," Sierra said. She jogged up the path to catch up with the three men.

"Good morning, Sunshine," Joe said without a smile.

"You have to release David. If he really took something, I'm sure he'll give it back. Or we can find some way to compensate for it. He can make it right."

Joe kept walking. "We already got it back."

Randall pushed past her, with Wayne's binoculars bouncing against his chest.

The third man gave her an awkward nod. He wore a knit hat and had a cartoon bug tattooed on the side of his neck.

Sierra hurried forward, catching up to Joe again. "Okay, then what's the point of tying him up? That doesn't help anything."

"Oh, that's where you're wrong," Joe said. "He's teaching everyone a lesson."

"That's insane," Sierra said.

Joe shook his head. "Insanity is letting everyone run around, doing whatever they want, without any rules. Look how that turned out."

She tried another tactic. "He's a doctor. You need his help."

"He let Charlie die," Joe went on. "He must not be very good. Besides, we don't need doctors. Nobody here gets sick."

"Nobody except Cameron, you mean," said the man in the knit hat. He spoke with a British accent.

Randall looked confused. Joe slapped him on the back. "You listen to Harold and stay away from Cameron. She's got the pox."

Randall grimaced. "How'd you find that out?"

Sierra felt disgusted. None of this was relevant.

"When we first got here, she went around asking for penicillin. Said she needed it for syphilis."

Randall sucked air.

Harold nodded. "I know, right? What good is surviving the end of the world only to have your knob rot off?"

Sierra rolled her eyes, doubting Cameron actually had syphilis. It sounded like she'd found a clever way to ensure these perverts left her alone.

They followed the burbling creek through the pine forest. The land rose slowly along the way and small boulders littered the ground.

"People still get hurt, even if they don't get sick," Sierra said. "David can help."

"Like I told you, he's helping," Joe said. "He's sending a message."

This was going nowhere. "How long are you going to keep him tied up?"

Joe worked his jaw for a moment. "Haven't decided yet. Right now, I'm focused on food."

They arrived at the canyon entrance, with its nearly-perfect vertical walls. Randall craned his neck. "How do we get up there?" The massive rock edifice rose above the treetops.

"There's a way up at the far end," Harold said. "It's a bit like a ladder, innit?"

Sierra didn't remember seeing any ladders, but she'd been a little distracted by the dead bodies. They entered the canyon. The walls felt close on both sides.

"What are we doing here anyway?" she asked.

"We? I don't remember inviting you along," Joe said.

"She does whatever she wants," Randall said, clearly annoyed.

Joe smiled at her, showing a wide row of teeth. "You've got more balls than most of the men here. I like that." The tight walls amplified his voice.

Harold sniggered.

The twists and turns of the canyon felt random and haphazard, but the stream always stayed right in the middle. Boulders leaned against the walls, as if they'd been placed there as decorations. They certainly hadn't broken off from the clean rock faces above.

"Tell me more about them rhinos," Randall said.

"You gotta see 'em," Harold replied. "Total mingers."

"But y'all killed one?"

"Charlie did," Joe said. "A small calf he found off alone."

Harold patted his belly. "We ate like kings, didn't we?"

"Why don't we just do that again?" Randall asked.

"Haven't found one by itself. They stay in herds." Joe rounded the last turn and stopped, placing his hands on his hips. Harold and Randall froze behind him.

This was where he'd shot Thad. The canyon widened to a space the size of a tennis court. Green moss covered the ground around the pool. Boulders sat along the walls, some short and round, others tall and slender. The waterfall gushed from a hole straight ahead, about fifty feet up, as if pouring from a pipe. It looked like a decoration at a water park.

"I had to do it," Joe said. "I didn't have any choice."

Sierra remembered thinking the same thing yesterday. Waldmire's words came back to her. *There's always a choice.*

She realized how right he had been.

Chapter Forty-Eight

David stood behind the main fire pit with his wrists bound over his head and tied to the wooden crossbeam above. He alternated between flexing his arms and rising up on his toes to keep his muscles from cramping. The routine helped his mind as well as his body.

After Sierra left, two young women had distracted Burt while a Black man roughly David's age crept up and gave him a sip of water. He wore a blue baseball cap and had a tired, sad face. He'd asked if David was doing okay.

David had simply nodded. Of course he wasn't okay, but what else could he say?

Burt wandered off an hour or so later, probably because it was lunchtime, judging from the rumbles in David's stomach. Even after he was gone, the villagers kept their distance. He couldn't blame them. Cutting him free would only make things worse.

He spotted Burt sitting on a bench, hunched over a plate.

David rose up on his toes, keeping the blood flowing and trying to get a look at whatever Burt was eating. Three villagers shifted together, blocking his line of sight.

He hung his head and looked at the ground. Were they trying to spare him from the torture of seeing food he couldn't have?

Two small shoes appeared, right in front of him.

"Daddy," Kim sobbed, touching his face.

The villagers were obviously blocking Burt's view, not his, so that Kim could visit. It touched him that they were doing that for a total stranger.

"You can't be here, Sweetie," he said. If Joe found out she was here, he didn't know what would happen. He also felt wretchedly embarrassed that she had to see him like this.

"It's all my fault," Kim said.

Tears welled in David's eyes. "No, no, no," he said, trying to be strong for her. "I'm fine."

"Bullshit," she sputtered.

Hearing his twelve-year-old daughter swear made him smile, considering the circumstances. "Is Barry okay?"

"Yes. He cried a lot. I tried to calm him down, but Dee did a better job than me."

"Dee?"

"One of the women here. Short blonde hair. She's nice. She made a game of pulling weeds and now he's filthy."

He nodded, grateful that so many people were helping out. "You need to go," he said. "It isn't safe for you to be here."

"No. I'm going to cut you loose." She pulled a small steak knife from a pocket in her cargo shorts and held it where he could see it. "I wanted someone to help me, but I couldn't find Sierra and Waldmire is busy cleaning up Barry."

David's mouth hung open. Another stolen knife. "Oh God, Kim, you can't." He looked from side to side, making sure no one was watching. "If you get caught, we'll both be in trouble. Big trouble."

Her eyebrows knotted toward each other. She returned the knife to her pocket.

"Put that back where you found it. And don't let anyone see you."

She blew out a sarcastic puff. "Half the people here barely know what's going on."

David nodded. "Some of them are in shock. I think they've been here so long they didn't realize how screwed up things were getting."

"The frog in the pot?"

He smiled. He had told her the fable of the boiling frog not too long ago. "Just help take care of Barry for me. I'll be out of here soon." In truth, he had no idea how long Joe would keep him tied up. But he had to believe. They both did.

Kim nodded, a glint of hope in her eyes. She fished a small pouch of leaves from a different pocket, then unwrapped them, revealing a portion of yellow vegetable. The inside of David's mouth felt like a washcloth that had been wrung out and left to dry. Kim broke off a piece of the food and placed it between his lips.

He let it dissolve on his tongue, soft with a buttery flavor. "Mmmh."

She fed him the rest of the vegetable. "I can bring you more. Or something else. They've been growing peanuts and Joe has them mashing peanut butter. I could sneak some away for you."

"No. Don't take anything that isn't given to you." He tried to appear stoic. "I'm not really hungry. Being tied up like this is an awesome diet plan."

"Dad." Kim sobbed the word into three syllables.

"Hey, listen. Your dad is tough. I'll be okay."

She wrapped her arms around him and squeezed, sending a sharp pinch to his ribs. He didn't care. The hug felt wonderful.

"Sweetie, go on now before Burt comes back. Take care of Barry. You guys stay out of trouble."

Kim squeezed him again and left.

He wanted her to come back. He almost called out to her, but he had to be strong.

A brawny figure pushed between the villagers lined up along the eating area. David tensed.

It wasn't Burt, though, it was Lily, the woman who'd allowed Thad to murder her son. She walked over and stopped in front of David, her dress a wall of blue.

"What do you want?"

"Tell me about the behemoth," Lily said. Her voice seemed too small for her body. Dark circles hung under her eyes.

"What're you talking about?" He wished Burt would come back and chase her away.

Lily stepped closer. She smelled sour, like a diabetic with bad ketoacidosis. "Is it true, the beast you saw? The dinosaur?"

"There's an island full of them," David said. "But I only saw the one that swam over."

"What did it look like?"

"A face full of teeth," he said. "A face full of teeth on two legs."

"Why did it go to your island?"

"I don't know. It followed the raft after it ate Wayne."

Lily stared into empty space. "An island full of them. Put there by God to do His bidding."

"How could you do it?" he asked. He knew he should keep his mouth shut, but he couldn't help himself. "How could you let Thad kill your boy?"

The big woman whispered, "Isaac was already dead. We all are. You, me, everyone here. We just need a little help moving on."

"You're insane."

She smiled thinly. "The Lord shall smite me with madness and dismay of heart."

Chapter Forty-Nine

Joe stared at the dried blood on the canyon floor. He pictured all that blood exploding from the back of Thad's head. Killing Pete in Yosemite Valley had made Joe feel sick. Killing Thad in front of the whole village had made him feel something different. He'd felt tough. Besides, if Thad had been allowed to live, what message would that have sent? Like his daddy always told him, *people must be punished.*

"You did the right thing," Randall said.

Joe snorted. "The right thing would have been to shoot Thad before he murdered children." Now that he was in charge, he would spot problems early and nip them in the bud, just like he'd done with David.

Harold took off his black beanie and shoved it in his pocket. Curly tufts of hair stuck out in all directions, making him look like a clown. He walked to the left side of the pool, swinging wide around the blood smear, and stopped at the column of horizontal lines running up the rock wall.

Sierra followed him, then looked back, her pert little mouth hanging open. "Did you guys carve this somehow?"

"Naw," Harold said. "That ladder was there when we got here."

It wasn't really a ladder. Ladders had rungs. But the openings in the wall served the same purpose. Each groove was three feet wide and about three inches tall, perfect for climbing.

"You first, Harold," Joe said.

Harold grabbed hold and started to climb. As he pulled himself up, his shirt rose from the back of his pants, revealing his Walther P22. It looked like Sierra noticed the gun. Good. A gun showed who was in charge. That's why Joe always kept the Smith & Wesson right up front, in plain sight.

When Harold was out of the way, she climbed after him.

Joe went next. The grooves curved downward inside the wall, making them easy to grip.

Halfway up, Sierra stopped and flexed the fingers on one hand. She looked down and drew in a sharp breath.

Randall, climbing last, let out a chuckle. "Dave would not like this one bit. You should'a made him climb this wall instead of tying him up, Joe."

"What're you talking about?" he asked, anxiety creeping up his throat. He hated it when people said things he didn't understand. It seemed to happen more and more often.

"He's scared of heights," Sierra said.

Joe relaxed. That wasn't surprising. David was like Charlie. Full of himself and soft as a worm.

Just like you, Joe's daddy said.

No, not any more, Joe thought. He was tough now. Maybe if he could figure out how to be as tough as his old man, the bastard would finally stop haunting him. "Keep moving," he barked.

They started climbing again.

Harold reached the top and pulled himself over the edge. "This is the worst part, innit?" He turned around and extended a hand to Sierra. His stupid curly hair made his head huge against the blue sky. "Come on. Wait till you see what I found."

Joe followed, crawling forward through the coarse grass before getting to his feet.

A giant woolly rhino stood twenty yards away, all alone.

He tensed. It was twice as big as a normal rhino and didn't really look like one. Normal rhinos had wise old eyes, but this monster had lifeless black eyes and a five-foot horn too big for its body. A massive hump rose from its shoulders and it was covered with coarse, shaggy fur like a yak.

A small herd grazed a quarter mile beyond it. This individual must have wandered off. Too bad it wasn't another calf. It had to weigh ten thousand pounds.

Sierra lifted Harold's shirt from behind and snatched his gun.

"Hey!" Harold grabbed at her, but she moved out of reach.

Joe's hand went to the Smith & Wesson in his belt.

Sierra crept toward the rhino, aiming at its face. Ropey strands of green slime hung from the creature's mouth, a mix of snot and spit and half-chewed grass.

"What the hell are you doing?" Joe hissed.

She kept her gaze forward. "I'm getting us dinner."

The animal was freakishly huge, its neck a mass of muscle, front-heavy like a buffalo. It laid its ears back and clicked its teeth. Sierra took two more steps. She studied Harold's gun for a moment until she found the safety.

She's gonna get herself killed, Joe's daddy said with a laugh.

The rhinoceros pawed the ground.

Sierra took aim, steadied her arm, and pulled the trigger. The gun popped, kicking up in her hands. A puff of dust appeared at the base of the giant horn.

The creature hunched low, dug its massive feet into the ground, and sprang off, tearing into the topsoil as it ran away.

Sierra shielded her face from flying dirt.

The rhinoceros thundered toward the herd, triggering a stampede across the plateau.

Joe marched over to Sierra.

"I hit it," she insisted. "I swear, I hit it."

"That gun is a twenty-two," he said. "It bounced off his skull like a rubber ball."

"Give it back," Harold said.

Sierra offered Harold's gun toward him, muzzle down.

Joe snatched it before Harold could and gave it to Randall. "Here, it's yours now."

"What?" Harold whined. "Wait a minute."

"You let a girl who doesn't know jack shit about guns take it from you," Joe said. He turned to Sierra. "What were you thinkin'?"

"It was off alone," she said. "Isn't that how you killed one before?"

Joe froze. She really didn't understand. There wasn't anything worse than being unable to understand. He took a slow breath. "The one Charlie killed was a calf, a third the size of that one. He lassoed it and staked it to the ground. Then he spent an hour spearing it."

"I see," Sierra said. "Well, I shot that terror bird we ate last night. I was trying to do the same thing here. Oh well, at least we learned what we needed to." She walked back to the edge of the canyon.

Joe's daddy snorted. *She's playing you, Joseph.*

He rolled his head from side to side, trying to get the goddamn voice to shut up. "What are you talking about?"

"We learned that they're skittish. We can use that. We need to get everyone up here, circle around behind the herd, and drive them forward. We'll make them stampede and fall in the canyon." She stood there with her back to the drop, a hundred feet straight down. Christ, this girl had some balls on her.

"What about the gap?" Harold asked, pointing past the end of the canyon. "It's twenty meters wide."

"Yeah," Randall said. "What's to stop them from running to the other side?"

Just past the end of the canyon, a narrow strip of prairie connected the two halves of the plateau. Beyond that, treetops rose from the back side of the island.

Sierra nodded. "Most of them will make it across, but we only need one or two to fall in. If they're panicked, it'll work." She made eye contact, as if seeking his approval. Joe stared right back at her, trying to figure out what he should do.

"I got a better idea," Randall said. "We should set this all afire. I saw a grassfire once in Texas with a hundred animals right in front. Deer, rabbits, and coyotes, all running side-by-side." He held his arms wide. "We could burn this whole plateau and maybe even cook some of 'em while we're at it."

"I like it," Harold said.

Randall grinned.

"But for a grassfire, you need wind, don't you?" Harold asked.

Randall's grin vanished.

"It would hardly burn," Sierra said. "Look how green everything is. Besides, you'd destroy their ecosystem."

"Ecosystem?" Randall threw back his shoulders. "We're trying to eat here."

"We also want to eat a month from now," Sierra said. "If we kill them all, there won't be any left."

Joe nodded. Sierra was thinking long term. It was exactly the kind of thinking they needed.

Joe's daddy laughed. *She's gonna be your downfall.*

Christ, he was sick of that asshole's voice. It muddled his mind. It made his thoughts bounce all over the place.

Randall and Sierra stared at him, waiting for a decision. Harold kept his distance.

Joe's daddy was wrong about Sierra. She'd been trying to help. She just needed to learn, and Joe would teach her.

"We'll do it your way, Sunshine."

Randall scowled and looked away.

"And David?" Sierra asked. "If you untie him, everyone will see that you're the right guy to be in charge. Firm but fair."

"Firm but fair," Joe repeated. His daddy had used those exact same words. "Alright."

Sierra nodded. "Thank you."

He decided to wait until after dinner, though. He couldn't let anyone think he was soft.

Chapter Fifty

Randall wanted to punch something. "If they knew what was good for 'em, they'd set a big fire and burn those goddamn alien rhinos. It'd be a hell of a lot safer." He sat with Waldmire and Josh at their little camping spot under the trees, angry that Joe hadn't listened to him and angry that Sierra had stolen his thunder. The trip to the plateau was supposed to have been Randall's chance to get in good with Joe. She'd ruined it.

Darkness had fallen and most of the village had turned in for the day. Josh poked the campfire with a stick. "They're not alien, they're prehistoric."

Randall turned on him. "What the fuck are you talking about?"

"The Indian woman says the rhinos are from the Plasta-seen Epic."

"Fuck. She uses fancy words to make herself sound better than everyone else. And now she's got you doing the same fucking thing. They're just big rhinos, and Sierra's dumbass plan is gonna get somebody killed. Maybe even your little girlfriend, Kim."

"She isn't my girlfriend," Josh said. "She's too young for me. Besides, I like Sierra better, even if she ..."

"What?" Waldmire asked, looking up all of a sudden.

It seemed to Randall that the old geezer had a crush on Sierra, too. The perv was always checking up on her.

Josh kept his eyes down. "My dad used to tell me if I ever dated anyone who wasn't white, he'd cut off my balls."

Waldmire pursed his lips.

Randall laughed. "Shit, my old man said worse than that. He didn't just talk, neither." He held up the back of his hand, displaying the little constellation of shiny spots.

Josh put his glasses on and leaned close to study them. "What happened?"

"Cigar burns."

"Whoah," Josh said.

Randall studied the burns. He'd never expected to impress anyone with them.

"What sort of plan did Sierra come up with?" Waldmire asked.

"It's a cattle drive," Randall said. "The canyon cuts the whole plateau in half, except for this little stretch at the end where one side connects to the other. We're going to make a skirmish line and drive them towards the crossing. Sierra thinks some of 'em will get knocked in."

Waldmire's face finally softened. "That's how the Blackfoot used to hunt bison."

Randall shoved a log in the fire, kicking up sparks. "I bet the whole herd just runs right across."

"Are you sure a fire would work better?" Josh asked.

Randall smiled. The kid really did look up to him. "Fuck yeah. A grassfire would take care of everything."

Josh nodded. "It sucks that they won't listen to you."

Randall blew out a huff of air. "They're worried about the goddamn environment. Fuck that. Light it all up and let the flames run every last one of them rhinos into the canyon."

A woman's voice came from behind him. "You would defile the most sacred place on this island."

Randall spun around. Lily stood at the edge of the firelight. The heifer had snuck up on them. "What the hell are you talking about?" he asked.

She looked down her nose at him. "The waters of Eden spring from that canyon. We were all reborn there by His holy hand."

"How do you know that?" Josh asked. "How do you know God brought us here?" The kid sounded like he wanted to believe her.

"God sent his heavenly messenger to shut the mouths of lions so they cannot harm me."

Her answer made no fucking sense. Randall had heard plenty of Jesus talk in lockup. It never helped anyone.

"That's from the Bible." Josh said. "Daniel and the lion's den."

Waldmire nodded. "Daniel six, twenty-two."

Lily studied him. "You know your Bible."

"It brought me through some tough times." Waldmire clasped his hands together. "But it helped me understand myself, not the world around me."

"I will pray for you." Lily turned back to Randall. "What is going to happen in the canyon?"

"That ain't for you to worry about, is it?" Randall said.

The woman looked down at the kid. "Do you miss your parents, Joshua? Do you want to see them again?"

"That's enough," Waldmire said. "You stay away from this boy."

Lily looked hurt. "I was only asking a question."

Randall stood and made a shooing motion. "Go on, git. Nobody wants to listen to your crap." She'd gotten off easy, considering what happened to her goddamned son.

Lily straightened, turned, and left.

Randall decided to follow her. "I'll make sure she stays gone." He was sick of the old man and the kid. He'd much rather be hanging out with Joe and Burt.

"What are you going to do?" Josh asked.

Randall laughed. "You want me to give her a beating?" The idea had a certain appeal. He needed to blow off some steam. He left the trees and hopped over the creek, letting the kid imagine whatever he wanted.

Up ahead, Lily disappeared into the women's cabin. From the sound of all the yammering inside, they didn't much like her either.

Randall followed her in.

One of the women stood in front of Lily with her arms crossed. "You're not welcome here. Go somewhere else." Six or seven other women, including Crystal, looked up from the floor, where they all had their own little spots.

Randall couldn't understand why anyone would stay in here. The air felt close, like it wanted to smother him.

Lily looked desperate. "Where am I supposed to go?"

Crystal came forward. "That's your problem. Now get lost."

"You want me to take care of her?" Randall asked.

Lily looked at him with defiance. "When we leave this place, we will go to our reward. You'll get what you deserve." She walked out.

Crystal stepped over a pile of clothes and touched Randall's arm. "My hero," she said with a teasing tone. The twinkle in her eye said something more.

She took his arm and led him out the doorway.

Lily walked away, disappearing in the dark.

Crystal pulled Randall in the opposite direction. "Let's go up to the canyon."

"Ain't that off limits?" Randall asked.

"It's okay." Crystal gave him a crooked smile. "Trust me."

They passed another cabin. A woman with short blonde hair stood in the doorway, with Kim peeking out from behind her.

"What're you lookin' at?" Randall barked. The last thing he needed was for someone to rat him out.

The reed door swung shut behind the woman as she disappeared inside.

At the high end of the village, Crystal slipped through the narrow gap where the creek flowed through the wall. Randall followed, and on the other side, he grabbed her arm, right on the row of diamonds. He knew the way to the canyon and he was done being led by a girl. He was going to blow off some steam after all.

Chapter Fifty-One

Sierra leaned against the perimeter wall in the dark. This spot was as far away from everything as possible while still remaining inside the village. Off to her left, the creek dissipated in a muddy bog. Somewhere to her right, the wall opened onto the path that led to the beach. People rarely came down here, even in daylight. Sierra had hidden her vial of pentobarbital under a rock just a few feet away.

Rows of tiny vegetables stood sentinel before her, gray outlines silhouetted by the campfires up in the center of the village, where David remained tied up, despite Joe's promise to free him.

Priya's voice came from the right. "Is that you?" The diminutive woman appeared, a shadow in the darkness.

"Yes. Thanks for meeting me here." She'd been looking forward to meeting Priya ever since hearing about her. She hadn't imagined it would be a clandestine meeting under the cover of night.

"Why the secrecy?" Priya sounded cold and guarded.

"I don't want to be overheard. I don't know who to trust here. You've got some frightening people in this village."

Priya snickered. "That's for sure. What do you want?"

"Two things. I want to ask a favor and I have a message for you."

Priya said nothing.

Sierra handed her the folded leaf pouch she'd saved from dinner. "Will you take this to David and check on him? It's just a few berries. Joe agreed to release him, but I'm worried he changed his mind. I'm trying to keep my distance. I don't want to give Joe any excuses to keep him tied up."

"That's probably smart," Priya said. "What's the message?"

"Right before Charlie died, he said to tell you that he loved you."

Dots of distant firelight glinted in Priya's eyes. She was silent for a long time and then said, "Thank you."

"I'm so sorry about what happened to him. He seemed like a truly good man."

"He was," Priya said.

"Will you take that to David?"

"Yes. But I want you to answer some questions first."

Sierra hadn't expected any conditions. "Okay."

"Do you remember your time in the pod?"

She thought for a moment. She remembered wondering if they'd brought enough supplies for whatever awaited them. They had water bottles, bags of spare clothing, and the first aid kit from Waldmire's medicine cabinet. Josh had been giddy with excitement.

"Not much," Sierra said finally, unsure what Priya wanted to know. "We were scared."

"Your pod opened thirteen days ago. Our pods opened seventy-seven days ago. That means you were in your pod for more than two months."

"What if we were all sent back in time?" Sierra asked. "Maybe your pods were sent a few months further back than ours."

Priya shook her head. "I don't think that's what happened. Woolly rhinos and terror birds were never alive at the same time as dinosaurs. They were separated by tens of millions of years. I think you must have been in some sort of suspended animation."

Sierra swallowed. The thought gave her an uncomfortable hollow feeling.

"Tell me about the dinosaurs," Priya asked.

"There were five or six different kinds," she said. "One was like Triceratops, but with more horns. There were little ones like turkeys and big ones that switched between two legs and four. Most of them had feathers."

"I would love to see one."

"Be careful what you wish for." Sierra's throat tightened at the memory of the Tyrannosaurus crushing Wayne in its jaws.

"Have you gotten your period since you've been here?"

The question was so far out of left field Sierra wondered if she'd missed something.

"It's been thirteen days since you arrived," Priya continued. "I know that isn't long enough to be sure."

"No, I haven't," Sierra said. "Why?"

"None of the women here have menstruated since we arrived. And no one has gotten pregnant. I think we've been sterilized."

Sierra's mind raced as she tried to juggle the information. "Wait. How could anyone risk getting pregnant here?"

Priya snorted. "People have made poor decisions around that topic for ages. Those of us with any actual sense used whatever birth control we brought with us, at least until it ran out."

"And by that point, you realized none of the women were getting their periods?"

"Bingo," Priya said. "Whoever brought us here must have done something to us. Chemically perhaps. Maybe even genetically."

Sierra crossed her arms, hugging herself. "Wouldn't we know?" She felt violated.

"You didn't know that two months had passed."

"We have to find whoever brought us here," Sierra said. "We have to make them undo what they did to us. If we don't, the human race is dead. We're the end of the line." Her emotions seesawed between deep despair and bitter anger. "Why? Why would they do that to us?"

Priya shrugged. "Maybe they're experimenting on us, like lab rats in a cage."

A cage. Those two words hung in the air and a piece of the puzzle snapped into place. "Holy shit." Sierra finally saw the picture.

Priya tilted her head.

"These aren't islands," Sierra said. "They're cages, habitats. It's all a big zoo."

"I already thought of that," Priya said. "It's too big. The islands go on for miles."

Sierra shook her head. "You're thinking in human terms. It's bigger than anything we would build, but it isn't too big for someone with magic floating pods." She huffed. "And suspended animation."

Priya was silent for a long time, then nodded slowly.

Sierra thought about everything she'd learned. It all fit. She flashed to a trip to the zoo with her grandmother, which brought back the smell of mothballs and coffee. Even as a little girl, Sierra could tell that the bear habitat was fake. The rocks, the pool, the waterfall, and a great hollow log were all arranged to form a scene from the Yukon, but everything was too perfect. There was even an artificial ramp to help the bears climb from the pool, just like that bizarre ladder running up the side of the canyon. "Each island is a different exhibit," she said. "A different ecosystem."

"Not just that," Priya said. "They represent different eras. Woolly rhinos *were* alive at the same time as early humans. And some terror birds coexisted with Entelodonts."

Sierra smiled. She was thrilled to have someone focused on finding answers with her. Someone smart. She only wished David was part of the conversation. "So where are the people from the rest of the pods?"

Priya shrugged. "Maybe they're in holding pens somewhere." She squinted. "I'm not sure it's a zoo, exactly. It's more like a wildlife preserve. A menagerie." Her voice grew sad. "Charlie and I thought this whole place was under some sort of quarantine. We thought we needed to be patient until whoever brought us here concluded we were safe." She looked down. "They aren't going to ever make contact, are they? We're nothing but specimens in a cage to them."

Sierra touched Priya's hand, which caused her to flinch. "We have to show them we're more than specimens. We're different from all the other creatures they've collected."

"How?" Priya asked.

"We're sentient. We've developed language and culture. We can be compassionate, we feel empathy. We cooperate, compromise, negotiate."

"No, I know all that," Priya said. "I meant, how do we show them we're different?"

"We have to find them, force them to acknowledge us. *We* need to make contact with *them*."

"They might not like that," Priya said. "What if they aren't friendly?"

"They saved us from extinction. They have to be friendly." Another piece suddenly clicked into place. "The dinosaurs went extinct because of a comet, too, didn't they?"

Priya nodded. "The Chicxulub impact."

Sierra felt giddy. Priya wasn't just smart, she was dorky-smart. It felt so good to be brainstorming, figuring shit out. This was how she wanted to spend her time, not dealing with people like Joe. "Maybe they send pods whenever there's an extinction threat."

"It's a solid theory," Priya said. "But it doesn't explain everything. How were dinosaurs collected, for example? They couldn't have climbed into pods on their own the way we did. And what about the woolly rhinos and terror birds? They weren't wiped out by comets."

Sierra shrugged. "I'm sure there's an explanation." That was all ancient history, literally. She was more concerned about the future. "If this is a cage, there has to be a way out. When we find our captors, we can ask them."

"What are you proposing?"

"We need to take the raft and search for the exit."

Priya shook her head. "Joe will never let you do that."

"If we get a large enough group together, we can stand up to him. How many people here would join us?"

"At least half," Priya said. "Probably more. But it won't be easy. Everyone's scared of him."

"Was he like this before?" Sierra asked.

"He's always been a bully," Priya said. "Charlie knew how to calm him down. But ..."

"What?"

"Something changed when we found Thad's people dead. Joe snapped."

Sierra puffed out a mouthful of air. "I can't imagine why. Look, if I was to talk quietly to people about standing up to Joe, who would you suggest?"

"Start with Reggie, Felicia, and Jasmine. Maybe Scott."

Sierra knew Jasmine and Reggie. She didn't recognize the other names.

"Until yesterday, I would have included Morrie," Priya added. "He's a good guy, but after what Thad did to his brother ..."

"I know," Sierra said. "What about Cameron?"

Priya flinched.

Sierra held up her hands. "Okay."

"No, no," Priya said. "Cameron is a good choice. It's just ... she and I have issues. She had a history with Charlie."

Sierra nodded. "I'll start asking around after the hunt tomorrow."

"Be careful," Priya said. "Everyone is on edge, traumatized. We've been here seventy-seven days, remember. It isn't purgatory, but it's definitely felt like limbo."

"I hear you," Sierra said. She started to rise, but Priya put her hand on her arm.

"Don't forget, Joe's got all the guns."

"If we get enough people together, he can't shoot all of us." Sierra meant it as a lame joke, but Priya didn't seem to take it that way.

"He doesn't have to shoot all of us," she said. "Just one. To make an example." She chuffed and pointed over her shoulder. "Like your friend, David."

Chapter Fifty-Two

David managed to doze in short stints by leaning back against the ropes. He woke up regularly to shift his position and keep blood circulating in his arms and legs. Burt abandoned his guard post at dinner time and didn't come back, but it didn't matter. David wasn't going anywhere. He'd begun to feel fuzzy, as if his head was stuffed with cotton.

About an hour after night fell, he woke up, sensing someone close by. Or something. Maybe a dinosaur. With his arms tied over his head, there was nothing he could do to defend himself.

"Who's there?" he asked.

A woman's voice said, "I brought you some berries." David detected an Indian accent.

Priya stepped from the shadows and placed fruit between his lips, one piece at a time, like inserting coins in a vending machine. He mashed them against his palate with his tongue and felt something close to euphoria as sweet juice watered the inside of his mouth.

He swallowed and summoned as much lucidity as possible. "There was nothing I could do for Charlie. I tried. I'm so sorry."

"Thank you," Priya said.

"Have you seen my children?"

"They're okay. Several people have been taking turns looking after them."

He forced a smile. "You're much nicer than Charlie's sister. She came by, but she didn't bring me anything to eat."

"What did she want?"

"I think she wants to kill us all so we can get sorted off to heaven or hell."

"Lily is crazy."

David snorted like a drunk. "There's a fair bit of that going around."

Priya laughed, short and curt.

"She still believes this is the afterlife," he said.

Priya grew serious. "Your friend Sierra has a better hypothesis. She thinks we're in a giant wildlife preserve. She wants to make contact with whoever put us here."

David blew out a long breath. "Good luck with that. You'll never get anywhere."

She squinted. "What do you mean?"

"Whoever put us here doesn't care what happens to us. They just want to watch."

"Why do you say that?"

"I think I saw one of them when Joe killed Thad. It didn't do a goddamn thing to stop him." David concentrated to keep from slurring his words.

"Wait, what did you see?" Priya leaned close. "What did it look like?"

"A blurry cloud floating overhead," David said.

"How big?"

"I don't know. It was hard to tell."

"Maybe if we can get their attention, they'll realize we don't belong in cages."

David looked up at the butcher's rack he was tied to. "You don't have to tell me that." He snickered. "But I still don't think you're—"

Priya cut him off, her tone suddenly loud and monotonous, as if lecturing. "You simply must not go into the storage sheds. You cannot take things that don't belong to you. If we don't all work together, the whole lot of us will suffer."

Why had she changed the subject so abruptly? David looked around, confused.

Joe stood a few feet away, a ghost in the dim light. "I appreciate you educating our prisoner."

David tried to keep from shaking. How long had he been listening?

Priya turned to face Joe. "He needs to be released," she said. "He can help us."

"Oh, he's helping, believe me." Joe said. "He's sending a message."

David took a deep breath. "Happy to be of service."

Joe chuckled and stepped closer. "Smells like you pissed yourself, Doc." His face was lined and weathered. Stubble covered his chin. "Tell you what. I'm here to commute your sentence."

David clamped his mouth shut, trembling. He didn't want to look eager, but he couldn't help it.

Joe pulled out Josh's knife and sawed at the fibrous rope above David's head. "I need you for the hunt tomorrow."

It took him forever to cut through the ropes. Finally, David's arms fell like dead weights. He dropped to his knees in the dirt. Every part of him ached. Electric pins and needles shot through his shoulders.

David knew he shouldn't say anything else, but he couldn't help himself. "I'm not going on any hunt. You tied me up like an animal. I can barely stand."

Joe crouched next to him. "Oh, you'll do exactly what I say. 'Cause if you don't, I'll tie your kids up here."

Chapter Fifty-Three

Cameron kneeled at the top of the cliff and helped Sierra climb over the lip. The last part was the most difficult. You had to pull yourself from the vertical wall over the edge onto horizontal ground, without any real handholds. Sierra nodded her thanks and moved out of the way. Word had gotten around that she thought this was all some kind of big zoo. Cameron didn't like the idea of being on display. If this was a cage, she wanted out.

For now though, she had to focus on the hunt. Burt came up the ladder next, huffing and puffing. His cheeks were red and sweat beaded on his forehead. He reached over the top with one hand. Cameron dug her feet against the ground and pulled.

Panting like a dog, Burt flopped over the edge, crawled across the grass, and rolled onto his side, cradling the MP5 submachine gun strapped to his shoulder.

Nearly everyone had been ordered up to the plateau. The only adults still in the village were Waldmire and Carol, who were keeping an eye on Josh, Kim, and Barry. Josh had bristled about being left behind, but Cameron thought he should count himself lucky. The plateau stank of rhino shit.

Three women came up the ladder next, a welcome change of pace after Burt. Cameron pulled up each one easily. They were all younger than her, and they always stuck together. She felt a pang of jealousy. She hadn't gotten close to anyone in the village.

Next up was Scott, the guy who never took off his sport coat. The jacket's shoulders bunched up around his ears as he climbed.

"That's a bit puckersome, don'cha think?" he said, looking back over his shoulder.

She pushed him out of the way and returned to the cliff.

A trembling hand reached over the edge. Cameron pulled it and David's face appeared.

In basic training, she'd seen new recruits pass out while running drills on hot, humid days. They turned a pale sickly blue and their eyes rolled up. David looked close to that point.

She squeezed his hand and helped him over the top. "You did it. Nice job."

He scurried through the grass and staggered to his feet. Color bloomed slowly on his face. "Thanks," he stammered. "I'm not so good with heights."

Joe and Burt snickered.

Cameron gave them an angry glare. David had to be sore as hell from being tied up, but he'd still made the climb. That should count for something. She turned back to the ladder and helped the last few people up.

"Everyone gather around," Joe said. He looked across the plateau with the fancy binoculars he'd taken from David's group. A herd of woolly rhinos grazed nearly a mile away.

Roughly thirty people formed a half circle around Joe. He lowered the lenses and addressed them, his voice stern. "I don't want any screw-ups today, understood?" His head did that goofy swivel back and forth.

Cameron clenched her jaw. *Way to build up your team, Captain.* Charlie's warnings had proven true. Joe was definitely trouble. And he wasn't calming down, he was getting worse.

"We'll head over to the back side first." He pointed across the thin stretch of land that connected the two halves of the plateau. All eyes followed. "We'll walk single-file along the back edge until we pass that herd." Joe's arm swung in a wide arc. "Once we're beyond them, we'll spread out to form a line and then march back this way."

Joe walked over to the little stretch of land between the end of the canyon and the back of the plateau. "Most of them will run across here, but one or two should fall into the canyon."

A few villagers nodded. Cameron had to give them credit. She saw more bravery on their faces than she'd expected.

"When we get close, I'll give the signal," Joe continued. "Everyone needs to yell and charge."

"What if they turn on us?" Crystal asked. She looked pale. Maybe not as bad as David had looked earlier, but definitely nervous.

"Those of us with guns will be spaced out in the line. We'll scare them away if necessary."

Only Cameron and four others were armed: Joe, Burt, Randall, and Morrie. It wasn't much.

"Why don'cha just pick one and shoot it dead?" Scott asked, miming a rifle shot.

"Do you have a bunch of spare ammo in that stupid jacket?"

Scott chomped his mouth shut.

Joe swiveled his head again. "Those of you with guns, do not fire without authorization."

Fuck that, Cameron thought. Joe carried their only AR-15, which still had three full clips by her last count, not to mention the stupid revolver in his pants. She had only her Beretta M9 and Charlie's Ruger.

"We have to startle them," Sierra said. "We have to trigger a stampede. That might require a shot or two."

Joe's neck reddened. "We need to preserve ammo. If everyone yells and charges like I said, they'll stampede."

The villagers looked at one another, clearly unenthusiastic about charging into a herd of giant prehistoric rhinos, but Joe didn't seem to care. "Let's move out. Morrie, take the lead."

Morrie carried an ancient M1 Garand. It wasn't exactly designed for big game, but a rifle was better than Cameron's handguns. He crossed the little strip between the two halves of the plateau and turned left. One by one, the villagers filed behind him. Cameron waited for the end of the line.

She wasn't sure what she should do about Joe. She didn't want to get into a shooting match with him, but she had to do something before he started killing people. She knew one thing for certain. If a fucking rhino charged her, she wasn't going to wait for his authorization to shoot it.

They skirted along the edge of the plateau, above the treetops on their right. Cameron wondered if there was an easy way down on the back side of the island. It might be nice to spend a few days exploring on her own. Maybe a few months. If Joe wasn't fit to lead the village, who was? She sure as hell didn't want the responsibility.

She marched along, careful to keep clear of the edge. If there was a way down, it wasn't here. She couldn't even see the forest floor below.

"We're coming for you," Harold shouted as they passed the herd. "You lot are going *down*."

Cameron rolled her eyes. The clown was trash-talking the wildlife.

The woolly rhinos clustered together in the center of the plateau, grunting and snorting. Charlie had identified four different herds, ranging from twenty head to more than forty. This was one of the larger ones. She spotted several calves, which probably made the adults extra protective. She wondered why they were allowed to reproduce when all the humans here were apparently sterile. Maybe the zookeepers were running low on giant rhinos.

Several of the beasts raised their heads as the villagers snaked along the edge of the plateau, but they didn't seem too concerned.

When Morrie passed the herd, he turned left and the line followed him. He walked a half mile across the plains to the other side, his curly orange hair easy to see against all that green. Once they were spaced out, each person was separated from the next by about a hundred feet. It wasn't a very solid line, but the gaps would shrink as they worked their way back toward the canyon, where the plateau narrowed.

The line was complete when Cameron finally turned left. Twenty-eight people stood across the open plains. Out in the middle, Joe held two fingers in the air, then lowered his hand in a chopping motion. Everyone started forward.

Everyone except Crystal. She froze in place with her arms crossed, clasping her elbows. Cameron waved, trying to get her moving, but Crystal stood motionless, staring at the herd.

Cameron hissed her name. Crystal shook her head.

The line continued forward, leaving a wide gap where Crystal should be.

"God damn it." Joe's voice boomed across the plains. The line halted. "Get moving!" Several rhinos looked up. One pawed the ground.

Cameron missed Charlie more than ever. Joe really was going to get them all killed.

"Hey," Sierra called out, her voice calm. "It's going to be okay." Crystal looked at her and Sierra continued. "If we stay in line, we're a wall. They'll move away from us."

Crystal lowered her arms, but still looked unconvinced.

"Everyone has to work together." Sierra wasn't shouting, but her voice carried across the grasslands. "The rest of us need you. We're counting on you. It's going to be okay."

Crystal squared her shoulders and took a step.

Sierra nodded, urging her forward. "You've got this."

When Crystal caught up with the rest of the line, the march resumed.

Cameron snorted. Sierra had known exactly how to handle the situation. Not only that, this hunt had been her idea.

Too bad she wasn't in charge.

Chapter Fifty-Four

David marched toward the rhino herd, still wobbly, but feeling better after a night's rest. Spending time with his children had helped him recuperate as much as the sleep. Barry had shown him a reed mat that Dee taught him how to weave, and Kim had told him about throwing rocks at targets with a woman named Felicia whose arm was deadly enough to take down squirrels.

He plodded forward, Kona's leash coiled in his fist like a whip. It wasn't much of a weapon, but it gave him some comfort to know that Kona was unleashed back at the village. Hopefully, she'd protect the kids if they needed it.

As he drew closer to the giant creatures, he realized the eight-foot length of nylon would be as useful here as twine. These animals were twice the size of any rhinos he'd ever seen at the zoo.

He forced himself to keep going. The sooner he got this over with, the sooner he'd get back to Kim and Barry. Of course, he still had to climb down that goddamn wall. One thing at a time. He marched toward the canyon, maintaining his place in the line. Two dozen yards to his left, Burt walked along with a big gun in his hands, probably keeping tabs on him.

David skirted around a two-foot pile of rhinoceros dung, wincing at the stink of ammonia and sulfur. At some point, they were all supposed to charge and trigger a stampede, but Joe hadn't been clear about when that would happen. David had considered pointing out how inadequate Joe's instructions were, but he'd kept his mouth shut instead. He was learning.

Several of the closest rhinos grunted. He didn't think animals that large could be frightened of humans, but as the line moved closer, the individuals on the outside of the herd shifted inward. They looked demonic, with giant horns, glaring eyes, and shaggy black fur. Their bellows sounded like the groans of some great steam machine.

He scanned the sky as he walked, searching for the cloud he'd seen in the canyon, but saw only blue. He wondered if he would ever see it again. He wondered if he'd imagined it.

Sierra marched on David's right. Maybe he could pull her and Waldmire aside while everyone else was feasting. They would grab Kim, Barry, and Josh, and rendezvous at the beach after dark. The six of them would fit in two dugout canoes, which would be easy enough to hide once they got back to their island. He didn't know what they would do after they got there, but he couldn't stay here, not with Joe making threats against his kids.

Ahead, a bull stopped grazing and looked up. Muscles quivered along its back, shaking the clumpy fur on its flanks. Its horn curved high in the air. Dark mean eyes locked on David.

He called out "Yah," hoping to make it trot toward the rest of the herd without actually starting the stampede.

The creature stood its ground, shoulders twitching.

David froze, afraid to move any closer, but also nervous about staying still. Joe had been furious when that skinny woman stopped. "Go on," he barked. He swung the leash in a whistling arc through the air.

The animal pawed the dirt. David looked from side to side. To his right, Sierra watched with wide eyes. To his left, Burt continued forward, either indifferent or oblivious.

There wasn't any cover out on the plateau. If the rhino charged, he'd be gored where he stood.

"We're far enough, Joe," Sierra called out. Her voice carried across the grasslands, not a shout, but loud and clear. "Let's do it."

Joe yelled, "Now! Charge!"

Everyone surged forward, shouting and hollering.

The bull clenched, contracting its muscles. It launched itself away from David, toward the herd.

He roared and ran after it. His leg ached and his ribs protested, but he ignored the pain. Their plan depended on everyone staying together. The crowd ran as one. Some waved their arms, others screamed and shouted. One guy had taken off his blazer and spun it in the air above him like a helicopter.

The rhinos fled in a great thundering mass. Their feet shook the ground as they barreled toward the thin piece of land at the end of the canyon. They knew exactly where to go.

"Come on," David shouted. The herd was spread out. They wouldn't all fit across that narrow space. If they kept their current trajectory, a few animals would have to fall into the canyon. Sierra's plan was going to work. David let out another yell. This would all be over soon. Everyone would celebrate and he could grab his kids and get the hell away from here.

Tendrils of white smoke rose from the stretch of land at the end of the canyon.

Joe hadn't mentioned anything about a fire. David slowed to a trot, confused. He looked for the source.

Beyond the herd, a gray figure crawled through the grass at the edge of the canyon. It was Josh, creeping along with his hoodie pulled over his head and a torch in his hand. He was supposed to be back at the village. This didn't make any sense.

Josh threw the torch onto the prairie and disappeared over the cliff at the top of the ladder.

The herd kept running toward the gap, straight toward the low flames. David felt a whisper of hope. The rhinos could easily dash through the fire to the other side. The flames weren't even high enough to singe the hair on their bellies.

The herd turned in unison like a flock of starlings, leaning as they ran.

"Oh shit." David stopped. The flames were low, but the white smoke from the grass created a solid wall.

The rhino herd broke apart. Every last animal circled back toward the line of people.

Shouts and yells came from both sides. Everyone turned and fled. David ran, pumping as hard as he could.

He glanced over his shoulder. A rhinoceros the size of a truck bore down on him. David lurched sideways, praying a creature that big couldn't turn quickly.

The beast thundered past, shaking the ground. Dust flew in David's eyes and a pungent stink washed over him. He kept running.

The rumble of another rhino approached on his right side. David glanced back.

Burt pumped his arms, lagging behind. The rhino closed on him.

"Look out," David shouted. As the words left his mouth, he wondered if he should have kept quiet. Burt terrified him as much as Joe. But David wasn't thinking, he was running on instinct, and his instinct was to help people.

The warning didn't help. The rhino lowered its head and accelerated.

David veered away, still running, still watching.

The rhino snapped its head and struck Burt. Its horn erupted through his belly with an explosion of gore, lifting him from the ground.

Someone screamed. David tried to speed up, but his burning thigh wouldn't let him.

The rhino passed by with Burt's arms and legs flopping wildly against its head. Burt's body tore on one side and slipped from the horn, falling under the animal's pounding feet.

David pushed on.

Somewhere in the distance, gunfire erupted.

Three woolly rhinos stampeded past, but none came as close as the first two. More animals than he could count were out in front of them now. Were any still coming from behind? David's leg threatened to give up, to bring him to the ground.

He glanced back. Only one rhino remained, a giant barreling straight toward him, its horn lowered.

David turned, trying to move sideways, to get out of its path, but his legs barely responded. He heard snorting from the creature's nostrils. He sensed it closing on him.

He glanced back. The creature was right there, towering over him.

Sierra hit him with a diving tackle, shoving him sideways.

They rolled through the grass, pain chomping David's ribs. A second later, the ground shook as the animal thundered by. He felt it as much as he heard it, like sitting next to the tracks while a train passed. A musky stench followed a moment later.

Sierra staggered to her feet, coughing from the dust.

David rolled onto his back and exhaled. "Are we in the clear?" He wasn't sure he could get up.

She turned around, scanning in all directions. "We're safe. They're past us, and still going. Except one." She pointed. "There's a group of people gathered around a dead one over there. Are you okay?"

"Yeah," he lied. Everything hurt. Still breathing hard, he managed to add, "Thank you."

"No problem."

He remained on his back. Everything hurt, but at least he was still in one piece.

The sky above him shimmered. David sucked in a gasp. The cloud had returned.

"Sierra." He had to show her before it vanished. He pointed straight up.

She walked over, looking right at the blurry shape. "That's what you saw before?"

"Yeah." David got to his feet. "A watcher."

Spotting it again, and having someone else see it with him, felt incredibly validating.

She stopped directly below it. "Who are you? Why are you keeping us here?" The shimmer, floating four feet above her, didn't respond.

"Maybe it doesn't understand English," he said. "Maybe it doesn't know we can see it."

Sierra scowled. "I'm going to make sure it knows." She snatched the leash from him.

The cloud drifted away. Sierra ran under it. "Hey!" She reared back and swung the leash in an overhand arc. Her aim was perfect. It would pass right through the thing.

The end of the leash hit something solid. The metal clip stopped with a *THUNK*.

The cloud ascended and the leash fell straight down.

David stared, gaping. For an instant, the leash had outlined an edge, giving shape to one side of the cloud. It looked as big as a small car. The blur rose until it became imperceptible against the sky.

He turned to her. "Holy shit. You just made first contact."

Beaming, she placed the leash back in his hand. "It isn't a cloud. It's invisible. I can't wait to tell Priya about this."

"What does that even mean?" David asked.

"They're hiding from us."

"Why?"

"We have to find it again and ask it."

David's mind raced. "Maybe we could throw dust or dirt onto one, to make it visible."

"Ashes," Sierra said. "The main fire pit is filled with ashes. But that isn't enough. We need to weave a net or something to throw over it."

"Do you really think it's a good idea to try to capture one?"

"They put us in a zoo. They captured us first."

"They also saved us from the Ender. Besides, we don't know for sure this is a zoo."

"Then we'll give them a chance to explain."

"Fair enough," David said. "But we've got more pressing issues. We need to get the hell away from this place."

"We can't just leave."

"We sure as hell can't stay. Joe is going to lose it after what just happened."

"At least he'll be focused on Randall."

David looked at her, confused. "What do you mean?"

"The fire was Randall's idea," Sierra said. "Joe's going to kill him."

"It wasn't Randall," David said. "It was Josh. He was right out in front of me."

"Shit." The color drained from Sierra's face. "Keep quiet about Josh. Maybe no one else saw him."

Chapter Fifty-Five

Joe held his AR-15 at the ready as he walked around the rhinoceros he'd shot. The monster had nearly killed him. Blood splotched the creature's fur. It smelled like rancid cheese. The horn looked too big for its head, a great curving spike that had to be at least six feet long.

"Nice job, man," Scott said. "You got him good."

Joe tightened his grip on the AR-15 and glared at him. "I had to use an entire magazine. This is not how it was supposed to go down."

Scott receded into the crowd. Seven or eight people had gathered beside the beast, which was as big as a van, even lying on its belly. Morrie stood close by, thumbing rounds into the top of his ancient Garand, which meant he must have fired off a few shots, too.

Harold ran up with Burt's MP5 in his hands. "Two dead," he puffed. "Burt and Matt."

"Oh no," Morrie said. "Where's Grace?"

Harold pointed. Across the grasslands, Grace knelt beside the body of her boyfriend. Four or five people were walking toward her.

The people standing around Joe lowered their heads and muttered quiet words of anguish.

I thought you were going to keep these people safe, Joe's daddy said.

"This was Randall's fault," Joe said. "That goddamn fire was his idea." He pointed toward the end of the canyon, where the flames had died away, leaving only thin wisps of smoke. "It drove them straight at us."

"Randall is coming this way," Reggie said, nodding past the body of the rhino. "Him and a couple of others."

Scott's hand jerked up, pointing at the Rhino. "Holy crap, look, this thing is still alive." The animal's sides rose and fell slowly. One of its dark eyes opened.

Joe brought the assault rifle up to his shoulder.

"Wait." Morrie held up his hand. "We can't spare any more ammo."

Joe's daddy laughed. *That baby-faced peckerwood has more sense than you.*

Joe glared at Morrie, then slung the gun over his back. He pulled a knife from his belt and looked at the eight-inch blade. It was Josh's knife. Bracing his feet against the ground, Joe buried it in the rhino's throat, all the way to the handle. When he jerked it out, blood sprang from its jugular, thick as oil.

Reggie put his fist up to his mouth and backed away.

"Everybody okay over here? Randall asked. He walked up to the group, along with Crystal and two other women.

Joe pointed at Randall's face with the bloody knife. "That fire was your idea. You got Burt killed and we just used up half our ammo. You're gonna fucking pay."

"He had nothing to do with it," Crystal said. "He was in the line. Everyone saw him."

The other women nodded.

Randall looked hurt. "You made the call, Joe. No fire. I wouldn't go against you like that. But I seen who set it."

Joe lowered the knife. "Who was it?" He hoped to God it was David. It would give him just the excuse he needed to kill that self-righteous bastard.

Randall's buggy little eyes narrowed. "It was Josh."

Chapter Fifty-Six

Sierra stood behind the corner of Joe's hut, listening from the shadows while Joe and three others argued. The aroma of cooking meat filled the village, but Sierra had lost her appetite.

Josh was tied to the butcher's rack, his hands over his head. His glasses were gone, making him look even younger than sixteen. Sierra thought that might work to her advantage. She needed to emphasize the idea that he was only a child.

Joe's shouts came from around the corner. "Two people are dead!"

"We knew there were risks," argued a voice. Sierra peeked past the hut. It was Morrie.

"We had a plan," Joe roared. "That little shit fucked everything up."

"What're we going to do now?" Harold asked. "What do we do without Burt?"

"This place is falling apart," Joe said. He stood frozen for a moment, staring off into the dark, as if listening to something.

Sierra's chest tightened. She felt pressure all around her, like she was at the bottom of a swimming pool. She looked up, wondering if the watchers were listening in. If so, they were impossible to spot against the jet-black sky.

"People will do whatever they think they can get away with," Randall said. "You can't let Josh get away with this."

"What are you saying?" Joe asked.

"People died 'cause of Thad," Randall said. "And people died 'cause of Josh."

Sierra couldn't believe what she was hearing. The son of a bitch had known Josh since the beginning.

Joe glared at him. "Are you saying I should execute a child?"

"Come on," Morrie said. "Thad intentionally drowned people. Josh thought he was helping."

Harold shrugged. "Thad thought he was helping, too, didn't he? He was sending them on to heaven."

Unable to stand by and listen any longer, Sierra marched over to the group. A small campfire sputtered in the middle of the gathering. "He's just a little boy."

"What the hell are you doing here, Sunshine?"

"Josh is a child. He needs you to help him, not murder him."

"He got my men killed," Joe said, as if that was the only thing that mattered.

"And you think killing Josh is going to help somehow?"

Joe looked uncertain. "Maybe. If it teaches people a lesson."

Sierra breathed, forcing herself to slow down. Everyone was exhausted. It had taken hours to carve the carcass, throw the pieces into the canyon, and haul them back to the village.

"Killing a little boy will not help. It doesn't make you a leader. It makes you a butcher. It makes you like Thad."

Morrie nodded. "Leave him tied up for a while. He won't disobey you again."

Randall worked his jaw. He looked nervous. The fire had been his idea. Sierra thought about pointing that out, but then decided against it. If Randall felt cornered, he might lash out even more.

Joe said nothing for a long moment. The fire crackled. Low murmurs wafted over from the workbenches, where the leftover meat was being hung on racks for smoking. "I'll think about it." He leered at her.

"Let me untie him," Sierra said.

"Absolutely not."

"Joe—"

"Don't make me change my mind."

Sierra left before he could say anything else. She marched through the village, reeling. She wanted to cut Josh free right now and row to the other island. She wanted to be back on Earth. She wanted her father. Rick Preston would know how to fix everything. She felt helpless and hopeless.

When she reached David's cabin, Kim burst through the door and wrapped her arms around her, almost toppling her. The girl's breath came in shaky gasps. "Oh my God, Sierra, we have to do something."

Sierra squeezed her. "I know. I'm working on it." Kim pulled away and looked up, hope in her eyes. Sierra nudged her back into the hut.

David sat on the crude bed with Barry cowered against him, their eyes tiny stars in the dark room. "Did you have any luck?" David asked.

"Josh isn't getting released tonight," Sierra said. "Will he be okay tied up there?"

David sighed. "Yeah. He's tough. He'll survive." His shoulders fell. He looked exhausted. "What about the other villagers? Could we confront Joe as a group?"

"Most of them are steering clear of Joe right now. They're scared. A bunch are busy taking care of Grace." She shrugged. "Honestly, Joe seems to dig in harder when he feels like people are ganging up on him."

"What about the aliens?" Kim asked. "Can we get them to help?"

"They haven't been interested in helping so far," Sierra said.

"We have to make them help," Kim said. "We have to capture one of them and force it to do something."

Barry looked up from David's lap. "How could you catch one? They're always above us."

"We have to get above them somehow." Kim looked back and forth between them, pleading with her eyes.

Her determination gave Sierra strength. "I think we need to deal with Joe directly."

"How?"

"Don't you worry about that." Sierra put her hands on Kim's shoulders. "Let me speak to your dad alone for a minute."

David stood. "You and Barry stay here and keep quiet until I get back." He followed Sierra out of the hut.

"We have to get out of here," David whispered. "Joe is a lunatic."

"Where would we go?" Sierra asked. "The first island? We can't leave without Josh, and I'm not willing to give up on this place. There are good people here. We can't just run away."

"What else can we do?"

"I think we should use the pentobarbital to sedate Joe. Once he's unconscious, we take his guns."

"Then what?" David asked. "Are we going to tie him up in the butcher's rack? Because if we don't, he's going to come after us when he wakes up."

"I don't know," Sierra said.

"And what about Harold and the others? How are they going to react?"

"Harold and Randall are just followers, latching onto whoever's in charge. The rest of the village will thank us."

"What you're talking about isn't easy. If the dose is too high, it could kill him."

Sierra took in a deep breath and let it out slowly. "That's a risk I'm willing to take."

"Well, I'm not. They sorta teach against that at doctor school."

"David, he's threatening to execute a sixteen-year-old boy."

A gasp came from the dark. Kim was listening. *"Execute?"*

"Shit." David went to his daughter. "It's okay, Sweetie."

"Dad, we have to do something."

"We're not doing anything tonight," David said, using a tone that made it clear he was done talking. "We need to give everyone time to cool off."

He looked back, his face grim, as he ushered Kim into their hut, leaving Sierra alone in the dark.

Chapter Fifty-Seven

Randall stood in the center of the village, bored as hell. He was supposed to guard the meat smoking on the racks and keep watch over Josh. The sky was pitch black and everyone else had finally gone to sleep. Nobody would touch the meat. They'd all stuffed their faces. And Josh sure as hell wasn't going anywhere. The boy stood in the butcher's rack with his hands tied tight over his head.

He walked a circuit around the bonfire, stopping in front of Josh. "What the hell were you thinking?"

"You said it was the safest thing to do. You said a fire would take care of everything." Tears ran down Josh's cheeks.

Had the kid really set that fire to impress him? He couldn't let this blow back on him. He was finally part of Joe's team. Hell, with Burt dead, he was practically his right-hand man now. He leaned close and poked Josh in the chest with the Walther P22 that had belonged to Harold. "I never told you to set that fire."

He started his circuit again, weaving through the maze of meat. Loins, flanks, and slices of rump were staked to wooden easels alongside smoky campfires. Ribs from one side of the rhino had been sawed apart and laid on slats two feet above the flames, each one as big as a man's thigh. The other side of ribs remained together in a single rack, almost as tall as Randall.

Cameron had been worried all that meat might attract wildlife from the other islands, but that was bullshit. There wasn't any breeze to carry the smell.

He stuck the Walther in his pocket and added branches to a fire that had died down. His belly couldn't hold another bite, but the savory aroma made him want to try. Rhino meat tasted like steak, but with a strange hint of licorice.

He completed his patrol and returned to Josh.

"You have to talk to Joe," the boy pleaded. "You have to tell him it was your idea. I didn't know any better. Please. He likes you." Fresh tears fell from his eyes.

"If you mention a word of that to anyone, I'll beat your ass." He wondered if he should just do it anyway, as a pre-emptive measure.

Movement caught his eye beyond the big rack of ribs. He drew the pistol but kept his distance. If a wolf-pig had somehow swum over, it could take whatever it wanted. The twenty-two-caliber handgun would only piss it off.

Crystal stepped into view. "Hi."

Randall lowered his gun. "Maybe I won't die of boredom tonight after all."

"Kim told me you were lonely." Crystal tilted her head. "She said I ought to check on you."

He didn't know why Kim would do him any favors, but he was smart enough to answer the door when opportunity came knocking.

Crystal walked over. Her shirt was unbuttoned almost all the way down. She ran her hand along Randall's forearm. "Kim said that you thought I was brave on the hunt today." She smiled, showing every one of those cocked-up teeth.

Randall actually thought Crystal had been a total pussy, but he couldn't quite tell her that. "You did good."

She moved her hand to the back of his neck. "Being so close to dying makes me want to live, you know?"

Randall felt the same way. He moved in for a kiss, careful not to probe past her lips.

She pulled away. "Let's go back to our spot in the canyon."

"I can't leave my post." He pointed his gun at Josh. "I don't want to end up like that."

Crystal reached for his crotch. "Everyone's in a food coma. Besides, Joe ordered the whole village to keep away from the kid. He isn't going anywhere."

"All right." He grabbed a torch soaked in rhino fat and held it over a fire until it flared to life. "Let's hurry." Judging from his throbbing cock, they wouldn't need long.

He took her hand and led her to the side entrance in the wall, which was only a dozen yards from the main fire pit, behind a little cluster of trees. When they reached the creek up near the high end of the village, Crystal tried to say something, but Randall shushed her. He wasn't in the mood for chit-chat.

The hike took longer than the fuck, and Randall got the sense Crystal was disappointed, but he didn't care. He left her to clean up in the creek while he hurried back.

When he finally reached the wall, he relaxed. The village was still dead, the cook fires were still going, and everything was fine. No one had seen him leave. Randall slowed down. The muscles in his back were knotted tight. He shook his arms, trying to loosen up, and walked to the central bonfire.

Josh was gone.

Randall's sphincter clenched. He'd been played. Kim had used Crystal to lure him away so she could free the little shit.

He stood motionless and considered his options. Josh could have gone anywhere. He'd never find him. Joe would be pissed beyond belief, and he was crazy enough to shoot Randall on the spot, just to make a point.

What if he took out Joe first? It'd be easy to kill him in his sleep, but then what? None of the others would ever trust him after that, even though he'd be doing them all a favor. And then there was Cameron. That army bitch might try to kill *him* in his sleep.

Maybe it was time to move on to greener pastures. So far, two out of three islands had people on them. There had to be more. He could take a canoe and find another one. If he showed up armed, he could rule the place. Hell, forget about finding a new one, he could simply return to that first island. He'd take Crystal with him. They'd rule the hilltop, just the two of them.

Randall made up his mind. But that island was crawling with dangerous creatures. He needed more than the ten measly rounds in his Walther. He would grab the remaining ammo, and maybe the binoculars. Crystal would be back any minute. They could set sail before everyone woke up. He wondered if anyone would try to stop them. He sorta hoped so. After the way things had gone tonight, he needed to smack the shit out of somebody.

Randall grabbed another torch and walked to the storage sheds.

Supplies littered the floor and a small figure crouched in the dark, searching the lower shelves.

It was Josh.

He turned to look up, eyes wide.

Randall's blood rose. He wouldn't have to leave after all. "Oh, you should'a run when you had the chance."

Chapter Fifty-Eight

David woke from a fitful sleep as the flat light of morning came into his cabin. He studied his kids' sleeping faces. An image of Kim tied under the butcher's rack popped into his head, sending a cold chill up his neck.

He needed to talk to Sierra again. The more he thought about it, the more he thought she was right about Joe.

First, he had to check on Josh. The boy had been okay last night when David went to bed. He was a tough kid. David pulled on his shoes and Kona followed him out of the cabin.

The forest canopy crowded in at the edges of the village. He saw nothing in the sky. The invisible aliens could be up there anywhere, hidden from view above the trees.

He pushed on to the main firepit.

Josh looked like a fly in a spider web. Six or eight new ropes had been added, stretching from different parts of his body to the frame around him. Blood dripped from his nose onto his shirt. Ropes ran from each of his ankles to the support posts, forcing him to stand with his feet apart. Ropes around his waist connected him to the posts in four places. Two ropes were knotted around his neck and tied to the upper corners of the structure.

"Jesus Christ, what happened?" This was not how Josh had looked the night before. He tried to loosen the vines around the boy's wrist. They were cutting off his circulation.

"Nothing," Josh managed. "I had it coming." He produced a fake and painful-looking grin.

Kona sniffed a spot of blood on the ground in front of the boy. David nudged her away with his foot. He felt sick.

He worked at the vines, but they were too tight. He needed a knife. He stepped back and studied Josh's injuries. A contusion covered one cheek and his black eye was swollen shut.

"My eye hurts, Mr. Williams. I can't open it." Red saliva dripped onto the dirt.

Once upon a time, David would have corrected him. *Doctor Williams.* The thought embarrassed him. How petty he had been.

Sierra was right. They had to do something. *I'm not willing to give up,* she had said. *We can't just run away.* Lindsey had said the exact same thing when David wanted to retreat to the wilderness in the last days before the Ender. If he'd done that, he never would have found a pod.

As soon as he was finished here, he would find Sierra and they would come up with a plan to use the pentobarbital.

He moved close to Josh again. "We've got to get you out of here."

Josh produced a tiny, terrible laugh. "That's a bad idea."

Another laugh startled him from behind. "He tried to escape last night," Randall said. "I took care of him."

David balled his hands into fists. "You did this?"

"It's your girl's fault," Randall said.

David shook, as if splashed with cold water. "Wh-what are you talking about?"

"She got Crystal to lure me away, then she came and untied him."

"She didn't," Josh whispered. "It wasn't her."

"Bullshit." Randall took another step closer to David.

A growl rumbled in Kona's throat.

David didn't know who Crystal was, but if Kim had been involved somehow, he would deny it until his dying breath. "Kim was asleep with me all night," he said, wondering if it was actually true. "Don't go blaming her for your screw-up."

"Joe'll be here any second. We'll see what he says about all this."

Panic squeezed David's chest. Randall was an idiot and Joe was insane. He took a deep breath, keeping those thoughts to himself. "Are you really going to tell Joe that a little girl tricked you into leaving your post? What's he going to think of you then?"

Randall's face fell and he stepped back.

"It wasn't Kim," Josh said. "It was Lily."

David and Randall both turned to look at him, but before he could say anything else, Joe walked over.

"You wanted to show me something, Randall?"

"Josh nearly got loose last night," Randall said. His eyes darted to David. "Harold didn't tie him up tight enough the first time."

"What the hell happened to him?" Joe asked.

"I had to rough him up a little," Randall said. "You know how it is."

For a long moment, Joe didn't speak. Finally, he whispered. "Sometimes boys got to be taught a lesson, I guess." He reached out and tugged at the network of ropes, jerking Josh's body. "He ain't going anywhere now."

"I need to tend to his injuries," David said.

Joe looked around. He seemed to be considering it.

Morrie, Jasmine, and a couple of other villagers had gathered by the main firepit.

"Let David look at him," Morrie said.

"Come on, Joe," Jasmine said. "He doesn't deserve that."

"He got two people killed," Joe said, moving his hand to the gun in his waistband.

"He's just a kid," said a young woman with dirty blond hair. "He didn't mean to get anyone hurt."

"He's sixteen." Joe pointed at them with two fingers. "You stay away from him. All of you." He glared until the group broke up and wandered off.

"Hey Joe, you better get over here," Harold called out. He stood over by smaller fires where the meat was smoking, waving his knit cap in the air.

Joe started his way, with Randall trailing behind him.

"What now?" David muttered to himself. He followed them both. He had to make sure Randall didn't mention anything about Kim.

The area looked like a slaughterhouse. Bright red meat hung on wooden racks of all sizes. A woman who'd been stoking the fires got up and moved out of Joe's way.

"That big old side of ribs is gone," Harold said.

"What do you mean, gone?" Joe asked. "Did somebody cut it up already?"

A large wooden tripod stood empty between two fires. Clumps of blood congealed on the rungs. The woman tending to the fires shook her head.

"It was right here, wasn't it?" Joe demanded, his voice rising.

Randall scurried around the racks, examining all the meat.

Joe trembled. "Are you telling me we've got a mother-fucking thief now?"

Chapter Fifty-Nine

Sierra followed the creek to the perimeter wall, hoping she looked casual. Just a woman taking a walk. People were arguing back near the middle of the village, where all the meat was smoking. Good. As long as their attention was focused over there, no one would notice her.

She passed the swampy marsh where the creek fizzled out, continued along to the spot where Priya had met her two nights earlier, and found the kidney-shaped rock leaning against the wall. She looked around to make sure no one was watching and nudged the rock aside. The amber bottle sat right where she'd left it.

Black dread crawled up her spine. She was going to poison someone. The idea made her feel flat and empty. Rick Preston's life lessons hadn't exactly covered poisoning people.

Wrong, she realized. That was his final lesson.

She snatched the bottle, shoved it in her pocket, and walked back toward the center of the village. Along the way, she passed four or five people in the fields, pulling weeds. She saw no sign of the alien overhead.

Josh was still tied to the butcher's rack. Behind him, Morrie and two men were building something. Crystal, the woman who'd frozen during the hunt, sat nearby in a mess of vines, braiding them into a rope with a noose at the end.

"What's going on here?" Sierra asked.

"Someone stole a bunch of rhino meat last night," Crystal said. "Joe thinks it happened 'cause he went easy on Josh. He's gonna hold an execution. He thinks people will stop breaking rules once they see the consequences."

"And you're okay with this?" Sierra spat. Crystal's attitude about the whole thing sickened her as much as the news.

Crystal merely shrugged and continued braiding.

Morrie took Sierra's arm, leaned close, and spoke quietly. "We're building a gallows." He led her off to the side, out of everyone's earshot. "Joe wanted to shoot him, but I convinced him to save the ammo." Anguish showed through trembling eyelids. "I suggested the gallows. I knew it would take us a while to build and I thought it might give him time to cool down. Maybe enough time to change his mind."

"What did Joe say?"

"He loved the idea. He said Josh could hang and rot, to remind everyone what happens when they go against him."

Disgust rose in Sierra's throat. "How long will it take you?"

Morrie looked over at the piles of wood. One man held a log in place while another chopped it with a primitive ax, a sharp stone tied to a stout branch. "I could have this done in a few hours if I wanted." He gave Sierra a conspiratorial sneer. "But I don't think we'll be finished until midday tomorrow at the earliest."

She put her hand on his arm. "Thank you. You're a good man. Where's Joe now?"

"He's walking the perimeter wall, looking for the meat." Morrie glanced around nervously. "He'll be back any minute. Cameron is with him. She's keeping an eye on him."

"Good."

Morrie shook his head. "If that kid hangs because of me, I'll never forgive myself."

"He won't." She didn't say anything else. The less Morrie knew, the better.

She walked over to Josh, who was tied up right in front of the construction, where he could hear it but not see it. Sierra shuddered. If the butcher's rack was a foot or two taller, he would be hanging already. Morrie had bought her a day. She had to act quickly.

"Hey," she said quietly.

Josh looked at her with one eye. The other was swollen shut. "I'm so tired," he said. "I never slept last night."

"Shhh. It's okay. We're going to get you out of this mess."

"Why? Why bother? I screwed up everything."

Josh had made some stupid choices, but he was a kid. It wasn't his fault. She put her hand on his shoulder and gave him a squeeze. "You aren't to blame for any of this. We're going to get you out of here, and everything's going to be better."

"You promise?"

"Yes. Of course. David and I have always looked out for you. You know that."

Josh's lip trembled. "You have," he whispered.

Sierra nodded and left, more determined than ever.

She marched over to the camping area, where Waldmire and David stood talking. Barry was playing fetch with Kona near the perimeter wall and Kim crouched by the closest tree. She had folded Josh's spare clothes for him and placed a small yellow flower on the pile. This was not the time to be delicate, Sierra thought.

"They're going to kill him," she announced.

"We know," David said.

Kim came over, a pained grimace on her face. "Why is this happening? Why doesn't someone do something?"

"Everyone's scared," Waldmire said. "Joe has all the guns."

"So they're just going to let him execute a kid?" Kim's lips pulled back in an angry grimace.

"No one's getting executed," Sierra said. "There are people keeping watch over Josh and there are people keeping an eye on Joe."

"What about Randall?" Waldmire asked. "He's known Josh since the beginning. How can he go along with this?"

David shook his head. "The meat disappeared on Randall's watch. He blamed Josh for it. He encouraged Joe to teach him a lesson."

"That's insane," Waldmire said. "We need to leave. We need to get out of here."

"No, no, no," Kim held up her hands, trembling. "We can't leave Josh."

"She's right," Sierra said. "We aren't giving up on Josh and we aren't giving up on these people. They need our help and we need theirs."

Waldmire gave her a smile so warm she could almost feel it. He still looked scared, but he also looked proud.

David drew in a long, slow breath. "Did you get it?"

She felt a wave of relief. He was onboard.

"What?" Waldmire asked. "What did you get?"

She pulled out the bottle of pentobarbital. "I'm going to put this on Joe's food. It will knock him out. Once he's unconscious, we take his guns, we untie Josh, and we gather everyone together. We'll all decide what to do next."

Waldmire looked at the bottle for a long time. "How can I help?"

She smiled. She had Waldmire's support, too. "We need to get Joe and his men away from the work tables. I'll mix this into the peanut butter. Joe is crazy about peanut butter."

David nodded. "We have to make sure no one else touches it."

"That's easy," Sierra said. "We'll tell everyone he made it off-limits."

"What happened to the meat?" Waldmire asked. "Why would someone walk off with it? There's plenty for everyone."

"Ask Lily," Kim said.

"What?" Sierra looked down at the girl, squinting. "What are you not telling us?"

"They were going to kill him." Tears welled in Kim's eyes.

David dropped to one knee. "Kim, did Lily take the meat?"

Her lips trembled. "I think so. Probably. She told me she would set Josh free if I could get Randall away from him."

"Kim, you cannot trust that woman," Sierra said. She looked at David. "We have to do this, now."

He worked his jaw. "I'll find a way to distract Joe."

She clutched the amber bottle and nodded, her throat too tight to speak.

Chapter Sixty

Tracking down the missing meat was the best way to lure Joe away from the center of the village. Finding it could even help defuse the situation. David wrapped Kona's leash around his fist and led the dog to the women's cabin. It was a long shot, but Kona might be able to help.

Carol Mulligan sat outside on a stump, as if everything was normal, just an old lady on her porch.

"I need to see Lily's belongings," David said.

"Lily? She doesn't like my shoes. Can you believe that?" Carol patted Kona's blocky head but made no move to rise.

David was suddenly back in the hospital, speaking with a patient who wasn't listening. "Does Lily sleep here?" Simple questions with simple answers usually broke through the mental fog.

"Oh, yes. She says I snore." Carol sounded deeply offended.

David pulled back the reed curtain hanging in front of the door. "Can you show me her things?" he asked again.

Carol pursed her lips and stood, taking an eternity to walk inside. How had this woman ever beaten anyone to a pod?

A path from the doorway branched between small nests of clothing. "Those are my things there," Carol said, sounding sad. "I don't have much anymore."

She shuffled to a spot in the back corner that was apart from all the others. "Nobody wants to sleep next to Lily now." Carol shook her head. "Poor, poor Isaac."

David pulled Kona over to Lily's belongings. Most of the women slept on mats made from woven reeds, with leaves or pine needles stuffed underneath for cushion, but apparently Lily slept on the hard floor. "Where is she, girl? Where is she?"

Kona sniffed the woman's clothes. David felt like a fool. Kona could barely find a tennis ball in two inches of snow. Still, he had to try something. He picked up a sweater and pulled Kona back through the doorway.

"She didn't sleep here last night," Carol said as she settled back down on her stump again.

David held the sweater in front of Kona's nose. "Find her, girl."

The dog zigzagged away from the cabin, pulling David straight to the meat racks. For a moment he thought she was actually going to help, but then he realized Kona just wanted what every golden retriever wanted. She hoovered up bits of gristle from the ground.

"Kona, come on," David said. "If you find those ribs, I'll let you eat the whole thing." He shoved the sweater in Kona's face.

She pulled him to the empty rack where the ribs had been.

"That's it, girl."

She jumped up, putting her front legs on the rack, and licked congealed blood from the wood.

"Shit." This was a waste of time. For all he knew, the watchers had taken the meat. He glanced skyward. Nothing.

Kona dropped back to all fours and pulled toward the fields, following the path between rows of leafy shoots that looked like carrot tops. David wished Lindsey was here. She would know what to do.

The dog pulled harder, sniffing the ground.

"Kona, there's nothing there." David looked down and saw that he was wrong. Lines ran through the dirt, leading down the path toward the opening at the low end of the village. He let out a dry, bitter laugh. *Of course.* Lily couldn't have carried the rack of ribs very far. It was too heavy. She must have dragged it.

Kona clawed forward against her leash and snatched a tiny scrap of meat from the ground.

"Good girl," he said, a laugh in his voice. He marched back to the firepit, where Joe was watching the construction of the gallows behind Josh. Cameron, Harold, and Randall stood around him.

"I know where the meat went," David said. "There are tracks leading straight out of the village." He pointed. "They're right there, plain as day. I think Lily took it."

Randall's eyes narrowed, watching him.

"Why would Lily want all that meat?" Harold asked.

David shrugged. "I don't know. Maybe she wants to make an offering."

"Whatever it is, it can't be good," Cameron said. "She's a nut job."

Joe's face darkened. "I should have killed that bitch when I had the chance." He turned to Harold. "You stay right here. If anyone comes within ten feet of that kid, shoot 'em. If he isn't there when I get back, you'll hang in his place."

David looked around. As long as Harold stayed right by Josh, he wouldn't be able to see Sierra mashing peanuts over at the work tables. He hoped it was good enough.

Joe drew his big silver pistol. "Lead the way, Doc."

He led them to the path, careful to stay off the tracks so the others could see them. When they reached the opening in the wall at the low end of the village, Kona snatched up another small piece of gristle and wolfed it down.

The tracks ran straight down the path through the woods. Kona led the way.

"This is bullshit," Randall said. "Why would she drag rhino meat out of the village?"

"She's having a big luau at the beach," Cameron said. "Didn't you get the invite, Randall?"

"You're fuckin' hilarious," Randall said.

Cameron walked beside David. She didn't say anything, but he was glad to have her there. He thought he could trust her.

The lines in the dirt never veered from the center of the path and eventually, the opening at the end of the woods appeared. After another five or ten minutes of walking, they reached the beach. The raft that had brought David and his companions sat empty on the shoreline.

The path of the dragged meat became even more obvious in the sand. The tracks ended next to two dugout canoes.

Joe stepped out in front, holding his gun up beside his head. "Where's the third canoe?"

"There." David pointed. "It's her."

A hundred yards offshore, Lily sat in the back of the canoe, paddling toward them.

The group walked across the beach. Kona barked once and then bent to lap at the water.

"What the fuck is going on here?" Joe growled.

"Trouble's coming," Cameron said.

Lily stroked three times on one side, then switched, bringing the canoe steadily closer.

"She's got it with her," Randall said. The rack of ribs sat propped against the bow.

David squinted. The meat looked like the giant ribs from the Flintstones cartoon, where a drive-in waitress placed them on the side of the car, flipping it over. "Why is she bringing it back?"

The dugout canoe drifted to a stop against the shore. Lily made no move to get up.

Joe pointed his gun at her. "Explain yourself."

"When your testimony is finished, the beast will come from the abyss to attack you, and overpower you, and kill you."

"I don't want to hear that bullshit," Joe said.

"What the hell is she talking about?" Randall asked.

"Each of us must go on from here," Lily answered. "We cannot remain."

Joe looked around, shaking his head.

Lily turned to David. "Your daughter helped me last night. She earned her reward."

"What's she talking about, Doc?" Joe asked.

"She's crazy," David said. "Kim had nothing to do with it."

Lily put her hands on the sides of the boat and gave David a canny look. "Tell the truth and shame the Devil."

"Enough," Joe shouted. He sloshed into the water and grabbed Lily by the arm, forcing her to her feet. The canoe wobbled and threatened to roll over.

"What are those?" Cameron pointed out to sea, behind Lily.

Two large lumps approached through the water, at least fifty yards away, but closing steadily. David shuddered. He recognized the nostrils and horrible yellow eyes.

Tyrannosaurus. Two of them, following the canoe back to the island.

Joe dropped Lily onto her seat and screamed at her. "*What the fuck did you do?*"

THE FALL

Chapter Sixty-One

Sweat dripped down Cameron's back. She'd been following Joe around, watching him, just like Charlie had instructed with his goddamn dying words, ready to pounce the moment the asshole finally lost it. Ready to shoot the bastard if he actually tried to hang Josh.

She didn't know what she was supposed to do about a pair of fucking dinosaurs.

"We have to get out of here," David said. "Now." He wrapped the dog's leash around his fist and started across the sand.

Randall darted past him, toward the path. He wasn't normally one to move quickly. This was serious.

Cameron backed away.

Joe stood motionless beside the canoe, water up to his shins. He whipped around, pointing his gun at David. "This is your daughter's fault."

A delirious laugh burst from David and he gestured at the canoe, fingers splayed. "My daughter isn't the one who just lured dinosaurs here."

Cameron chuckled. He had a strong argument.

"Joe, we got to go," Randall called out, halfway across the beach.

Lily folded her arms on her lap, sitting back in the dugout. "A tribulation is coming, like nothing since time began."

Joe sloshed ashore. "You're fucking insane."

He was right about that. Cameron snickered. Of course, he was something of an authority on the subject.

Kona barked. The lumpy heads of the swimming dinosaurs closed the gap, just over a hundred feet away.

Randall disappeared into the dark tunnel of the forest path. Cameron took off after him, glancing back as she went.

David stopped in the middle of the beach, looking torn, like maybe he wasn't willing to leave Lily behind. If so, he needed a good smack across the face.

Lily gave him a thin, sanctimonious grin, one Cameron had seen many times before. David started moving, thank God, with Joe right beside him.

Cameron stopped in the shadows a few yards up the path, solid dirt under her boots. The village was just over a half mile away. She peered through the trees to the shoreline, where Lily sat motionless in the canoe, her back to the open sea. She seemed to be humming.

The creatures rose as they reached the shallows, water dripping from thin layers of matted feathers. Cameron gaped in awe. She'd seen the wooly rhinos and the terror bird. Neither had prepared her for the sight of these towering beasts.

The larger one stepped forward and sniffed the rack of ribs. Its head was pink and black, like burned skin. It snatched the meat with its jaws. Lily grabbed the sides of the wobbling canoe to steady herself.

David and Joe caught up to Cameron on the path, where they were hidden behind the first few yards of trees. With any luck, the dinosaurs would wander off along the beach.

Joe aimed his revolver back toward the end of the path. "If they come this way, open fire." He rolled his head from side to side.

"Are you nuts?" Cameron spat, keeping her voice low. "These handguns won't hurt anything that big. Not unless you hit it in the eye." He had to know that.

"What do you suggest we do?" he growled. "I have to protect my people."

The smaller Tyrannosaurus approached the back of the canoe. Bright orange streaked its head, highlights over dull gray skin, like the pattern on a tiger. Lily stared straight ahead, humming loudly. The tiger-head dinosaur bent and grabbed her. She screamed for a heartbeat, then the jaws clamped shut. One arm tore off, falling into the shallows. The larger Tyrannosaurus plucked it from the water, a heron darting a tadpole.

Joe snorted. "Bitch got what she deserved."

"Come on," Randall shouted, another two hundred yards up the path.

The dinosaur's head snapped up, facing them. It took a step in their direction.

"We gotta get out of here," David said.

All three of them took off after Randall.

"Let's head for the plateau," Cameron said. "It's the only place they can't go."

"Then what?" Joe asked.

She didn't know. She hadn't thought far enough ahead.

They caught up to Randall, who'd slowed to a jog, holding his side and breathing hard.

"We have to get everyone into the canyon," Joe said. "We'll climb up to the plateau."

Genius.

The path grew dark. Behind them, one of the dinosaurs stepped onto the trail, blocking the light from the beach.

"Those things are gonna catch us," Randall wheezed. "We won't even make it to the village. Joe, we have to buy some time."

Joe skidded to a stop and aimed his revolver at David. "I've been waiting for an excuse to do this."

Cameron had been waiting for something like this, too. She lowered her arm and shifted her hand toward her Beretta, moving slowly so Joe wouldn't notice.

"Wait a second, hold on," David said, one hand up, his eyes darting back and forth. Kona pulled at her leash, trying to continue up the path.

Cameron slid her fingers around the grip.

Joe cocked the hammer.

He was right about one thing. A dead body on the path might buy them a few extra minutes. Cameron nudged off the safety with her thumb.

"Let's just go," David said. "There's still time."

Cameron brought up her gun.

Randall was one step ahead of her. *Fucking Randall.* The hole at the end of his Walther pointed at her heart.

She wasn't close enough to grab it from him, so she twisted sideways, giving him a narrow target.

She wasn't fast enough.

Randall fired.

An explosion of pain turned the world black.

Chapter Sixty-Two

A shot rang out as Sierra mashed a bowl full of peanuts with a stone pestle at one of the work tables in the center of the village. She flinched, chafing her knuckle against the edge of the rock mortar. Blood dripped onto the peanut butter. She mixed it in. A little blood was nothing compared to what she was about to add.

Priya stood at one of the other tables, carving slices from a hunk of smoked meat. "What was that?" She rose up on her toes, peering across the fields to the forest beyond the wall, where Joe and David had gone. Several villagers pulling weeds turned that way as well.

The gunshot had been distant, maybe as far as the beach. Sierra tried to think of a scenario where that sound meant something good. She couldn't.

She glanced back at Josh, the sight gutting her. She'd only known him for two weeks, but he was like a little brother now. An annoying little brother sometimes, but wasn't that how little brothers were supposed to be? She was responsible for him.

Harold popped up from the edge of the fire pit where he'd been sitting, halfway between Sierra and Josh. The big bonfire had died down to embers. "That was a gunshot." He walked toward her, his own gun hanging from his shoulder by a thick black strap.

If he came any closer, he'd notice the bottle of pentobarbital nestled in her bra, especially if he looked at her chest, and the mop-haired British prick was always looking at her chest. Sierra hadn't added any poison to the peanut butter yet. If he took the bottle, she was screwed.

She turned away, facing Priya. "Go find Waldmire. He's in the camping area with Kim and Barry. Something's happening. Find a safe place." Sierra jerked her thumb at Crystal, who sat on the gallows platform behind Josh, still weaving the rope for his hanging. The damn thing was already more than three times as long as they needed. "Take her with you."

Priya put down her knife, but Crystal only glared.

A deep, bellowing roar came from the woods below the village.

Crystal dropped the rope and scrambled after Priya.

"What the bloody hell was that?" Harold asked.

"No idea," Sierra lied. Fear chilled her veins. It sounded exactly like the Tyrannosaurus that had chased them up the mountain. "Go see if Joe needs help." If Harold left, she could cut Josh free.

Harold looked back and forth between Sierra and the path leading out of the village. "No, no, no. Joe said to watch the lad, and that's what I'm gonna do, innit?" He looked back toward the butcher's rack. "Bloody hell!"

Kim stood in front of Josh, tugging at the ropes that held him to the frame.

"You get away from there," Harold shouted, running toward them.

Sierra followed. She grabbed a heavy log from the woodpile next to the fire pit and raised it high over her head, gripping it in both hands like an ax. "Hey, Harold."

He turned around.

She swung with all her might, grunting. The log struck Harold's forehead with a heavy thud and he crumpled to the ground.

Sierra gaped, unable to believe what she'd done. Unable to believe it had worked. She bent over Harold. A blue welt swelled on his forehead and blood leaked from the corner of one eye.

"Did you kill him?" Kim asked, her voice small.

Sierra shook her head. "I don't think so."

"We have to get Josh free," Kim said.

A second roar came from the woods, closer than before.

Chapter Sixty-Three

David dropped to his knees beside Cameron. Blood swelled through the top left quarter of her shirt. Jesus, had she been shot in the heart? He pressed two fingers against her neck and felt a faint pulse. Kona backed away, tail tucked, her leash dragging on the ground.

Joe and Randall were gone. Randall had snatched Cameron's gun and they both disappeared up the path.

Cameron groaned through gritted teeth. "Motherfucker."

Thank God. She was conscious. She couldn't have been hit in the heart. Her skin was cool and pale, her pupils huge. Signs of shock.

David pulled her shirt down at the neck. The bullet had pierced the top of her pectoral muscle just below the clavicle. Just *above* her heart. He leaned over and lifted her a few inches, spotting the exit wound high on her back. She was damned lucky.

He was lucky too. She'd taken a bullet for him.

The second Tyrannosaurus entered the path behind the first one.

"We gotta move." He yanked off his overshirt and pressed it against the wound. "Hold this."

A wistful smile grew on her face as she stared straight up. "Thad's angel. It's come for me."

Twenty feet above them, a blurry shape floated beneath the forest canopy. "Yeah, I've seen those before. All they do is watch. They're useless." He took her good arm and hoisted her up. "Come on."

Kona whimpered. God bless that dog, she stayed right beside them.

The dinosaurs were maybe eighty yards back. Each step brought them ten feet closer.

David pulled Cameron's arm over his shoulder. "Kona, come." They started creeping toward the village. There was no way they'd make it.

"Do something," David grunted at the shape floating overhead. The aliens always showed up when everything went to hell, but they never did a damn thing to help.

Cameron got her legs moving a little faster.

Kona led the way, dragging her leash. She looked back every few steps and barked. The dinosaurs were gaining.

David had to come up with a different plan. At this rate, the tyrannosaurs would catch them long before they reached the village, and he was leading the monsters straight to his kids. He didn't know where else to go. The ladder to the plateau was the only place the dinosaurs couldn't follow, but it felt like a hundred miles away.

Cameron huffed and hissed, cradling her arm, holding his shirt against the wound.

A deep roar barreled up the path, rattling David's lungs. He studied the trees on either side. "We have to get off the trail."

Kona's barking picked up. The dinosaurs were only thirty yards back now.

David and Cameron veered off the path toward a dense clump of trees. Branches clawed David's face as he helped Cameron scramble between a tight row of trunks.

"Kona, come," he shouted. "Come on, girl."

The dog stopped on the trail, looked through the trees at David, then faced the dinosaurs. Her hackles were up and her lips drawn back.

"Keep going," Cameron hissed.

David's mouth trembled. "Kona!"

The lead Tyrannosaurus stopped in front of the golden retriever, towering above her. Kona barked and barked, froth spewing from her mouth.

David took a deep breath and put all of his anger into his voice. *"Kona, come!"*

The dinosaur snapped downward. Kona dug in her claws and bolted off the trail, running straight toward him. The monster's jaws came up empty.

Deeper in the woods, Cameron called back. "Hurry."

Kona ran to David and turned around, still barking.

David stayed planted and shouted at the dinosaurs. "Hey! Over here!"

Both tyrannosaurs looked at him through the forest.

Kona kept barking. She didn't know it, but she was helping. They had to lure the dinosaurs off the path. The forest would slow them down. It would buy time for his kids.

"Come on!" David shouted. *"This way!"*

The lead tyrannosaur's head drifted from side to side as it peered into the woods. Then it turned forward and continued straight up the path toward the village. The second creature followed close behind.

Chapter Sixty-Four

Sierra grabbed the knife Priya had been using to slice meat. It was Josh's knife. She raced to the butcher's rack.

Kim tugged at the ropes, desperation in her eyes. "It's going to be okay, Josh. We're going to get you out of here."

Sierra held the blade so he could see it. "I got your dad's knife for you." She sawed at one of the ropes tied to his waist.

"Just let me sleep," Josh said.

"It's going to be okay," Kim said again, patting his hair while Sierra worked.

It took more than a minute to slice through the first two ropes, and there were at least seven more. Sierra moved to the rope tied around his wrist and worked the tip of the blade into the knot, trying to pry it loose, thinking it might be faster to work the knot free.

Kim put one hand on Josh's cheek. "Dad will patch you up. Nothing else bad will happen."

Josh's good eye fell shut.

Shouting came from the forest. Sierra looked over her shoulder as Joe and Randall ran through the opening at the low end of the village. David and Cameron weren't with them.

"Kim, get out of here, now," Sierra hissed. "You can't let them see you. Get to the canyon."

The blocky teeth on the back of the knife blade caught in the knot. She tugged, but it wouldn't come free.

Kim's eyebrows swam toward each other. "What about Josh?"

"I won't leave him."

"What about you?"

Joe ran to a group of villagers working in the fields. He herded them up the path, straight toward them.

"I'll figure it out. Go." Sierra left the knife hanging from the knot and shoved the girl away from Josh.

Kim ran across the gallows platform and disappeared through the cluster of scraggly trees behind it, heading toward the side entrance in the wall.

Sierra kissed Josh on the cheek. "I'll be right back. I promise." She turned and raced toward the sheds, ducking behind the work tables to stay out of sight.

Harold lay unconscious where he'd fallen, with his gun next to him. It looked more complicated than a pistol. She grabbed the barrel and pulled, but the damn strap was still looped around his shoulder and neck. She lifted his arm.

"Whuudda?" Harold slurred, his eyes still closed.

"Harold," Joe shouted. He sounded close. "Where the hell are you?"

There wasn't time. Keeping low behind the work tables, Sierra darted into the first shed and scrambled to the back, squeezing under a crude shelf. She tucked herself behind a pile of gourds and pulled her legs against her chest, trying to make herself small. Her breathing thundered in the dim space.

Flat light spilled through the entrance to the shed, which was barely bigger than a closet. She couldn't see anything out the opening except the closest work table and the distant treetops beyond.

"Holy shit, somebody knocked him out." Randall must have found Harold.

"Joe, what's going on?" This new voice was Morrie. Sierra felt a spark of hope. Morrie wasn't like the others.

"Lily brought the goddamn dinosaurs here," Joe bellowed.

"Dinosaurs? What? Why?"

"We need to go," Randall said.

"Morrie, get the ammo from the shed," Joe barked. "All of it."

Sierra tensed, then remembered that the supplies were in the other shed. The one she was in contained only food.

Another bellowing roar came from the distance.

"Harold, wake up," Joe shouted. "What happened?"

"Hey, check this out," Randall said. "Somebody was cutting Josh free."

Sierra held her breath. He'd found the knife stuck in the knot. She pressed herself into the corner, cold and helpless.

"Shoot him," Joe said. "This is his fault. He was in on it with Lily. The Doc's girl, too."

Sierra squeezed her eyes shut, bracing for the gunshot.

"Joe, he's unconscious and he's tied up," Morrie pleaded. "We can't spare the ammo. You know that."

"Harold, wake the fuck up," Joe shouted.

"I got snucked," muttered a new voice, sounding groggy and drunk.

Sierra's heart sank. Harold was awake now. If he told Joe what she'd done, he'd kill her.

Another roar came, louder than the last.

"It's almost here," Randall yelled. "Josh ain't going nowhere. Come on, let's go."

The sound of their footsteps moved away from the shed.

Sierra listened and waited, anxious to go to Josh, but terrified the others would spot her if she ventured out too soon.

Chapter Sixty-Five

Joe ran to the huts in the middle of the village, shouting for everyone to clear out. He couldn't lose anyone else. He couldn't let his daddy be right.

Oh, you know I'm right. They're all gonna die, and it's gonna be all your fault.

He stopped at the first cabin. "Out," Joe shouted. "Everyone out. Get to the canyon."

Three women got to their feet. "What's happening?" one of them asked.

"Just go," Joe yelled. The AR-15 shook in his hands.

"Where's Crystal?" Randall shouted.

None of the women answered. They were already out the door, heading toward the village's side entrance.

Joe raced to the next cabin. It wasn't his fault. It was everyone else's fault. None of this would have happened if they'd just listened to him.

That's a good one, Joseph. I love it. His old man had said the exact same thing a million times.

Harold stumbled along behind, with Morrie helping him keep his balance. The stupid Brit was slowing them down.

Four people came streaming out of the next cabin, two men and two women.

A roar came from the woods below the village.

One of the men froze. It was Scott, tugging on his stupid dress jacket. "What was that?"

"It's a goddamn dinosaur," Randall said.

"Huh?" Scott stammered. "I don't under—"

"Just get to the canyon," Joe yelled, shoving him toward the exit.

Joe started in the opposite direction, toward the camping area. Harold stumbled as they crossed the creek, soaking himself. Morrie steadied his arm.

Several people were clustered together under the trees, looking confused.

"What was that noise?" Jasmine asked.

"Everyone, get moving," Joe shouted. "Get to the canyon."

"What the hell is that?" Reggie pointed downhill, past the fields.

The Tyrannosaurus with the orange head appeared at the base of the village, just beyond the eight-foot wall.

"Oh, that's not good," Harold said, slurring. "We can't go out that way, can we?"

"You're a fucking genius," Randall said. He checked the chamber in the Beretta he'd taken from Cameron.

Joe's daddy let out a coughing laugh. *You let this happen, Joseph. These people needed you, but you ain't strong enough.*

"I am," Joe shouted.

Morrie took his arm. "Joe, it's time to go. We need to leave."

Joe nodded and they started back across the village toward the side entrance.

Chapter Sixty-Six

Sierra peeked out from the shed. Joe and the others were gone.

She ran over to the butcher's rack, terrified she would find Josh's throat slit or his guts spilling out. Josh's head hung forward. He was asleep. She saw no new injuries.

Shouts came from further up in the village, on the other side of the trees behind him.

The knife was gone and at least seven ropes still tied him to the wooden frame.

Sierra pulled at the vines knotted around one wrist. Her fingernail ripped, but she kept pulling. "Shit." She wasn't getting anywhere. The knot wouldn't budge. "Somebody help." Her voice cracked. She was all alone.

A roar came from behind, close now.

At the low end of the village, a Tyrannosaurus emerged from the forest, just beyond the wall. It was smaller than the one that ate Wayne, but still as big as an elephant. The wall only came to its knees. Its orange head shifted slightly, as if searching for prey, then it moved through the opening. One foot caught on the edge of the wall and the dinosaur lurched.

"Fall," Sierra whispered. A hard fall would have to injure an animal that size. With those stupid little arms, it might not even be able to get back up.

The Tyrannosaurus brought its other leg under its massive body and caught itself, then stomped forward onto the fields.

Sierra froze. Maybe if she remained motionless, it wouldn't spot her. Maybe it would be drawn to all the commotion higher up in the village. The orange streaks on its head seemed to flare as it sniffed.

Sierra breathed slowly through her nose, trying not to make a sound. The copper tang of blood filled her nostrils.

Oh, fuck.

Ten yards away, hundreds of pounds of fresh meat sat on racks by the smoke fires.

Chapter Sixty-Seven

Randall kept close to Joe, Harold, and Morrie as they ran along the huts toward the side exit. Ahead of them, three people darted through the opening in the wall, then turned left, toward the canyon.

Joe carried the AR-15 and the big Smith & Wesson stuck in his pants. Harold had Burt's MP5 and Morrie held an ancient hunting rifle. Randall carried a Winchester long gun, plus the twenty-two he'd taken from Harold and the Beretta he'd snagged from Cameron. Seven guns. Not nearly enough for two *T. rexes*.

"Hurry, let's go." Harold raced out in the open.

Randall finally spotted Crystal, in the middle of a small group running in the same direction. "Hey," he called out.

"No, no, no, wait," Morrie pointed. "There's another one." He stopped by the corner of the last hut.

"Shit," Joe hissed, backing up next to Morrie. "Shit. Shit. Shit."

Harold kept running, clearly still dazed from getting knocked in the head. He froze at the gap in the wall.

The Tyrannosaurus with the ugly pink skin emerged from the woods outside the village. It closed the distance to the outhouses in four strides, then stopped, jerking its head back and forth, tracking the crowd, which split in two. Some people ran uphill outside the wall, while Crystal, a man wearing coveralls, and two others retreated back into the village. Screams came from both groups.

Randall held his breath. Somewhere deep in the back of his mind, he cared for that woman, fucked-up teeth and all. He hadn't cared for anyone since he was seven and found his mother dead from an overdose on the bathroom floor.

The asshole in the coveralls shoved Crystal out of the way and ran along the inside of the wall, toward the high end of the village.

Harold remained frozen in the opening, looking up at the monster.

Cold terror swept over Randall. One dinosaur was directly ahead. The other was off to his right, coming up through the fields below the sheds. They were blocking both exits. He was trapped.

Chapter Sixty-Eight

"Josh, wake up!" Sierra glanced over at the work tables, hunting for another knife she could use to cut him free. There was nothing. She kept pulling at the knot. Beyond the tables, the Tyrannosaurus was halfway across the fields and coming straight toward her.

She turned back to Josh as screams came from further up in the village. A second Tyrannosaurus appeared at the opening near the outhouse exit, bigger than the one behind her. She tensed. If this new one turned her way, it would spot her.

"Come on, Josh, please," she whispered, digging into the knot. Pain lanced her bleeding fingernails. She yanked on the vines. It was useless. She couldn't free him.

The larger Tyrannosaurus stepped forward, which put it behind the small cluster of trees.

She looked over her shoulder. The first Tyrannosaurus arrived at the rhino meat and plucked a chunk from the wooden racks. Another half-dozen racks stood between it and her.

She didn't know what to do. She couldn't free Josh, she couldn't leave him, and she couldn't stay here. She had zero options.

Chapter Sixty-Nine

Joe leaned back against the corner of the cabin next to Randall and Morrie. Twenty yards in front of them, the Tyrannosaurus loomed over the side entrance.

Harold stood below it, right at the gap in the wall. His paralysis broke. He threw his hands up in the air and ran back toward them.

Randall raised the Beretta, pointing it straight at Harold.

Joe clutched his arm. "No."

"That asshole will lead it here," Randall hissed.

He's got what it takes, Joe's daddy said. *Too bad you don't.*

"I do," Joe growled. He raised his AR-15.

Before he could pull the trigger, the dinosaur lunged, striking like a snake, clamping its jaws around Harold's shoulder and lifting him from the ground. He screeched.

"Goddamn it," Joe stammered.

Harold screamed from inside the monster's mouth. He pounded on the creature's face with his free arm. The jaws crunched tight and the pounding ceased. A fountain of blood sprayed the ground. Harold's headless body fell, a half-circle missing where his shoulder had been.

The beast stepped into the village, ignoring the corpse. It gave a throaty bellow that shook Joe's bowels.

He pressed himself into the side of the cabin. Morrie fidgeted, like maybe he was about to bolt, but Joe threw his arm across his chest, keeping him there. He couldn't lose any more men.

The Tyrannosaurus tramped along the perimeter wall, moving in the direction Crystal and the others had gone, up toward the high end of the village.

Behind it, the side exit was clear.

"Come on," Joe growled. He ran toward the opening, with Morrie and Randall close behind.

"Oh, shit." Morrie pointed past the little cluster of trees on their right. The other dinosaur, the one with the orange head, was coming up through the fields. "It's gonna get Josh."

"Good," Joe spat. "This is his fault."

It's your fault, Joe's daddy said. *It's always your fault.*

Joe ground his teeth. He ran towards the opening, where Harold's body lay in a heap. Shards of white bone glistened inside the hole in his chest.

Randall snatched the MP5. A dark hunk from one of Harold's organs spilled out as he yanked the gun free.

They ran through the opening and turned left, toward the canyon.

"It's not my fault," Joe muttered through gritted teeth. "It's not my goddamn fault."

Chapter Seventy

Sierra was out of time. She had to run. The Tyrannosaurus with the orange head had gorged itself on the rhinoceros meat. It was less than forty feet from her.

In the other direction, the second Tyrannosaurus stomped away, heading up toward the high end of the village. She had to flee while she could.

That meant leaving Josh.

The Tyrannosaurus behind her inhaled, a sound like an angry ghoul, and snatched the last mouthful of meat. Smoke from a half-dozen cook fires surrounded it. She had to try to lure it away.

She kissed Josh on the temple. "Don't wake up," she whispered. Tears streamed down her cheeks.

The dinosaur turned toward her, now less than thirty feet away. It wove through the smoke, its orange head glowing from the light of the fires.

If she couldn't lure it away, it would eat Josh alive.

Sierra froze as a terrible idea came to her.

She yanked the pentobarbital from inside her bra, twisted loose the cap, and placed the bottle in the hood of Josh's sweatshirt, hanging between his shoulder blades. She hated herself. This was beyond horrible.

But if it ate him, it would eat the poison too.

Chapter Seventy-One

Randall raced along the wall outside the village, catching up to the Tyrannosaurus stomping along on the inside.

Crystal still had a chance. She could get out through the tiny gap where the creek flowed in. A dozen people clumped at the opening, which was only big enough for one person to squeeze through at a time. Crystal bounced from side to side at the back of the group, trying to push through.

The Tyrannosaurus was almost to her. Joe fired his AR-15 over the wall. Shots flicked across the dinosaur's flanks.

"Save the ammo," Morrie shouted. He and Joe ran to the opening as a woman squeezed out.

The dinosaur lunged into the crowd, biting. Its head rose, lifting two people in its jaws. The man in the coveralls dangled by one leg, screaming. The other victim, a woman, was crushed in the center of its mouth. It dropped them both. The man crawled away, dragging his destroyed leg behind him. The Tyrannosaurus pounced and snapped. The man collapsed, no longer moving, riddled with holes from dagger-sized teeth.

"Goddamn it," Joe shouted.

The fucking thing was killing everyone in sight, and not even bothering to eat them. In Oklahoma, they called it henhouse syndrome, when a coyote killed more than it could eat, to save the rest for later. The Tyrannosaurus was doing the same thing. Or maybe it just liked to kill.

The villagers still inside the wall shoved one another, desperate to get through the narrow opening. Hands reached, choking the gap. Morrie grabbed a man by the collar and jerked him through.

Crystal called out, "Randall!" His heart tightened. He dashed to the opening.

Another guy jumped and caught the top of the wall. He pulled himself up and swung a leg over. The Tyrannosaurus plucked him off, shook him, and dropped his corpse.

Randall grabbed a woman who came through the gap and shoved her out of the way. She fell on her face.

Joe pulled her up. "Get to the canyon. Climb the ladder."

Two more squeezed through and joined the others running up the path.

The Tyrannosaurus loomed over the three remaining villagers, oily gore dripping on them. Crystal was still in the back. The monster leaned down, but she dodged away. It chomped a middle-aged woman in half. Blood sprayed Crystal, soaking her hair.

The other villager pushed forward. Randall yanked him through the opening. "Move!"

Crystal was right there. Their eyes connected.

The head of the Tyrannosaurus came down again.

Randall grabbed Crystal's bicep, right on the lucky diamonds, and pulled. She screamed, a high thin sound like air escaping from a balloon, and slipped through the wall. The dinosaur's teeth snapped shut behind her.

Randall gulped. He'd saved her.

"Let's go," Joe shouted.

At least four bodies lay inside the wall, enough to keep that giant fucker occupied while they fled to the canyon.

Randall ran, still gripping Crystal's arm. They were in the back of the crowd. They had to get to the front. There'd be another bottleneck at the ladder, and they wouldn't be safe until they were on the plateau.

A crack came from behind, then a crumbling crash. Crystal's arm jerked and she pulled free from his grip, rising somehow. Randall looked back, still running.

The Tyrannosaurus had broken through the wall and snatched her. Its jaws sank into her torso as it lifted her high in the air. She opened her mouth in a silent scream. The dinosaur bit down and her body fell in two pieces. Blood landed on pine needles in thick, pattering globs.

Randall kept running, fury and fear pounding in his ears.

Chapter Seventy-Two

Sierra stumbled toward the gallows platform behind Josh. "Come on," she cried, shouting at the dinosaur, trying to lure it away from the boy. The distant screams of villagers grew louder. She shuddered. Where was the other one, the larger one? For all she knew, it had come back down and was right behind her.

The first Tyrannosaurus followed her, but stopped next to Josh, still suspended in the web of ropes. It looked at him, tilting its head.

"This way!" Sierra waved her arms in wide arcs. "*Come on!*" Her voice cracked as she screamed.

The Tyrannosaurus turned its head toward her.

"That's it! Here!" She backed away, ready to sprint to the exit. If she made it through the wall, she could try to lose it in the woods.

The monster turned back, opened its mouth wide, and bent toward Josh. Sierra brought her arms up over her face, but it didn't help. She heard the butcher's rack break apart. Wood splintered and vines snapped. She wailed, a raw, involuntary sound, then retched on her shoes. When she opened her eyes, Josh was gone.

She stumbled backwards across the half-built gallows and fell onto the coils of rope. Josh's noose.

The Tyrannosaurus bent to snatch some part of Josh that had fallen onto the ground.

No no no no no.

Haze filled Sierra's head. She didn't know what to do, but she had to move. Shuddering and dry-heaving, she scooped up the rope,

throwing the coils over her shoulder. Maybe she could use it to climb
out of the canyon somehow. Maybe she could use it to hang Joe.

Chapter Seventy-Three

Cameron clenched her jaw, trying not to pass out. Her shoulder was wrecked and she'd lost a lot of blood. The gun had only been a twenty-two, but it hurt like a motherfucker.

Randall would pay.

She shuffled along the path behind David. They'd staggered out of the woods after the dinosaurs passed and David had screamed and hollered, but the creatures had ignored them.

Roars came from the village.

"Goddammit." David ran harder. His kids were up there.

Cameron tried to keep up, but she didn't have the strength. David's long-sleeve shirt was tied around her neck, a makeshift sling immobilizing her arm.

They reached the opening in the wall. One of the dinosaurs stood feeding at the center of the village, near the big rock fire pit. She saw no other signs of life.

David stood in the opening and shouted, "Barry! Kim!"

Kona ran into the fields, barking at the Tyrannosaurus. It raised its head and looked in the dog's direction.

Cameron caught up to David, dizziness tingling the back of her skull. She couldn't keep going much longer.

Smoke rose from the campfires. The wooden structures that had held rhino meat lay splintered on the ground, as well as the butcher's rack. There was no sign of Josh.

"Where are they?" David cried.

"Canyon," Cameron said. It was the only place to go.

Kona darted back and forth in the dirt, barking nonstop. The Tyrannosaurus shambled toward her through the smoke, its head down, looking at the dog.

Kona's barks grew hoarse.

Cameron grabbed David by the back of his neck and pulled him close. "Listen. I got this." Her voice was low and sultry. She didn't mean for it to be that way, not now at least, but it was all she had left. "Go around. Find your kids."

The Tyrannosaurus was halfway across the fields.

Cameron pulled Charlie's Ruger from the small of her back, where it rested against the tramp-stamp she had gotten to impress him, all those years ago.

David raised his eyebrow. "You've got another gun?"

"I've always got another gun."

A thin smile lit his face. She wished she'd gotten to know him better. They could have made a good team.

"Go," Cameron shouted, raising the Ruger.

David started left, outside the wall. He probably didn't realize that a nine-millimeter wouldn't do jack shit against an eight-thousand-pound monster.

The dinosaur stumbled closer, staggering as it walked. Something was wrong with it. This was the one with the orange stripes on its head, the one that had eaten Lily. Maybe that fundamentalist cunt had made it sick.

Cameron took a firing stance, legs shoulder-width, knees bent, her weight slightly forward. Her only hope was to hit it in the eye, and for the bullet to pass through the socket to its brain. She pulled the trigger. A flicker appeared on the dinosaur's cheek from her shot. She steadied her arm, wishing she could use both hands. Her shoulder burned like hot oil.

The Tyrannosaurus lumbered forward, then paused, wobbling.

A blurry cloud passed above it. Another watcher, or maybe the same one she'd seen earlier. Cameron tracked it with her gun. David said they were useless. If she shot the damn thing out of the sky and it landed on the dinosaur, maybe it wouldn't be so useless after all. "Fuck." She aimed back at the Tyrannosaurus. She couldn't spare the round.

Kona danced at the monster's feet, still barking. The dinosaur ignored the dog. It had spotted Cameron.

She pulled the trigger again. Her hand kicked up and a flicker of blood burst from the creature's nose. In four more steps it would reach her. She backed down the trail.

Five rounds left. Each one had to count.

The Tyrannosaurus roared and she fired twice more. One shot exploded on the roof of its mouth. Hopefully, that did some damage.

Sulfur and saltpeter burned her nostrils. She breathed in, relishing the smells one last time.

The Tyrannosaurus stepped through the opening in the wall. Kona circled its feet, barking madly but keeping just out of reach. Cameron retreated down the path.

The dinosaur's lower jaw dropped and black bile poured from its mouth. It raised its leg to take another step, but then brought it back down and stood still. Something was definitely wrong with it. Maybe the nine-millimeter rounds were doing more damage than she thought.

She pulled the trigger twice more, placing both shots between the creature's eyes. Chunks of gore sparked from its skin, but she couldn't possibly have pierced its skull.

One shot left. She considered putting the gun to the bottom of her chin. Immediate death would be better than getting eaten alive.

The dinosaur lurched and tumbled forward, crashing on the path with a ground-shaking thud. Frothy blood oozed from its nose. Kona yelped and sprinted away.

Cameron couldn't decide if she should flee or fire another shot directly into the dinosaur's face. She couldn't concentrate. She couldn't feel her shoulder. The world swam around her and she felt like she was falling. Dizziness won over. Her knees buckled and she collapsed to the dirt.

Chapter Seventy-Four

Sierra raced outside the village toward the canyon, trying to focus on what to do, trying not to think about Josh. She slowed at the sound of wet crunching. The larger Tyrannosaurus stood inside the wall, its tail high and its face down, hidden from view. The gap where the creek trickled into the village had been torn open.

The monster rooted around, feeding. Sierra pressed her fist into her diaphragm to keep from puking again. *Please don't let that be Kim. Or Barry. Or David. Or Waldmire.*

Hopefully, it was Joe.

She circled away into the woods, stepping lightly on pine needles. The coiled rope on her shoulder weighed her down but she couldn't leave it behind. It might help them climb to the plateau somehow, or maybe rappel down on the back side of the island.

She reconnected with the creek further upstream and ran to the canyon. Inside, she couldn't hear anything but the sound of her footsteps and her heaving gasps. Maybe the others were already up top. If Joe was there, she would shove him off the cliff. The piece of shit had left Josh to die, beaten and helpless.

Her legs shook. She wanted to drop to her knees to scream. He was just a teenage boy. She remembered him on her motorcycle in Brentwood. She pictured him sitting tall next to Wayne on the hilltop, trying to be a man.

A low-frequency bellow boomed through the canyon. The Tyrannosaurus was following her. Sierra groaned, pumping her legs. Terror turned the world red. Hadn't it eaten enough already?

She tried to focus, to push her grief and fear aside. There had to be something they could do. They could shove rocks onto the dinosaur from above or maybe they could somehow block off part of the canyon, trapping it.

Boulders sat here and there along the walls. If they gathered enough rocks, and everyone worked together, maybe they could build a barricade. It wouldn't even need to be high, just enough to trip the dinosaur if it tried to climb over.

That's it, she thought. *The rope.*

The smaller Tyrannosaurus had stumbled on the wall when it entered the village. Falling had to be dangerous for creatures that big. She needed to find a way to use her rope as a trip line.

Crowd noises came from ahead. Sierra rounded the last corner and faced a pair of gun barrels. Joe and Randall. She slid to a halt, her mouth wide, unable to breathe. They'd shoot her for knocking out Harold. For planning to poison Joe. Or maybe just on principle.

"Sierra." Joe lowered his big assault rifle and beckoned her closer. "Get over here."

Her breath came back. He didn't know what she'd done, what she'd been planning. She had to keep it that way, to put on a performance. She couldn't rage at them about Josh.

"One's coming this way," she said. "I don't know about the other."

"Get up the wall," Joe said. "We have to get up top, where they can't reach us."

Behind him, in the back left corner, eight or nine people stood below the ladder, with five or six others climbing above them. Kim led the group, about halfway up.

"Kim!" Sierra called, swelling with joy. She was still alive.

"She's to blame for this," Joe hissed.

Sierra didn't respond. Kim must have gotten here before Joe. Otherwise, he would have sent her to the back of the line, or worse.

At the bottom of the ladder, Morrie held the crowd back to keep everyone from swarming the lowest climber. Priya and Jasmine stood among them, waiting for their turns. Waldmire, David, and Barry weren't here. Sierra swallowed and forced herself to forget about them for now.

Harold wasn't here either. He must not have told Joe she'd attacked him.

Judging from the speed of the people climbing the ladder, the Tyrannosaurus would get here long before they all reached the top, and Sierra would be at the back of the line.

Two women shoved each other, fighting for the next spot. Morrie pulled them apart. "One at a time."

Another roar reverberated through the canyon. Screams came from the crowd. The guy wearing the blazer pushed past Morrie, but he grabbed him and shoved him back in line.

Sierra lifted the coils of rope over her head. "I need help. Somebody come help me make a trip line."

"You'll just piss it off," Joe said.

"No. I saw one stumble. If it falls, it'll break its bones." They had to try something. "We can at least slow it down."

Kim was almost two thirds of the way up. Near the halfway point, a young woman slapped the heels of the woman above her. It was Carol, frozen on the ladder. Sierra winced. Carol was in her seventies. She might not have the strength to make it to the top.

Beyond the small crowd, the waterfall spilled into the knee-deep pool. There was nowhere else to go.

"It's worth a shot," Morrie said, looking even more pale than usual. "If it goes down, we can shoot it in the head."

"Where?" Joe asked. "How are you gonna tie it?"

Sierra crept downstream, keenly aware she was moving toward the dinosaur. The first turn was about fifty yards back. When the Tyrannosaurus appeared, it would be only seconds from her.

She found a perfect pair of boulders sitting across from each other. One was chest-high and spherical. The other stood fifteen feet tall and leaned against the wall like a column. "Here." Sierra waved for Joe and his men to follow her. "Come help." She ran to the round boulder.

Morrie appeared beside her a moment later, grabbing an armload of rope. Joe and Randall hadn't moved.

Another roar bellowed up the canyon. "It's getting close," Morrie grunted. Sweat dripped down his face.

Sierra wrapped the end of the rope around the smaller rock. "Feed it through," she said, holding the noose open. Morrie shoved the rope through the loop, then gathered the coils and splashed across the creek to the opposite side, doling out the line behind him. Sierra cinched the rope tight around the boulder and gave it a tug. It felt secure.

She followed the line across the canyon, where Morrie shoved coils through the gap between the column-shaped rock and the wall. She grabbed the rope as he fed it to her. Thirty feet back, Joe and Randall just stood there, waiting.

"Get ready," she shouted, then added, "*assholes*" under her breath.

"No shit," Morrie muttered.

The pink and black head of the Tyrannosaurus appeared at the far end of the canyon. Dark blood dripped down its chin. Sierra shuddered. It looked like a vulture.

Morrie fed the slack rope through the gap while Sierra pulled, scraping her knuckles raw on the rocks.

The rope snapped tight, lifting the section that ran across the canyon floor. It was a perfect trip line, but only as long as she pulled on the loose end.

"We've gotta tie a knot," Sierra said. Chills shot up her neck. The Tyrannosaurus was fully around the corner, fifty yards away, each step bringing it three yards closer.

"There's no time." Morrie shook his head, lips trembling. "Come on." He ran back to the others.

Twenty or thirty feet of rope remained. Sierra wanted to shriek. Why the hell had they needed so much rope to hang a teenage boy? Morrie was right. There was no time to tie a knot.

The dinosaur roared again. It had cleared half the distance to her. Screams of terror came from the back of the canyon.

Chapter Seventy-Five

David stopped in the mud where the creek seeped out from under the wall. Behind him, one Tyrannosaurus lay on the path, just outside the village. He couldn't see Cameron. "Shit." It wouldn't take long to go back. He had to check on her, to make sure she wasn't crashing.

Water oozing under the wall flowed red with blood.

"Shit, shit, shit."

He'd survived his own gunshot wound. Cameron was tough. She could hang on a little longer. He had to save his kids, assuming it wasn't too late. Praying, he pressed on, running along the wall.

Halfway around the village, the trees crowded close, growing thick on both sides.

Barry's voice rang out. "Daddy!"

Relief shuddered through him. He grabbed the top of the wall, craning to see over it. "Barry? Where are you?"

"Up here, David." Waldmire sat twenty feet up, in the branches of a tree over the camping area, one arm around the trunk and the other around Barry.

"Oh my God, thank you, thank you." David looked from branch to branch, but the rest were empty. "Where's Kim?"

"I don't know," Waldmire said. "The other dinosaur followed everyone to the canyon."

"Daddy, I'm scared." Barry's voice broke.

"I know, Bud." David swallowed. "You stay there. Both of you."

Waldmire nodded and David started off.

"Hurry," Waldmire called out. "Please find Sierra, too."

Chapter Seventy-Six

The Tyrannosaurus tilted its head, taking in the crowd.

Sierra fled deeper into the canyon, unspooling the extra rope as she went. Behind her, the line ran along the wall, then wrapped around the tall rock and extended across to the other side, two feet off the ground.

"Get your guns ready," she shouted. No one was doing a damn thing to help. She searched for some place to tie off the end of the rope, to hold it taut.

The Tyrannosaurus stomped closer. The man wearing the blazer broke out of line and fled to the rear of the canyon, cowering near the waterfall.

A small boulder near the ladder looked like it might be heavy enough to anchor the rope. Sierra ran to it, keeping the line tight as it slid through her hands, burning them. The end came up just shy of the rock. Now the goddamn thing was too short.

"We can still trip it," she shouted, pulling the end of the rope. The line ran from her hands to the rock, then turned across the canyon, where it trembled just above the ground. She shouted at the villagers. *"Help me."*

Priya abandoned her spot in line and took up the rope behind Sierra. She barely weighed over a hundred pounds. Not nearly enough.

"Gimme that," Jasmine said, grabbing the end of the rope.

Sierra felt a spark of hope. One by one, other villagers joined them, even the guy wearing the blazer.

The trip line held tight, a tug-of-war wrapping around the rock column, then crossing in front of the dinosaur's shins.

The monster stopped and sniffed the air, flexing its fingers. Prey was plentiful here at the end of the canyon. It could kill them all and feed at its leisure.

As each person joined on the rope, Sierra scooted forward. Several people on the ladder came down off the wall to help. One man cradled an injured arm against his chest while pulling with his other hand.

The Tyrannosaurus stepped closer.

"Hold the line!" Sierra shouted. The rope trembled, taut and alive in her hands.

"Come on, you big mother," Jasmine shouted from the back. She wrapped the end of the rope around her wide belly.

Joe, Morrie, and Randall lined up next to them, raising their guns like a firing squad.

The toes on the dinosaur's foot slid under the rope. It lifted, yanking everyone toward it. Sierra floundered, almost dropping to her knees. Grunts and shouts came from behind.

"Pull!" Sierra clenched her teeth and dug against the ground with her feet. Her palms burned.

The crowd moved back, an inch at a time, pulling the rope tight against the column.

The body of the Tyrannosaurus shifted forward. Its front leg reached, trying to get beneath its massive weight, but the foot was still caught under the rope.

The line held.

Momentum kept the creature moving. Its tail thrashed, smacking the canyon walls. A putrid snarl burst from its mouth.

It toppled and slammed to the ground, whipping the rope through everyone's hands.

The canyon shook. Creek water sprayed Sierra and dirt rained down from above. She backpedaled, shoving the others out of the way.

"The eyes." Morrie held his rifle to his shoulder. "Aim for the eyes." He fired first.

As the Tyrannosaurus began to rise, Joe, Morrie, and Randall shot its face from less than ten feet away. Its eyes exploded, splattering the canyon.

The others receded along the wall, huddling together.

The dinosaur roared, exposing nine-inch teeth with strings of flesh and tatters of clothing wedged between them.

Sierra pressed her hands against her ears as deafening gunfire filled the canyon.

Morrie threw down his rifle, apparently empty, grabbed a second one from Randall's back, and started shooting again. Randall dropped one handgun and switched to another.

Pale chips of bone flew from the dinosaur's eye sockets. All three men fired until their weapons clicked empty. Joe dropped his assault rifle, pulled out his revolver, and fired six times. Blue smoke clouded around them. The echoes of Joe's final shots continued after the gunfire ended.

The Tyrannosaurus lay motionless, with gaping craters where its eyes had been. Chunky blood carried bits of bone down the sides of its face.

Sierra gasped. "We did it," she whispered.

"Holy shit." Morrie panted. A goofy smile covered his face.

Joe and Randall stood on either side of him with their mouths hanging open.

Jasmine whooped and began hugging everyone around her.

The guy in the blazer ran over and put his hands on Sierra's shoulders. His cheeks puffed red on either side of a beaming smile. He looked like he might try to kiss her. He opened his mouth, but couldn't seem to find any words.

"It's okay," Sierra said. "We're all okay."

He released her shoulders and stepped back, still beaming.

Behind him, Reggie took off his baseball cap and rubbed his bald head. "That was amazing, Sierra. You saved us."

"We did it together," she said.

Almost everyone was smiling. A few of them were laughing.

The people still on the ladder descended. Carol climbed down even more slowly than she'd gone up, preventing Kim from joining the celebration.

A small group gathered around the head of the monster. Gray gore oozed down its cheeks. Its body lay in a twisted heap, blocking the canyon. Water from the creek pooled alongside its contours.

Priya walked over to Sierra and held up her knuckles for a fist bump. "You did it. I don't know how, but you did it."

"Simple physics, right?" Sierra said.

"No," Priya said. "Not that. Getting everyone to work together. You saved us all."

Sierra nudged Priya's arm aside and gave her a hug, meaning to keep it brief because Priya wasn't the touchy sort. Priya surprised her, bringing her arms tight behind Sierra's back.

Sierra shuddered, feeling a mixture of grief and relief. She hadn't saved *everyone*.

"What do we do now?" someone asked from the crowd.

"Yeah," someone else shouted. "What now?"

They were all looking at her.

Joe swiveled his head back and forth, his mouth hanging open.

Over on the wall, Morrie helped Carol down the last few feet. As soon as she was out of the way, Kim hurried to the bottom.

Sierra pushed past the others and met her, wrapping her arms around the girl. *Don't ask about Josh.*

Kim pulled back and looked up at her. The question was there in her eyes.

Sierra didn't say anything. She couldn't.

A dog bark came from somewhere down the canyon, beyond the carcass.

Kim turned away. "Dad?"

Sierra stood on her tiptoes, craning to see over the huge corpse. She'd gotten the reprieve she needed.

"Kim!" David called out, desperation in his voice. "Where are you?" He appeared around the final bend in the canyon with Kona by his side.

"Where's the other one?" Morrie shouted.

David climbed onto the leg of the fallen Tyrannosaurus. "It's dead. Cameron killed it."

Cameron or the poison? It didn't matter. Sierra couldn't share what she'd done.

"Dad!" Kim ran forward.

Joe snatched her wrist as she passed.

She looked up, shaking her arm. "Let me go."

"My people are dead because of you," Joe said, his voice a low growl. "Someone has to pay."

Chapter Seventy-Seven

David staggered across the body of the dead dinosaur. "Let her go," he shouted.

"She's a child," someone yelled.

Another person cried, "Come on Joe. This is crazy."

Reggie stepped forward and grabbed Joe's arm.

Joe shook free and pointed his gun at him. "Get back."

The crowd shifted away. Reggie held up his hands, pure terror on his face.

David's legs stopped obeying him. He dropped to his knees and crawled across the carcass. Clumps of downy fuzz came loose in his hands.

Joe swung around, looking at the villagers, his words low and livid. "People died because of her." He kept his grip on Kim and swung the barrel of the gun toward the crowd.

No one moved.

"Harold's dead," Joe growled. "And a bunch more back at the wall." He sounded ready to explode. "Someone has to pay."

Randall leaned over Kim. "Crystal died 'cause of you."

Kim trembled, her mouth frozen wide in a grimace. She tried to pull free, but Joe jerked her back.

David's heart hitched. The world had gone insane.

"She didn't do anything," Sierra said. "It wasn't her."

David slid down the shoulder of the Tyrannosaurus and lurched to his feet. His gorge rose in his throat from the moldy smell of the dinosaur and its rancid blood.

Kona barked behind him, still on the other side of the carcass.

"Lily told us everything," Joe hissed. "The girl was in on it."

Kim sobbed. "Yeah, because you were going to kill Josh." She twisted and pulled, trying to break free from his grip.

David's heart sank. *Oh Jesus, Kim, don't admit it.*

Joe's mouth closed, forming a wide straight line.

David ran forward. Joe raised the revolver and pointed it straight at his heart. David froze.

Kim wailed and covered her face with her hands.

"You can't blame a kid for having a shitty father, though, can you?" Joe said.

Screams came from the crowd.

"Joe, don't," someone shouted.

Joe pulled the trigger. The hammer clicked on an empty cylinder.

Barely able to breathe, David lunged forward, reaching.

An arm snaked around his neck, jerking him back. The hard metal of a gun barrel pressed against his head. "Don't move, Dave," Randall said into his ear.

David tugged Randall's arm. It constricted even tighter around his neck.

Joe dug into his pocket and pulled out a single bullet. He punched it into the revolver and swung it toward the crowd, which had been creeping closer. Everyone froze, except Morrie, who kept coming.

"Is that the only round you got left? We need it." Morrie kept voice low and even. "Come on, Joe."

Joe brought the giant silver gun back to David's chest.

Hissing gasps came from the villagers. Several whispered Joe's name. He looked off in the other direction, as if listening to something else. He cocked the hammer.

Kim cried in her hands.

A vicious tirade bubbled up inside David. Joe was as much to blame for what had happened as anyone. He'd lost his mind after Thad killed children and then only two days later, he'd decided to hang a teenage boy.

David kept his mouth shut. It wouldn't change anything. Joe was too far gone, lost in a twisted confusion of insane rationalizations.

Still holding his neck, Randall marched him over to the canyon wall and stepped away.

David stood tall, clenching his raw throat.

Joe raised the barrel, aiming at his forehead, right where he'd shot Thad.

"*Noooooooo.*" Kim's shout turned into sobs.

"Joe, we need the ammo," Morrie whispered. "We need it to keep people safe. Tie him up and let's figure this out."

Fury darkened Joe's face. "The last time we tied somebody up, all of this happened!" Spit flew from his mouth.

"That's fine," Morrie said, taking another step closer. "But we need that ammo. Be smart. Let's find another way."

"What other way?" Joe spun on him, cords popping from his neck.

Morrie flinched back.

"You're insane," Jasmine shouted.

Joe glared at her. She receded into the crowd.

David looked up, praying for an end to this madness. A blurry shape floated in the canyon above them. He opened his mouth to point it out, then lost sight of it against the mist of the waterfall.

Randall, watching him, let out a giggling hiss. "I got it, Joe. He's terrified of heights. Throw him from the top. That's how they kill queers in the Middle East, ain't it."

"That's it." Joe nodded so hard his whole body shook. "Take him up there, Randall."

Randall grabbed David's shirt at the neck.

"You're gonna splat like a mother fucker," Joe whispered.

David looked up at the wall, his breath coming in short hitches. He imagined the fall, the tumbling rise in his stomach, the ground rushing toward him.

Randall shoved him toward the ladder.

"Joe, please don't do this," Sierra said.

"He falls," Joe said, aiming the revolver at Kim. "Or I shoot the girl."

David looked Joe square in the eye. "I'm going."

"*Dad, noooo!*" The anguish in Kim's voice shriveled his heart.

"It's okay," he muttered, barely able to get the words out. "Barry needs you."

"Somebody, do something," Priya said. "This is madness."

"Come on, he's a doctor," someone else shouted, taking a step forward.

Joe swung the gun around. "Back off."

David reached for the ladder, curving his fingers inside the horizontal slit, but Randall shoved him aside. "Me first, Dave. Can't let you kick me off and run away up top."

Randall started up the ladder.

David stole a final look at Kim and climbed up behind him.

Chapter Seventy-Eight

Sierra stepped closer to Joe, trying to hold her expression neutral.

"Keep your distance." His eyes narrowed to thin slits. "You're not going to stop this. People must be punished. We went easy on Thad and he killed children. We went easy on David and Josh. Look what happened."

Sierra wanted to grab his gun and shove it down his throat. Instead, she said, "I know. Thad should have been stopped long before any of that happened."

Joe nodded, but the motion was so slight he might have only been trembling.

She ran with it. She had to do something. Anything. "You were right all along."

He tilted his head.

The villagers drifted back from the wall as they watched Randall and David climb.

Kona jumped down from the dead dinosaur and ran to the bottom of the ladder, barking. Morrie grabbed her collar. "Easy, girl."

"You've been right about David all along," Sierra said. "He thinks he's better than you. He wanted to take over. He thought he could lead these people better than you. But he's soft. You ... you've been right about everything. You keep people safe. David couldn't even save Charlie."

Joe looked off to one side. He nodded.

She was getting through to him. She had to be.

Joe swung his head back. "Quit trying to play me, bitch."

Chapter Seventy-Nine

David stopped halfway up the cliff, paralyzed. He shoved his toes into a crevice, pulled close against the rock wall, and told himself not to look down. It would only make things worse.

He couldn't help it. He looked. His heart pounded against the inside of his chest like a war drum. On the canyon floor, everyone had moved to the opposite side, clearing the ground below him.

"You wanna jump from here?" Randall called down, glee in his voice. "Might not kill you. Might just break you." Randall's feet were three slots above him, out of reach.

"It wasn't Kim's fault," David said.

He imagined Lindsey chastising him. *Why do you bother arguing with someone like him?*

"Fuck you." Randall hawked and spat. A wet glob splattered David's shoulder.

He squeezed his fingers tight in the slots to keep from flinching, then began to climb again. He tried to focus on the handholds in front of him, but his eyes kept wandering down. He imagined the fall, flailing, reaching, grabbing as the ground raced up. The worst part was knowing Kim would watch.

"Things were going good for me. Then your daughter got my girlfriend killed," Randall said. "Maybe she'll be my girlfriend now."

David looked up, his acrophobia replaced by a red haze. He climbed three rungs and reached for Randall's foot. He would grab the piece of shit and pull him down with him.

Randall grinned, his eyes thin slits under greasy hair. "Go for it." One booted foot moved out, ready to kick David off the wall. Red laces dangled from scuffed black leather.

David stopped. He turned his head and pressed his cheek against the cold rock, shuddering. How had it come to this?

The blurry shape of a watcher floated in the canyon, out over the shallow pool. They always showed up when something happened, observing, never helping. They just floated overhead, out of reach.

Except this time, it wasn't above him, it was straight out.

He would make it help.

He had to get higher. "Keep climbing," he muttered.

Chapter Eighty

Sierra took a step forward. "Of course I'm playing you."

Joe's jaw clenched, muscles flexing at the corners. He kept his gun trained on Kim, who sobbed into her hands. Every few seconds, her eyes darted in her father's direction.

Sierra stood straight, pushing her chest out, trying to appear strong. "I want to be in your circle." She stepped closer. "I want to learn from you. I'll do whatever it takes to be on your team." Her stomach lurched at the putrid stink of his sweat.

Power through.

"Back off," Joe said, the sides of his neck flushing red. "When this is done, I'm going to give you a fucking lesson." He looked her up and down. "That's for damn sure."

Bile rose in her throat. She swallowed it back, lowered her chin, and raised her eyebrows to look up at him, trying to show eagerness instead of utter disgust.

The flush on Joe's neck rose up the sides of his face.

If she could just get him to point the gun away from Kim, she would charge. She would tackle him and claw out his throat. Morrie and Jasmine and the others would help. They had to.

Sierra took another step toward him.

"Don't you come any closer," he said.

"This ain't right," Morrie called out.

"Why are you doing this?" someone shouted.

Joe trembled with rage. *"Shut up."* His finger shook against the trigger.

Kim turned away. The grimace on her face grew red and tight.

Sierra held up a hand. If Joe didn't calm down, he'd shoot Kim by accident. She turned to the crowd. "Don't you understand? It has to be this way."

Kim sobbed, *"Sierra!"*

She ignored her. She was beginning to lose hope she could save David. She had to focus on Kim. She had to get her out of this horrifying situation. If she could get Joe to calm the fuck down, maybe he would let Kim leave. Maybe he wouldn't make the girl watch her father die.

Chapter Eighty-One

David craned his neck as Randall pulled himself onto the plateau. He prayed for a rhino to knock him over the edge, but a moment later, Randall's face appeared, safe and sound. The herds had surely fled from the dinosaur roars and the gunfire that followed.

If he wanted a last-second miracle, he had to create it himself.

The canyon floor was eighty feet below. The watcher hovered halfway down, still off to the side, drifting over the pool.

David closed his eyes, his fingers clamped so hard in the handholds they felt frozen.

Randall brought his gun over the edge and pointed it at him. "Keep moving, Dave."

"Just a second," he whispered, letting terror show on his face.

Randall smiled, relishing it.

Lindsey's voice was silent. He was all alone.

On the canyon floor, Sierra was pleading with Joe. The villagers clumped in a group on the far side, holding each other near the pond.

The watcher floated through the canyon. David waited, timing its movement. Every muscle in his body tightened. Cold sweat ran into his eyes. He didn't want to do this. Not this. But he had to. It was the only option.

The blurry shape floated closer.

Chapter Eighty-Two

The crowd craned their necks up at David and Randall, most of them sobbing. Sierra kept her eyes on the gun. Nothing was working, but she couldn't give up. She spoke quietly.

"Let Kim leave," she said. If Kim was gone, Joe couldn't shoot her, accidentally or otherwise. "She doesn't need to see this."

"She has to watch," he growled. "Afterwards, she can scrape him up and bury him in the woods."

Kim slid down the wall and sat, her palms covering her eyes. Joe's pistol followed her.

"Please," Sierra said. "What if it was your father?"

Joe barked hysterical laughter. "I would give everything to see it."

"Keep your eyes covered, Kim," Sierra said. "You don't have to look." Kim curled on the ground, crying.

Joe's mouth hinged open and closed, as if too angry for words. He stomped over, grabbed her wrist, and jerked her to her feet.

Kim wailed, holding her arms over her face.

Joe shoved the pistol into the waistband of his pants and yanked her arms down to her sides.

Sierra sucked in a quick breath and held it. The gun was no longer pointed at Kim.

"You watch this." Joe held her biceps and walked her backwards to the middle of the canyon.

Kim's hands clenched into fists. She looked up at her father, her lower lip trembling, tear-snot running from her nose.

Joe raised his face skyward and shouted, "Hurry up, Randall. Throw him off."

Sierra took a deep breath and charged, reaching for the pistol grip sticking out of Joe's pants.

He turned toward her, fury on his face.

Kim broke free and staggered out of the way.

Sierra grasped the pistol and slipped her finger into the trigger guard. If the safety was on, she was fucked. She squeezed the trigger.

The gun roared, shaking her hand. A white flash exploded in the front of Joe's pants. The bullet pinged off the rocks somewhere, but the muzzle flash had done more than enough damage.

Joe screamed and elbowed her away. The gun pulled free from her grip, still caught in his waistband.

Chapter Eighty-Three

The blurry shape passed under David, maybe ten feet out from the wall. He pushed himself off the side of the canyon, twisting in the air.

A gunshot rang out. *No. Not Kim. Please, God.*

Randall cackled.

Every instinct told David to close his eyes, but he held them open. His stomach tumbled. His lungs seized. He spread his arms wide and roared, a scream of anger and terror.

He fell, certain that he had miscalculated. He would miss the watcher, or it would dodge out of his way. He would smash into the canyon floor.

Halfway down, David slammed into the invisible shape.

It plunged under his weight. David felt the impact from head to foot. His lip went numb. Pain shot through his cracked ribs. Something crunched beneath his toes.

The watcher plummeted, propelled by his momentum. It listed sideways, threatening to dump him. David clawed and grasped at a broad, rough surface, his eyes squeezed shut.

Below, he heard the buzzing whine of a million mosquitoes, as if the thing was fighting to remain airborne.

The sensation of falling continued. David pressed his face against something that felt like leather and smelled like rot. He braced for impact.

Chapter Eighty-Four

Sierra gasped. David fell, arms out like a skydiver, then vanished into a blurry shape. He must have landed on it, because now the blur was coming down fast.

A watcher.

Joe roared, grasping his blackened crotch with both hands.

Sierra crossed her wrists in front of her face and shoved him with everything she had.

He tilted back and looked up.

The invisible shape caught the top of Joe's head and slammed him to the ground with the crunching metal of a car crash. His legs kicked up and his arms flailed as he collapsed flat on his back.

The object crushed the top half of his head, pancaking everything from his mouth up. His lower jaw jutted from his neck, but above that, his head was gone. Blood and brains blossomed across the stone, impossibly flat.

A warbling blur distorted the air above Joe's head. The watcher was on the ground, right in front of Sierra.

Gasps came from the crowd.

At the top of the blur, eight feet above the ground, David's head, shoulders, and torso appeared. The rest of his body was missing from the waist down. Red flesh was visible from below, as if he'd been sliced through, but somehow he continued to move around.

David turned, looking everywhere, until he spotted Kim. Relief washed across his face.

Sierra tried to make sense of what she was seeing. Beneath David, the air looked bent. His waist and legs were obviously still there, but they were hidden by an invisible bubble that went right through him. From below, she was able to see inside his body, right where the bubble bisected him.

"What the fuck?" someone blurted.

"What's happening?"

"Goddamn!"

Kim ran forward, reaching, crying for her father. "Dad, Dad, Dad." Her legs collided with whatever was underneath him. "Ow!"

Joe's foot twitched, then grew still. Wisps of smoke rose from his body.

The blurry shape flickered and materialized, along with the rest of David.

He was kneeling on a brown, eight-foot-long creature that lay motionless on top of a mechanical platform. The creature's body was a shapeless bulge, a giant sack of potatoes. A cluster of wiry appendages protruded from one end, like antennae, but other than that, it had no apparent arms or legs.

David slid off, groaning. When his feet hit solid ground, he collapsed in his daughter's arms. "Are you okay, Sweetie?"

Kim shook as she sobbed. *"Daddy."*

"Holy shit." Morrie took a step back.

Kona barked, keeping her distance.

The creature lay on a silver and yellow platform with a two-foot wall curving around one end, almost like the headboard of a bed. Nozzles and rods extended from the sides, some bent from the crash.

"Our keeper," Sierra said, dizzy from shock and adrenaline. "A watcher."

She sidestepped around the bloated creature, looking for a face. Its body reminded her of sea lions on the docks at Marina del Rey. Dark orange fluid beaded at a gash on its side. The cluster of stalks and limbs protruding from one end looked like the mouthparts of a bug, or maybe a shrimp.

David leaned on Kim, holding his ribs.

"Is it dead?" someone asked.

"What is it?"

"What the hell is going on?"

Priya took off her shoe and pressed the toe against the skin beside one of the cuts on the creature's body. Thick slime oozed out. "It isn't moving. Maybe the fall killed it."

Sierra stooped over Joe's corpse. The yellow metal base of the alien vehicle obscured everything above his lower jaw.

Wincing from the smell of burned flesh, she grabbed his gun and pried it free.

Chapter Eighty-Five

David squeezed Kim, unwilling to let her go. His ribs groaned in his chest. His lip swelled like he'd been punched. His thigh throbbed. Even his toes ached. He'd kicked something solid when he crashed into the watcher. He ignored all the pain and simply hugged his daughter.

"What the hell just happened?" demanded the man in the blazer.

The villagers crept closer, gathering around the body. It made David think of produce, a giant gourd maybe, with a cluster of strings growing at one end, like the roots of an onion.

Reggie took off his baseball cap and shook it at the creature. "What is that thing?"

"A watcher," David said. "It's been watching us since we got here."

"Bullshit," said a grim-faced woman, looking around. "This is bullshit, right?"

"It's what Thad saw," Priya said. "He thought it was an angel."

A man cradling his arm against his chest huffed. "That's no angel."

Kona put her front legs up on the vehicle and sniffed the body, her hackles raised.

More shouts came from the crowd. "Are you sure it's dead?"

"What do we do with it?"

"Where did it come from?"

"Does it have a face?"

As far as David could tell, there wasn't anything to do with it. His kids were safe now that Joe was dead, and— "Shit. Where's Randall?"

Everyone looked up. Randall was gone.

"I have to get back to Barry." He didn't think Randall could reach the village from the plateau, but he wasn't going to take any chances. "And Cameron, too. Randall shot her. I have to help her." He prayed it wasn't too late. She'd been there for him when he needed it. Hell, she'd saved his life. He glanced around. "Is anyone else hurt?"

Jasmine looked him up and down and chuffed. "You are, Shug."

"I think I broke my arm," said the man holding his wrist against his chest.

"Come with me," David said. "We'll splint it."

"Who else is missing?" Sierra asked. "Where's Waldmire?"

"He's safe," David said. "He climbed a tree with Barry."

Relief brightened Sierra's face. "Thank goodness."

"The dinosaurs killed Lily at the beach," David said. "She lured them here."

Heads shook in disbelief.

"Why?" someone asked.

"She was trying to finish what Thad started," David said.

"She was out of her goddamn mind," someone else said.

No one disagreed.

Sierra stood rigid. "Josh is dead too. The other Tyrannosaurus killed him." She looked like she wanted to say more, but her face tightened, anguished.

Kim wailed and kicked Joe's corpse in the kidneys until David pulled her away. She broke free and got in one last stomp, crunching his fingers. He pulled her tight, and she buried her face against his side, sobbing.

"A bunch of people were killed at the creek," Morrie said. He put his gun on the ground and stood with his hands raised slightly. He was the only one left who'd been helping Joe, and he seemed to realize he'd been on the wrong side. Morrie listed off five names. David didn't recognize them, but of course everyone in the crowd did. Several shook their heads. One dropped to her knees, her face in her hands. Jasmine blew out a long wail.

Reggie took off his baseball cap again and twisted it in his hands. "Are you sure?"

Morrie nodded. "I'm sorry, Reggie."

Reggie clutched his hat and shook.

"Come on, Kim. Let's get back to the village." David ushered her toward the carcass.

Jasmine wiped her eyes with her thumbs and snatched up Morrie's gun. "I'll go with you."

A woman with short blond hair and torn clothes stepped forward. Dirty tear-trails lined her cheeks, one of which had a nasty cut. "Me, too. I want to check on Barry."

David nodded. "You're Dee, aren't you?" She'd been looking after his kids while he was tied to the butcher's rack. "Come on. We'll get you patched up."

Four other people followed Jasmine, including the guy cradling his arm against his chest.

"Wait." Morrie fished around in his pocket. "Here's a few more rounds." He handed them to Jasmine and put his hands back in the air.

Still sobbing, Kim helped David climb over the Tyrannosaurus carcass. Jasmine, Dee, and the others followed.

"If you see Randall, kill him," Sierra called out.

"Gladly," Jasmine called back, with a hint of song in her voice.

Chapter Eighty-Six

Sierra studied the alien creature, surrounded by the small group that remained at the end of the canyon. Apart from her, there were five women and three men. So few. She only knew four of them by name. Priya, Morrie, Reggie, and Carol.

"I still don't understand what that is," said a woman standing next to her.

Five, Sierra corrected herself. The woman was Grace, famous for the tryst on the beach that had triggered Thad. Grace, whose boyfriend had been gored on the plateau.

Grace winced. "I mean, is it a bug or what?"

"It doesn't look like anything from Earth," Priya said, leaning over the end with all the appendages.

"Is it really dead?" Reggie asked, looking around at the others. His eyes were red and his pupils were distant. Someone he'd cared for had been killed by the Tyrannosaurus.

"It has to be," snorted the guy in the blazer. "You can tell from the smell."

Sierra prodded the creature with the muzzle of Joe's gun. The bloated mass barely yielded. She gave Priya a questioning look.

Priya shrugged. "I can't find any signs of life." She circled the eight-foot body, stepping over Joe's corpse like it was nothing more than a log. "Maybe this machine provided life support and it got damaged when it hit the ground." She stopped back where she'd started, by the stalks protruding from folds in the alien's skin. "This seems like the head, maybe."

"Where is its face?" asked Carol. The old woman had turned away in disgust, but glanced back periodically over her shoulder.

"In here somewhere, I think," Priya said. "I can't tell if these are mandibles, or antennae, or something else altogether." She had to stand on her toes to see over the short wall that curved around the end of the creature. "Some of them must be appendages, because all the controls for the vehicle are here."

Several of the spidery fingers were mottled, as if they'd been bruised. A few were cracked, with yellow fluid leaking out.

Priya leaned over and used her shoe to move a couple of the thin limbs out of the way. "That might be a mouth." She pointed to a small slit buried between flaps of skin.

One of the women hissed. "Don't get so close." She turned to Sierra. "We should burn it. It's nasty."

Priya stepped back. "Oh, come on, Felicia. We have to examine it. We need to learn everything we can about it."

"Priya is right," Sierra said, facing the woman. "We need to study it. But we also need to keep watch over it. Felicia, could you organize a guard rotation?"

She'd used two tricks she'd learned from her father, Rick Preston trademarks. She said the woman's name, which showed she cared enough to remember it, and she asked for her help, which would make the woman feel trusted.

Felicia looked confused. "Why do we have to guard it if it's dead?"

Sierra tilted her head. "On Earth, when a zookeeper gets mauled in a tiger cage, they retrieve the body. Sooner or later, this guy's friends will come for him."

Everyone looked up.

"Be careful," Carol said. "When a tiger mauls someone, they usually put it down."

Sierra nodded. "That's another reason we should have people standing guard."

"I'll do it," Felicia said. She had a hard face, like she'd been through a lot. They all had that much in common, at least.

"Thank you," Sierra said.

Felicia gave her a stern nod in return.

"If the other zookeepers come, what are we supposed to do then?" Priya asked.

"We're going to get some answers," Sierra said. "We're going to find out where the rest of the pods went and we'll show them we don't belong in cages. We're an intelligent species."

Morrie, hands still in the air, said, "If they've been watching us, they may have concluded differently."

Faces fell in the crowd. Every one of them had played a part in what had happened, through inaction, if nothing else. Sierra couldn't hold that over them. What good would it do?

She pulled one of Morrie's arms down. "You weren't responsible for Joe."

Morrie winced and lowered both hands. "My brother believed in Thad and got killed for it. I believed in Joe because he took care of Thad." He looked down. "I was wrong."

"It was a shitty situation," Sierra said. "From what I saw, you were trying to steer him in the right direction."

He nodded and stepped back into the ring of people, as if trying to disappear.

"What're we going to do with that?" Reggie wagged his cap at the dinosaur carcass, which lay diagonally across the creek, filling the canyon from one side to the other. Blood ran from its cratered eye sockets and yellow-green bile seeped from its mouth. The creek pooled in front of its body.

"We should cook it," Felicia said. "We need the food."

"No way," Reggie growled. "That thing ate people. Leave it be."

Sierra stepped up to him, choosing her words carefully, trying to be sensitive to his loss. "We have to do something with it. We can't just leave it to rot on our water source."

Reggie rubbed his bald head and looked at the carcass. "We should haul it out of here and burn it." He had the look of someone trying desperately to keep it together.

Sierra nodded. "That would give its victims a proper cremation. Can you figure out how to make it happen?" A task to focus on might help him with his grief.

Reggie took a deep breath. "Yeah. I can do that. I'll need help, though."

"We'll help you," Grace said.

It was nice to see people working together, and it looked as if a load had been lifted from Reggie's back.

Later, Sierra might propose that they cut strips of meat from the tail, and maybe the muscles in its legs, but nothing near the dinosaur's stomach. They did need the food. All the rhino meat was gone. This simply wasn't the right time to bring it up. They would also need to address the other dead Tyrannosaurus before it rotted.

The man wearing the blazer put his hands on his hips, which made his pot belly protrude. "What about you?" He sounded accusatory. "What're you going to do?"

She'd saved the worst job for herself. She looked down at Joe's corpse, where dark blood oozed from beneath the alien sled. "I'm going to scrape him up and bury him in the woods."

Blazer guy backed off.

Sierra released a long breath. As far as she could tell, they had a plan for everything urgent. The crowd began to dissolve. A few people kept looking at the alien, but several others started climbing over the dinosaur carcass.

Morrie and Felicia crouched beside the alien vehicle. "If we could figure this out, we could fly over the islands," Felicia said.

"Yes," Sierra said. It was exactly the kind of thinking they needed. She felt a hint of hope, along with the exhaustion that came after a surge of adrenaline died off.

Felicia pulled her aside, away from the others. She tipped her head toward Joe's body. "You did good. You did what none of us were able to do. Your father will be proud." Her eyes glistened.

Sierra's throat clenched. Felicia was right. Rick Preston would have been impressed. "Thank you," she managed. "I hope he's up there watching." She didn't really believe it, but that wasn't the sort of thing you shared with a stranger offering words of comfort.

Felicia looked confused. "David said that he's safe up in a tree."

"What?" Sierra felt equally confused. "Oh, Waldmire? He was my neighbor."

"Sorry," Felicia said. "I thought he was your dad. You've got the exact same smile."

She turned and walked over to the alien body, which was fortunate, because Sierra had no idea how to respond. The more she thought about it, the more she wondered if Felicia might be onto something.

Chapter Eighty-Seven

After two days of recuperation, David's patients seemed to be on the mend. He'd finished checking in on Dee and Kevin, who'd both been injured by the mob squeezing through the wall. Kevin suffered from a hairline fracture in his ulna and was also afflicted with a tedious penchant for stating the obvious. Dee, a twenty-something from Wisconsin, was covered in cuts and bruises. Both were lucky. Five people had died at the wall. Lily, Harold, Josh, and Joe brought the death toll to nine. The village population was down to twenty souls.

David wished there was someone to care for him. Nearly every part of his body ached, from the gunshot wound on his thigh to the swollen lip he'd gotten when he crashed into the alien creature.

He made his way uphill to meet with his third and final patient of the morning. Cameron sat waiting for him beside the creek, several yards upstream from the village.

She pulled her shirt from her shoulder and he dipped a clean piece of cloth in the water, then dabbed at the crusted blood around the gunshot wound. The tissue looked pink and healthy, with no sign of infection. The bullet had missed the shoulder joint capsule and exited right above her scapula.

He took her hand and raised it up to the side, testing her range of motion. "Does that hurt?"

She locked eyes with him. "It's ... sore."

Cameron was tough as nails. The motion had to be painful.

She placed her hand on his shoulder and leaned into the stretch. "I need to be straight with you about my medical history, as my doctor, you know. I don't actually have syphilis."

David folded the cloth and held it against her wound. "No?" Of course she didn't, and this wasn't a medical discussion. It was flirting. Bizarre Cameron flirting.

"Most of the assholes here left me alone thanks to that story." Her lips formed a small smile. "You can't tell anyone. Doctor-patient confidentiality."

A jolt of longing ran through him. He wasn't sure he'd ever seen her smile. He loved it.

Her eyes widened, waiting for his response.

He raised an eyebrow. "I'm gonna need to give you a thorough examination." He cringed as the words left his mouth. His own flirting was even worse. Who could blame him, though? He was out of practice after more than a decade of marriage. *Lindsey.* The thought of his wife doused his desire. "I'm still married, though."

Cameron huffed. "Your marriage got annulled by the Ender."

David took a deep breath, which sent pricks of pain into his side. There was still a chance Lindsey had survived. Until they found the rest of the pods, he had to hold on to hope. "I can't," was all he could manage to say.

She removed her hand from his shoulder. "Your loss, Ace."

He wanted to take it back. Lindsey was gone and Cameron was here. She was a beautiful woman, lean and strong. He swallowed. "I'll still need to keep an eye on that wound."

Cameron pulled her shirt up over her shoulder. "We can play doctor any time you want." She ran her tongue across her lip. "Just let me know."

David blushed, then turned at the sound of someone approaching. Sierra and Barry walked downstream from the canyon.

Barry ran to him, waving a ten-inch curved white spike.

"What've you got there?"

Barry showed off his prize. "A *T. rex* tooth. Sierra says we can use them as tools."

Sierra carried a woven basket overflowing with teeth. "We just lit the bonfire. Reggie and Felicia stayed up there to keep an eye on it."

An enormous pyre had been built outside the canyon for the dinosaur carcass. Chunks of meat from the tail and the legs had been carved off and carried to the village for food, but the rest of the creature was being burned, to dispose of its body and to cremate the human remains in its stomach.

Reggie and Felicia had devised a system of rolling logs to haul the carcass from the canyon. They'd used the same technique to move the alien vehicle down to the village.

"What about the one I killed?" Cameron asked.

Sierra looked at her feet. "We'll burn that one soon."

She had told David about placing the poison in Josh's hoodie and asked him to keep it a secret. She was self-conscious about what she'd done, and Cameron had been more than happy to take all the credit. Everyone simply assumed she'd made enough lucky shots to kill the dinosaur.

They walked together to the village. It seemed a different place now without Joe. People were talking to each other, working together.

"Dad, come quick," Kim shouted. "We got a light." She and Morrie crouched over the alien vehicle, which now sat where the butcher's rack had been. Kim was obsessed with the machine. To her, it was a puzzle to solve.

David had been hesitant about letting her near the thing until Cameron called him an overprotective grandma. He relented after Morrie promised to keep a close eye on her. He was grateful she had something to distract her, considering everything she'd gone through.

The alien corpse had been removed and now lay a few yards away on the wooden platform that had been built for the gallows. Reggie had devised a system using ropes to lift the body. It had taken half the village to move it just a few yards. He estimated the creature weighed between seven hundred and nine hundred pounds.

The ropes now anchored the creature's sled to several small trees and stumps. David doubted the aliens would have any trouble cutting through woven vines, but at least it couldn't just float off, the way their pods had.

"Show me the light," Priya said, rising from a crouch by the alien body. "What caused it?"

Kim and Morrie sat on the black, foam-like material that covered the surface where the creature's body had been, similar to the lining of the capsules. A two-foot-high dashboard ran along the front of the vehicle, around the corners, and extended back a third of its length, giving the whole thing the shape of a Roman chariot that had been stretched and squashed. Panels and knobs crowded the inside of the wall, where the alien's limbs had been, along with clusters of shallow holes.

Kim touched one of the holes in the front corner of the dashboard, while Morrie touched a similar hole on the opposite side.

A concave panel in the center of the console cast a sickly yellow glow on both of them.

David tensed, ready to grab Kim and pull her away.

"Terrific," Cameron said with an exaggerated twist of her head, clearly underwhelmed.

He forced himself to relax. It was just a light, after all.

Cameron gestured at the alien. "How much longer do we have to keep that thing around?"

Felicia had organized a round-the-clock watch schedule. The zookeepers wouldn't be able to retrieve their property or their fallen comrade without making themselves known, assuming there were actually more of them. No one had seen another blurry cloud, and some were starting to wonder if others would ever appear.

"I'm with Cameron," Kim said. "That thing stinks."

"I want to perform an autopsy," Priya said. "I want to find out what's inside."

David winced. "Yum."

"As our physician, I would expect you to assist." Priya made a stern face.

He held up his hands. "Yeah, yeah. I'll do it."

"Have you learned anything yet?" Sierra asked.

"Barely. I can't categorize it. I don't even know if it's a vertebrate."

"I call it a bag bug," Barry said.

Priya's eyes narrowed. "Yes, the appendages look like something from an arthropod, or maybe a crustacean, but it doesn't have an exoskeleton, so it can't be a bug."

David raised an eyebrow. "I think maybe it could be classified as *alien*."

"That word only means 'different' or 'unknown.' It doesn't accurately describe a phylum."

He smiled. Priya was smart, but not so good with sarcasm.

"Why aren't there more of them?" Barry asked.

It was good to hear him asking questions again. David ruffled his son's hair and gave him the only answer he could. "I don't know. We'll find out, won't we?"

The smile Barry gave him made his heart swell.

"We just might have our answer," Sierra said quietly, gazing past him. "Look."

Waldmire stood down in the fields, pointing at the sky back toward the plateau. A few other people walked over beside him and followed his gaze.

David looked up, wondering if he should get his kids to cover, but he couldn't see anything.

They all walked down to join Waldmire and turned around to look back over the trees.

It wasn't a watcher. Instead, a dark column of smoke rose above the forest. It had to be coming from the burning Tyrannosaurus.

The rising column ended abruptly, flattening out and spreading in every direction. It looked like a mushroom cloud, but the top was paper-thin.

"It's like the smoke is hitting something in the sky," Cameron said. "Something invisible."

David estimated the height at roughly two thousand feet. "That isn't sky," he said. "It's the roof of our enclosure."

Chapter Eighty-Eight

Sierra sat down to a plate of smoked dinosaur meat and baked tubers. Everyone had gathered for lunch on the benches by the main firepit. It had been a rough couple of days, but they'd gotten a lot done.

Joe's body lay in an unmarked grave near the spot where Thad was buried. Wooden markers had been placed for the people who left no remains. Sierra and Kim had collected flowers for Josh's memorial.

After lunch, they planned to burn the second Tyrannosaurus. Its body still lay on the path below the fields. They would burn the whole thing. David had told Sierra privately that he thought the flesh from the poisoned dinosaur would probably be safe to consume, but they decided not to take any chances. They already had more meat than they could hope to eat before it spoiled.

Hunks from the first dinosaur hung smoking by the fires. It was flavorless and jaw-numbingly tough, but it provided much-needed fat and protein.

Carol leaned over from the bench next to her. "When are you going to get rid of that creature?" she asked. The old woman had kept her distance from the alien's corpse, which still sat on the wooden gallows platform.

"Priya and David are going to perform an autopsy tomorrow," Sierra said. "After that, we'll dispose of it."

"You should just bury it right now." Carol wrung her hands together. "Aren't you worried about upsetting its friends?"

Sierra shrugged. "If it makes them talk to us, so be it."

She realized that everyone had grown silent. The rest of the village was listening in.

"Have we learned anything at all about it?" Reggie asked. He'd organized the group into work parties, and most of them had put in long hours.

For some, the work seemed to help them atone for what they'd done, or, in many cases, what they hadn't done. For others, the labor probably helped take their minds off the horrible things they'd seen. For most, it was probably some of both.

Sierra extended a hand toward Priya, who had studied the alien nonstop, making sketches and jotting observations in a notebook someone had brought from Earth.

Priya set down her plate. "All of the alien's features are at one end," she said. "There are fourteen appendages. I believe six of the smaller ones are mandibles. They surround a fold in the skin that seems to be its mouth. The longer limbs appear to be arms. Eight of them are more than a meter in length, with multiple joints. Two end in hooks, two end in small pincers, and four end with just a single claw. I haven't identified any sensory organs or sex organs, but I honestly don't know what to look for."

"Eww," Kim said. She sat on the other side of the group with her father and Barry.

"Yeah, but what is it?" asked the guy in the blazer, a man from South Dakota named Scott.

"I don't know," Priya said, her tone defensive. "It isn't like anything on Earth."

"What about its machine?" Scott asked.

Sierra gestured to Morrie.

He looked around. "Uh, Kim and I are working on it. We got a light to come on. And we think we've identified some parts that were damaged." He smiled. "If anyone has a soldering iron, let me know." This earned a few chuckles.

Morrie seemed desperate to make up for his allegiance to Joe. He'd shown Sierra a box of ammunition hidden in Joe's cabin and cobbled together a holster from an old boot so she could wear Joe's revolver on her hip.

"Any sign of Randall?" Jasmine asked.

"One of the canoes is missing," Sierra said. "We think he's gone back to the island where we first arrived."

"We should go after him," Cameron said. "I don't like the thought of him running free out there. He's dangerous."

"How much ammo did he have?" Sierra asked, looking around.

Morrie shrugged. "There wasn't much left. He may not have any."

Sierra wanted to go after Randall, too, but Joe's words came back to her, shaming her. *People must be punished*. She didn't think Randall was capable of causing too much trouble without someone else telling him what to do, and she didn't think he would last very long over there all alone.

"We don't need to be vengeful," she said. "We can't go down that path. We'll stay vigilant, though."

Cameron stared, stone-faced. She didn't look happy, but she didn't protest any further.

Sierra pointed toward the alien sled with her fork. "That machine needs to be our priority. If this is all a giant enclosure, it can help us find the exit."

Everyone had heard about the zoo theory, but seeing the dark smoke fan out overhead when they burned the Tyrannosaurus had made it real. The discovery had been pure chance. White smoke from small campfires wasn't thick enough to see against the sky, and big bonfires were always lit after dark. Sierra wondered what other secrets were out there, just waiting to be discovered.

"Why should we even try to leave?" Dee asked, glancing nervously from face to face. "I mean, if this place was made for us, aren't we safer here?"

Sierra put her fork down and sat up straight. "I'm not willing to live in a cage. I don't want to be a zoo animal or a lab rat."

Judging from the murmurs in the crowd, many others felt the same way, but not all.

Sierra changed the subject before anyone could protest further. "In the meantime, Cameron is going to take a team on the raft to look for people from the other pods. There were thousands. We have to find them."

"Her injury needs time to heal before she goes anywhere," David said.

"Yeah, yeah, yeah," Sierra said with a grin. "Don't worry. We'll spend a couple of days coming up with a plan."

David smiled back.

Reggie took off his hat and clenched it in both hands. "Is that a good idea? I'm not sure I want to find more people. We got a decent group now. We don't need another psychotic asshole."

One or two other people whispered in agreement.

Sierra's shoulders fell.

"Our track record for exploring other islands hasn't been very good," Waldmire added.

She studied his face, searching for any resemblance to her own. Sierra's mother had left when she was nine and Waldmire had always been there, across the street. He gave her a present each year on her birthday and another at Christmas. Sierra hadn't confronted him yet. Rick Preston was Dad. He'd raised her. So much had already turned upside down in her life. She wasn't ready for another upheaval.

"Cameron can handle whatever is out there," Sierra said. "She took down a *T. rex* by herself, after all." This comment brought a few grunts of approval.

Across the group, David stood. Sierra clenched her jaw, steeling herself for an argument. He'd been wary since the beginning about what kind of people they might find.

"I'm with Sierra," he said. "We can't just stay here and wait for something to happen. That's giving up." He looked down at his kids. "We need to find the rest of the survivors and we need to find a way out of this cage. We sure as hell aren't safe here. Our captors stood by and watched while people died, again and again. We can't trust them to take care of us." He looked around the group. "I'm not giving up. I'm going to keep trying."

She nodded to him across the crowd, thankful for his words.

Reggie crossed his arms and shrugged. "Gotta do as we can, I guess."

Felicia looked up at Sierra. "We're with you. I appreciate you laying it all out for us."

Her words surprised her. The group saw her as a leader.

The best way to become a leader is to do what needs to be done, Rick Preston had told her once. She wished he was here. She missed him.

She made up her mind to speak with Waldmire about him after lunch, and see where the conversation took them.

"What's that noise?" Barry asked.

Sierra held her breath and listened. A low hum came from across the fire pit, the sort of sound she associated with electric motors.

Morrie ran to the alien's vehicle and leaned over the front console. "Something turned on."

Everyone rose and followed him, crowding around. Teal blue light glowed from three panels inside the front wall.

A snuffling sound came from the alien's body where it lay a few yards away.

"Whoa, whoa, look out." Reggie jumped back. "It's moving."

Sierra drew her pistol.

The cluster of limbs shifted slightly. A sucking hiss came from the opening that Priya thought was its mouth.

Several people gasped. Someone shrieked.

"It's alive," Kevin said. He stepped back, cradling his broken arm.

Cameron moved close, training her gun on the creature.

Jasmine shook her head and moved away. Carol was already three steps ahead of her.

"Another light," Morrie pointed. A new panel flashed on the sled. Mustard yellow light glowed inside the short front wall.

Low murmurs came from the alien, like the sound made by tires when they veered onto the rumble strip alongside a highway.

"What's happening?" Barry asked. David pulled him close on one side, and Kim on the other.

Sierra leaned over the alien, squeezing the grip of her pistol. Her breath came in short, frantic bursts. Several of the creature's limbs twitched in the air. She kept just out of reach.

The humming from the sled modulated, until it sounded almost human, like questions. *Whu-whu-whu. Wha-wha-wha.*

"Trouble's coming," Cameron said.

The alien hissed, then produced another series of rumbles from the flaps between its limbs. When it finished, a voice came from somewhere on the machine, robotic and gravelly. *"Caretakers must not be imprisoned."*

Sierra looked at the sled, then back at the alien. The machine had translated its rumbles into English. She stepped forward. "You imprisoned us first."

She held her breath, wondering if she should've come up with something more diplomatic for humanity's first interplanetary conversation. No, it was best to get right to the point. Besides, no one else appeared to have any better ideas. The others stood gaping. Several people looked ready to run.

The machine produced a series of rumbling sounds, apparently translating her words so the alien could understand.

When it finished, the alien rumbled back and after a moment, the robotic voice from the vehicle said, *"Human specimens have been saved from extinction."*

"That's great. Thank you. Now let's work together. We can learn from each other, help each other." Sierra looked around at the group while the translation commenced. David nodded.

"Caretakers need no assistance."

"Then what's the point?" she stepped back. "Do you just go around and save a bunch of species every time some random comet is about to wipe them out?"

The alien paused for several long seconds before responding. *"The comet was not random."*

A shiver ran up Sierra's spine. "What do you mean?"

"The comet was sent by gorgers."

"Holy Christ," Reggie said. "There's more aliens out there?"

A numb feeling washed over Sierra. Earth had been deliberately destroyed. "What are gorgers?" she asked. "What do they want? Why did they attack us?"

The alien didn't answer.

"Ask it about the other animals," Priya whispered, keeping her distance. "The woolly rhinos, the dinosaurs, the terror birds."

Sierra turned back to the alien. "What about all the other species on the islands? Why are they here?"

The alien rumbled again. *"Preservation and observation."*

Sierra's chest grew tight. It really was a giant zoo. "Did you save all of those creatures from the gorgers, too?"

"Some." The alien paused and produced another rumble. *"Some specimens are collected between attacks."*

A dull ache clouded Sierra's mind. *Attacks.* Earth had been attacked more than once. It was almost too much to process. "We aren't specimens."

The alien didn't respond.

She tried another tactic. "What do you want?"

It repeated its first statement. *"Caretakers must not be imprisoned."*

"Fine. Show us how to get out of here and we'll release you."

"Specimens cannot leave."

"Why not?" Sierra asked. "What's your world like? What's outside this place?"

The alien didn't answer.

"What about the other people?" David asked.

Sierra nodded. "Help us find the rest of the people from Earth. Take us to them, or bring them here." Several villagers nodded. Sierra bit her tongue and added, "The other human specimens."

The alien remained infuriatingly silent.

"At least tell us which islands they're on."

It rumbled a response. *"The remaining human specimens are not on other islands."*

Her heart dropped. Were they dead? Was humanity really down to just twenty people? "What happened to them?"

"Excess specimens remain in storage."

Several people gasped.

Sierra felt like she'd been kicked in the gut. "What? Where is storage? Take us there."

The alien didn't respond.

She kneeled in front of the flaps at the end of the creature. "You're not going anywhere until you release our people."

It folded its limbs alongside the flaps and grew still.

She tightened her fingers around the gun she'd taken from Joe and fired off more questions. "Where is storage? How big is this refuge? What's outside? How do we get out? Why do you observe us? Why didn't you stop the gorgers?"

She waited for answers, but the alien didn't respond. It simply lay there, silent and motionless.

Sierra stepped back, trembling with fear, but also determination. "This thing clearly doesn't want to help us. We're on our own. We have to find a way out of here, and we have to find the people in storage."

The story continues in

PART II

STRUGGLE FOR EXISTENCE

PREHISTORIC SPECIES

Phorusrhacos longissimus (Terror Bird)

Branisella boliviana (Sky Monkey)

Entelodont daedon (Wolf-Pig)

Velociraptor osmolskae (Blue and Red Bird-Creatures)

Corythosaurus casuarius (Horse-Faced Dinosaur)

Pentaceratops sternbergii (Horned Dinosaur)

Tyrannosaurus rex (Tyrannosaurus)

Coelodonta antiquaitatis (Woolly Rhinoceros)

THE PRESERVATION OF SPECIES

PART I

RULE OF EXTINCTION

PART II

STRUGGLE FOR EXISTENCE

PART III

BEASTS OF PREY

ACKNOWLEDGEMENTS

I couldn't have written this book without my family. Thank you Erin, Shannon, and Sydney for your patience, encouragement, and support. And also to River, who often lay curled at my feet.

My editor, Jacquelyn Ben-Zekry, provided insights that helped me find the book's rhythm and a sense of balance. Her work elevated mine.

Jim Stigall's excellent cover design sets the mood and entices the reader, all while balancing a tremendous load of words.

If you ever want to revisit this story, I recommend the audiobook. Stacy Carolan's narration truly brings these characters to life.

Special thanks go to Andrew Caldwell and Michael Smith for providing astronomical information. Their knowledge made the book stronger, though any inaccuracies should be attributed to the author.

Additional thanks go to my many critique partners for their feedback along the way. Look them up and read their work!

Laura Blegen	C. R. Hodges	Kyle Massa	Jason Rush
Heather Caspi	Lena Johnson	Beth McCabe	Danaeka Scrimshaw
Dani Coleman	Steven Johnson	Becky Munyon	Kate Tailor
Heidi Farmer	Laura Kelsay	Kay Olsen	Neil Williams
Amber Herbert	Laura Lauda	Nathan Pipelow	
Casey Hinkson	Kimberly Mallek	Margot Romary	

I'm also indebted to beta readers who gave valuable feedback:

Bridgette Braig	Ingrid Herve	Shannon Jones	Nathan Stormzand
Trinh Bui	Jordan Itkowitz	Sydney Jones	Benjamin Talavera
Greg Chiarella	Bill Jones	Genevieve Knight	Danny Talavera
Ben Gomez	Christopher Jones	Carol Pahl	
Mike Giese	David Jones	Greg Rhem	
Beau Hall	Erin Jones	Josef Richardson	

Thank you all so much for your time.

Finally, thank you, the reader, for coming along on this adventure. If you enjoyed *Rule of Extinction*, please take a moment to leave a review and share your thoughts on social media.

Every single review helps a book find its audience.

Now, take a deep breath and buckle up. In *Struggle for Existence*, Sierra and David face terrifying new dangers and monumental discoveries as they learn what's outside the menagerie and unravel the mystery of the gorgers.

Geoff Jones
Broomfield, Colorado